SCHOOL-LIVE!

ART BY SADORU CHIBA
STORY BY NORIMITSU KAIHOU (NITROPLUS)
VOLUME 5

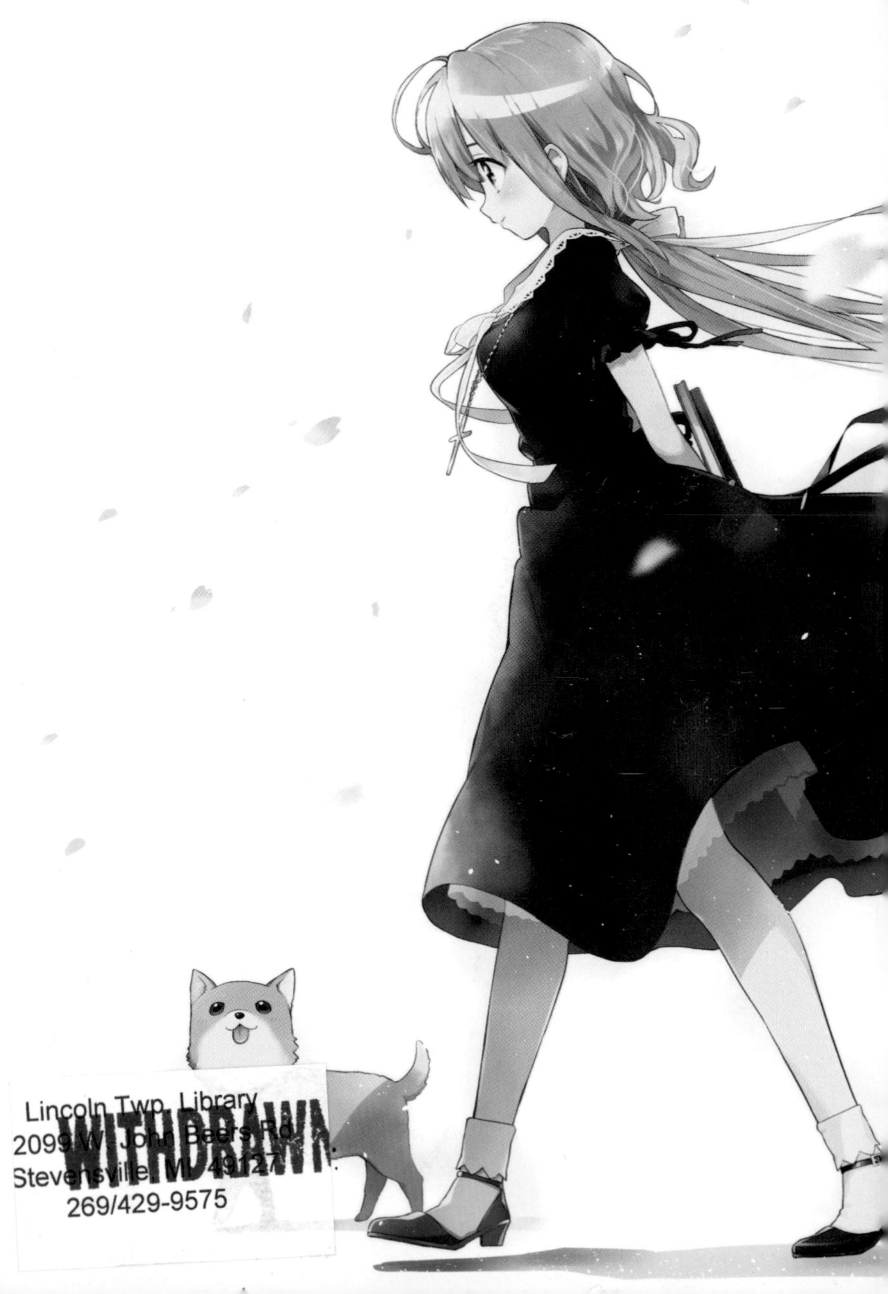

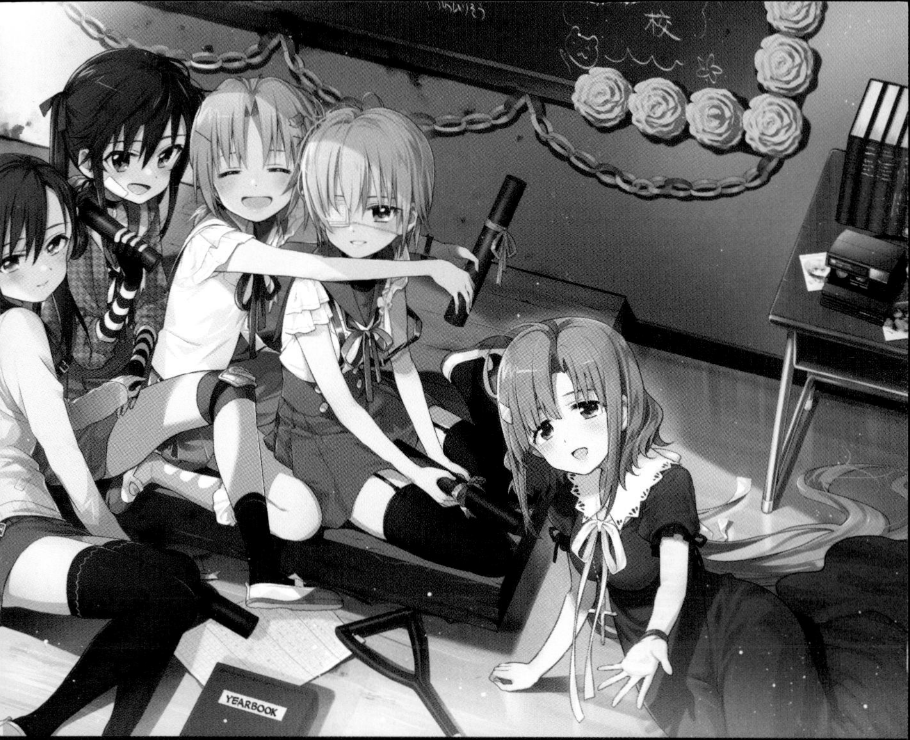
校
YEARBOOK

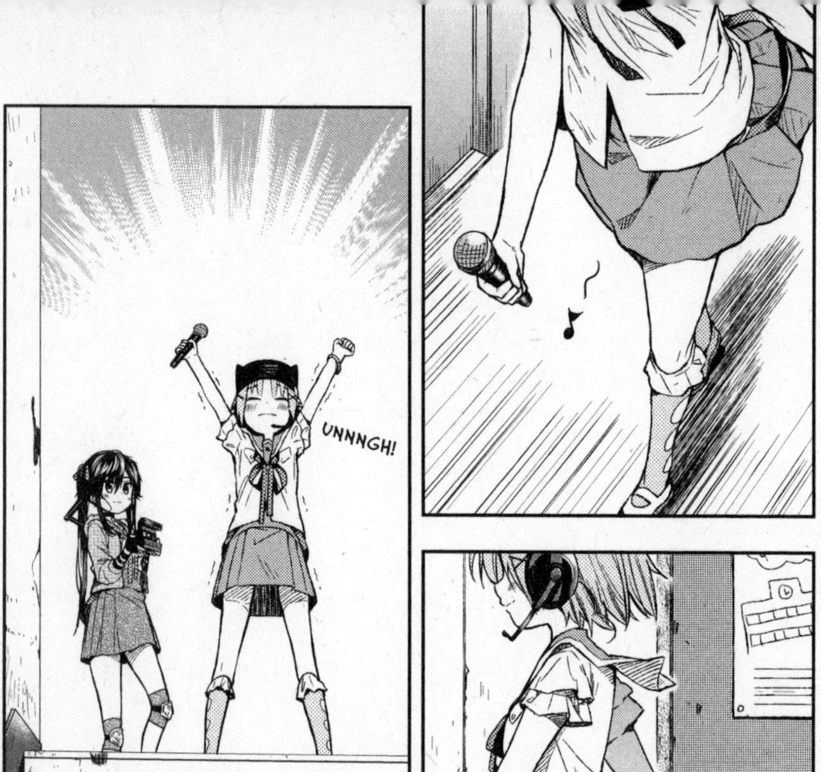
UNNNGH!

POSTER: 2XTH! MEGURIGAOKA ACADEMY MEGU FESTIVAL!

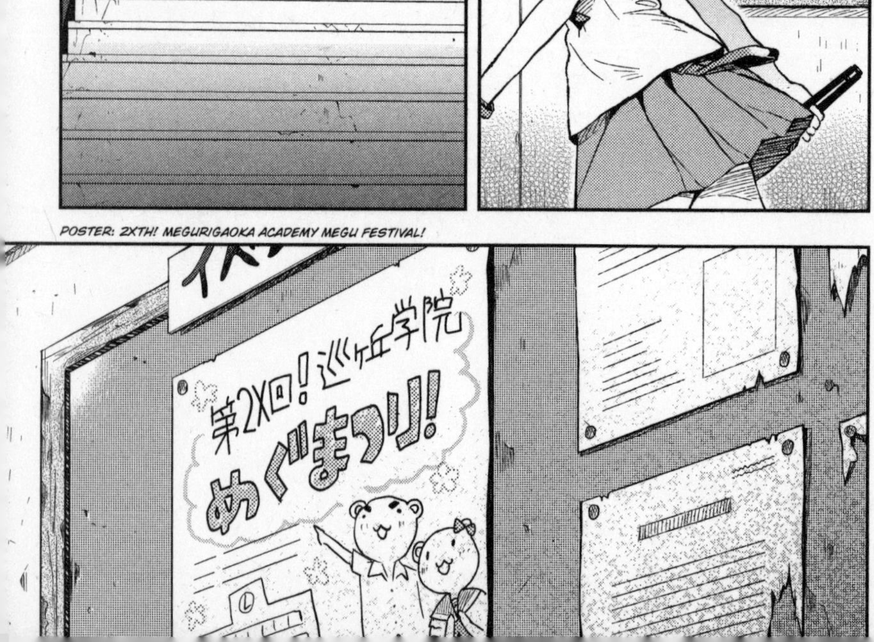
第2X回！巡ヶ丘学院
めぐまつり！

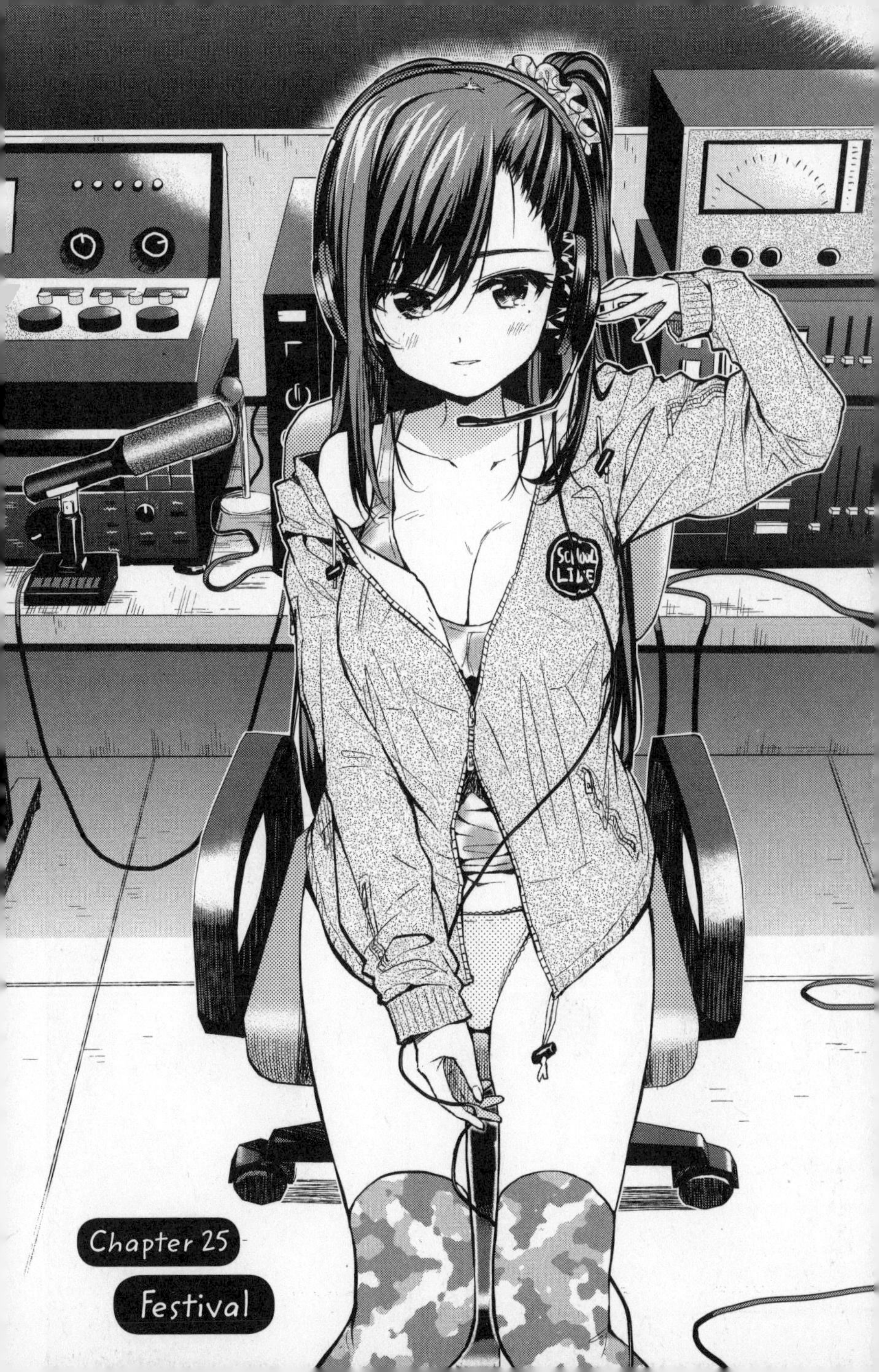
SCHOOL LIVE
Chapter 25
Festival

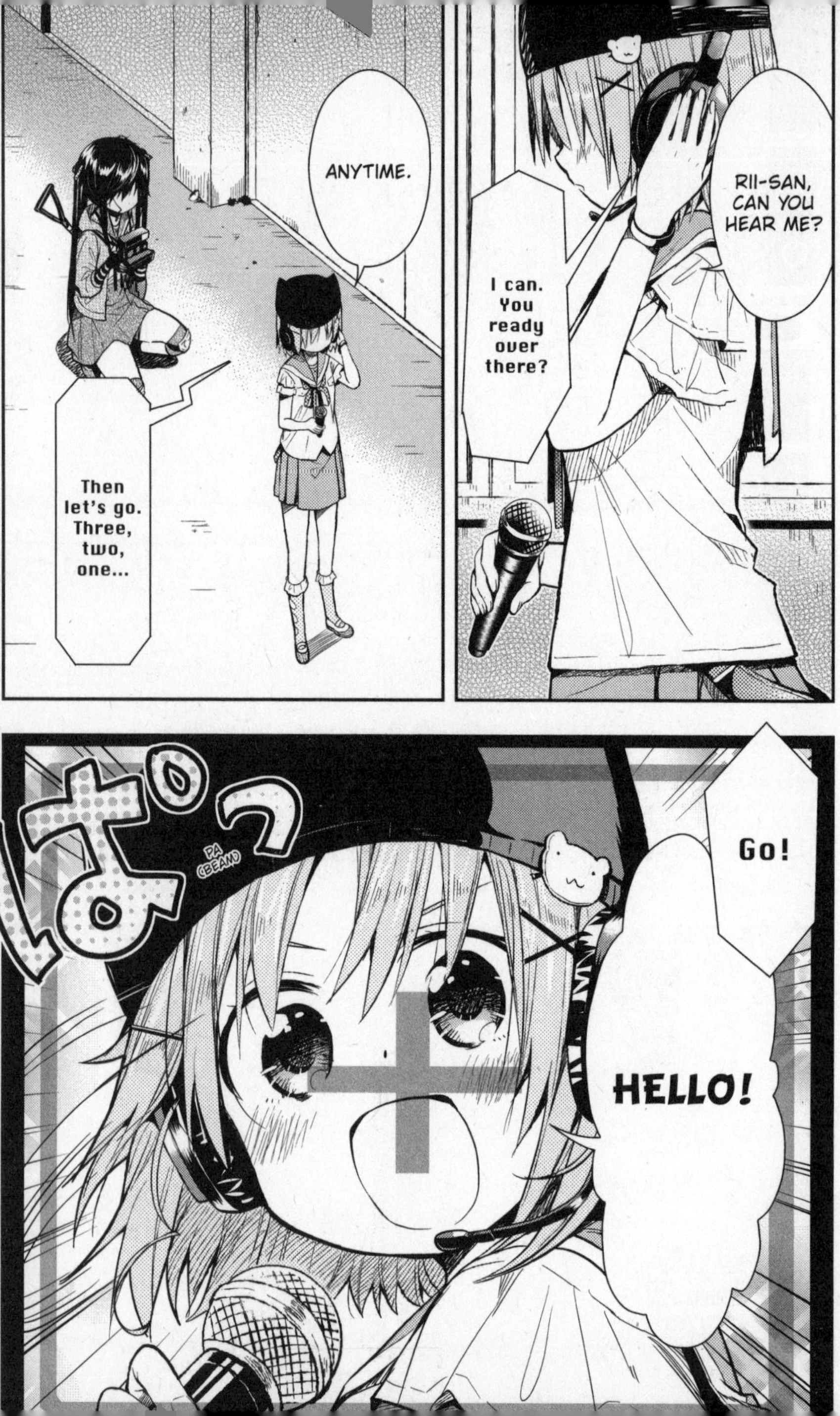
RII-SAN, CAN YOU HEAR ME?
I can. You ready over there?
ANYTIME.
Then let's go. Three, two, one...
Go!
HELLO!
ぱっ
PA (BEAM)

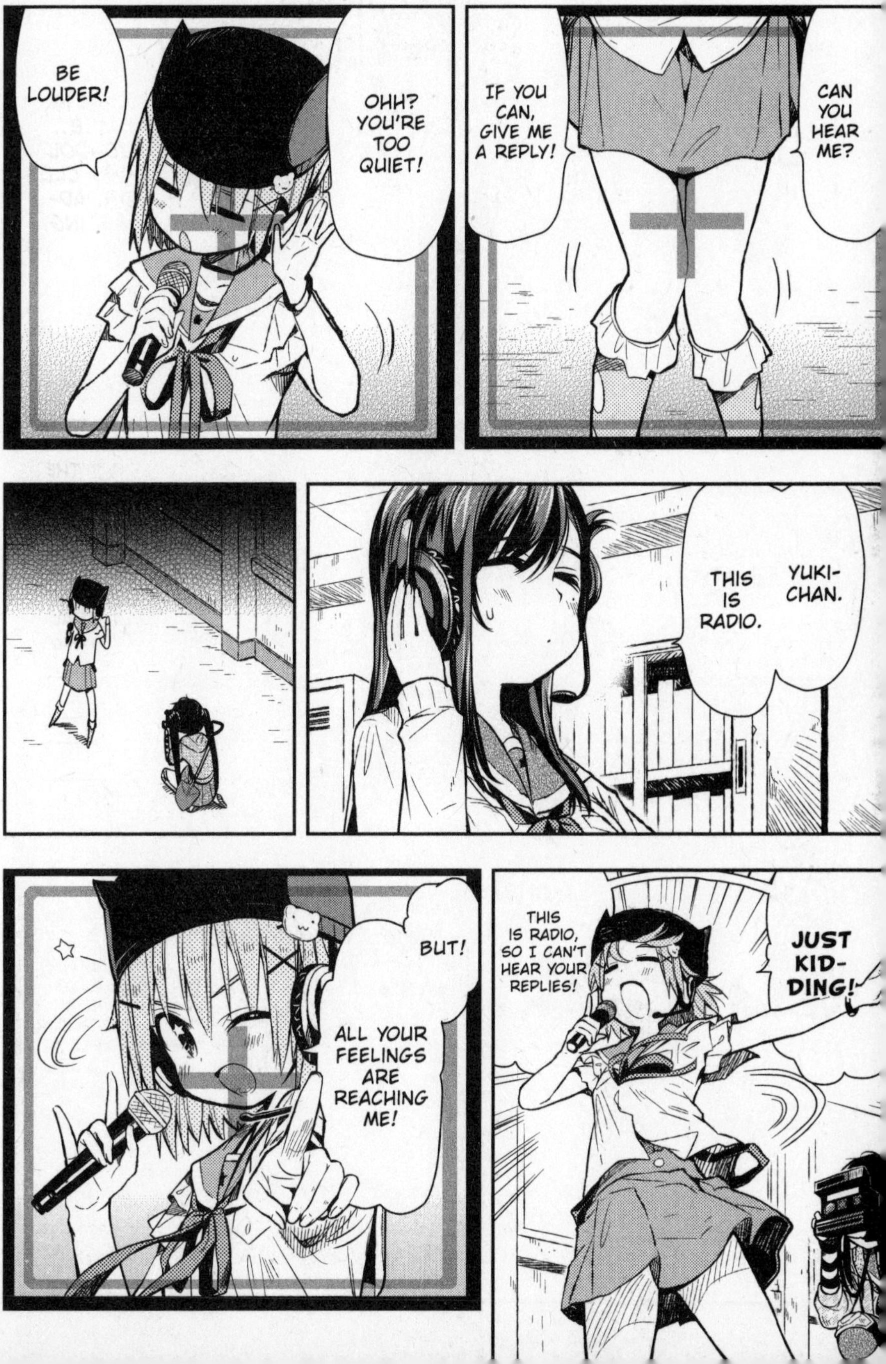
CAN YOU HEAR ME?
IF YOU CAN, GIVE ME A REPLY!
OHH? YOU'RE TOO QUIET!
BE LOUDER!
YUKI-CHAN.
THIS IS RADIO.
JUST KID-DING!
THIS IS RADIO, SO I CAN'T HEAR YOUR REPLIES!
BUT!
ALL YOUR FEELINGS ARE REACHING ME!

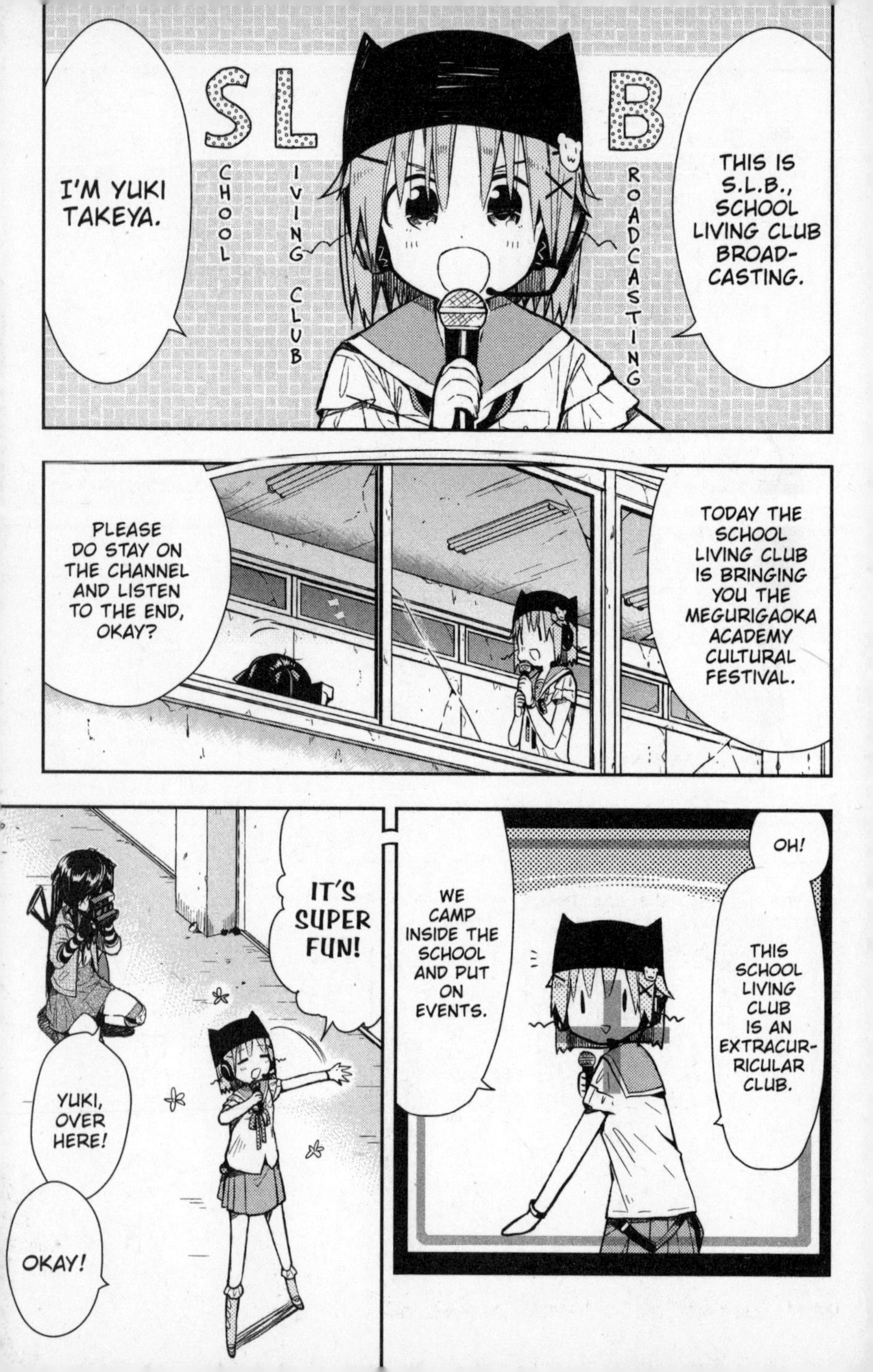
THIS IS S.L.B., SCHOOL LIVING CLUB BROAD-CASTING.
S L B
CHOOL
IVING CLUB
ROADCASTING
I'M YUKI TAKEYA.
TODAY THE SCHOOL LIVING CLUB IS BRINGING YOU THE MEGURIGAOKA ACADEMY CULTURAL FESTIVAL.
PLEASE DO STAY ON THE CHANNEL AND LISTEN TO THE END, OKAY?
OH!
THIS SCHOOL LIVING CLUB IS AN EXTRACUR-RICULAR CLUB.
WE CAMP INSIDE THE SCHOOL AND PUT ON EVENTS.
IT'S SUPER FUN!
YUKI, OVER HERE!
OKAY!

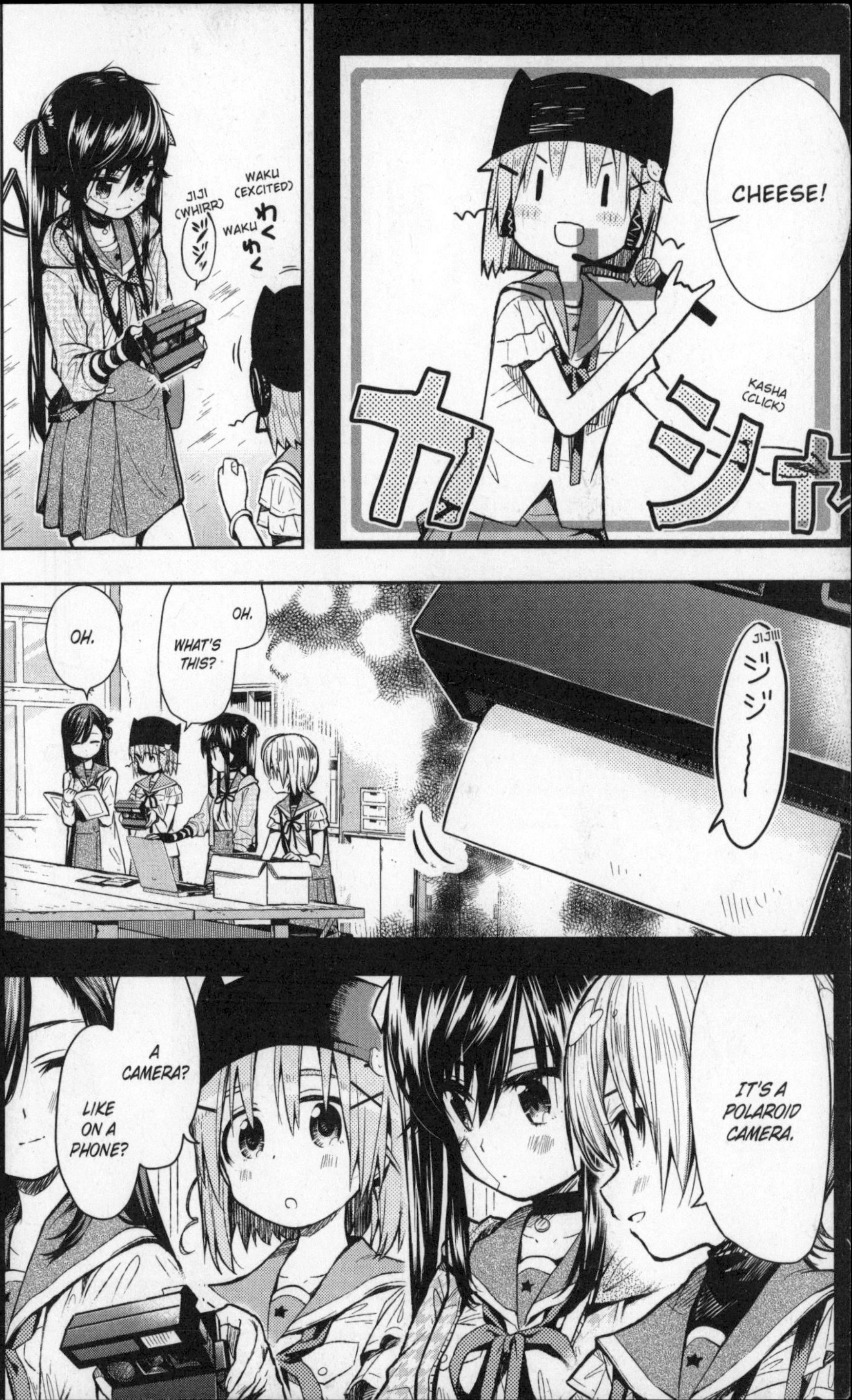
CHEESE!
KASHA (CLICK)
カシャ
WAKU (EXCITED) WAKU
わくわく
JIJI (WHIRR)
ジジ
JIJIII
ジジジ〜〜
OH. WHAT'S THIS?
OH.
IT'S A POLAROID CAMERA.
A CAMERA? LIKE ON A PHONE?

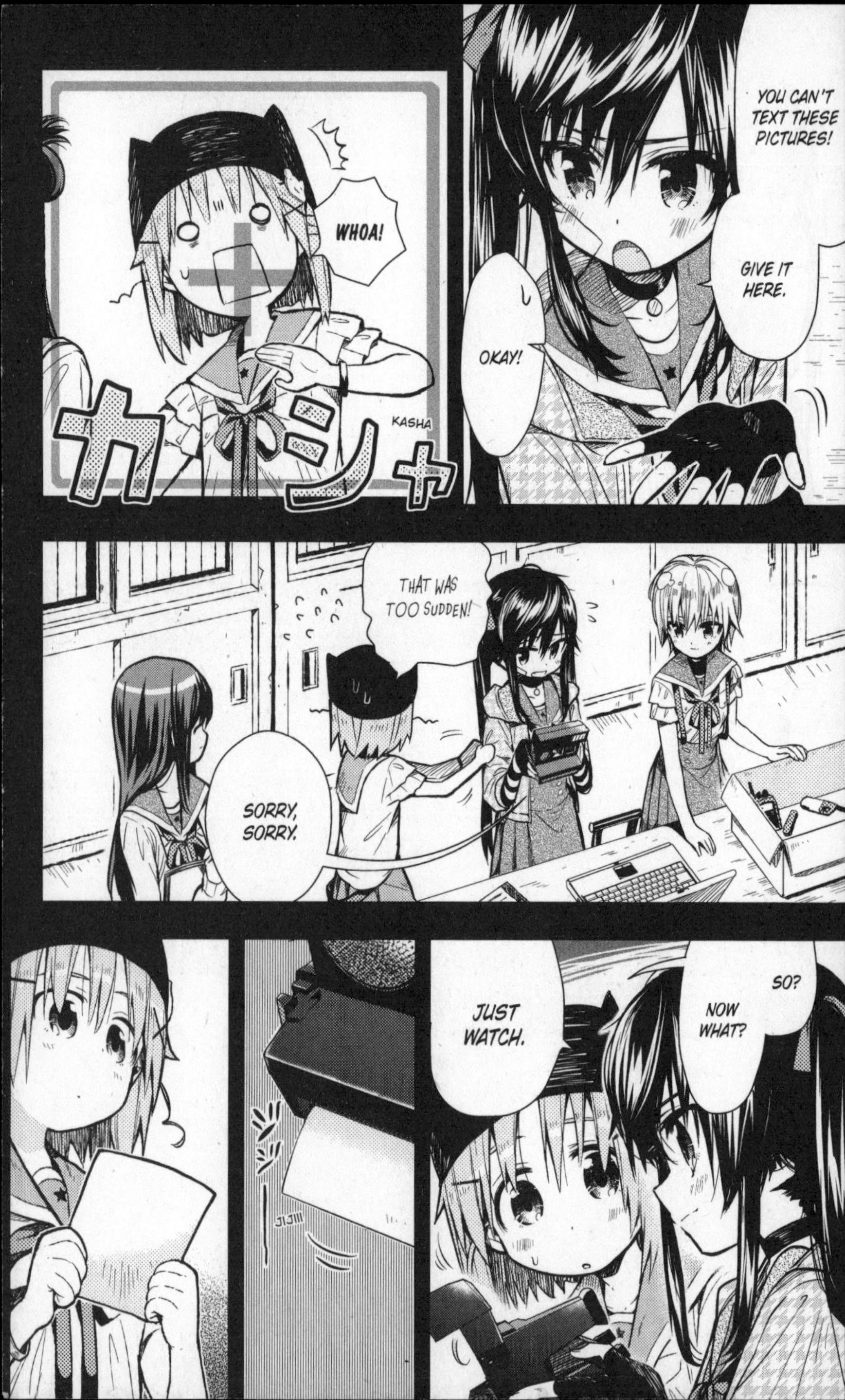
YOU CAN'T TEXT THESE PICTURES!
GIVE IT HERE.
OKAY!
WHOA!
KASHA
THAT WAS TOO SUDDEN!
SORRY, SORRY.
SO?
NOW WHAT?
JUST WATCH.
JIJIII

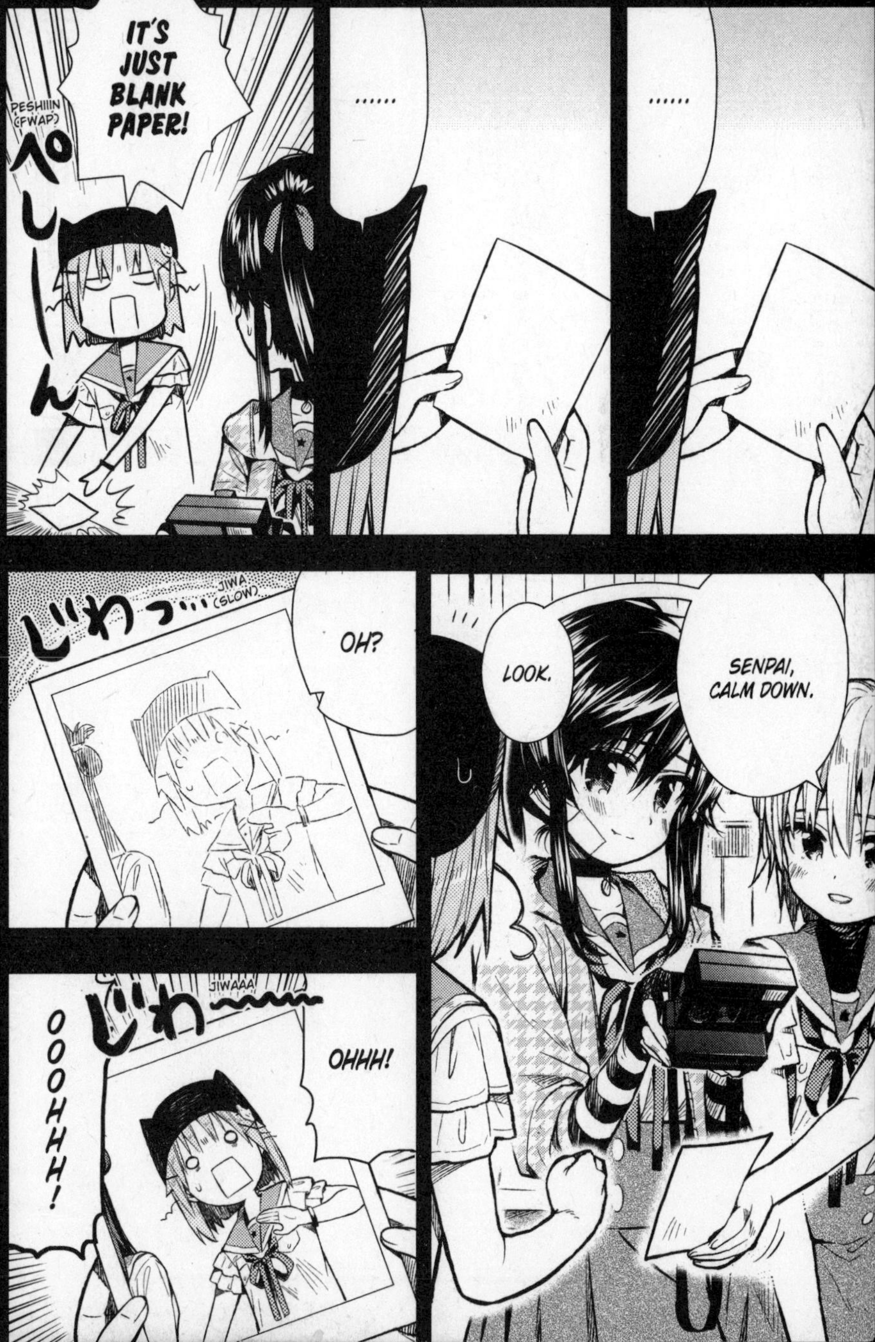
......
......
IT'S JUST BLANK PAPER!
PESHIIIN (FWAP)
へしーん
SENPAI, CALM DOWN.
LOOK.
OH?
じわっ...
JIWA (SLOW)
OHHH!
じわ~~
JIWAAA
OOOOHHHH!

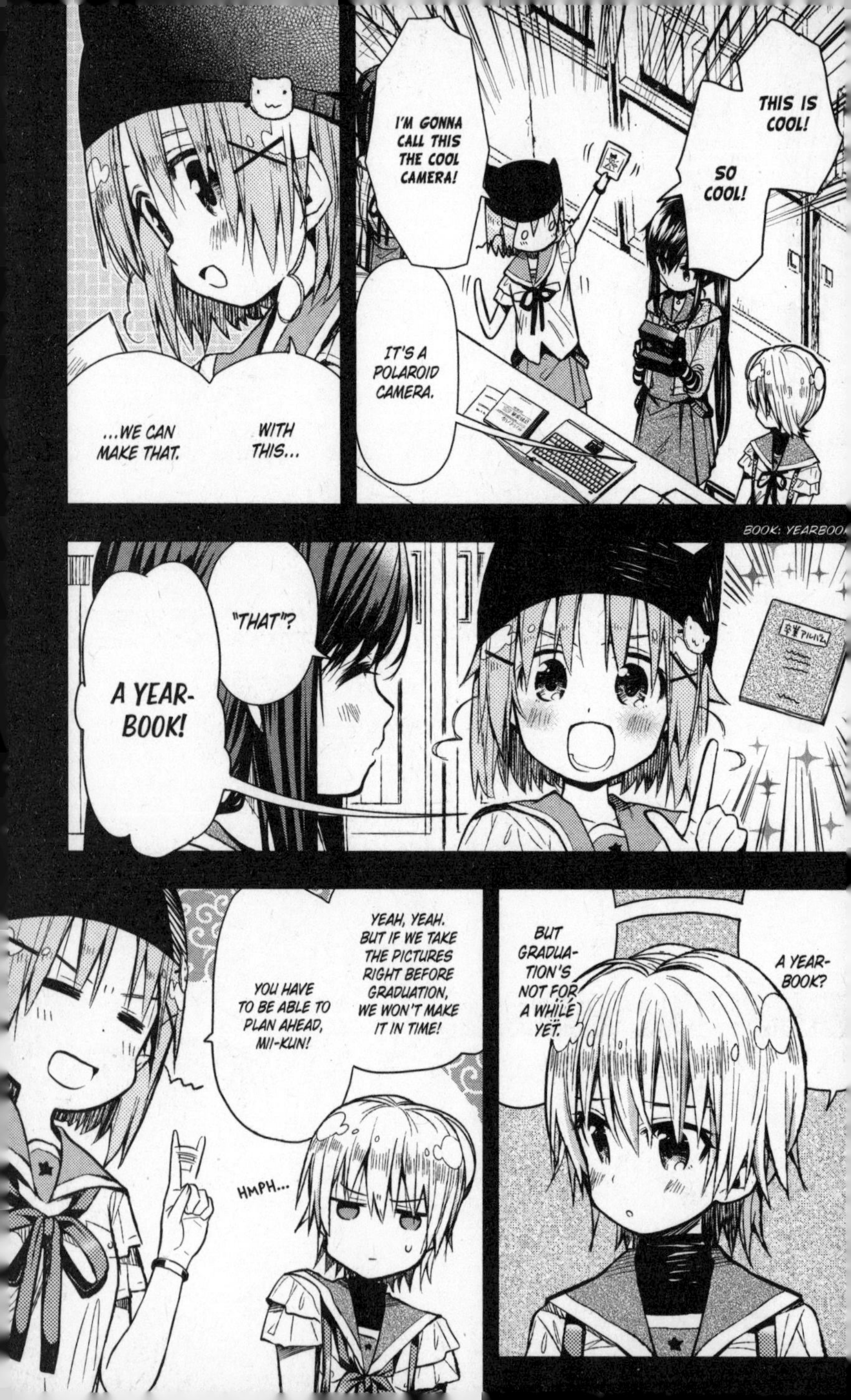
THIS IS COOL!
SO COOL!
I'M GONNA CALL THIS THE COOL CAMERA!
IT'S A POLAROID CAMERA.
WITH THIS...
...WE CAN MAKE THAT.
BOOK: YEARBOO
"THAT"?
A YEAR-BOOK!
A YEAR-BOOK?
BUT GRADUA-TION'S NOT FOR A WHILE YET.
YEAH, YEAH. BUT IF WE TAKE THE PICTURES RIGHT BEFORE GRADUATION, WE WON'T MAKE IT IN TIME!
YOU HAVE TO BE ABLE TO PLAN AHEAD, MII-KUN!
HMPH...

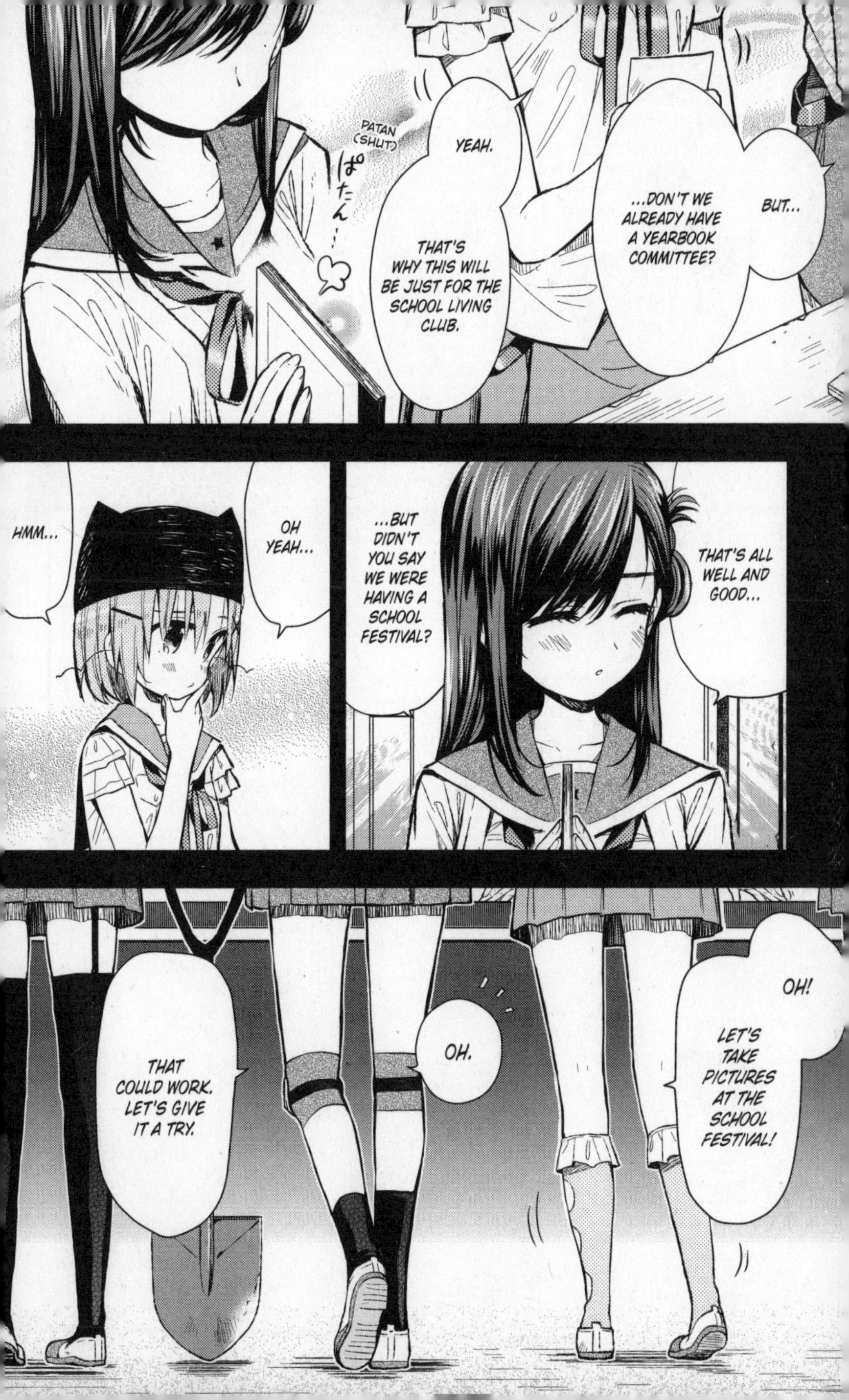
BUT...
...DON'T WE ALREADY HAVE A YEARBOOK COMMITTEE?
YEAH.
THAT'S WHY THIS WILL BE JUST FOR THE SCHOOL LIVING CLUB.
PATAN (SHUT)
ぱたん…
THAT'S ALL WELL AND GOOD...
...BUT DIDN'T YOU SAY WE WERE HAVING A SCHOOL FESTIVAL?
OH YEAH...
HMM...
OH!
LET'S TAKE PICTURES AT THE SCHOOL FESTIVAL!
OH.
THAT COULD WORK. LET'S GIVE IT A TRY.

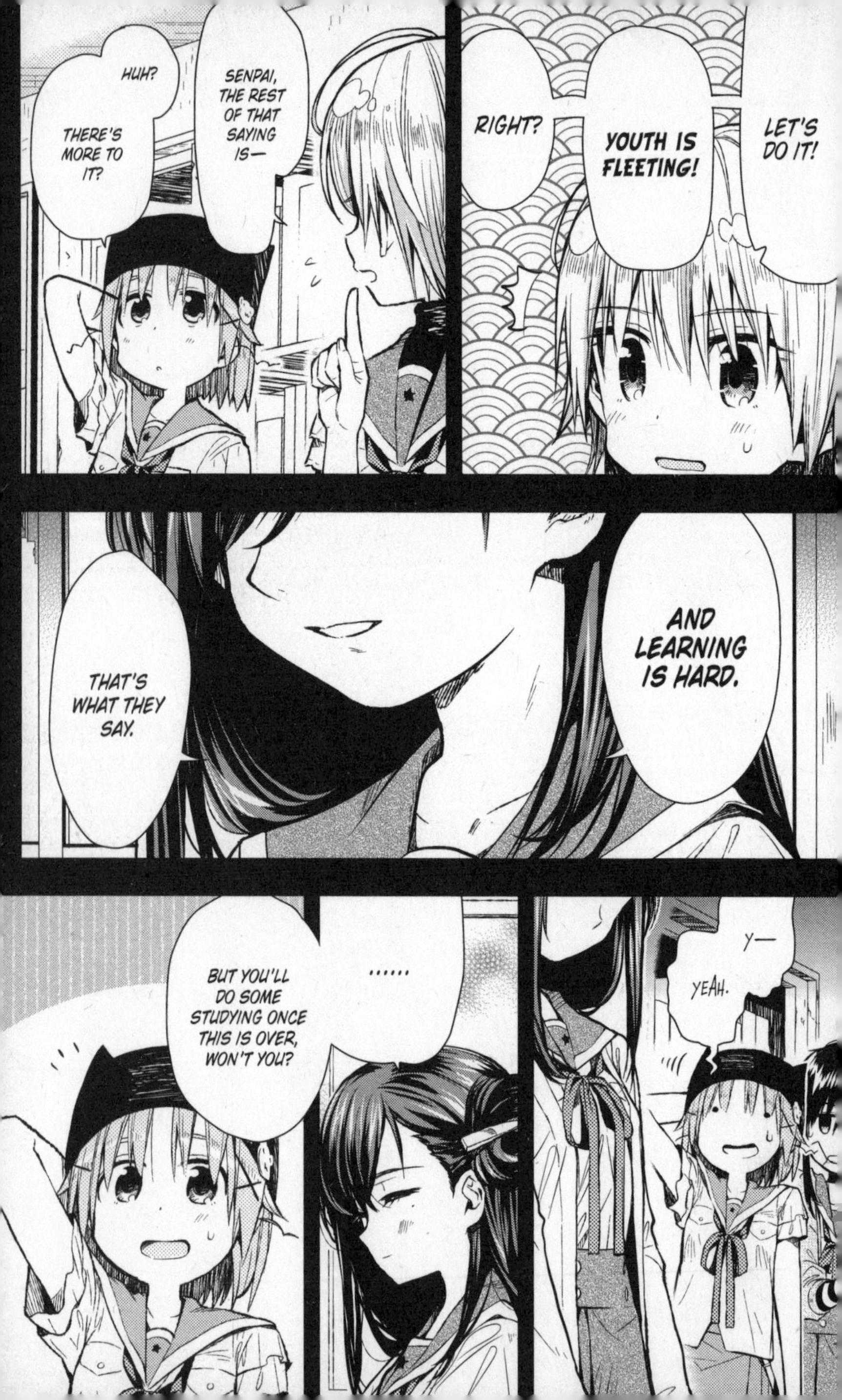
LET'S DO IT!
YOUTH IS FLEETING!
RIGHT?
SENPAI, THE REST OF THAT SAYING IS—
HUH?
THERE'S MORE TO IT?
AND LEARNING IS HARD.
THAT'S WHAT THEY SAY.
BUT YOU'LL DO SOME STUDYING ONCE THIS IS OVER, WON'T YOU?
......
Y—
YEAH.

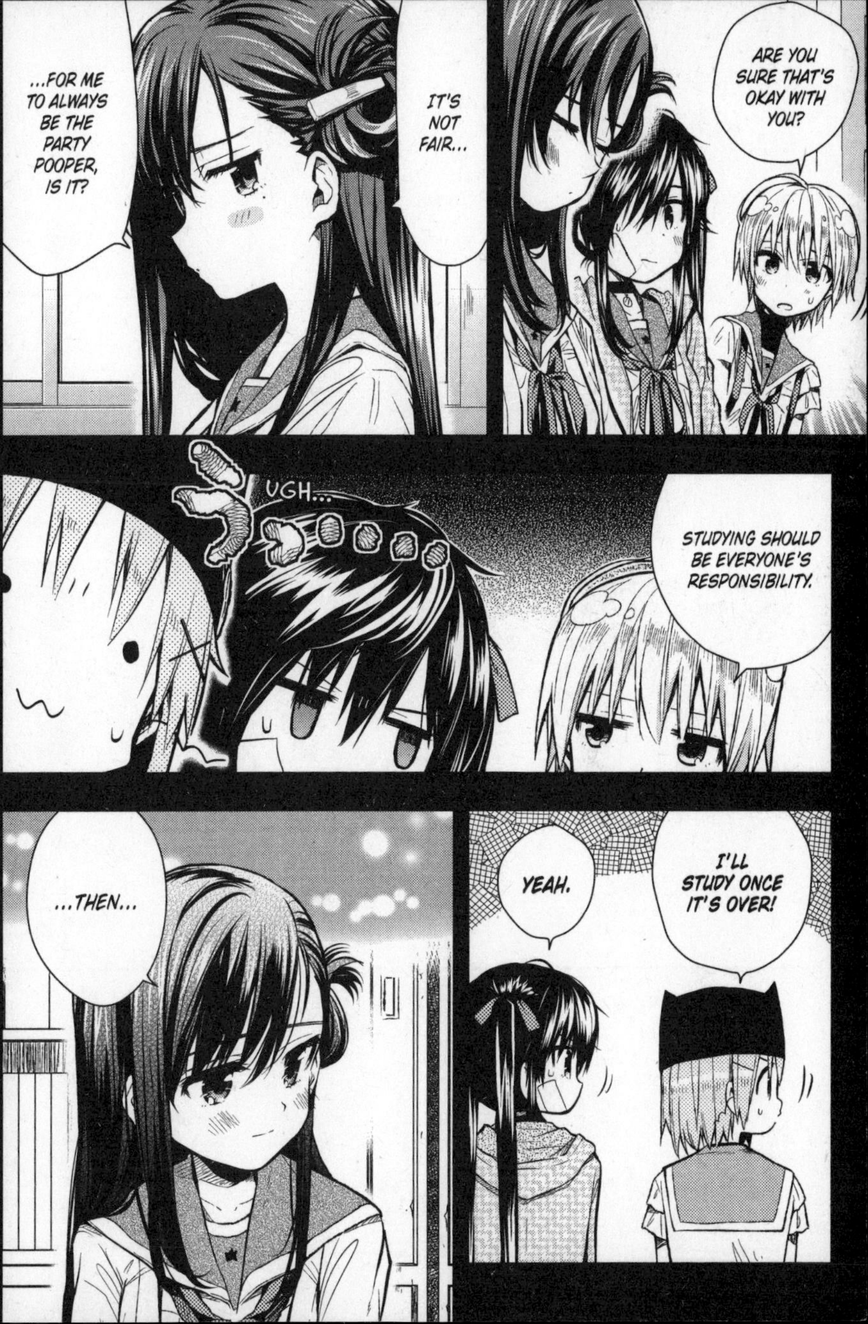
ARE YOU SURE THAT'S OKAY WITH YOU?
IT'S NOT FAIR...
...FOR ME TO ALWAYS BE THE PARTY POOPER, IS IT?
STUDYING SHOULD BE EVERYONE'S RESPONSIBILITY.
UGH...
I'LL STUDY ONCE IT'S OVER!
YEAH.
...THEN...

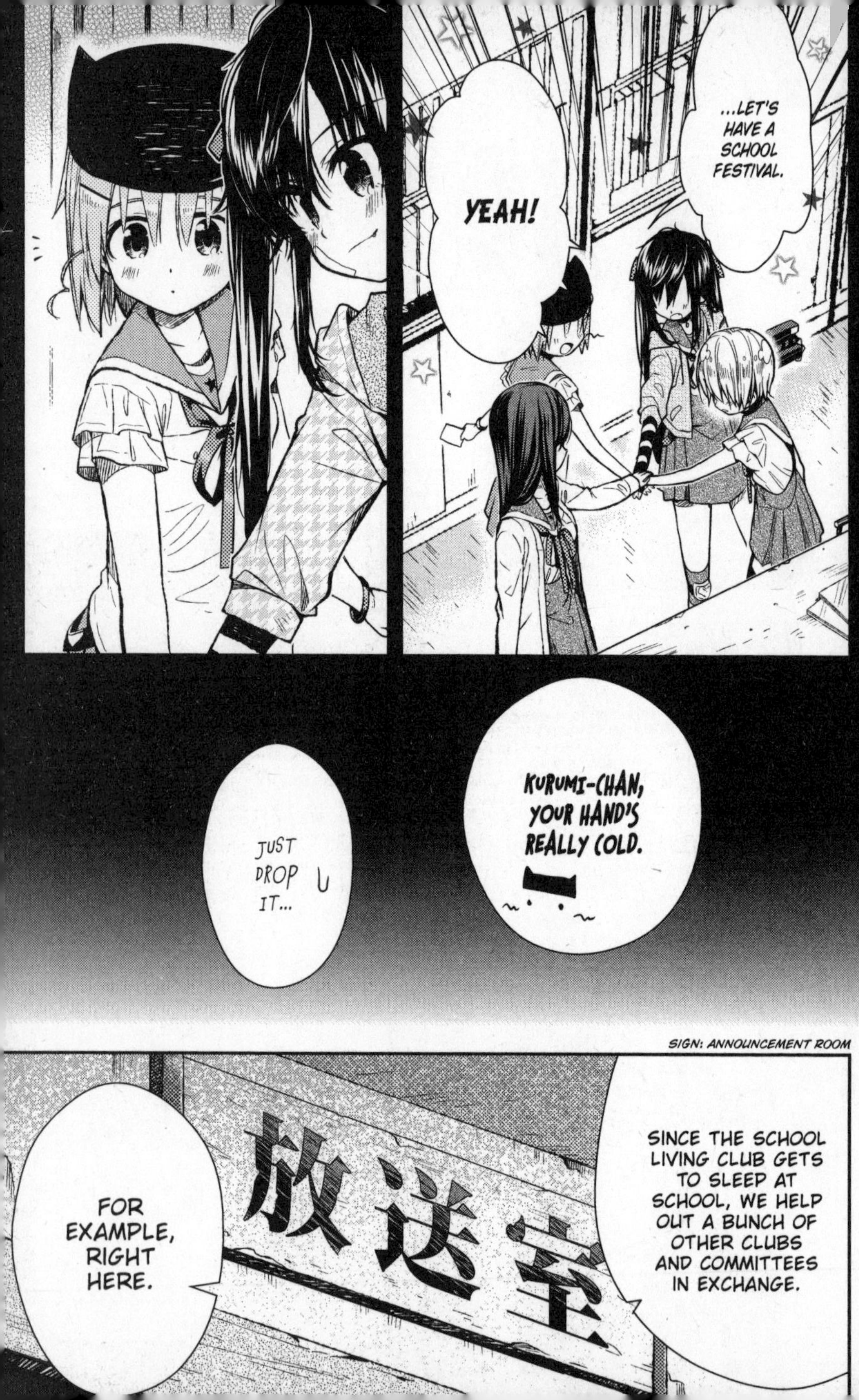
...LET'S HAVE A SCHOOL FESTIVAL.
YEAH!
KURUMI-CHAN, YOUR HAND'S REALLY COLD.
JUST DROP IT...
SIGN: ANNOUNCEMENT ROOM
放送室
SINCE THE SCHOOL LIVING CLUB GETS TO SLEEP AT SCHOOL, WE HELP OUT A BUNCH OF OTHER CLUBS AND COMMITTEES IN EXCHANGE.
FOR EXAMPLE, RIGHT HERE.

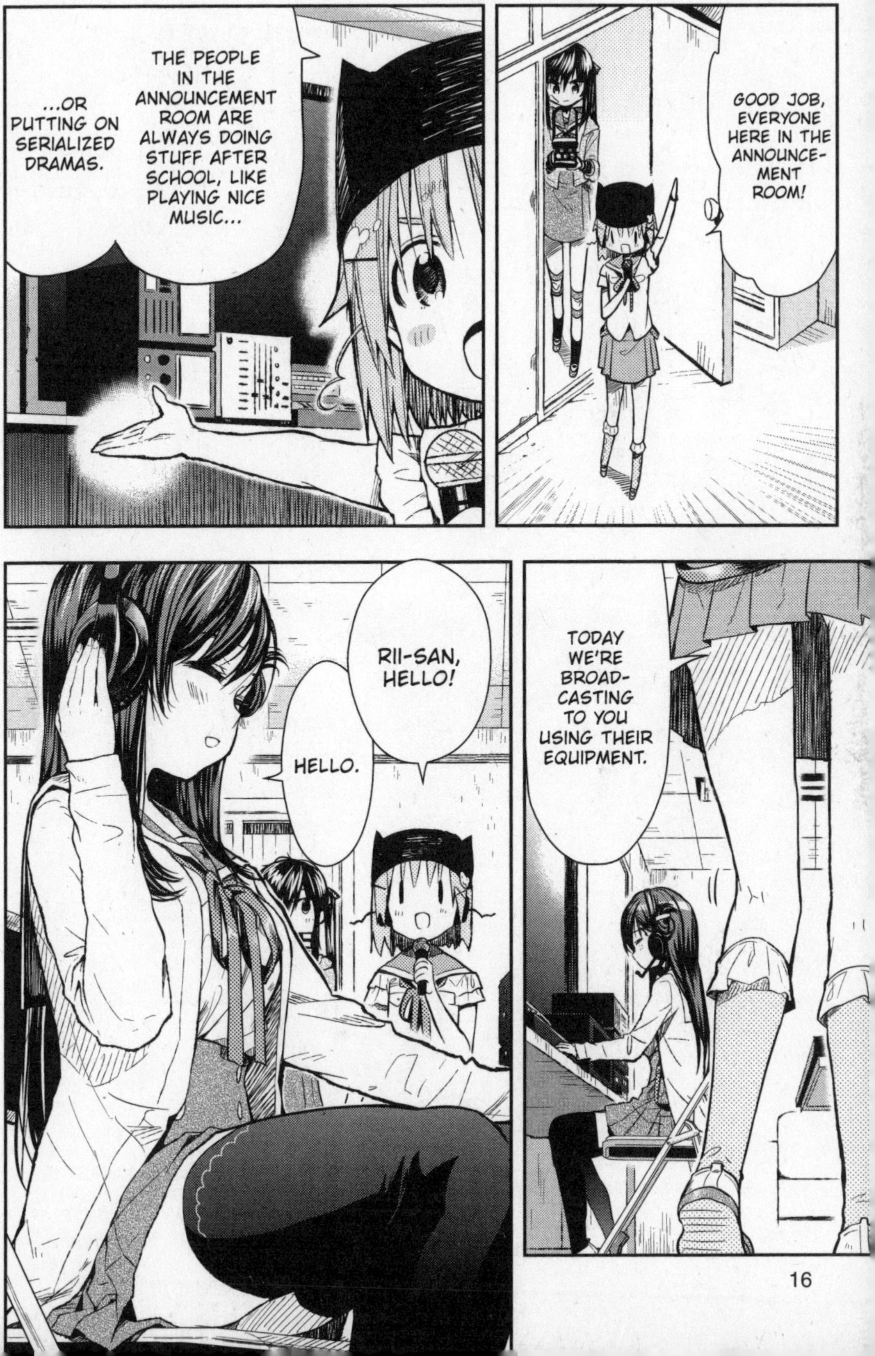
GOOD JOB, EVERYONE HERE IN THE ANNOUNCEMENT ROOM!
THE PEOPLE IN THE ANNOUNCEMENT ROOM ARE ALWAYS DOING STUFF AFTER SCHOOL, LIKE PLAYING NICE MUSIC...
...OR PUTTING ON SERIALIZED DRAMAS.
TODAY WE'RE BROADCASTING TO YOU USING THEIR EQUIPMENT.
RII-SAN, HELLO!
HELLO.

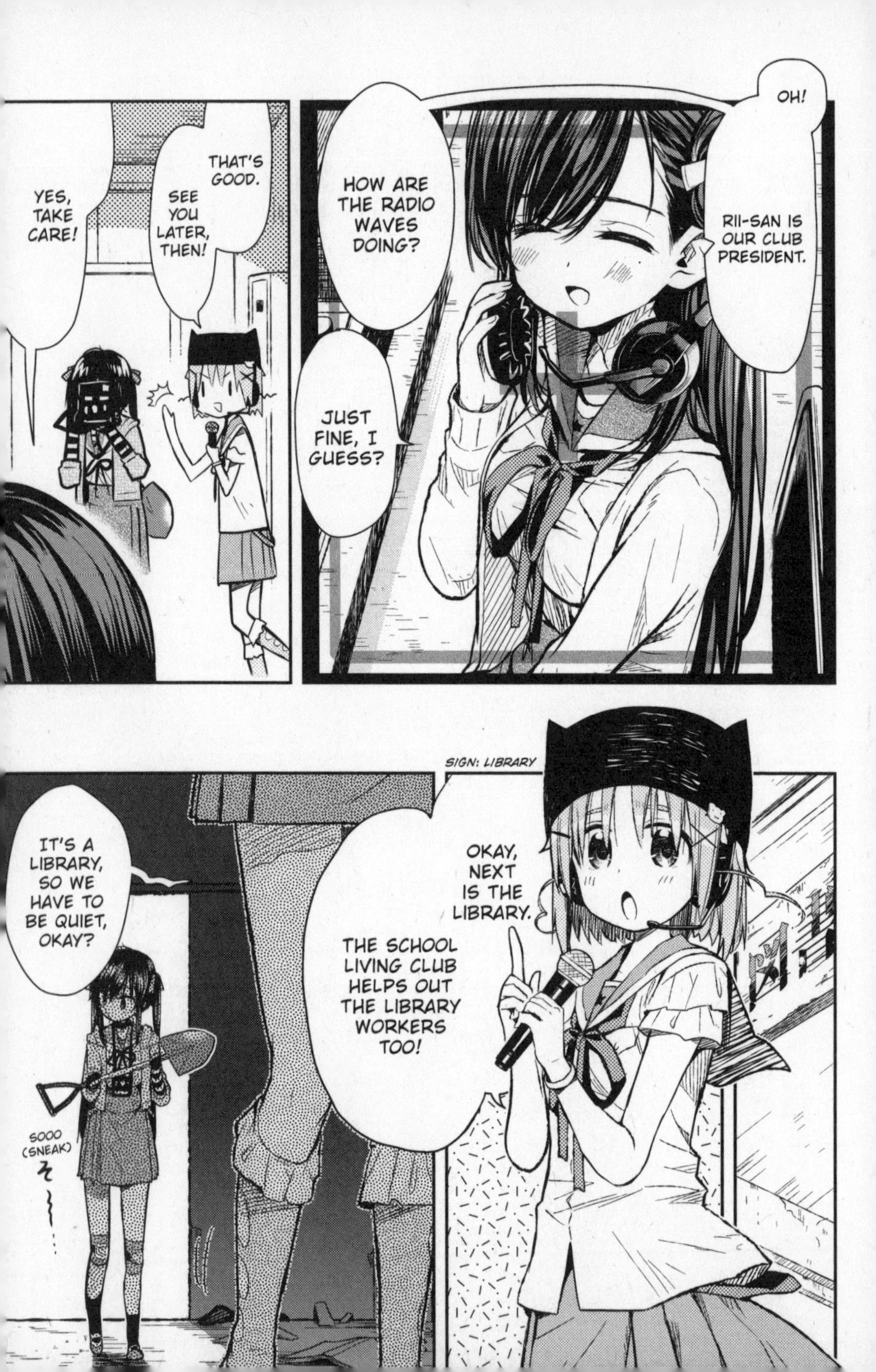
OH!
RII-SAN IS OUR CLUB PRESIDENT.
HOW ARE THE RADIO WAVES DOING?
JUST FINE, I GUESS?
THAT'S GOOD. SEE YOU LATER, THEN!
YES, TAKE CARE!
SIGN: LIBRARY
OKAY, NEXT IS THE LIBRARY.
THE SCHOOL LIVING CLUB HELPS OUT THE LIBRARY WORKERS TOO!
IT'S A LIBRARY, SO WE HAVE TO BE QUIET, OKAY?
SOOO (SNEAK)

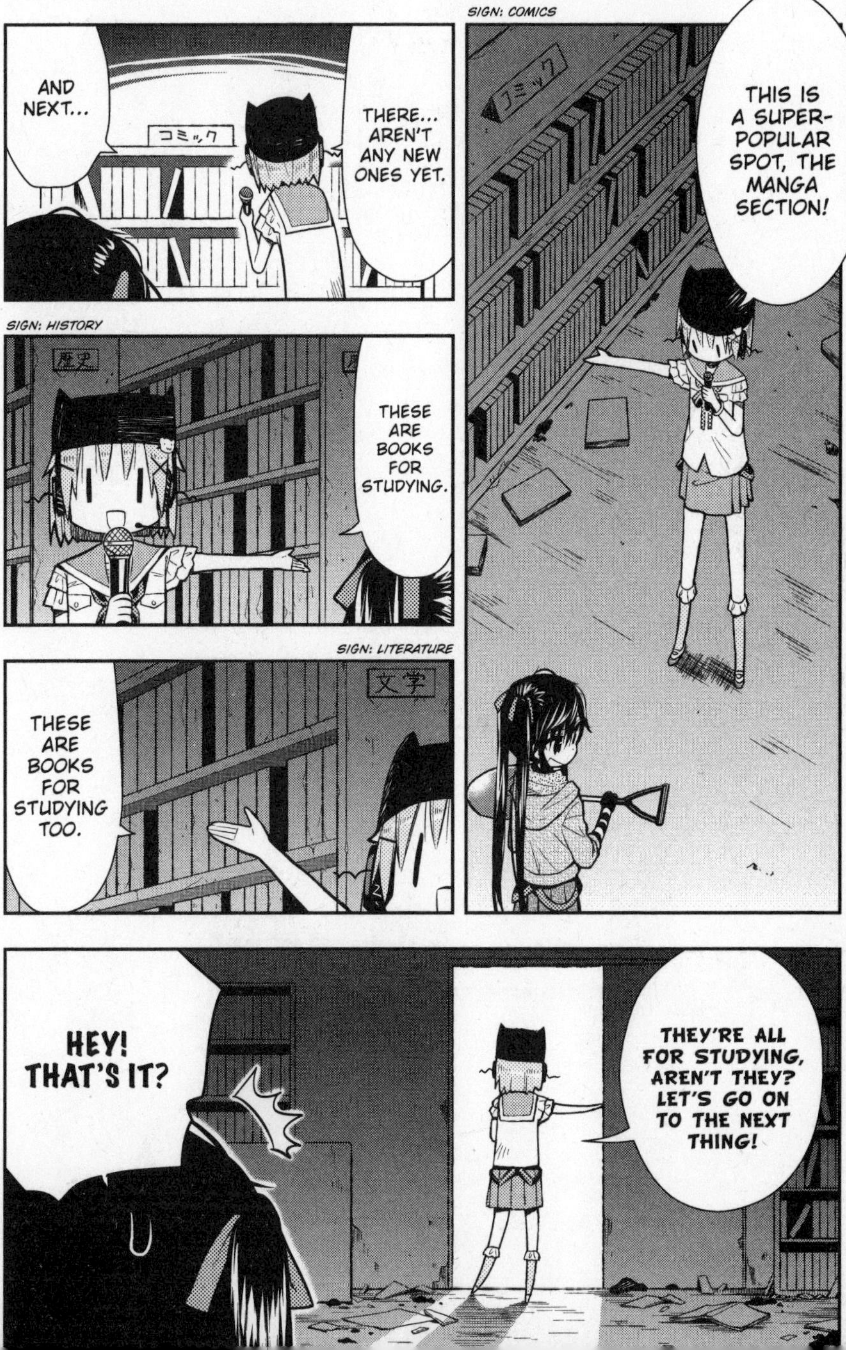
SIGN: COMICS
THIS IS A SUPER-POPULAR SPOT, THE MANGA SECTION!
AND NEXT...
THERE... AREN'T ANY NEW ONES YET.
SIGN: HISTORY
THESE ARE BOOKS FOR STUDYING.
SIGN: LITERATURE
THESE ARE BOOKS FOR STUDYING TOO.
THEY'RE ALL FOR STUDYING, AREN'T THEY? LET'S GO ON TO THE NEXT THING!
HEY! THAT'S IT?

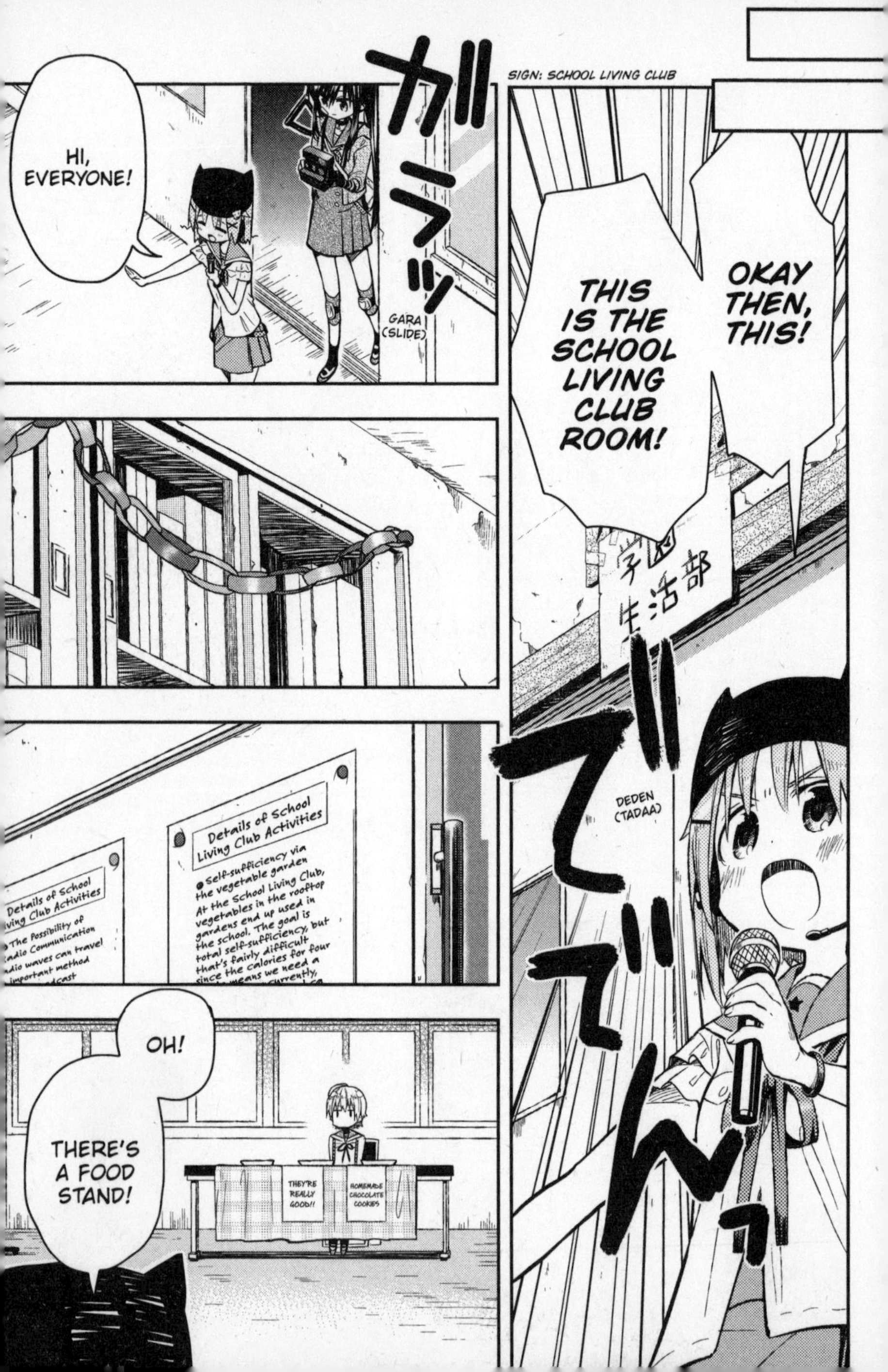
SIGN: SCHOOL LIVING CLUB
OKAY THEN, THIS!
THIS IS THE SCHOOL LIVING CLUB ROOM!
学園生活部
DEDEN (TADAA)
GARA (SLIDE)
HI, EVERYONE!
Details of School Living Club Activities
Self-sufficiency via the vegetable garden
At the School Living Club, vegetables in the rooftop gardens end up used in the school. The goal is total self-sufficiency, but that's fairly difficult since the calories for four
Details of School
The Possibility of
OH!
THERE'S A FOOD STAND!
THEY'RE REALLY GOOD!!
HOMEMADE CHOCOLATE COOKIES

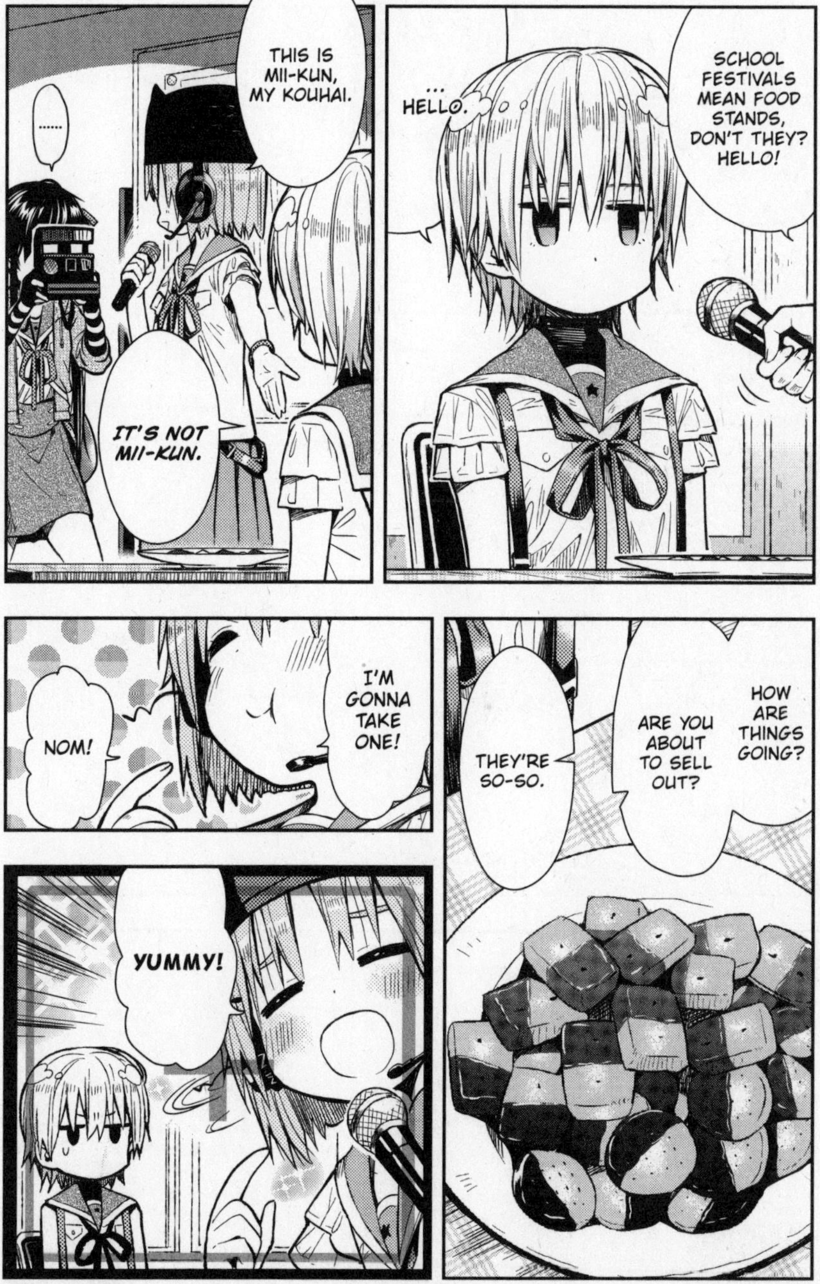
SCHOOL FESTIVALS MEAN FOOD STANDS, DON'T THEY? HELLO!
... HELLO.
THIS IS MII-KUN, MY KOUHAI.
......
IT'S NOT MII-KUN.
HOW ARE THINGS GOING?
ARE YOU ABOUT TO SELL OUT?
THEY'RE SO-SO.
I'M GONNA TAKE ONE!
NOM!
YUMMY!

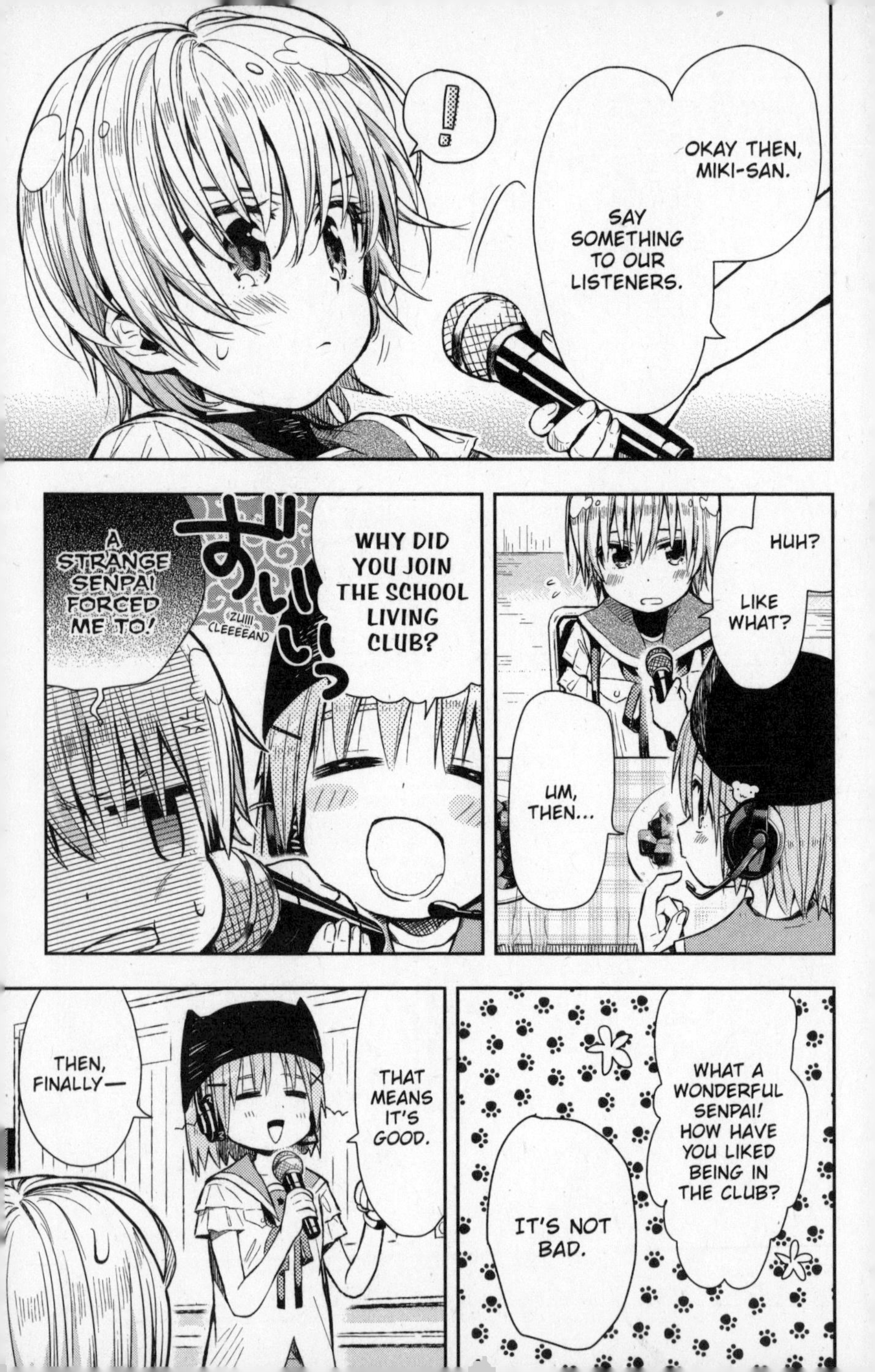
OKAY THEN, MIKI-SAN.
SAY SOMETHING TO OUR LISTENERS.
!
HUH?
LIKE WHAT?
UM, THEN...
WHY DID YOU JOIN THE SCHOOL LIVING CLUB?
ZUIII (LEEEEAN)
A STRANGE SENPAI FORCED ME TO!
WHAT A WONDERFUL SENPAI! HOW HAVE YOU LIKED BEING IN THE CLUB?
IT'S NOT BAD.
THAT MEANS IT'S GOOD.
THEN, FINALLY—

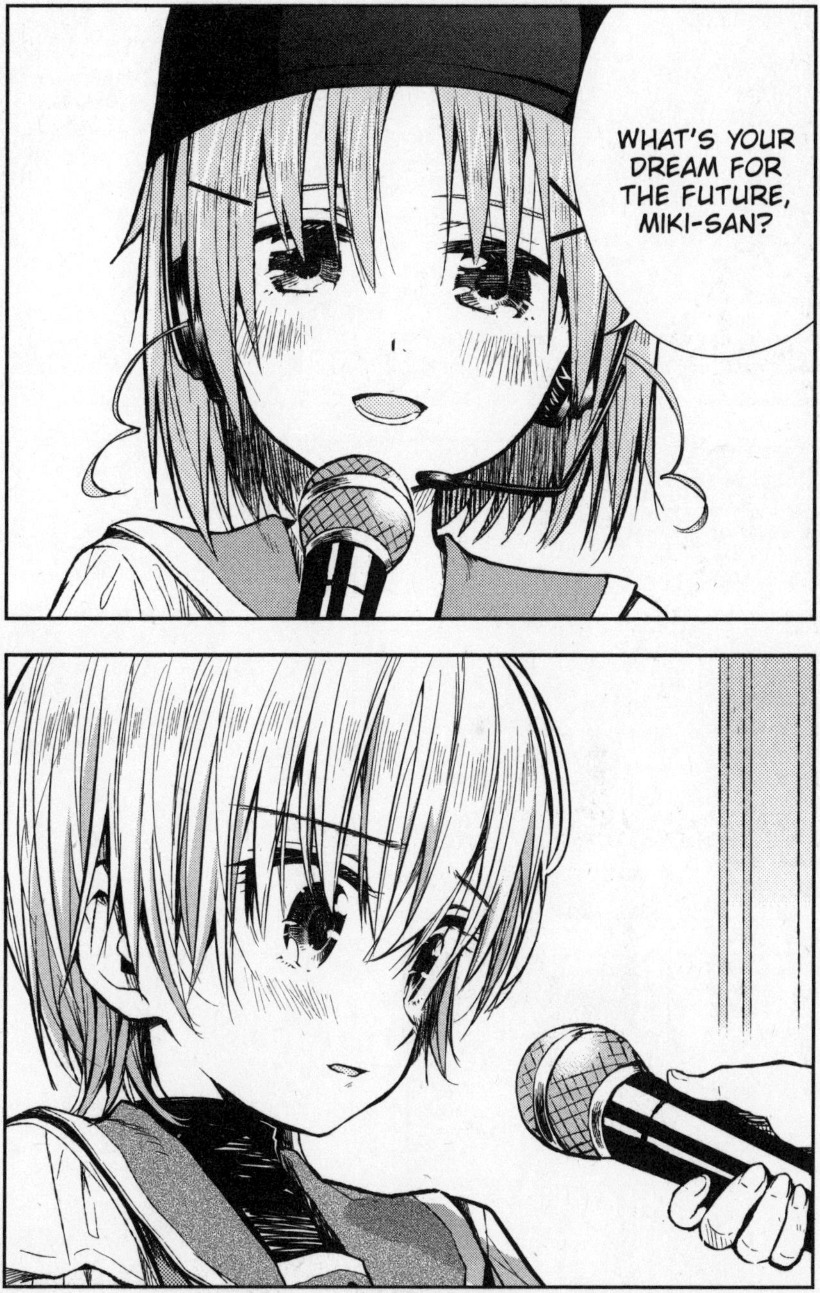
WHAT'S YOUR DREAM FOR THE FUTURE, MIKI-SAN?

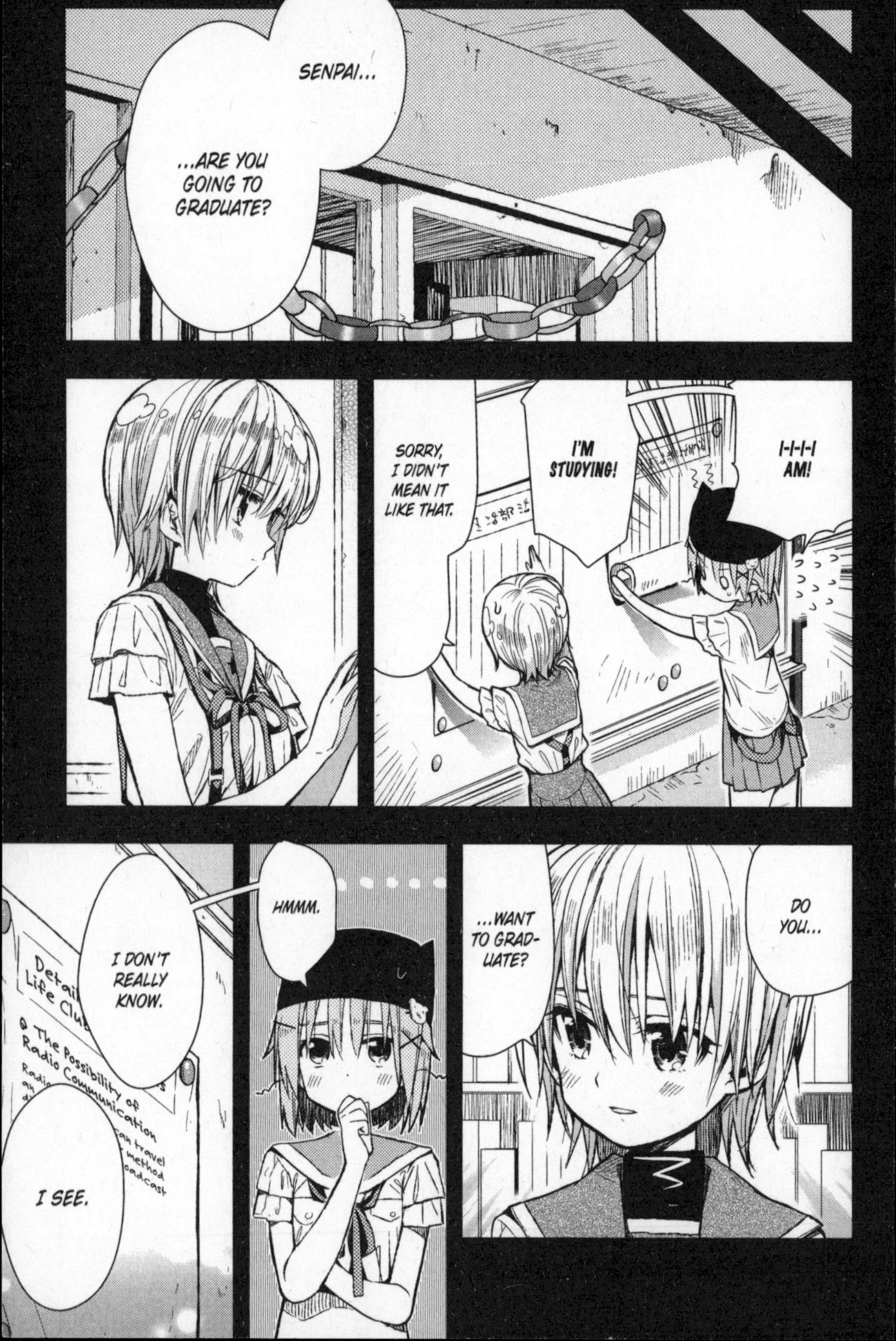
SENPAI...
...ARE YOU GOING TO GRADUATE?
I-I-I-I AM!
I'M STUDYING!
SORRY, I DIDN'T MEAN IT LIKE THAT.
DO YOU...
...WANT TO GRAD-UATE?
HMMM.
I DON'T REALLY KNOW.
The Possibility of Radio Communication
I SEE.

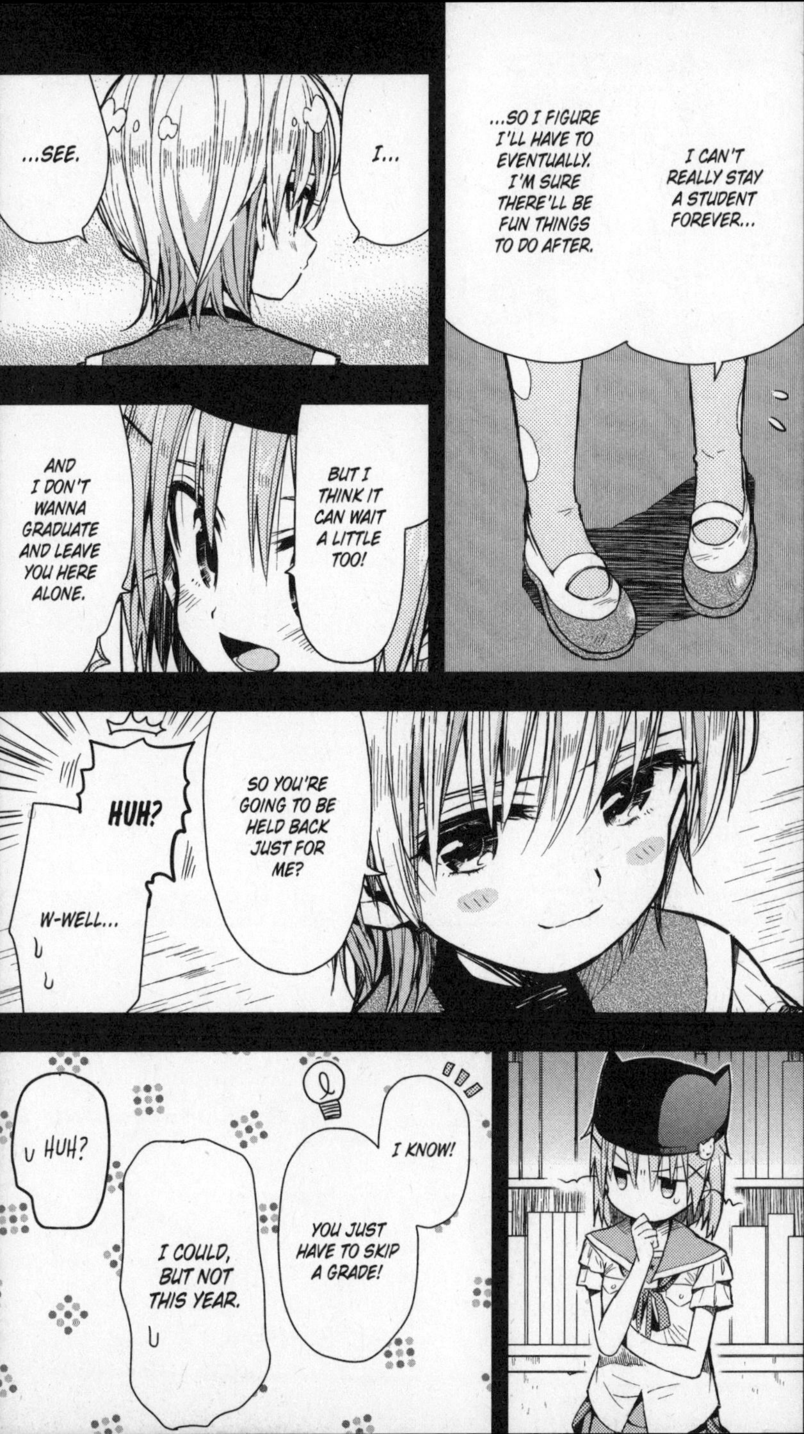
I CAN'T REALLY STAY A STUDENT FOREVER...
...SO I FIGURE I'LL HAVE TO EVENTUALLY. I'M SURE THERE'LL BE FUN THINGS TO DO AFTER.
I...
...SEE.
BUT I THINK IT CAN WAIT A LITTLE TOO!
AND I DON'T WANNA GRADUATE AND LEAVE YOU HERE ALONE.
SO YOU'RE GOING TO BE HELD BACK JUST FOR ME?
HUH?
W-WELL...
I KNOW!
YOU JUST HAVE TO SKIP A GRADE!
HUH?
I COULD, BUT NOT THIS YEAR.

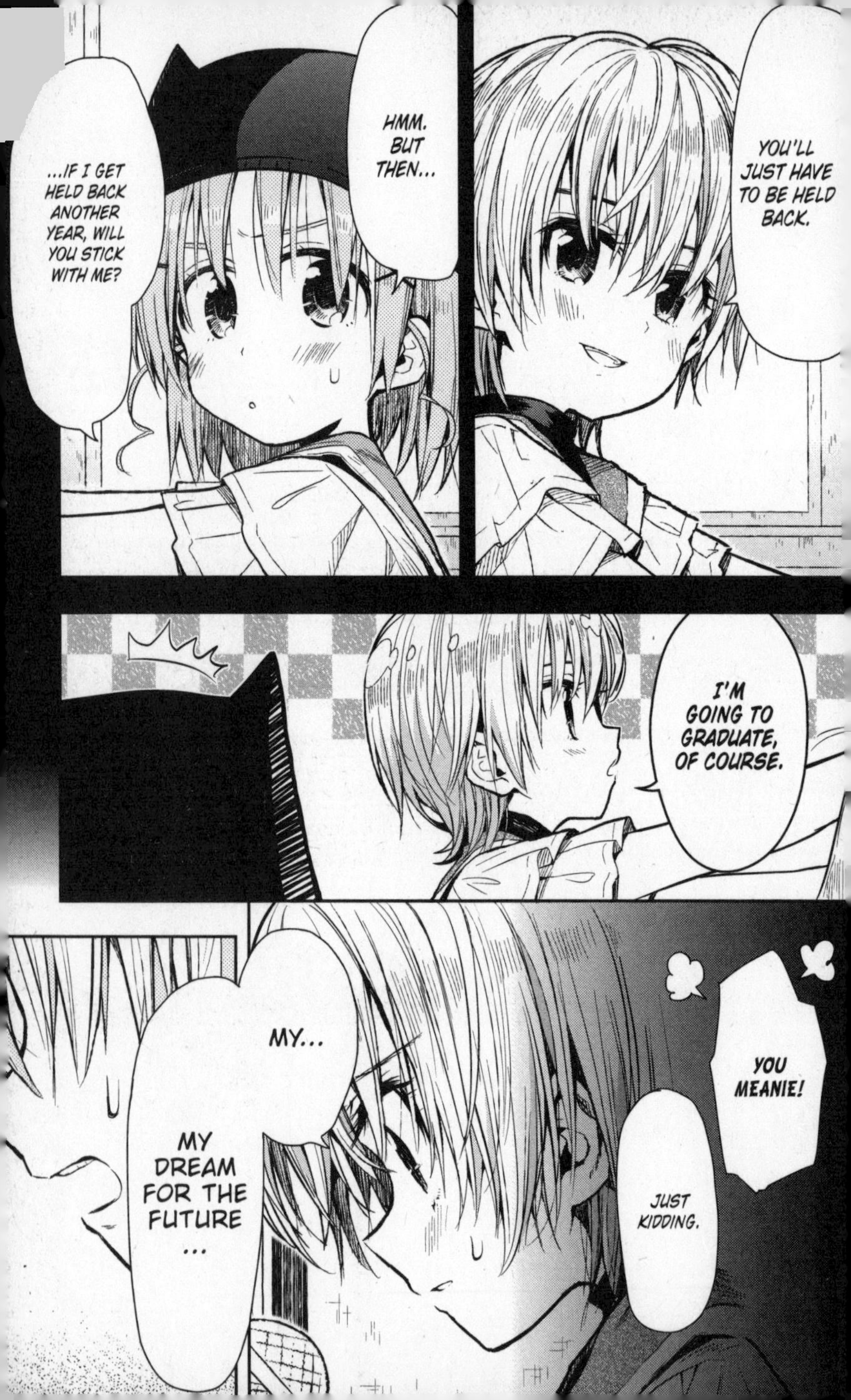
YOU'LL JUST HAVE TO BE HELD BACK.
HMM. BUT THEN...
...IF I GET HELD BACK ANOTHER YEAR, WILL YOU STICK WITH ME?
I'M GOING TO GRADUATE, OF COURSE.
YOU MEANIE!
JUST KIDDING.
MY...
MY DREAM FOR THE FUTURE ...

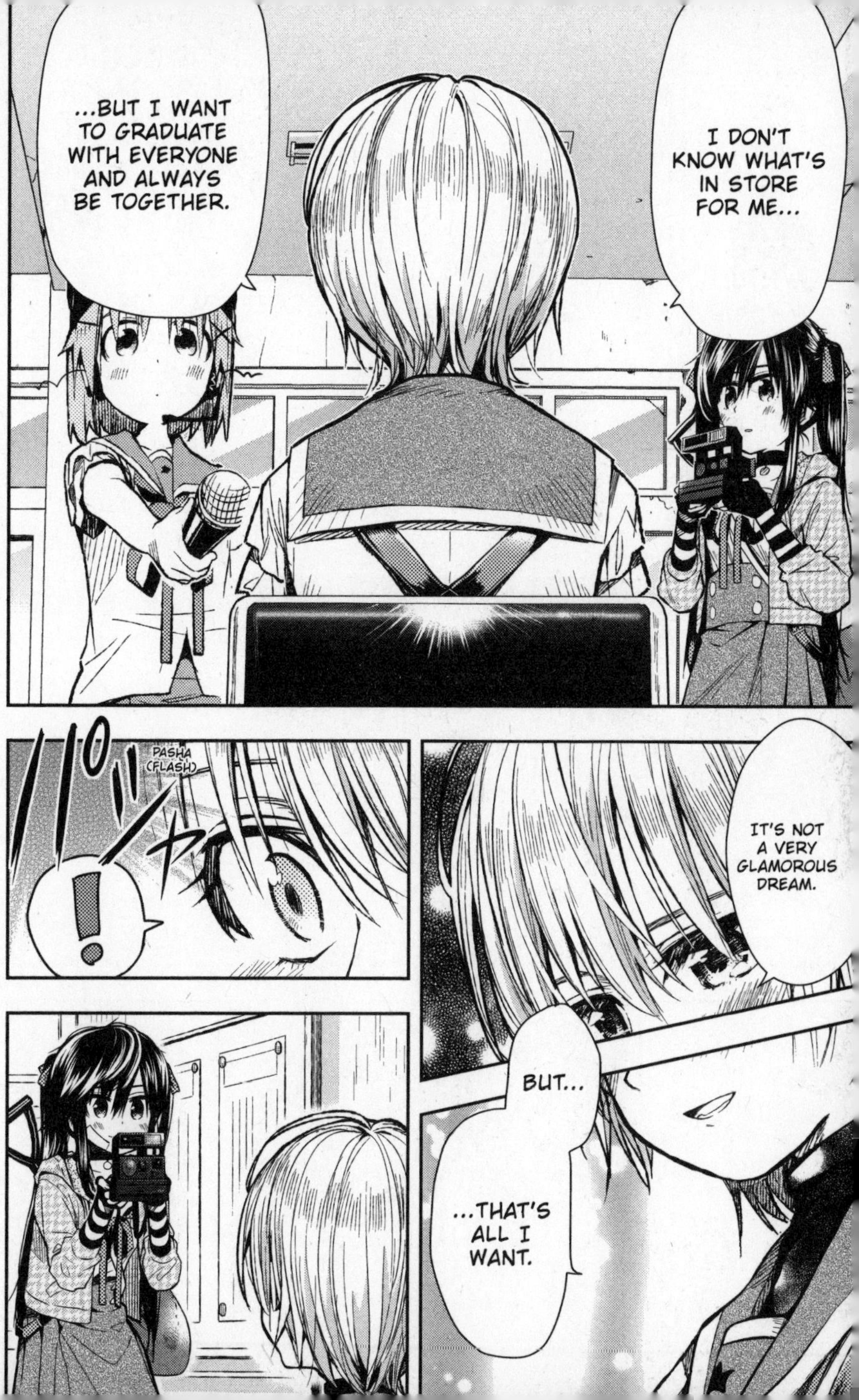
I DON'T KNOW WHAT'S IN STORE FOR ME...
...BUT I WANT TO GRADUATE WITH EVERYONE AND ALWAYS BE TOGETHER.
IT'S NOT A VERY GLAMOROUS DREAM.
PASHA (FLASH)
!
BUT...
...THAT'S ALL I WANT.

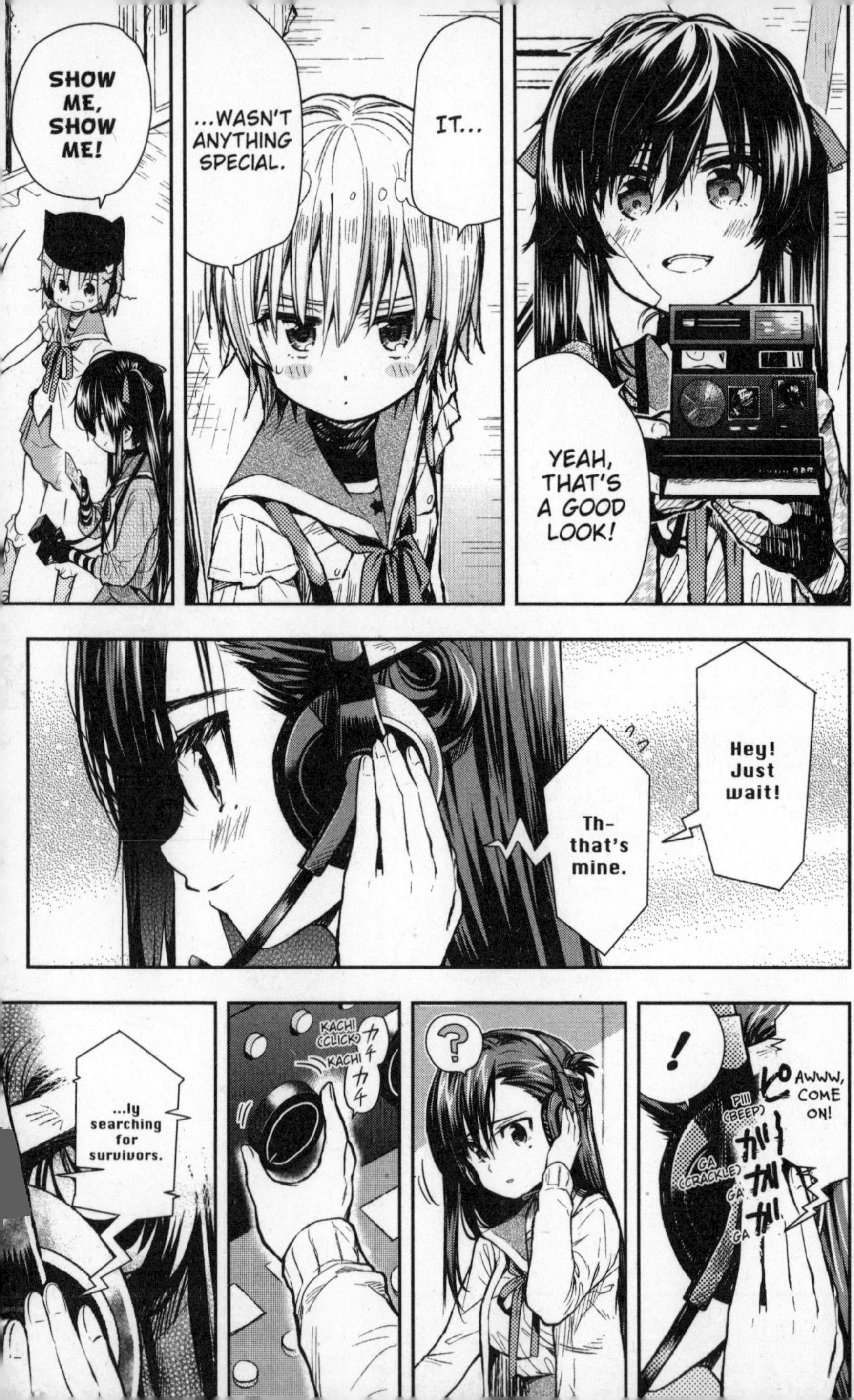
YEAH, THAT'S A GOOD LOOK!
IT...
...WASN'T ANYTHING SPECIAL.
SHOW ME, SHOW ME!
Hey! Just wait!
Th- that's mine.
!
AWWW, COME ON!
PIII (BEEP)
GA (CRACKLE)
GA
GA
?
KACHI (CLICK)
KACHI
...ly searching for survivors.

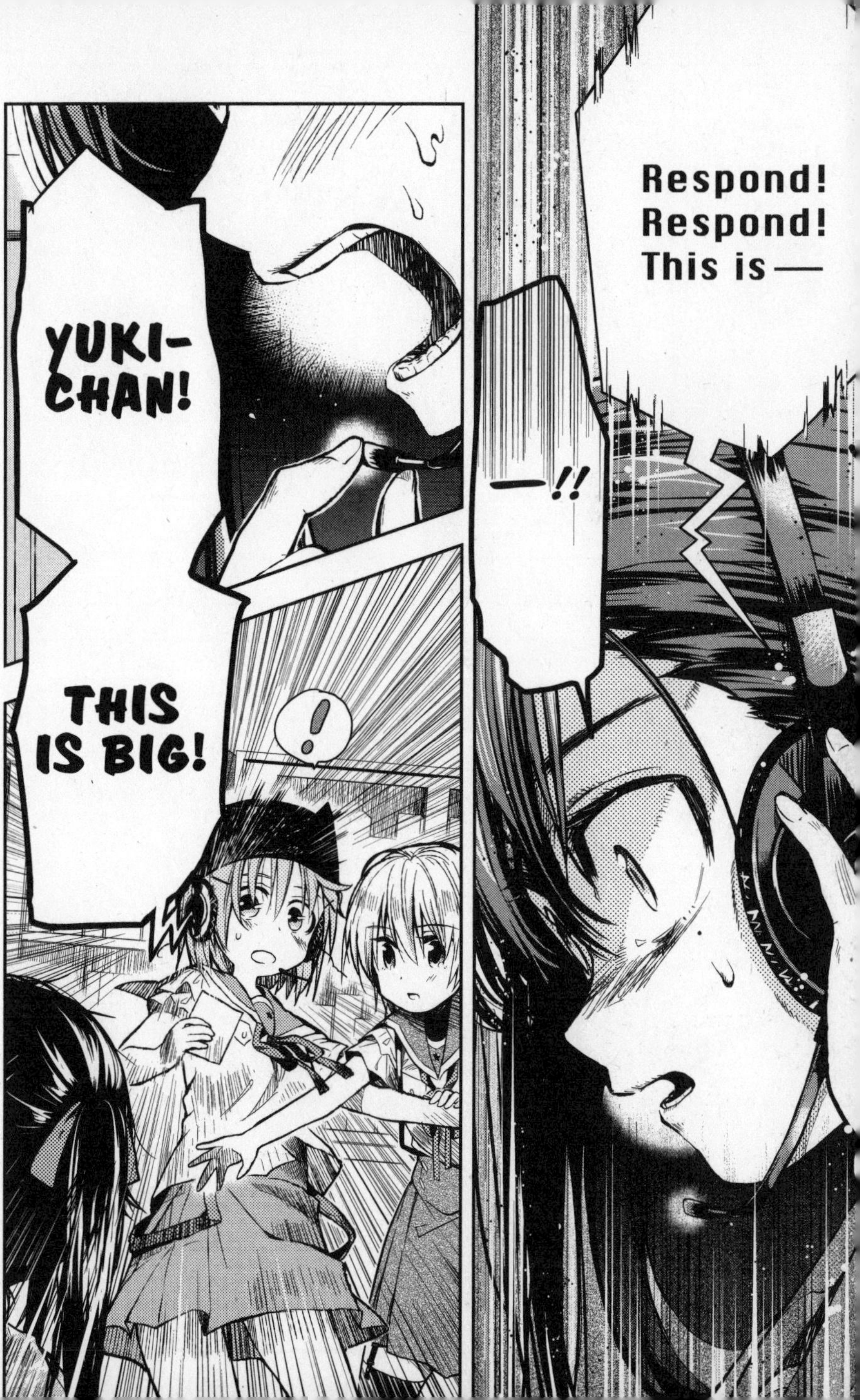
Respond! Respond! This is—
—!!
YUKI-CHAN!
THIS IS BIG!
!

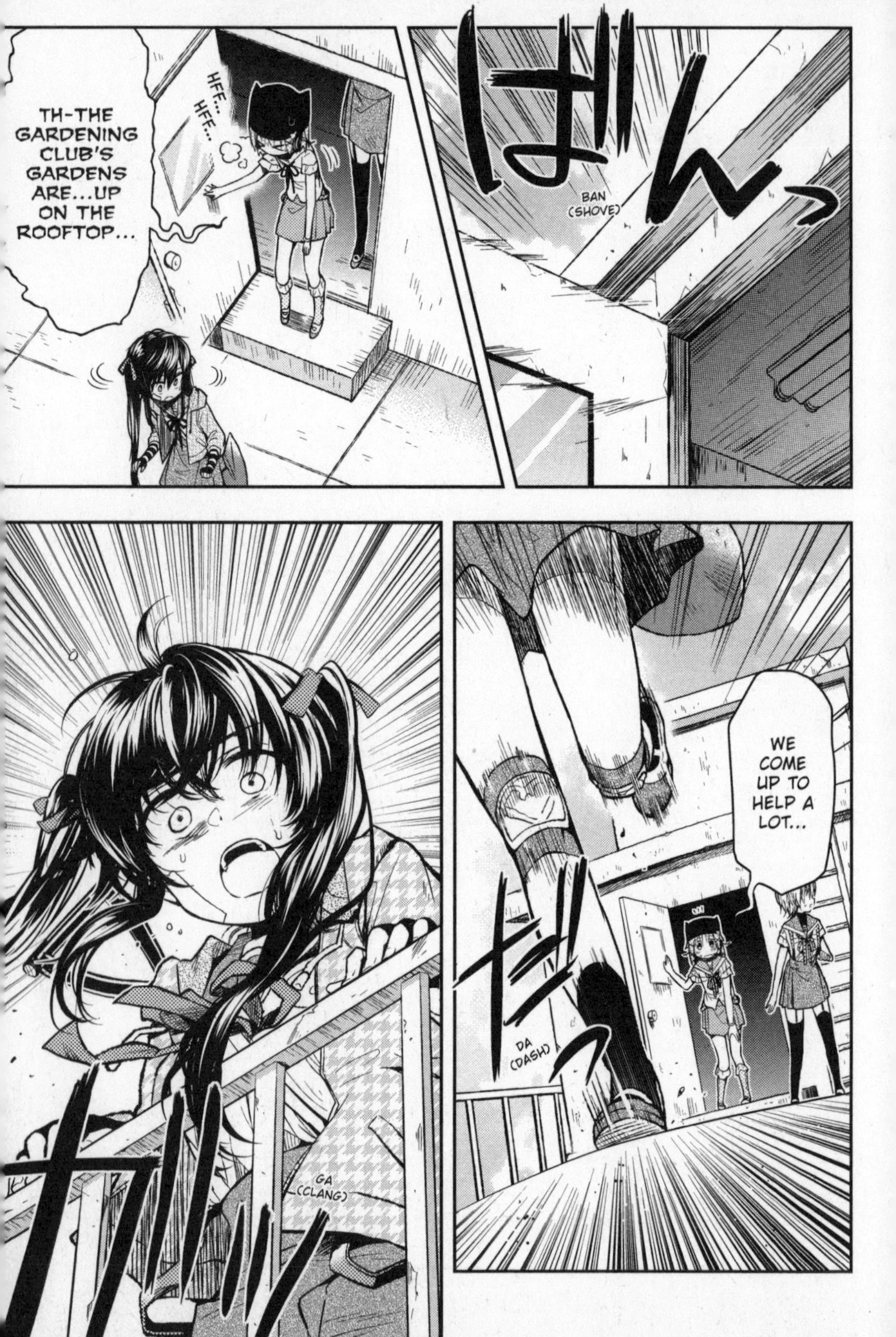
ばんっ
BAN (SHOVE)
HFF... HFF...
TH-THE GARDENING CLUB'S GARDENS ARE...UP ON THE ROOFTOP...
WE COME UP TO HELP A LOT...
DA (DASH)
GA (CLANG)

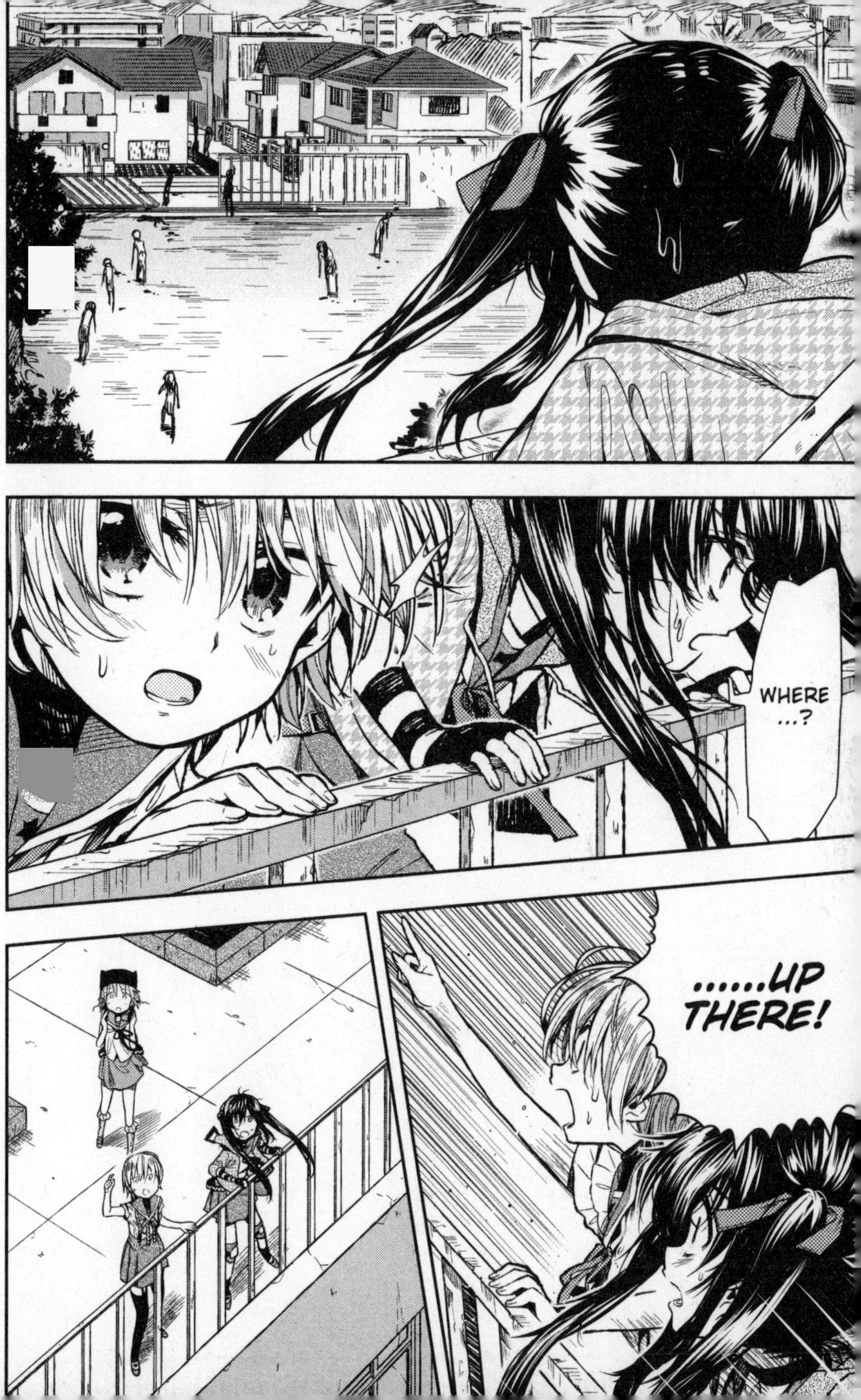
WHERE ...?
......UP THERE!

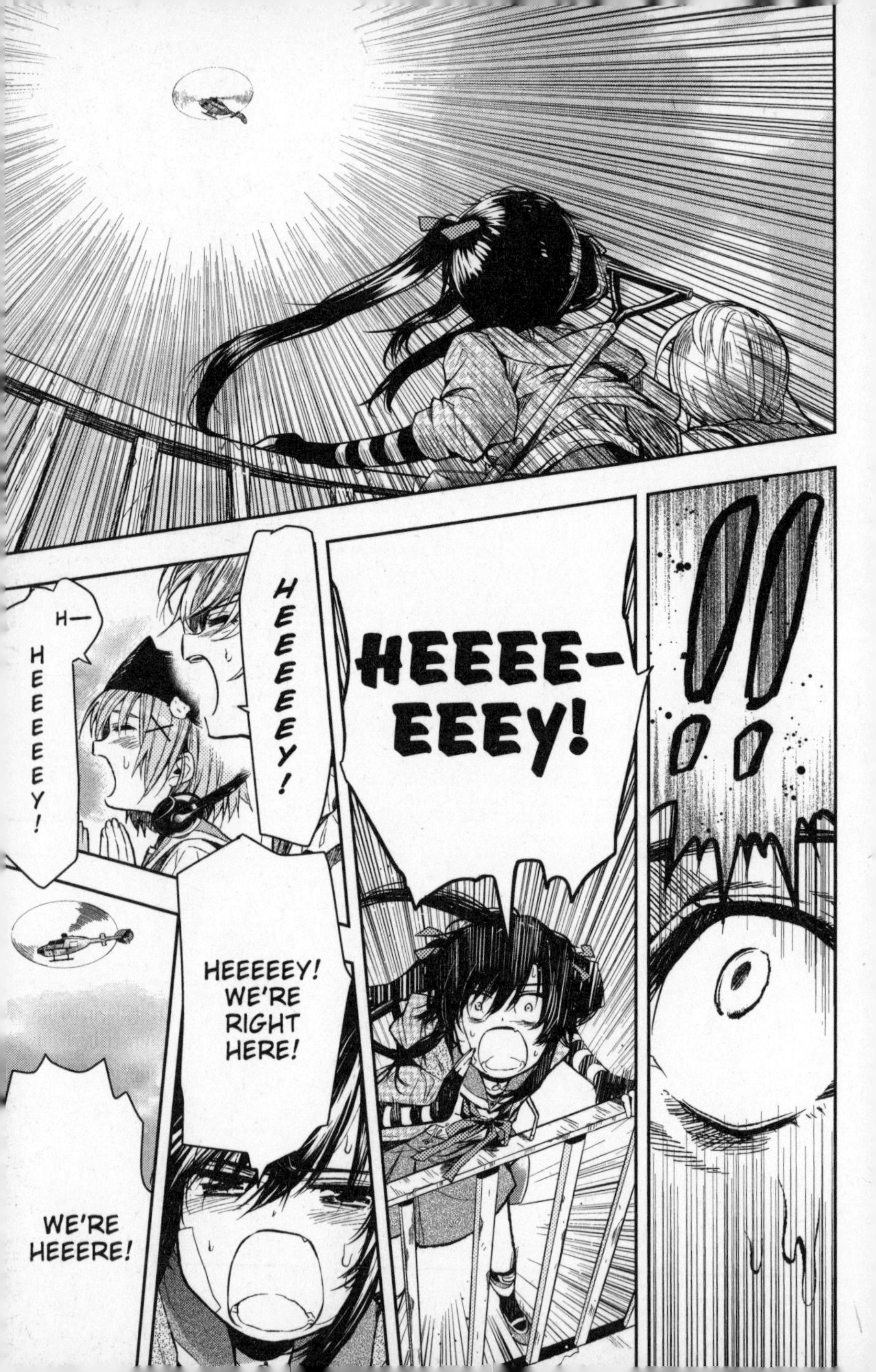
!!
HEEEEE-EEEY!
HEEEEEEY!
H— HEEEEEEY!
HEEEEEY! WE'RE RIGHT HERE!
WE'RE HEEERE!

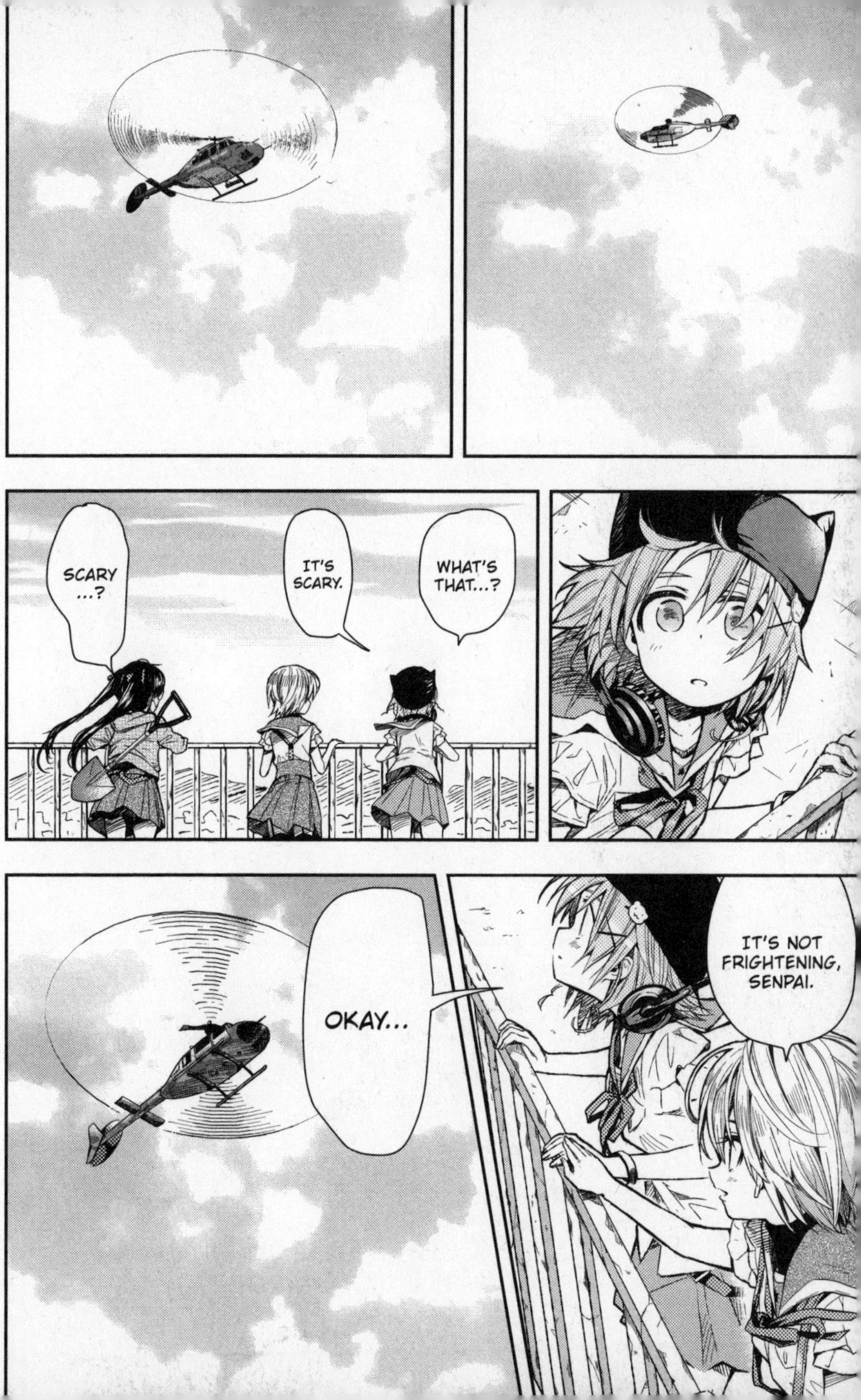
WHAT'S THAT...?
IT'S SCARY.
SCARY ...?
IT'S NOT FRIGHTENING, SENPAI.
OKAY...

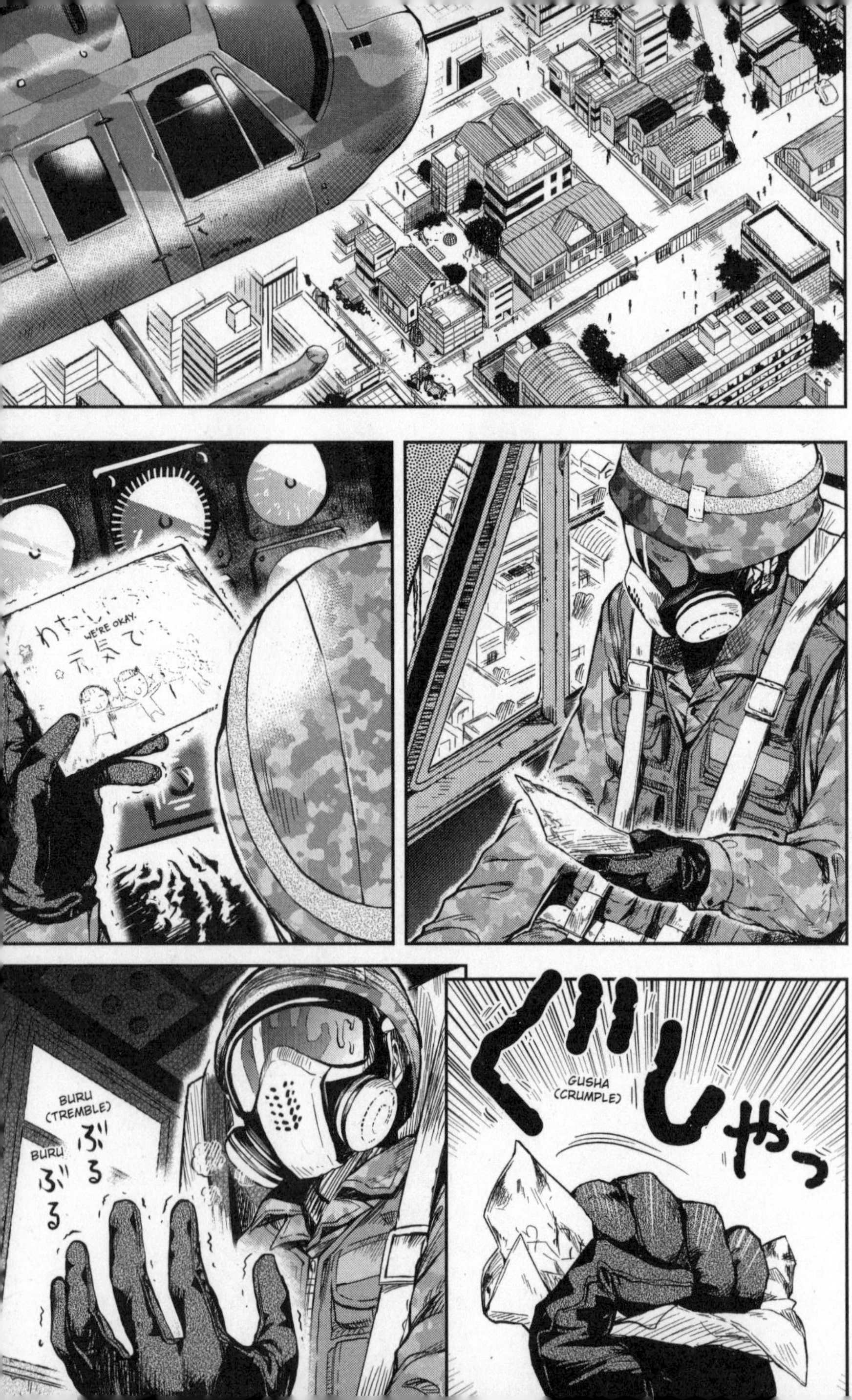
WE'RE OKAY.
ぐしゃっ
GUSHA (CRUMPLE)
ぶる
BURU (TREMBLE)
ぶる
BURU

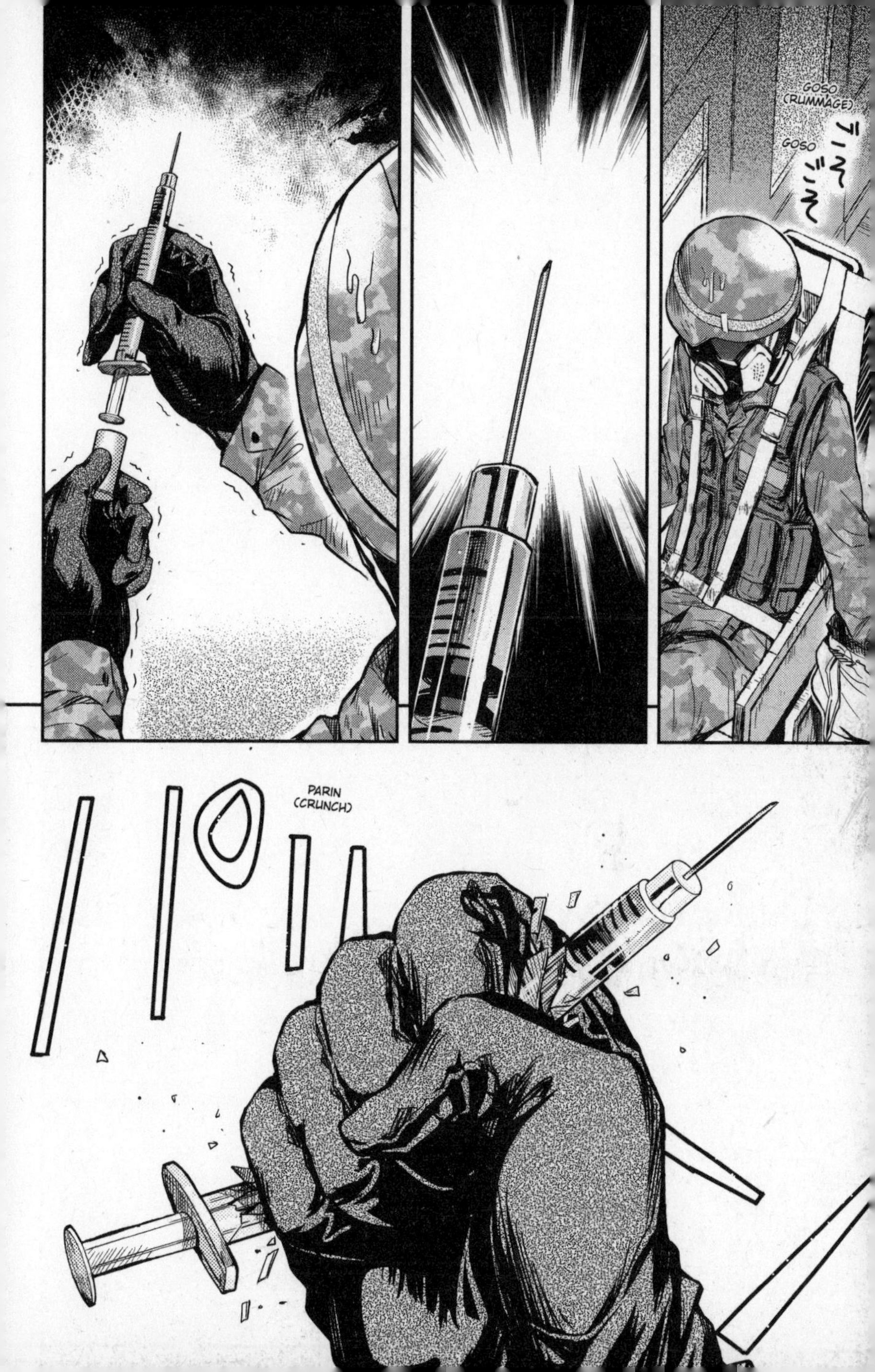
GOSO
(RUMMAGE)
GOSO
ゴソゴソ
PARIN
(CRUNCH)

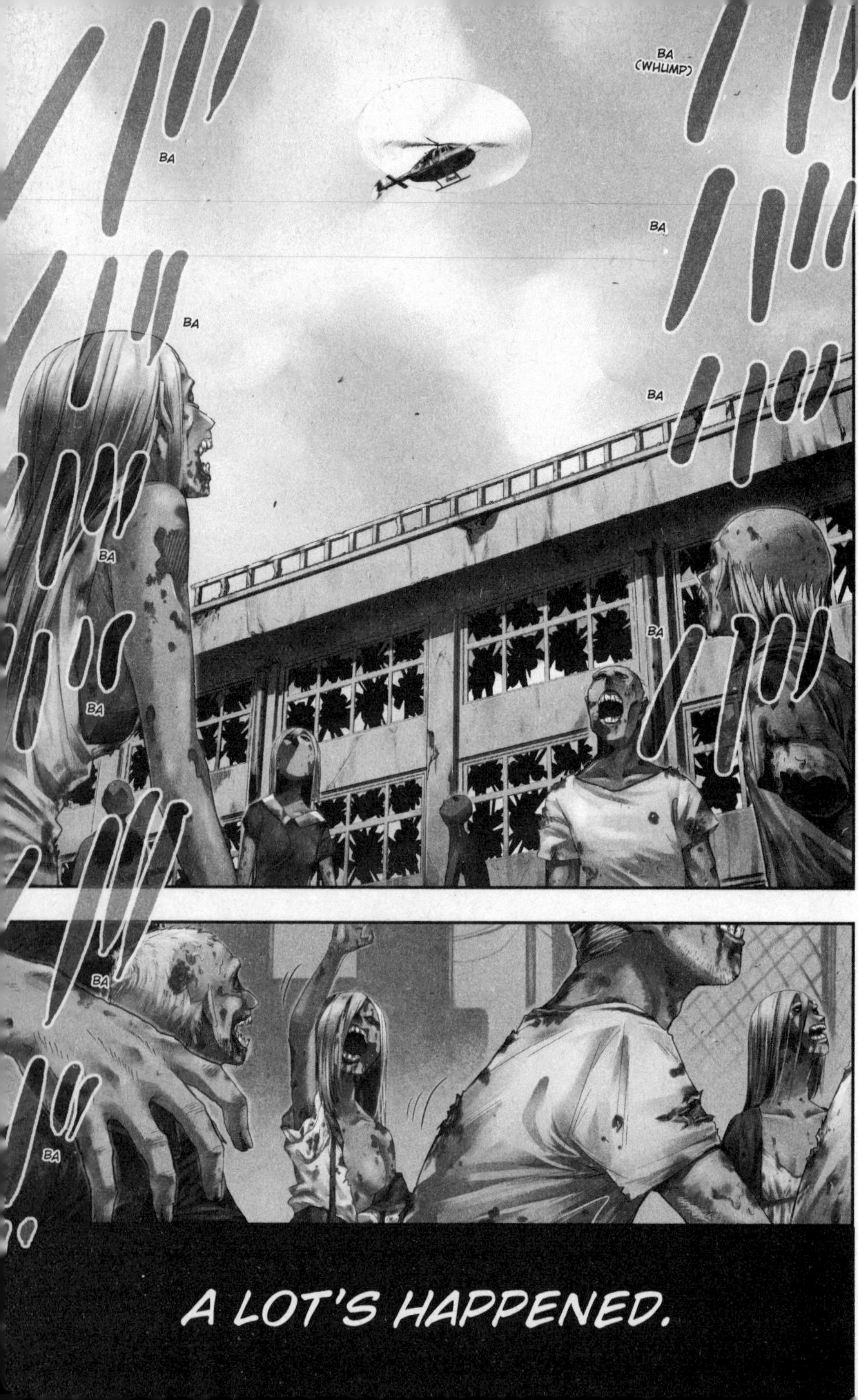
BA
(WHUMP)
BA
BA
BA
BA
BA
BA
BA
BA
BA
A LOT'S HAPPENED.

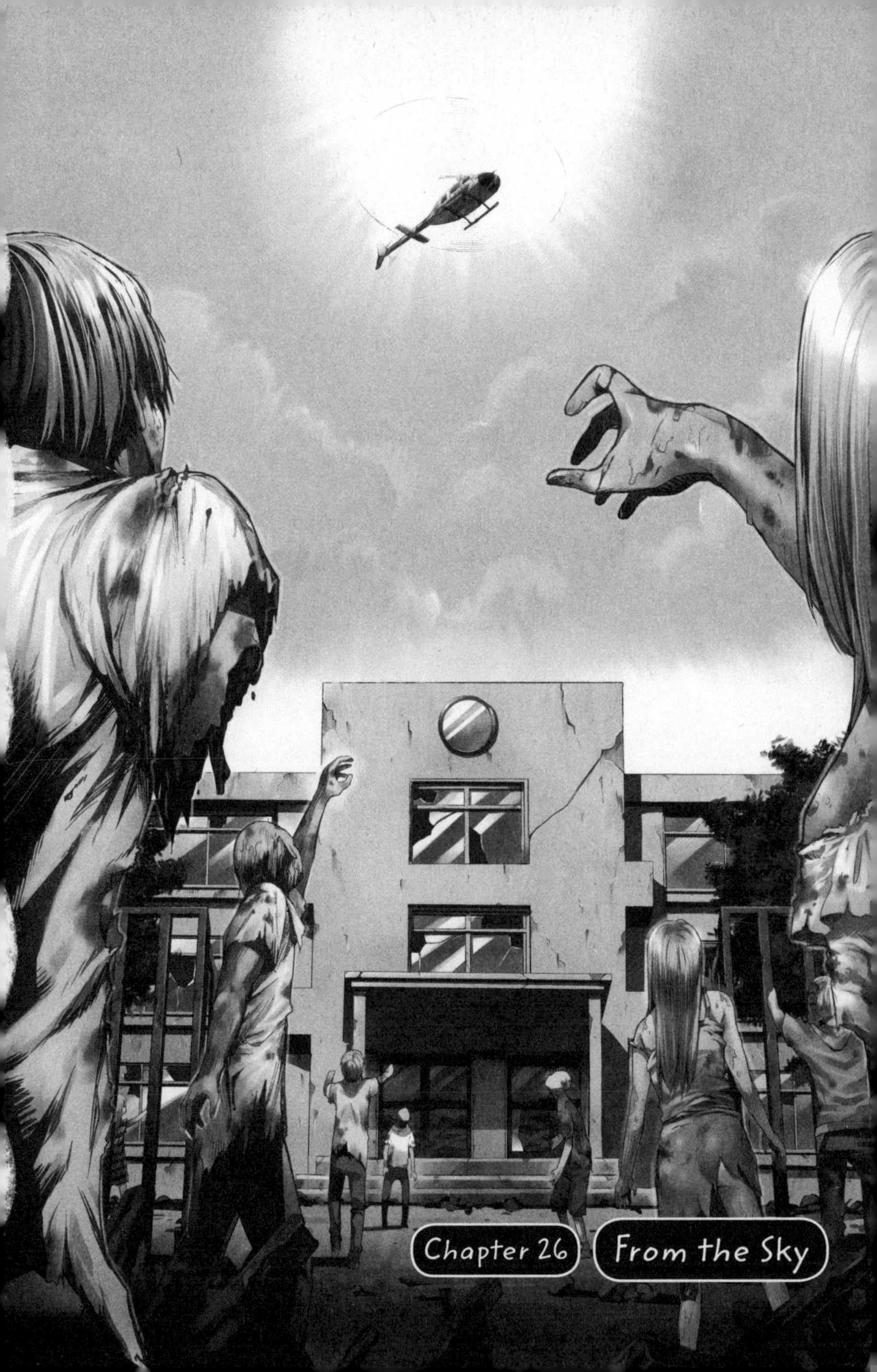
Chapter 26
From the Sky

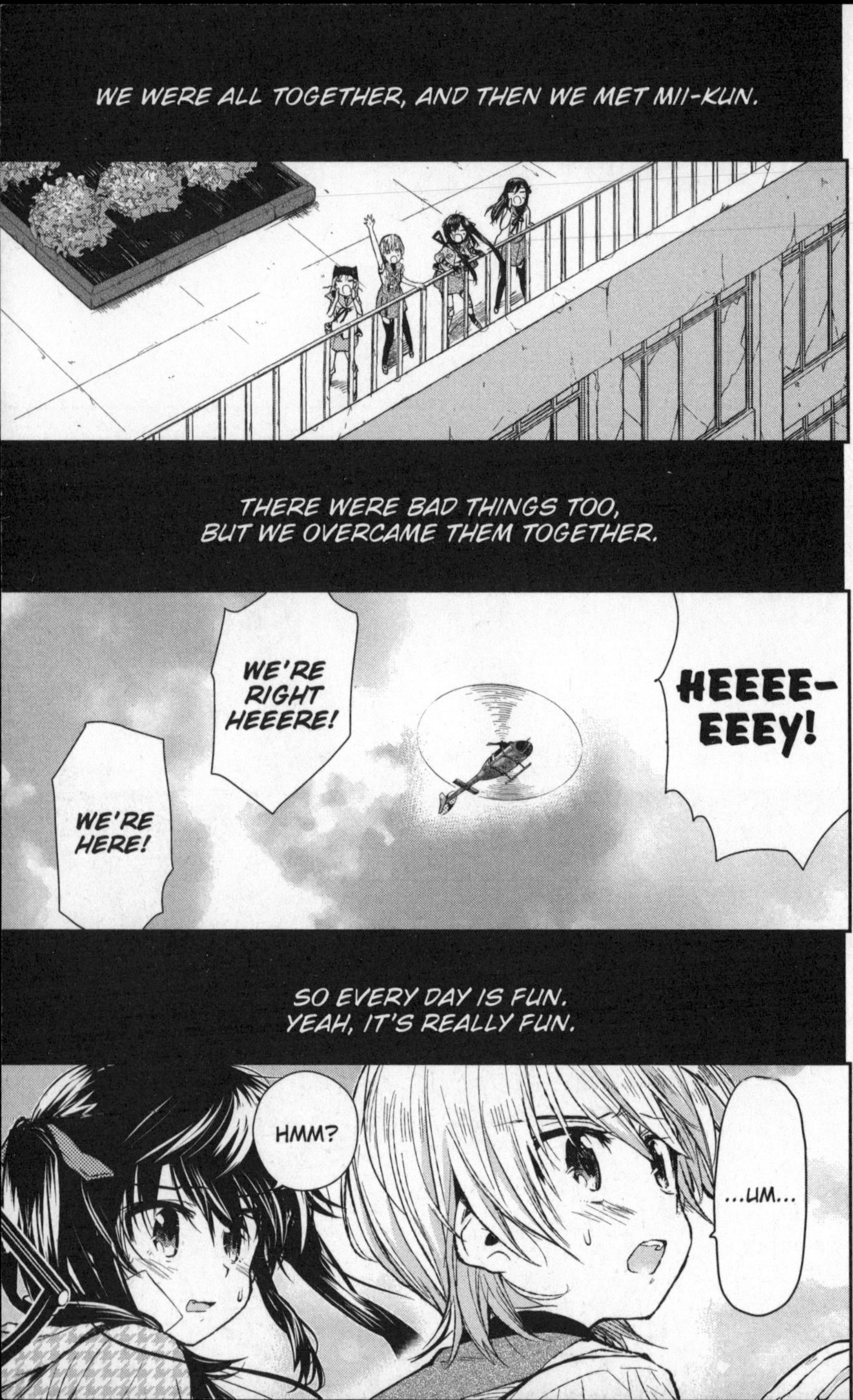
WE WERE ALL TOGETHER, AND THEN WE MET MII-KUN.
THERE WERE BAD THINGS TOO, BUT WE OVERCAME THEM TOGETHER.
HEEEE-EEEY!
WE'RE RIGHT HEEERE!
WE'RE HERE!
SO EVERY DAY IS FUN. YEAH, IT'S REALLY FUN.
...UM...
HMM?

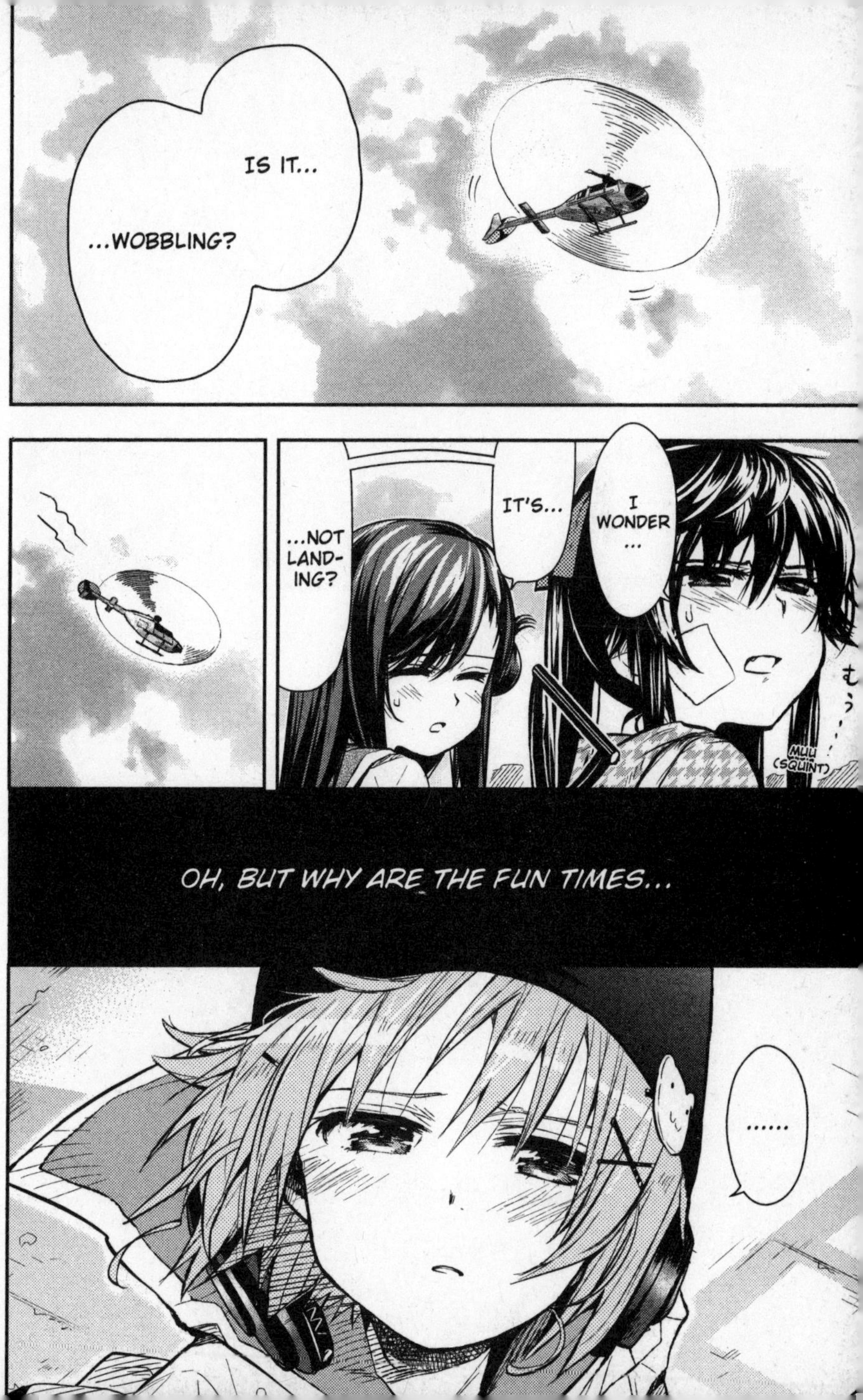
IS IT...
...WOBBLING?
I WONDER...
IT'S...
...NOT LANDING?
むう
MUU (SQUINT)
OH, BUT WHY ARE THE FUN TIMES...
......

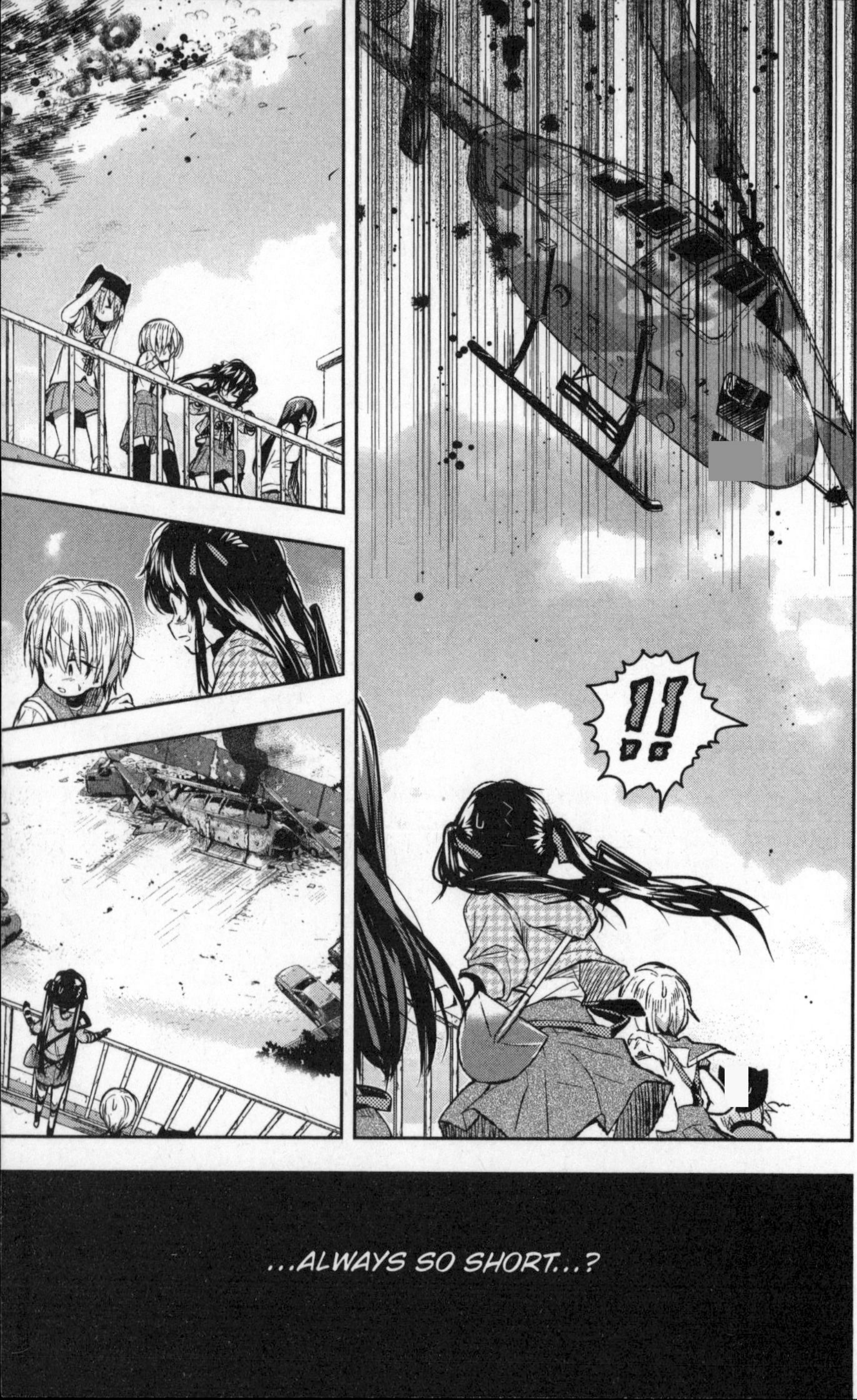
!!
...ALWAYS SO SHORT...?

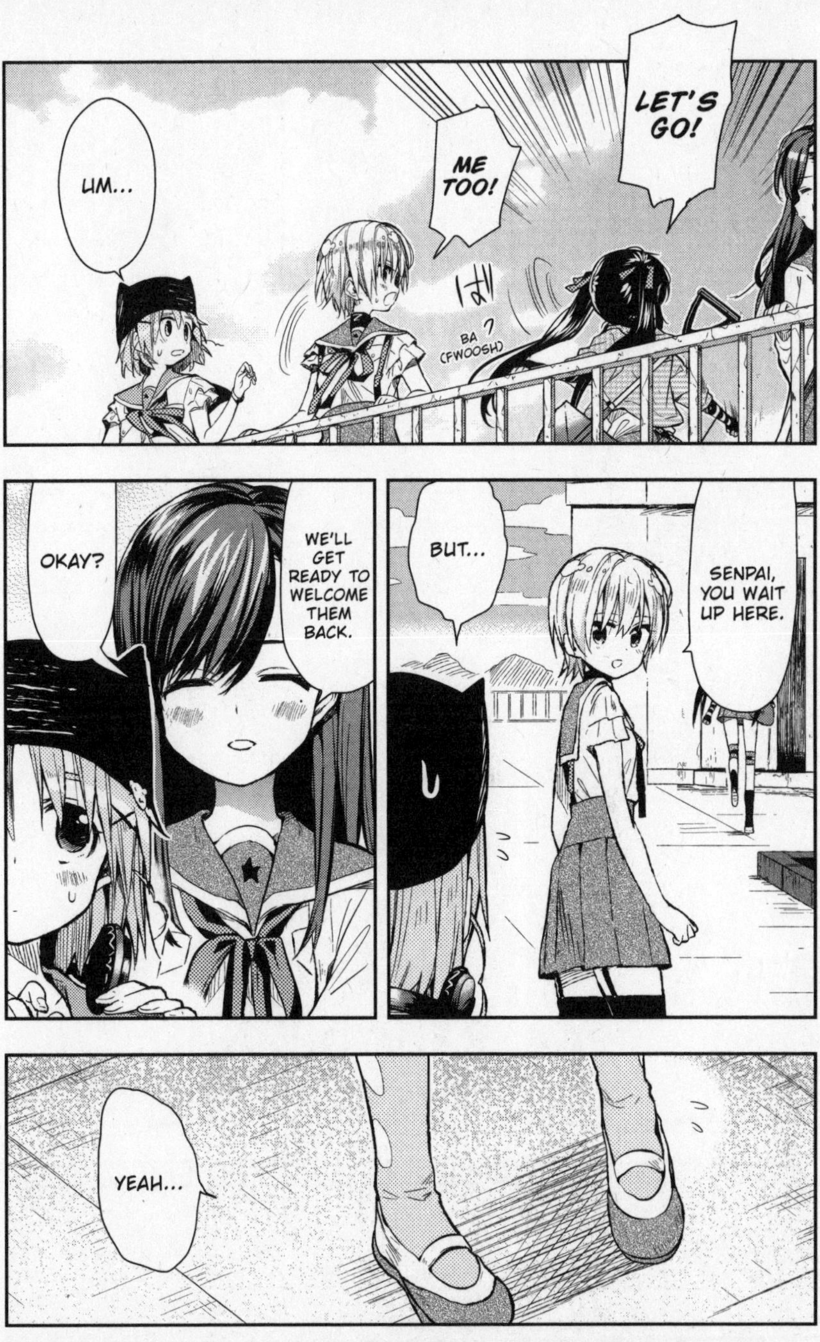
LET'S GO!
ME TOO!
ぱっ
BA (FWOOSH)
UM...
SENPAI, YOU WAIT UP HERE.
BUT...
WE'LL GET READY TO WELCOME THEM BACK.
OKAY?
YEAH...

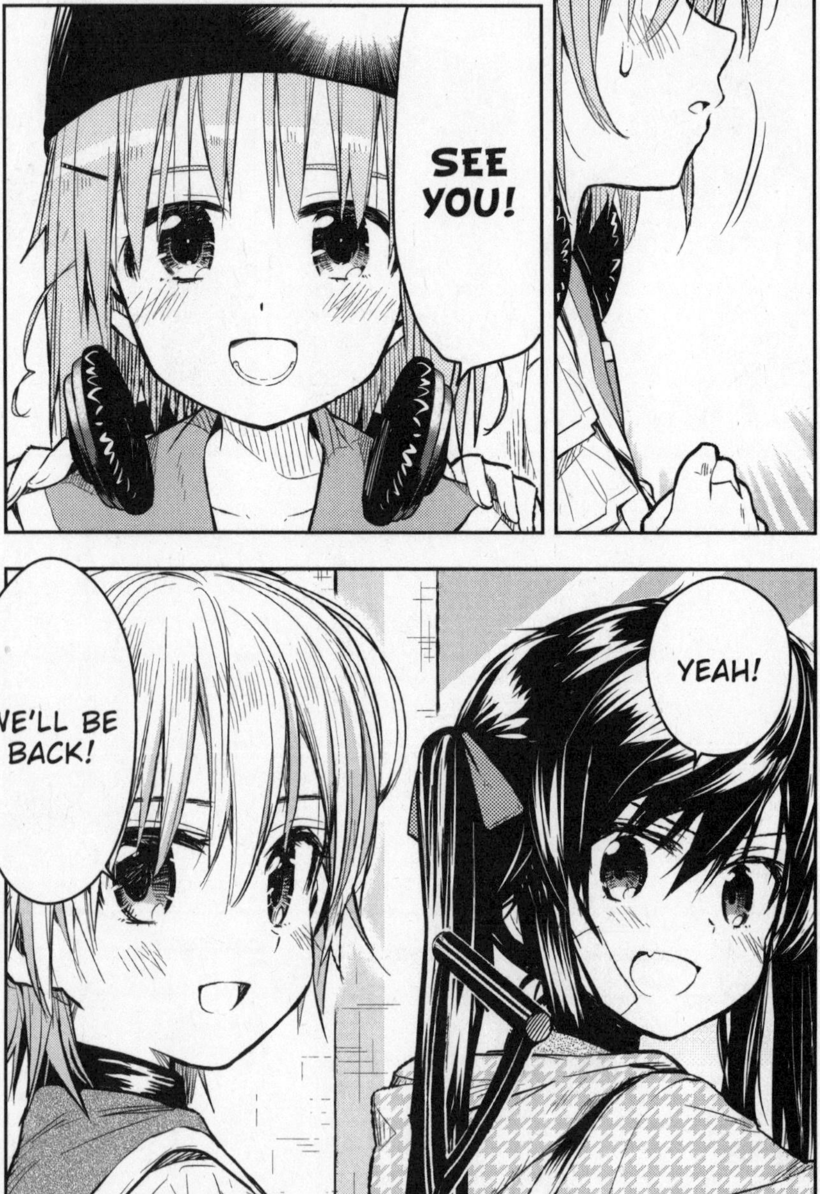
SEE YOU!
YEAH!
WE'LL BE BACK!

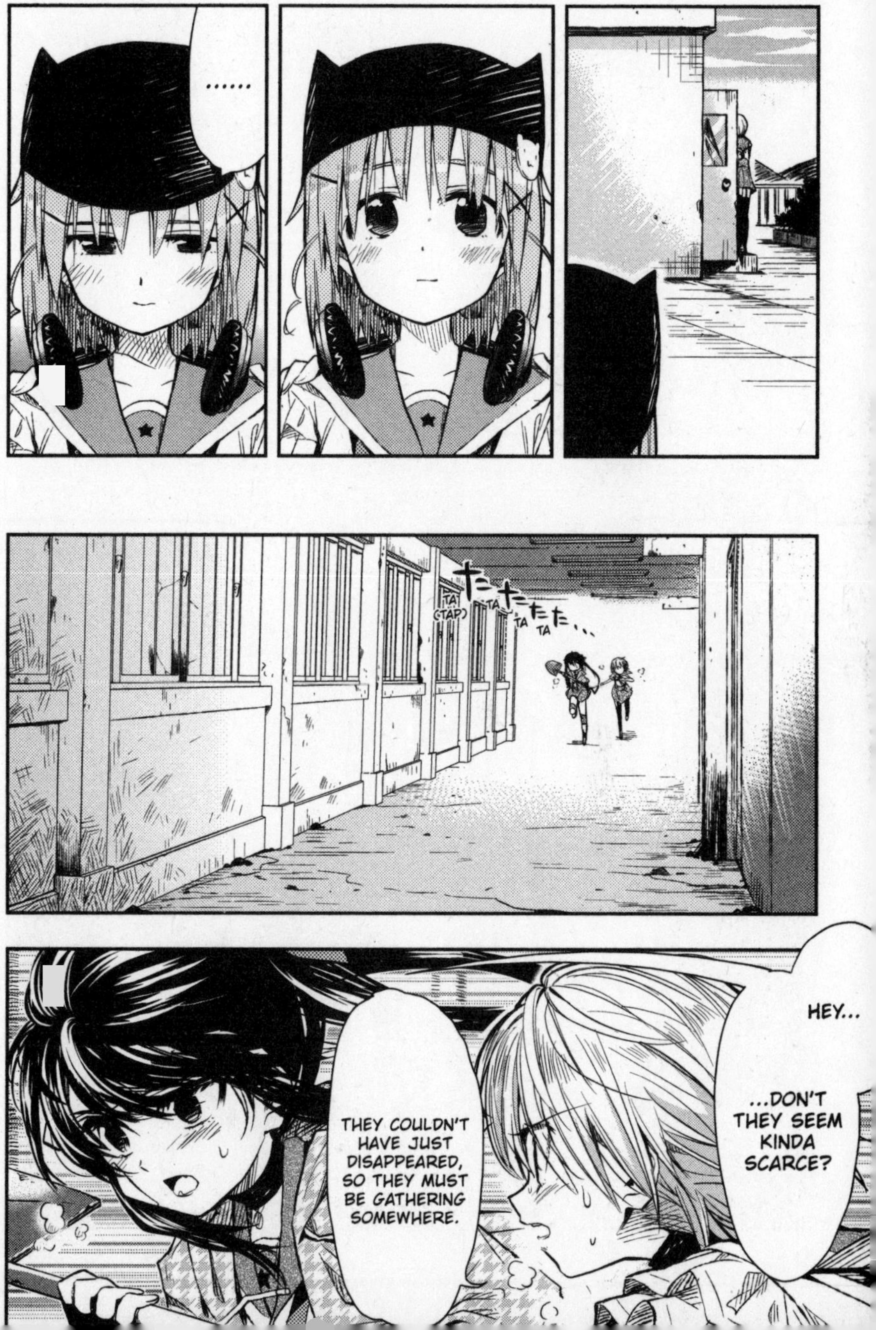
......
TA (TAP) TA TA TA
HEY...
...DON'T THEY SEEM KINDA SCARCE?
THEY COULDN'T HAVE JUST DISAPPEARED, SO THEY MUST BE GATHERING SOMEWHERE.

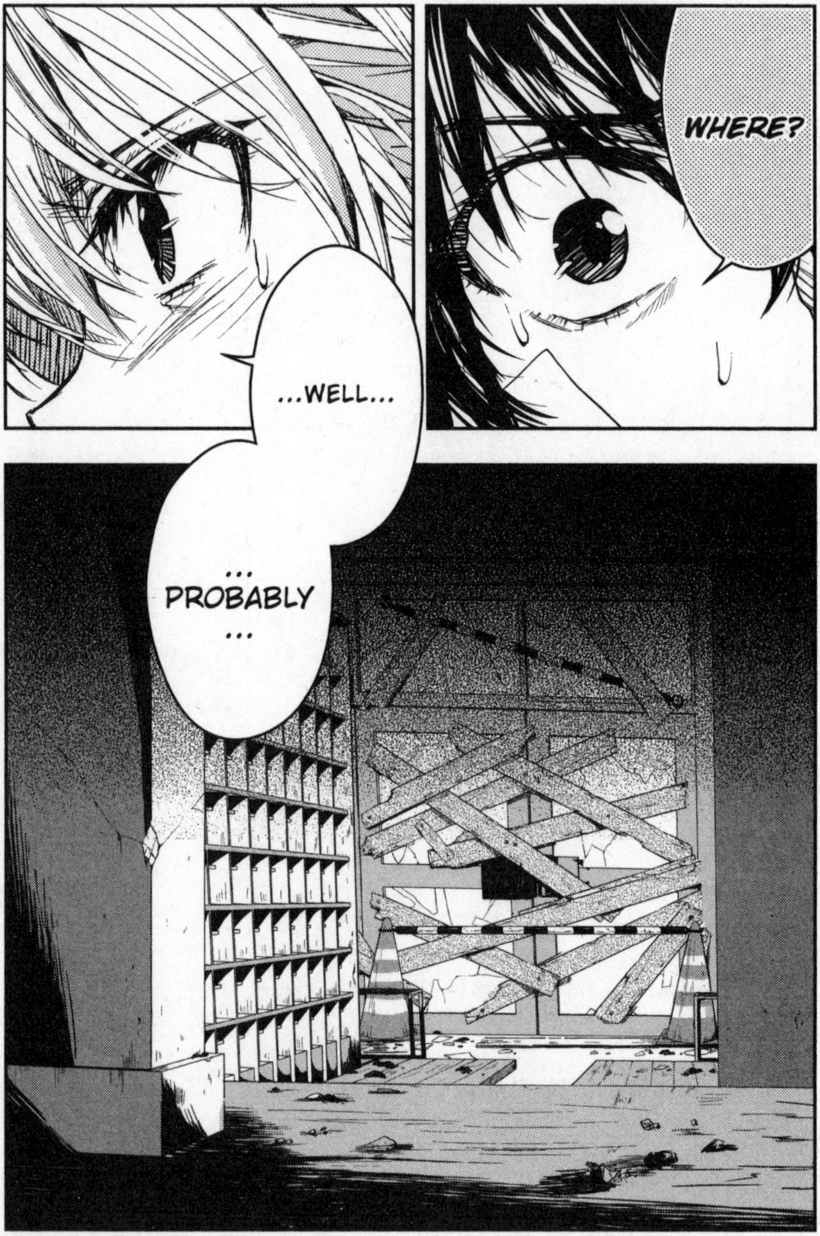
WHERE?
...WELL...
... PROBABLY ...

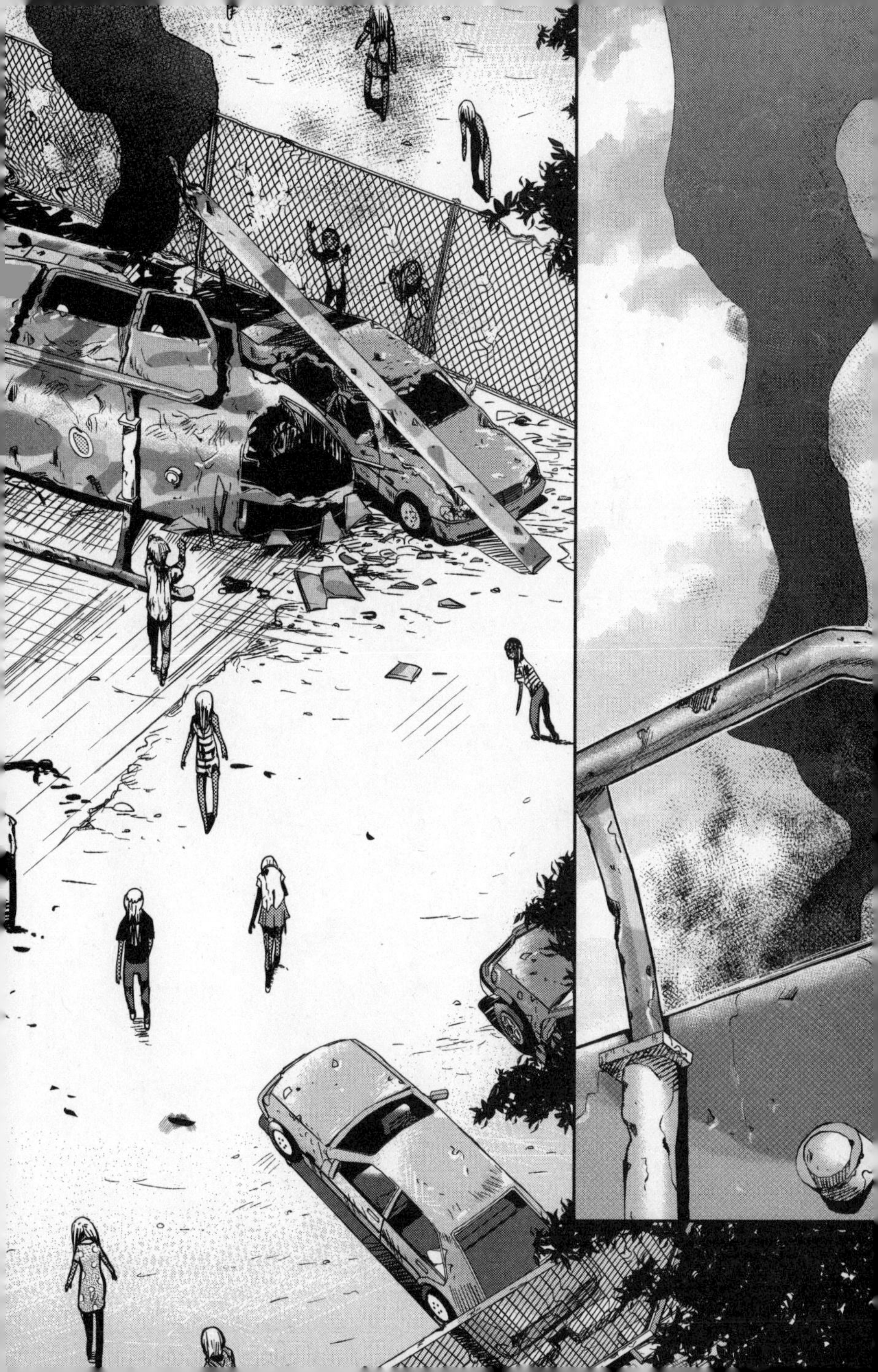

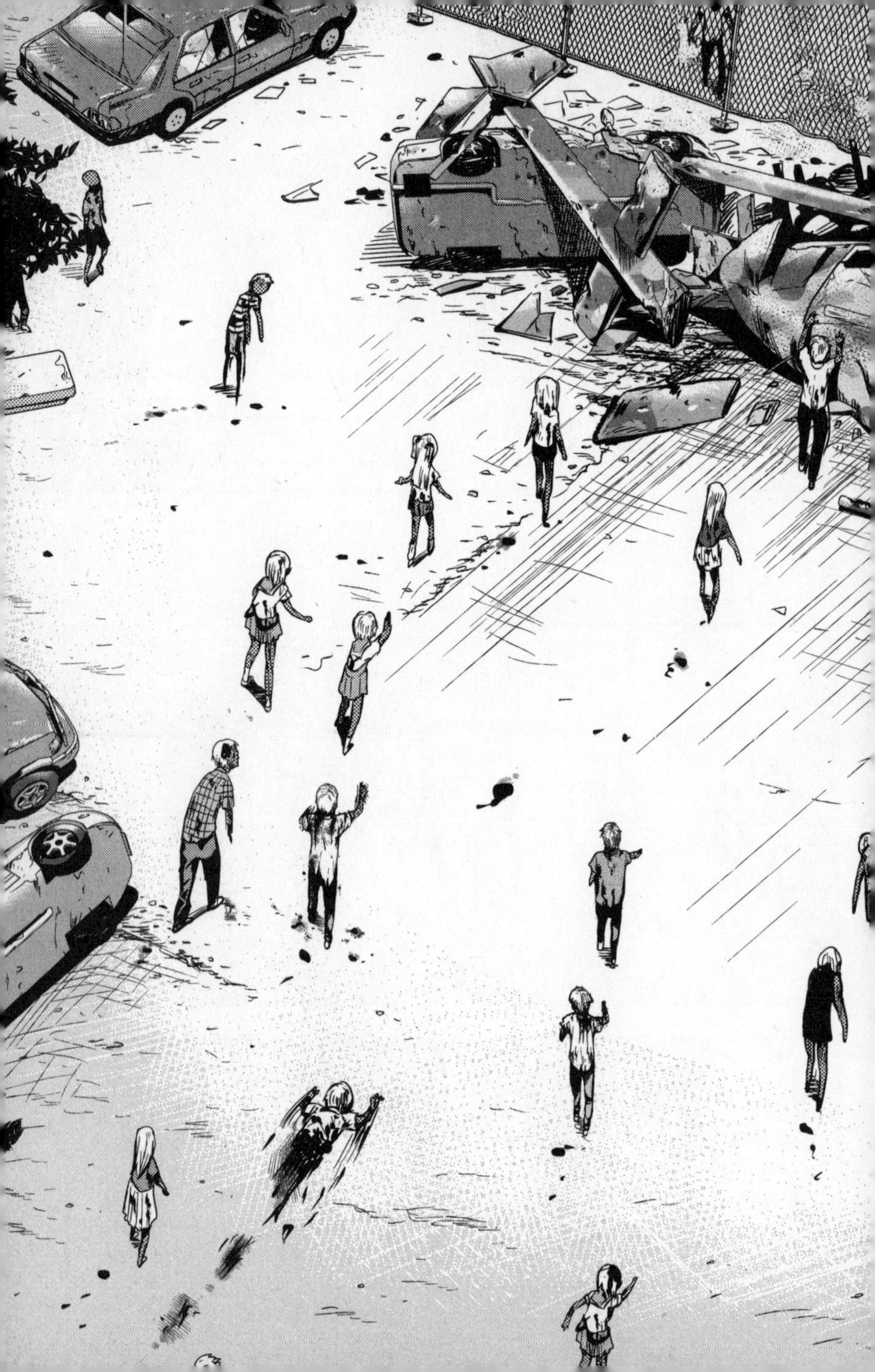

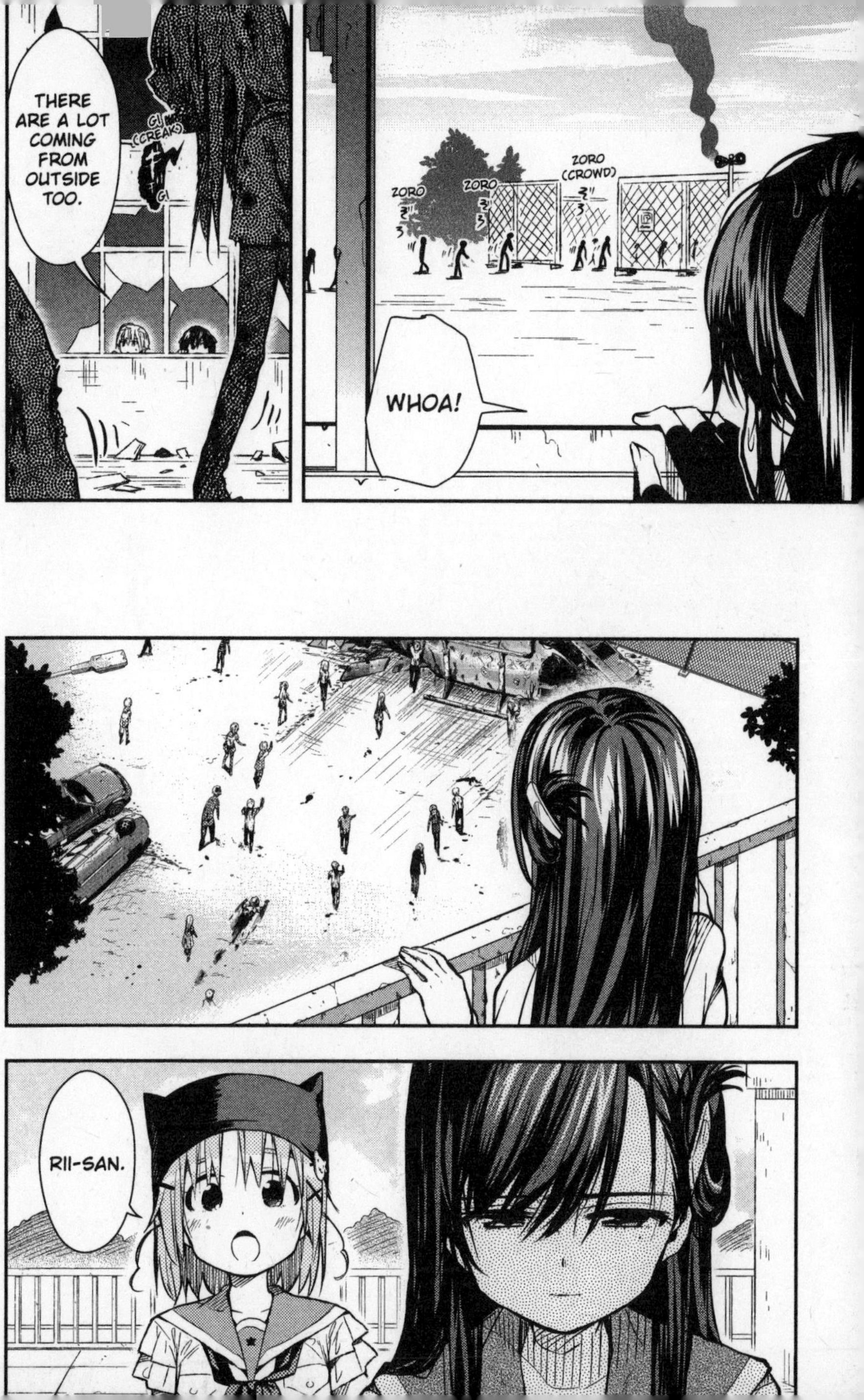
ZORO (CROWD)
ZORO
ZORO
WHOA!
GI (CREAK)
GI
THERE ARE A LOT COMING FROM OUTSIDE TOO.
RII-SAN.

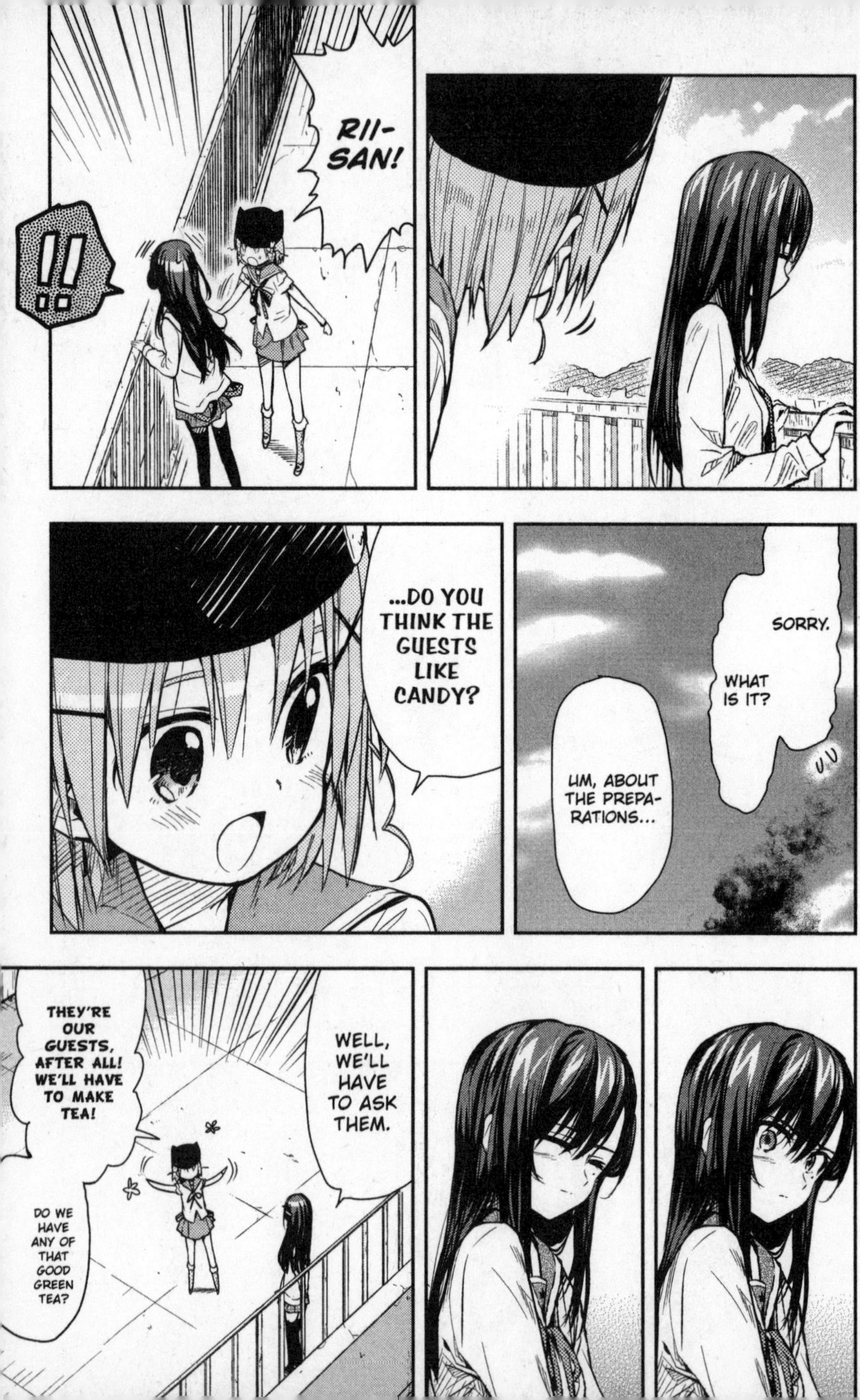
RII-SAN!
!!
SORRY.
WHAT IS IT?
UM, ABOUT THE PREPARATIONS...
...DO YOU THINK THE GUESTS LIKE CANDY?
WELL, WE'LL HAVE TO ASK THEM.
THEY'RE OUR GUESTS, AFTER ALL! WE'LL HAVE TO MAKE TEA!
DO WE HAVE ANY OF THAT GOOD GREEN TEA?

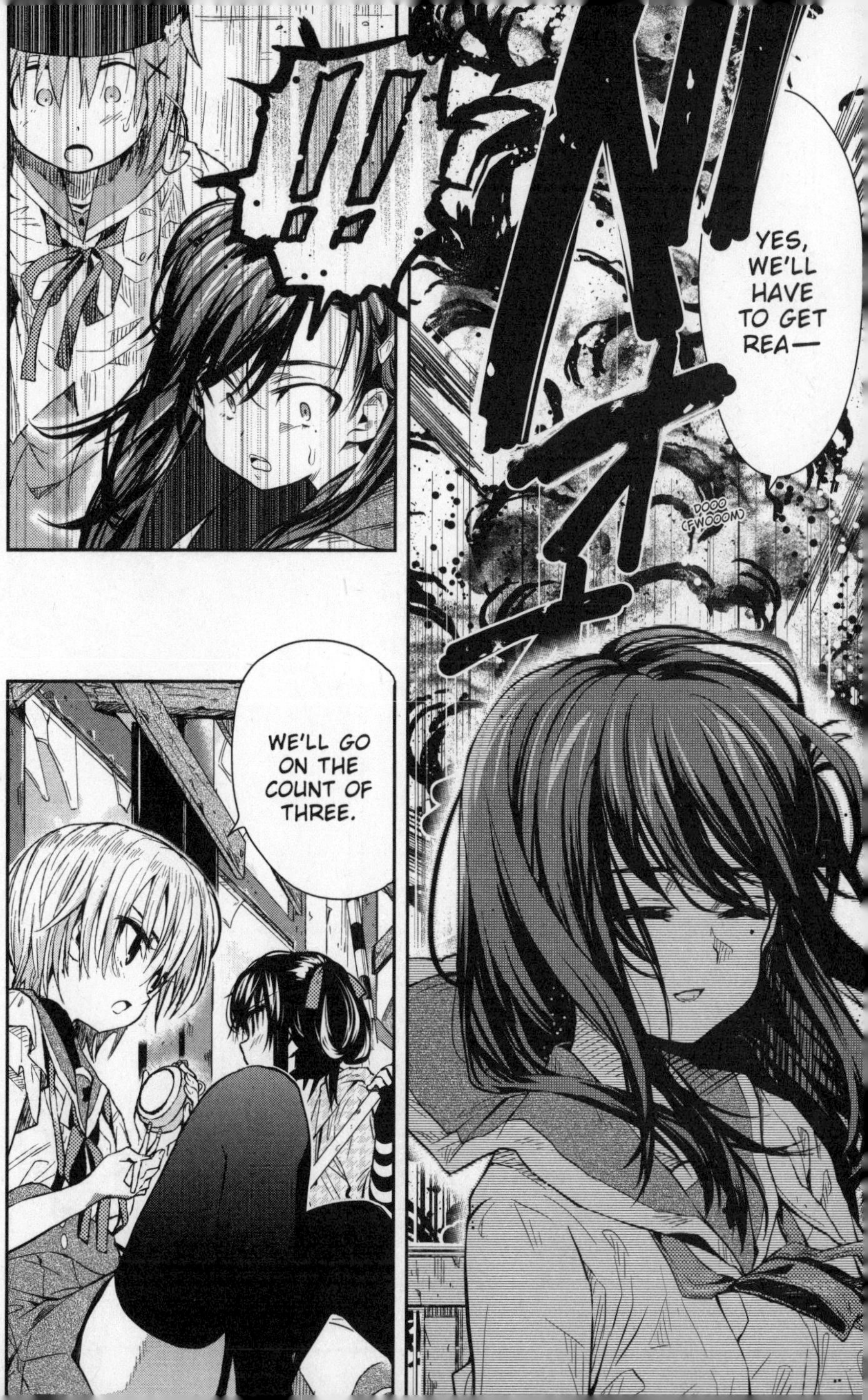
YES, WE'LL HAVE TO GET REA—
DOOO (FWOOOM)
!!
WE'LL GO ON THE COUNT OF THREE.

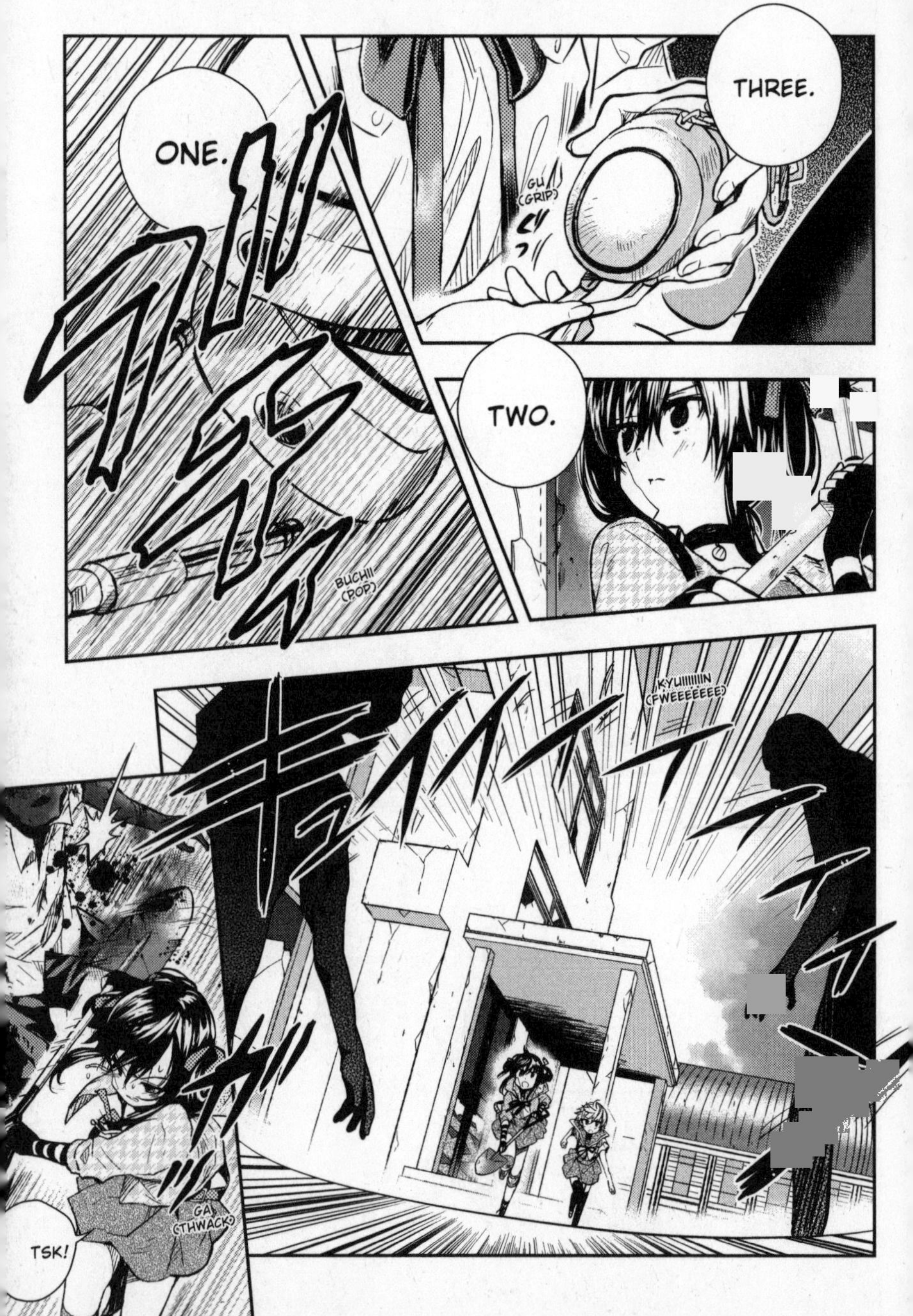
THREE.
GU (GRIP)
TWO.
ONE.
BUCHII (POP)
KYUIIIIIIN (FWEEEEEEE)
GA (THWACK)
TSK!

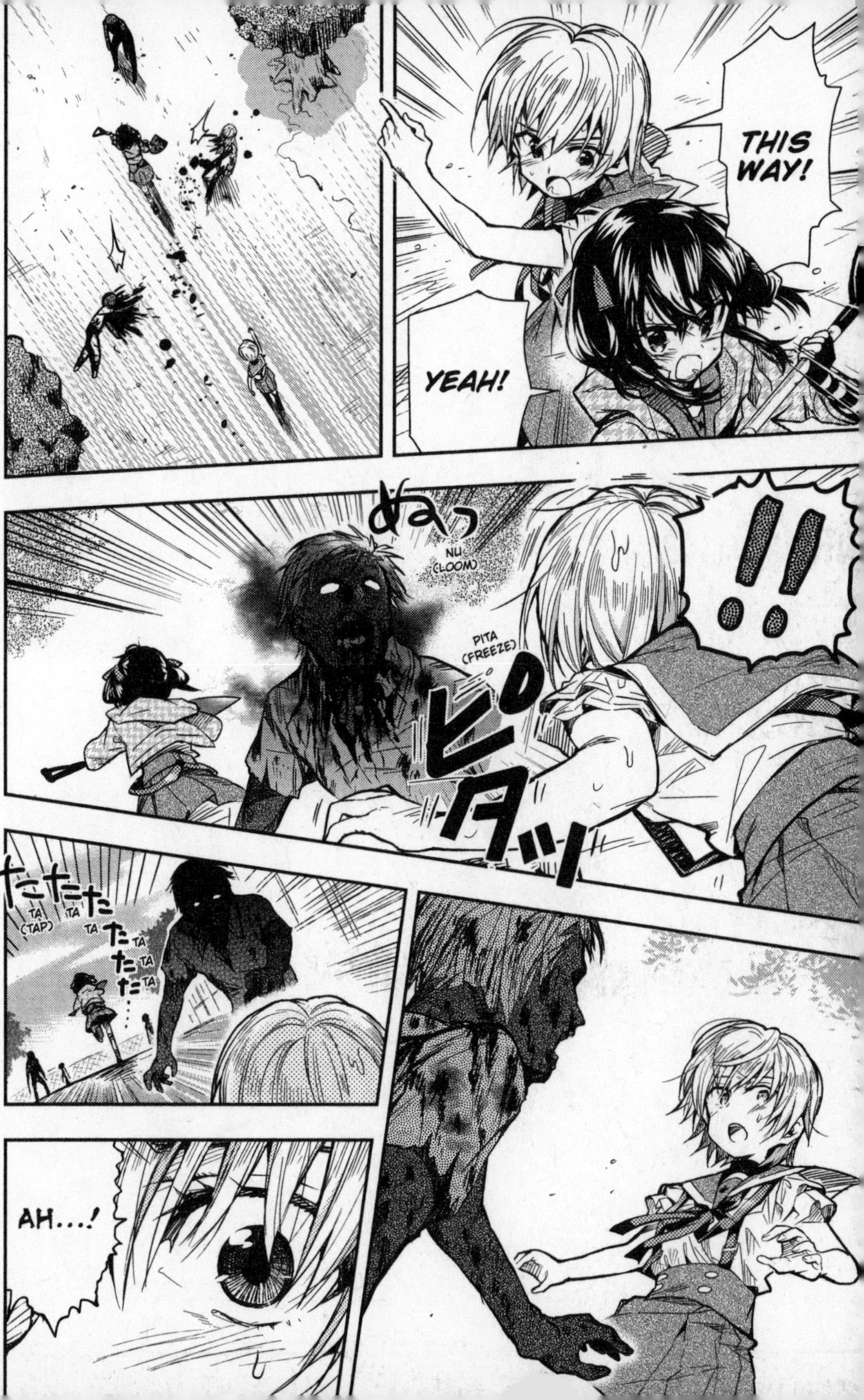

THIS WAY!
YEAH!
!!
ぬっ
NU (LOOM)
PITA (FREEZE)
ピタッ
たたたた
TA TA (TAP) TA TA
たたた
TA TA TA
AH...!

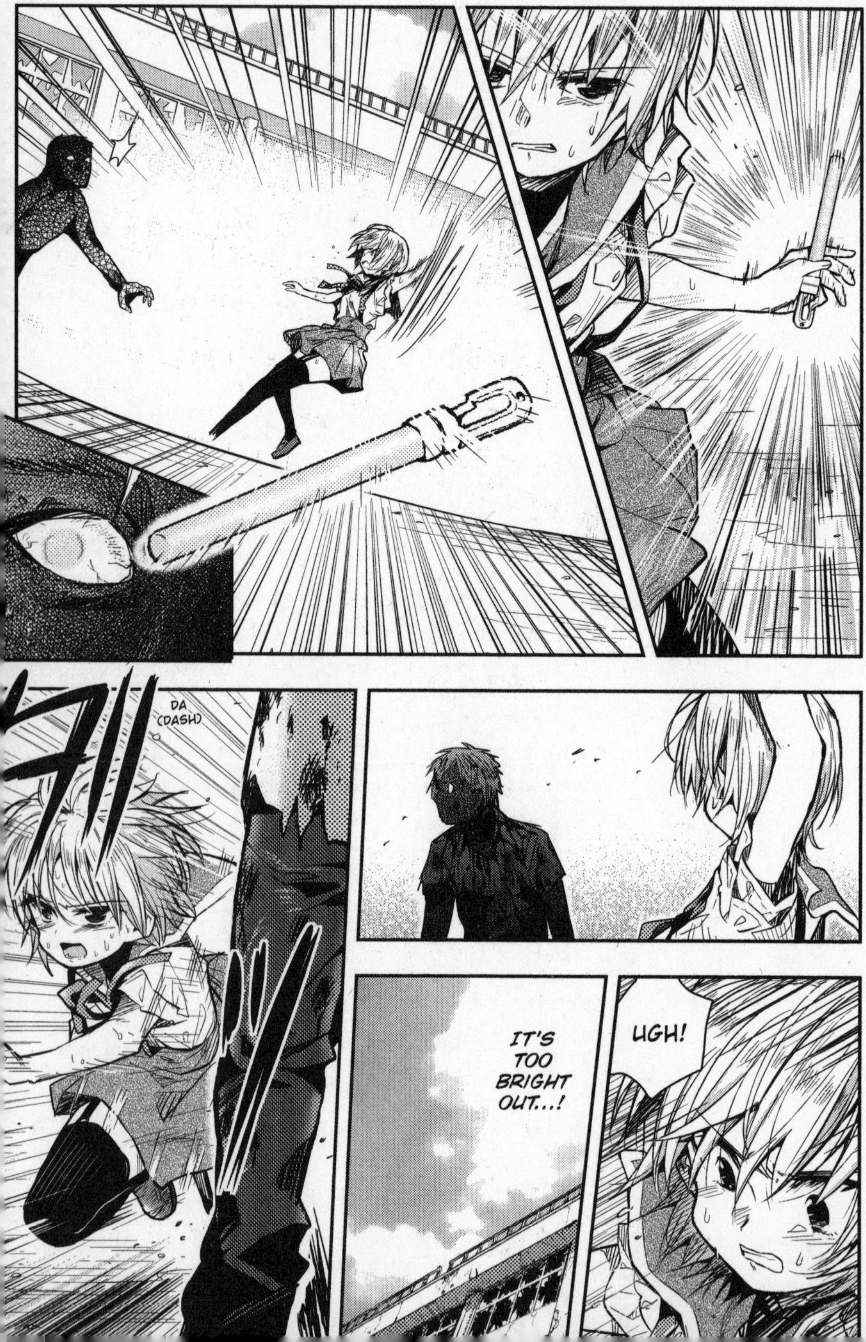
UGH!
IT'S TOO BRIGHT OUT...!
DA (DASH)

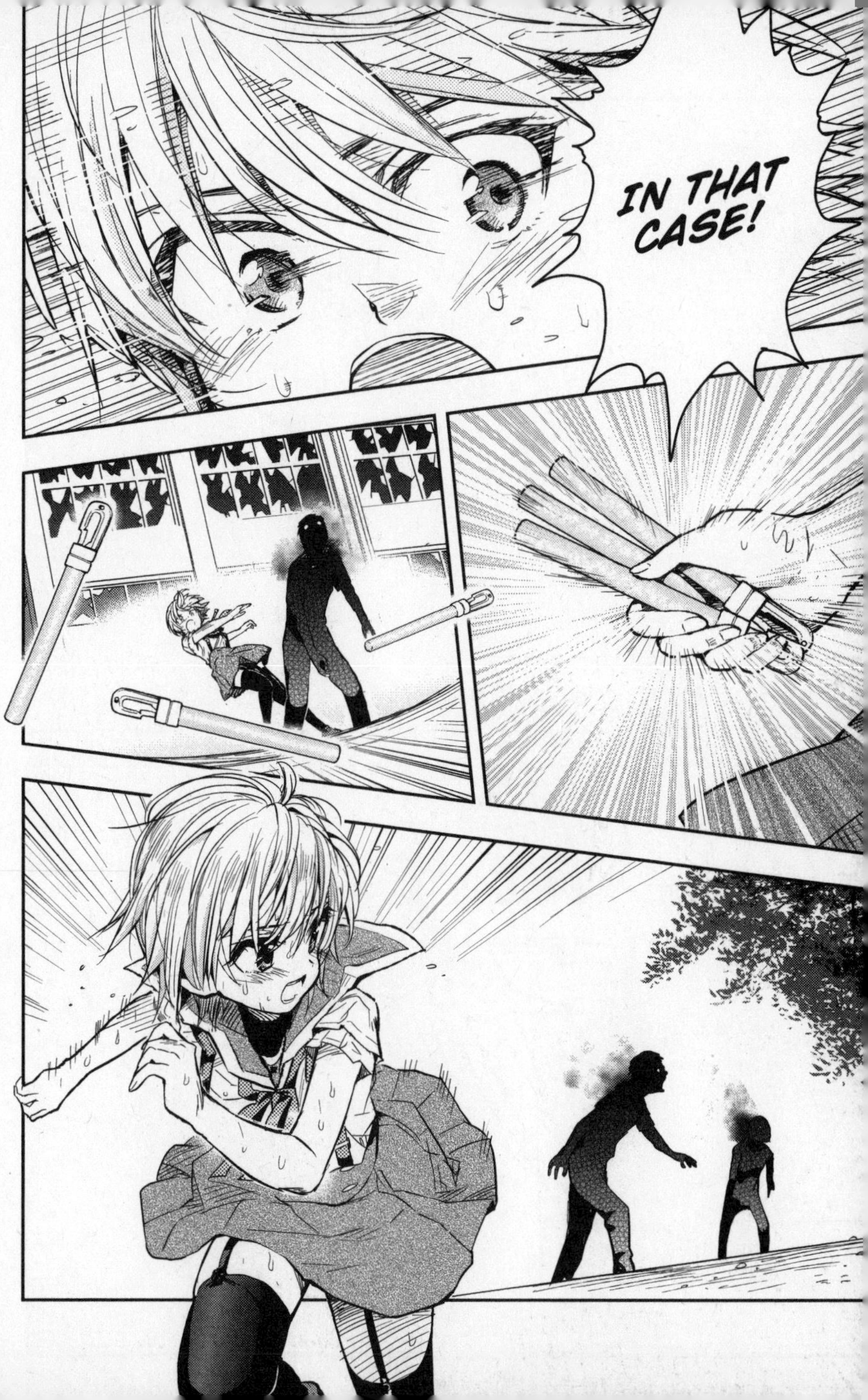
IN THAT CASE!

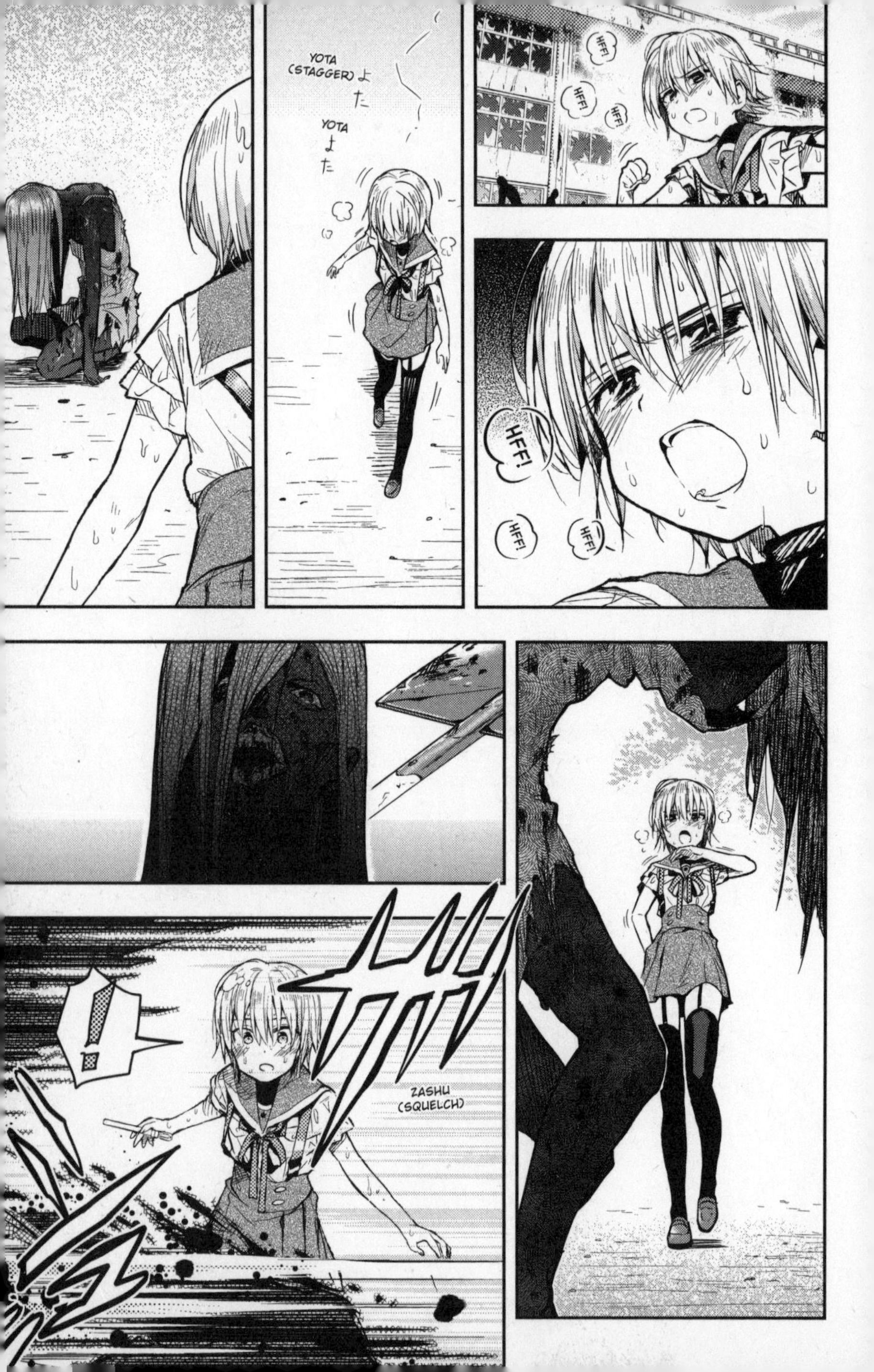
HFF!
HFF!
HFF!
HFF!
HFF!
HFF!
YOTA (STAGGER) よた
YOTA よた
ZASHU (SQUELCH)
!

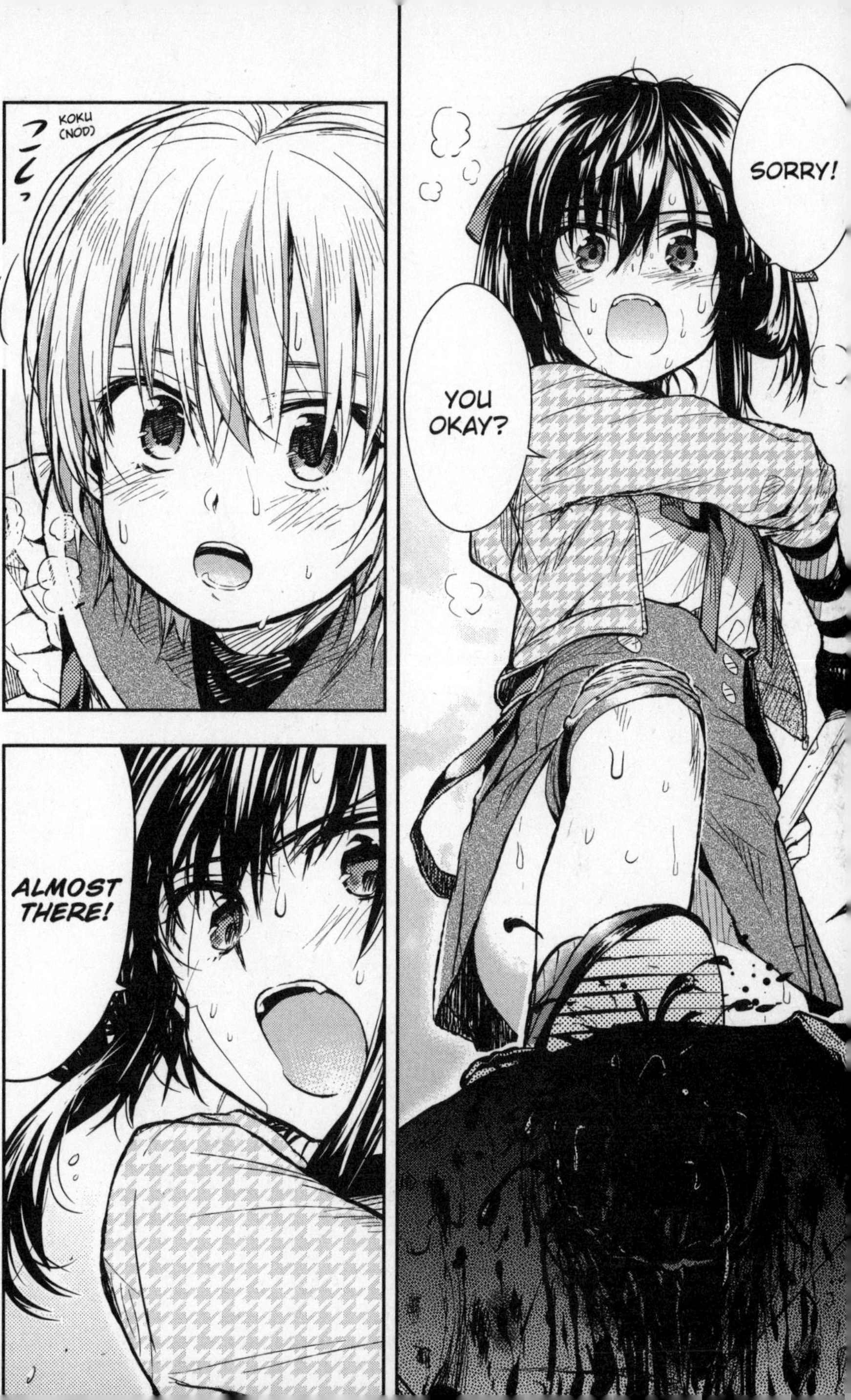
SORRY!
YOU OKAY?
KOKU (NOD)
ALMOST THERE!

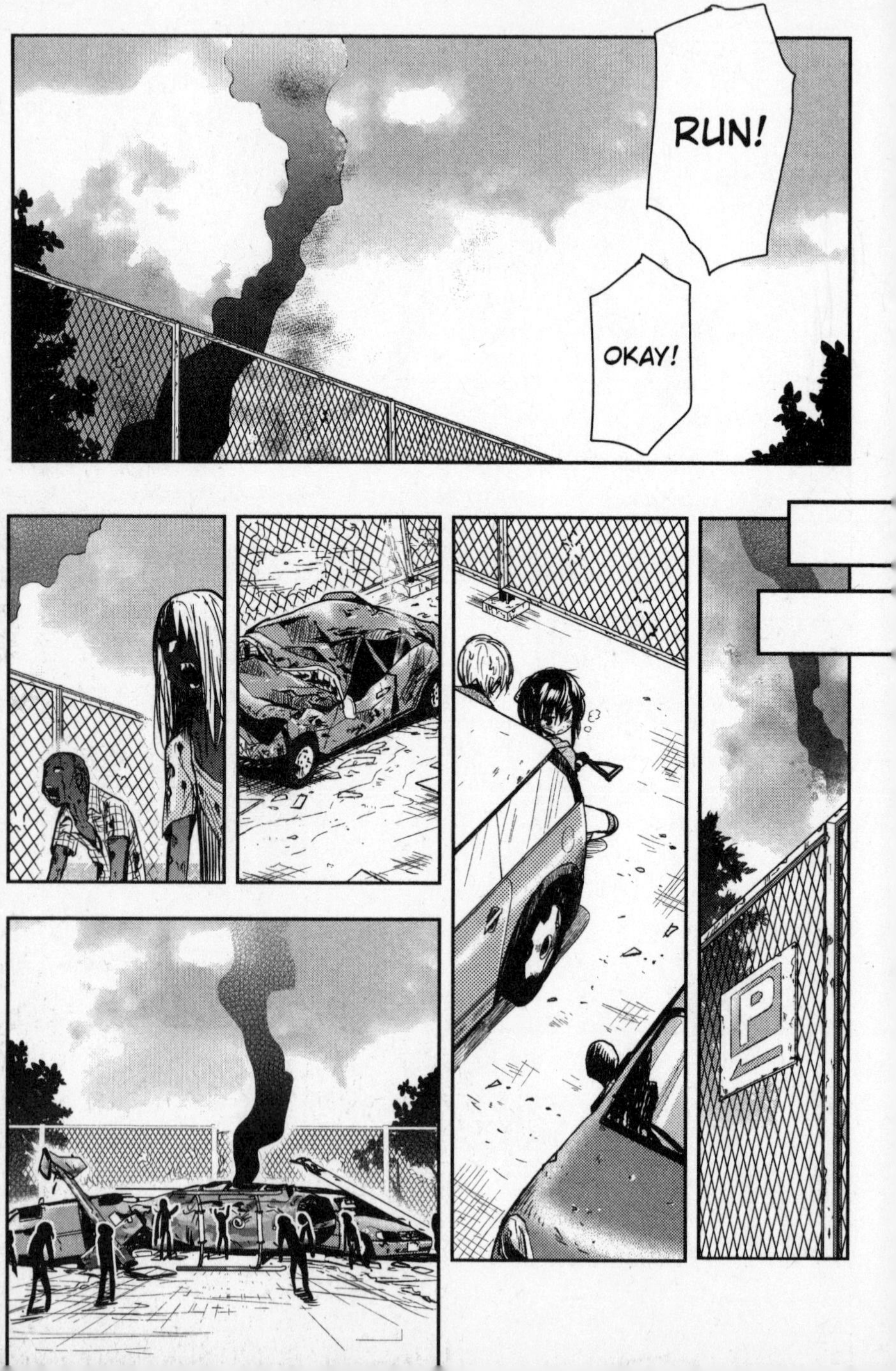
RUN!
OKAY!

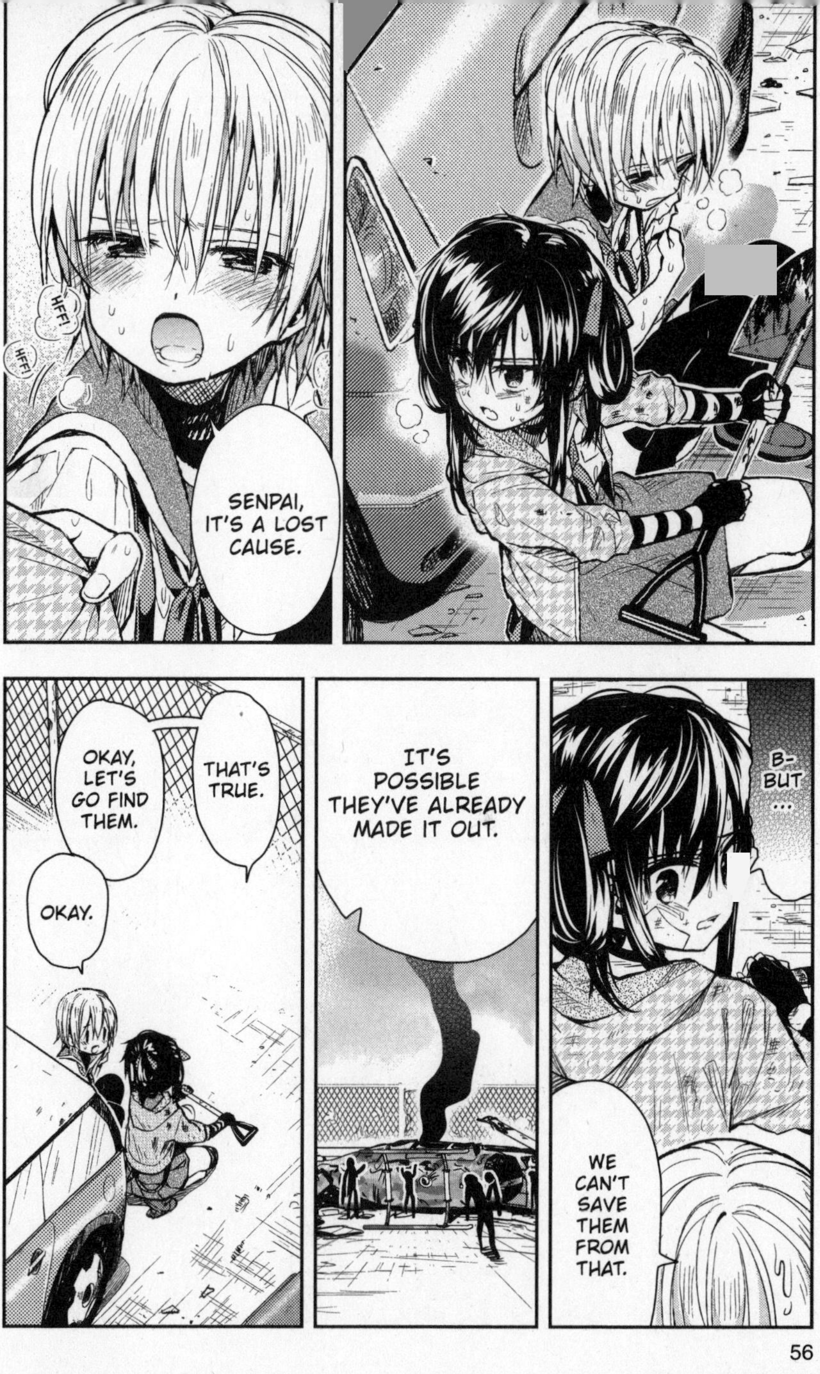
HFF!
HFF!
SENPAI, IT'S A LOST CAUSE.
B-BUT...
WE CAN'T SAVE THEM FROM THAT.
IT'S POSSIBLE THEY'VE ALREADY MADE IT OUT.
THAT'S TRUE.
OKAY, LET'S GO FIND THEM.
OKAY.

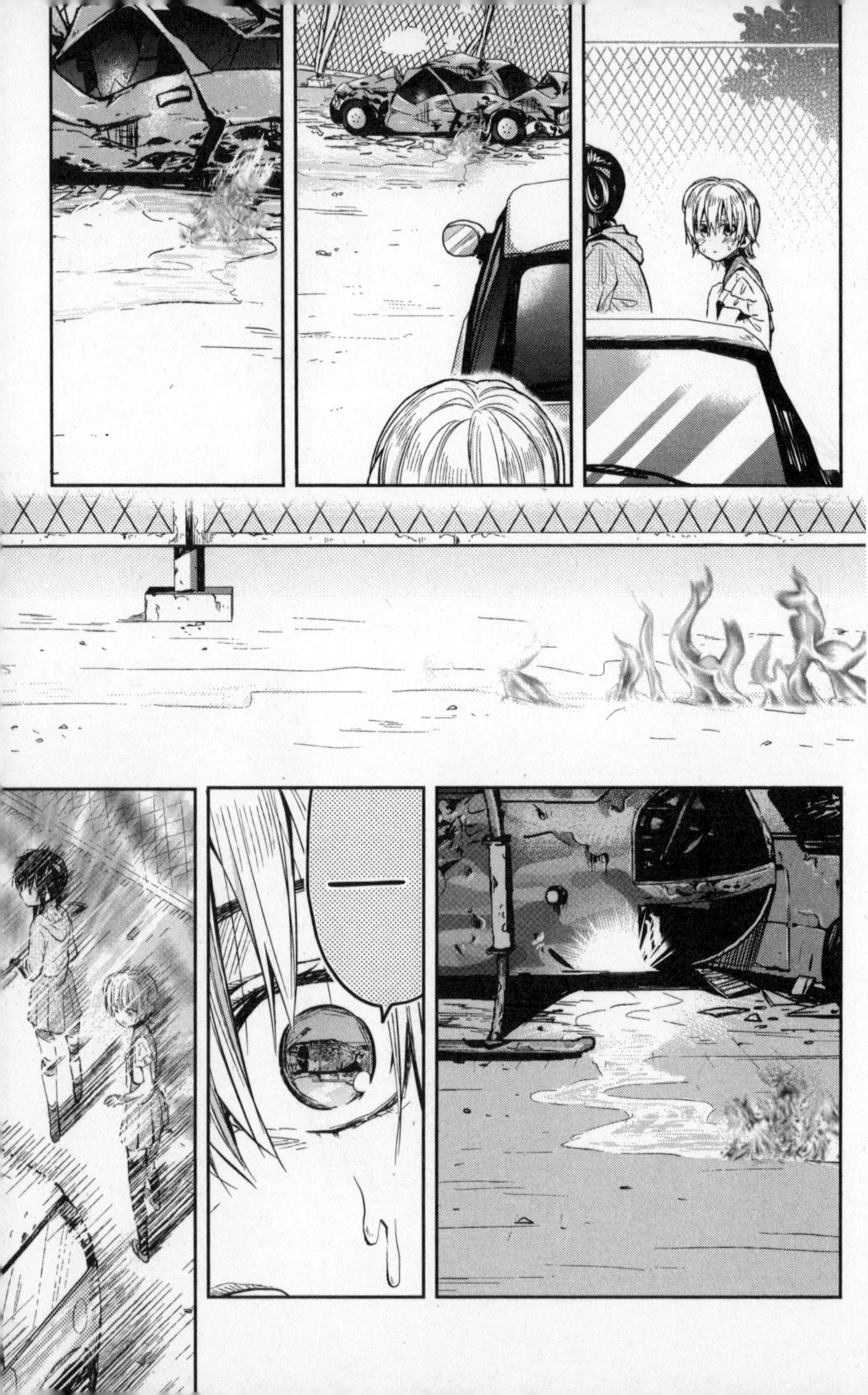
—

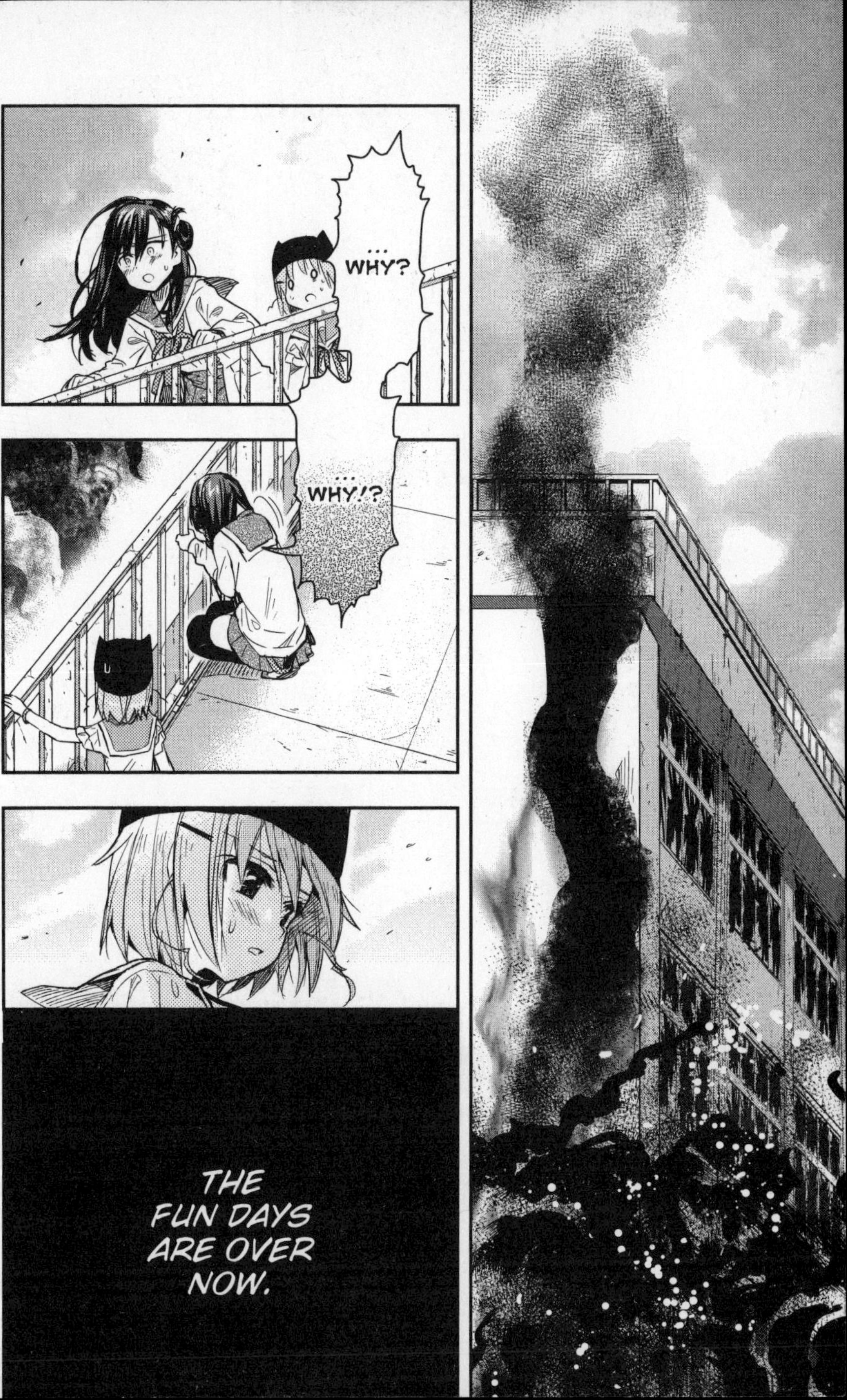
...WHY?
...WHY!?
THE FUN DAYS ARE OVER NOW.

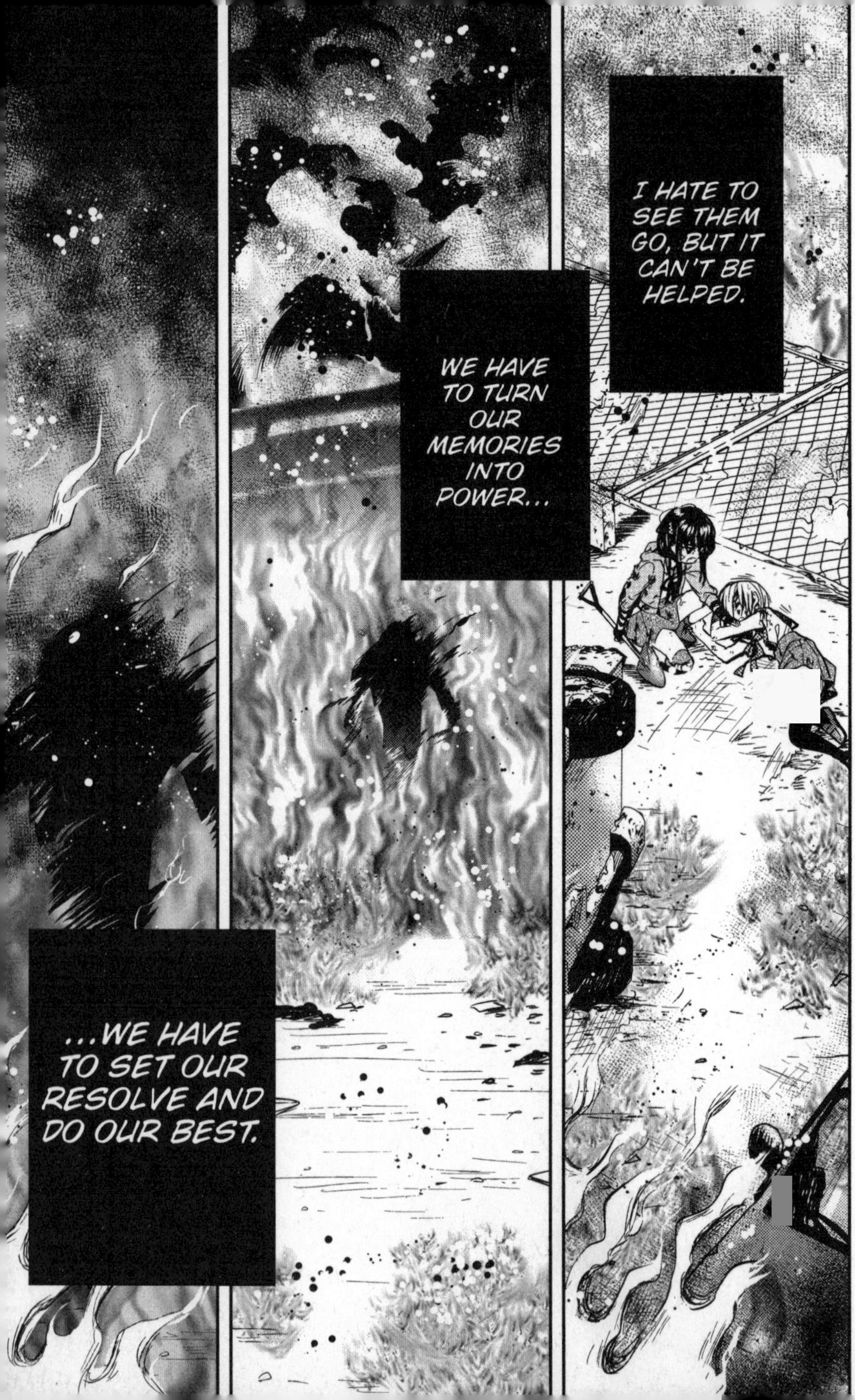
I HATE TO SEE THEM GO, BUT IT CAN'T BE HELPED.
WE HAVE TO TURN OUR MEMORIES INTO POWER...
...WE HAVE TO SET OUR RESOLVE AND DO OUR BEST.

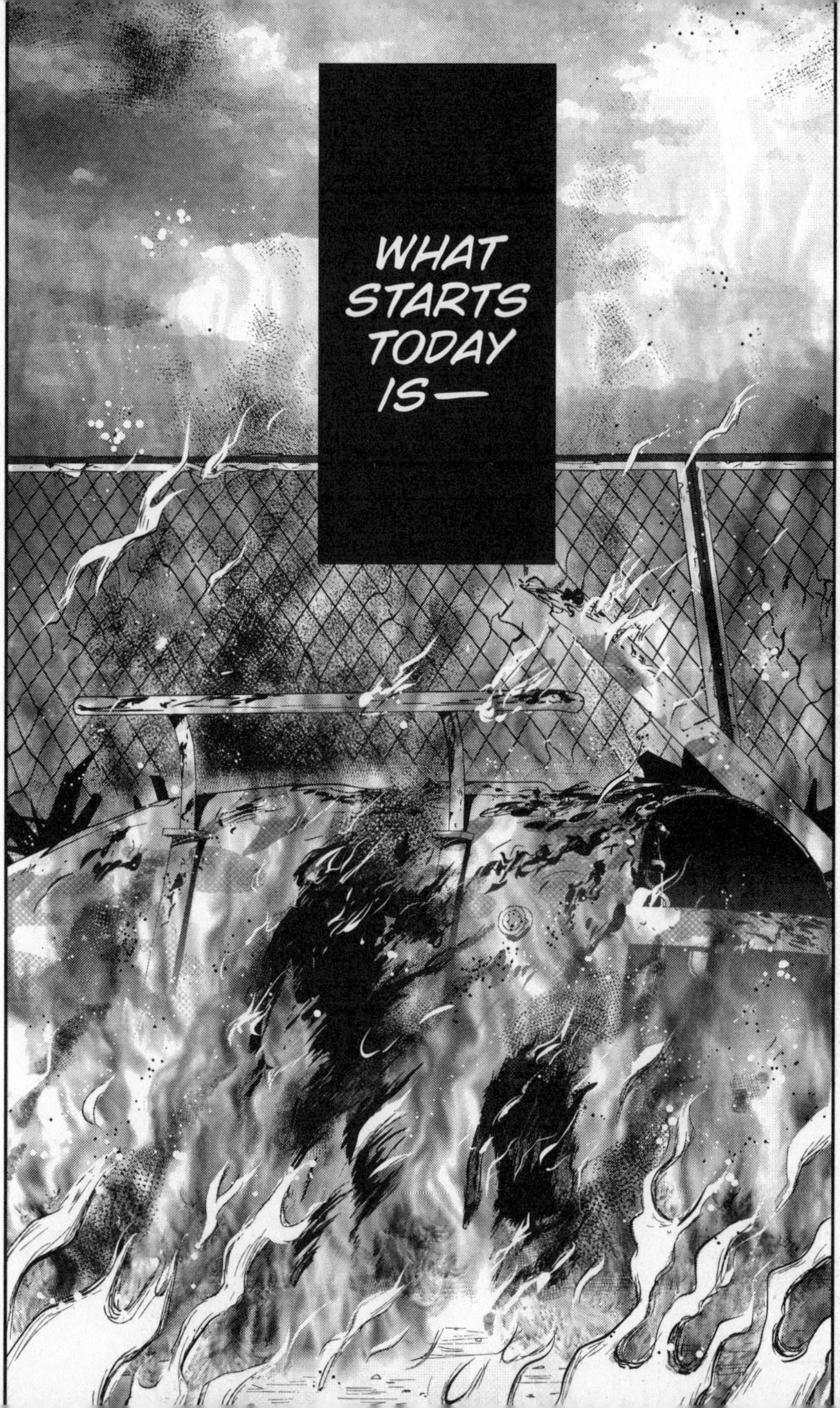
WHAT STARTS TODAY IS—

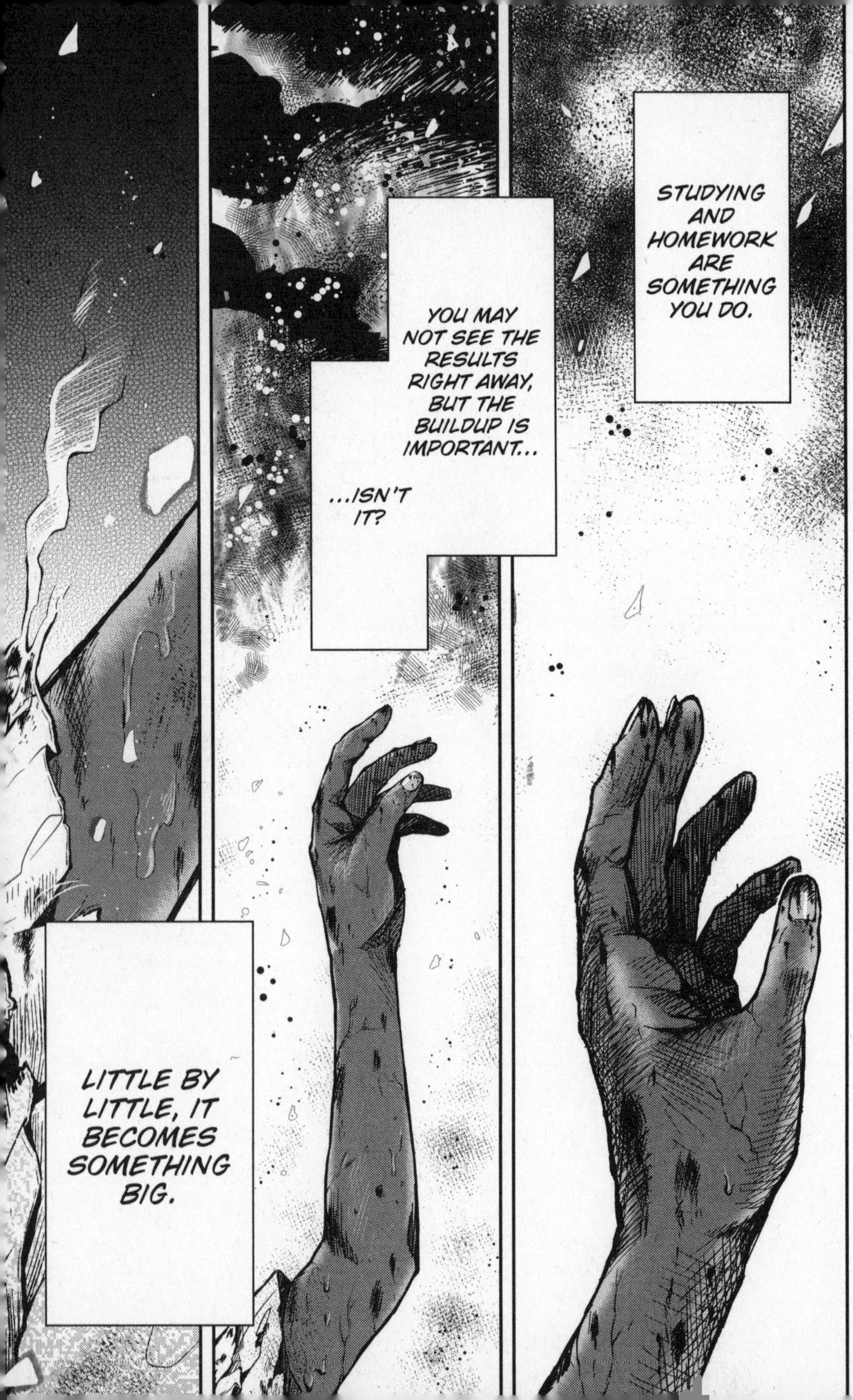
STUDYING AND HOMEWORK ARE SOMETHING YOU DO.
YOU MAY NOT SEE THE RESULTS RIGHT AWAY, BUT THE BUILDUP IS IMPORTANT...
...ISN'T IT?
LITTLE BY LITTLE, IT BECOMES SOMETHING BIG.

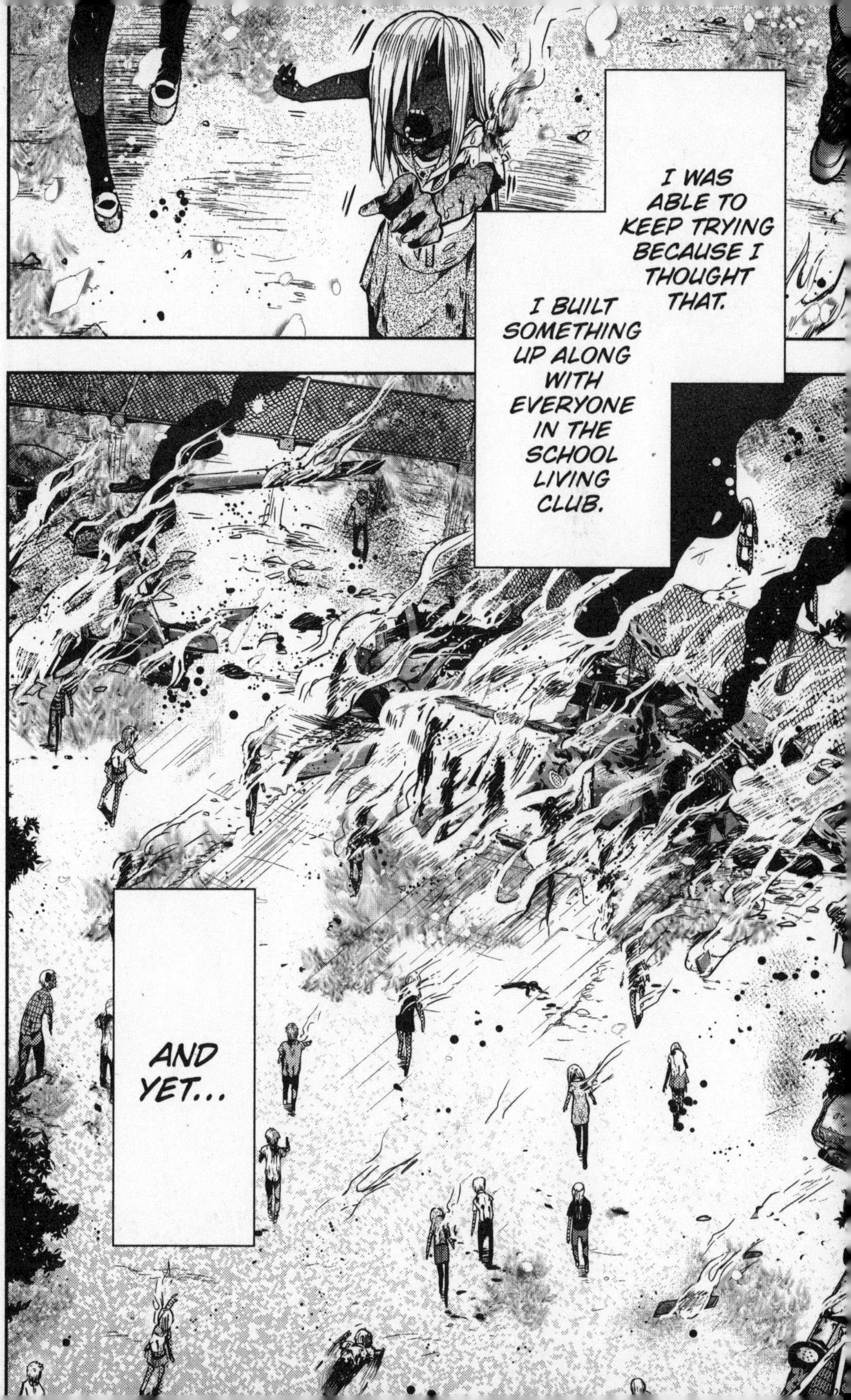
I WAS ABLE TO KEEP TRYING BECAUSE I THOUGHT THAT.
I BUILT SOMETHING UP ALONG WITH EVERYONE IN THE SCHOOL LIVING CLUB.
AND YET...

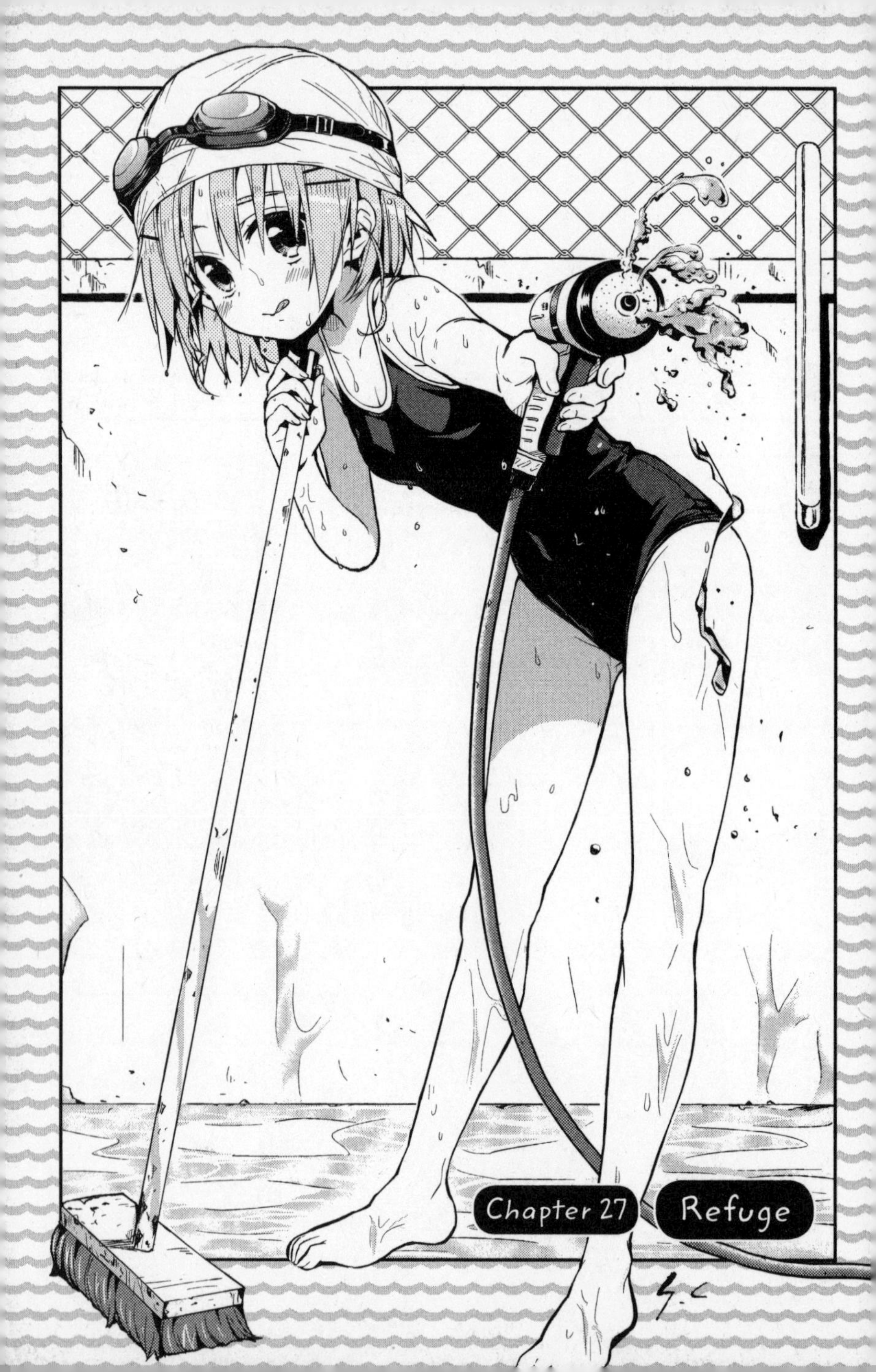
Chapter 27
Refuge

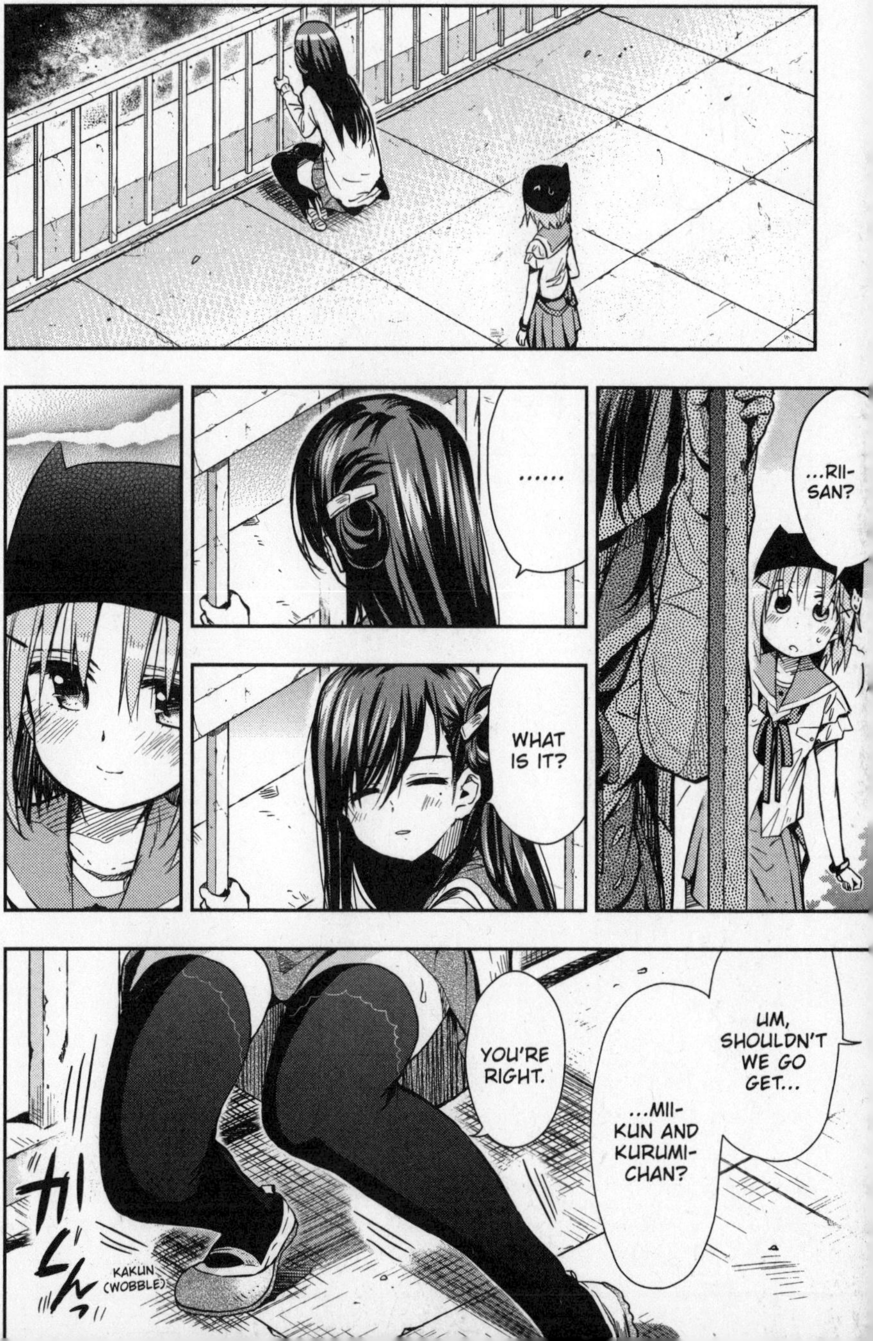
...RII-SAN?
......
WHAT IS IT?
UM, SHOULDN'T WE GO GET...
...MII-KUN AND KURUMI-CHAN?
YOU'RE RIGHT.
KAKUN (WOBBLE)

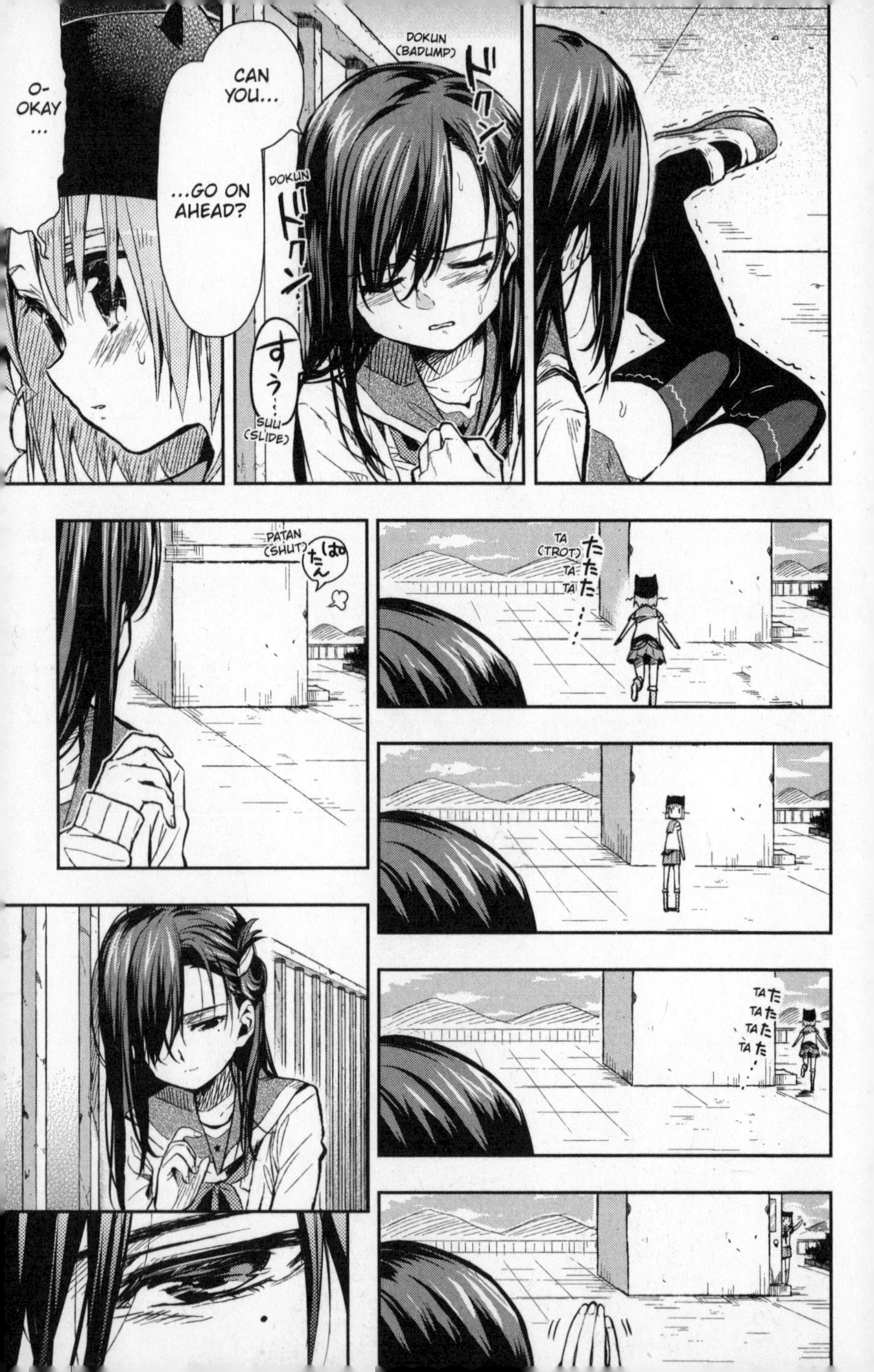
DOKUN (BADUMP)
ドクン…
DOKUN
ドクン…
CAN YOU...
...GO ON AHEAD?
すぅ…
SUU (SLIDE)
O-OKAY ...
TA (TROT) TA TA
たたた…
TA TA TA TA
たたたた…
PATAN (SHUT)
ぱたん

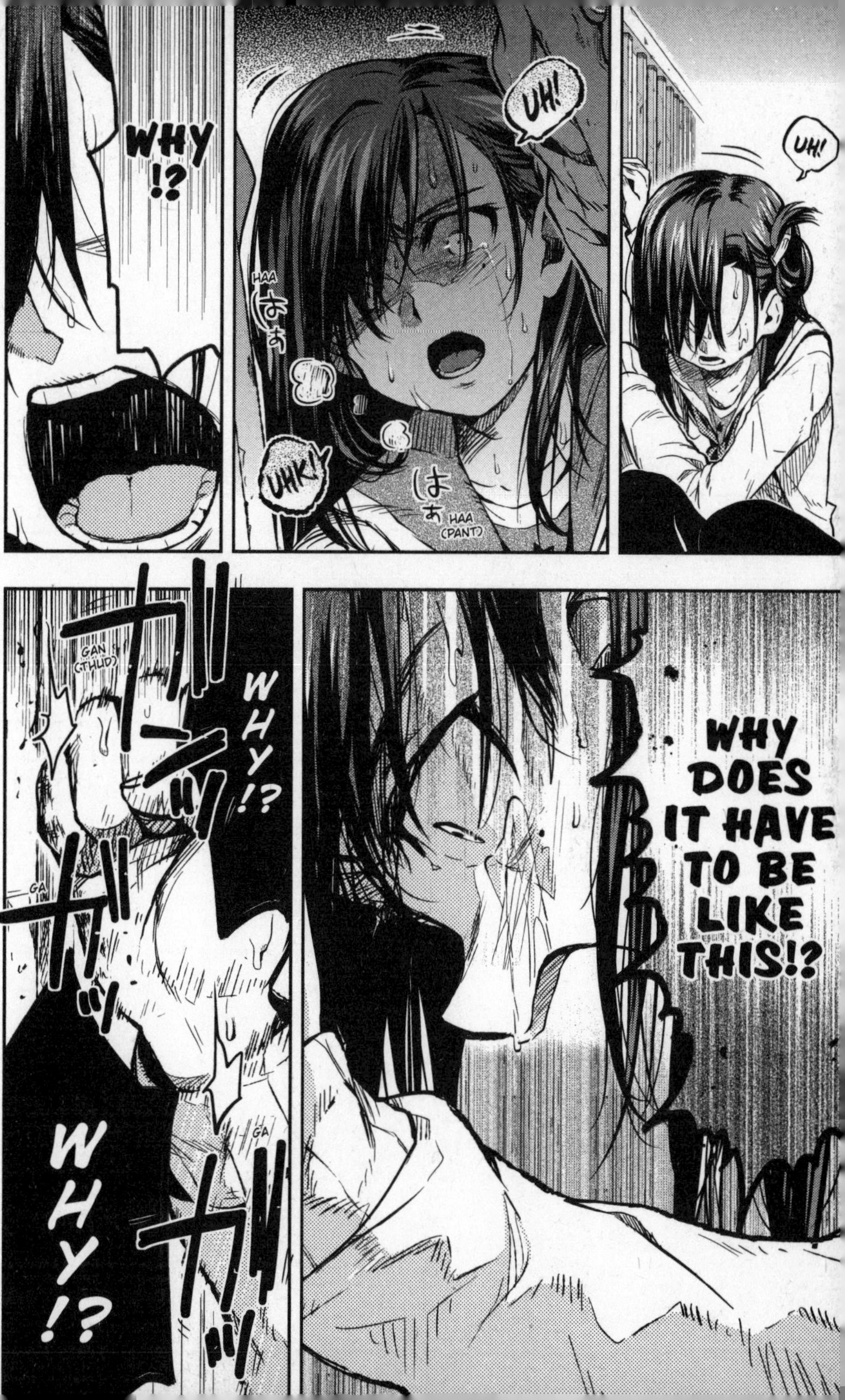
UH!
UH!
HAA はぁ
UHK!
はぁ HAA (PANT)
WHY !?
WHY DOES IT HAVE TO BE LIKE THIS!?
WHY!?
GAN (THUD)
GA
GA
WHY!?

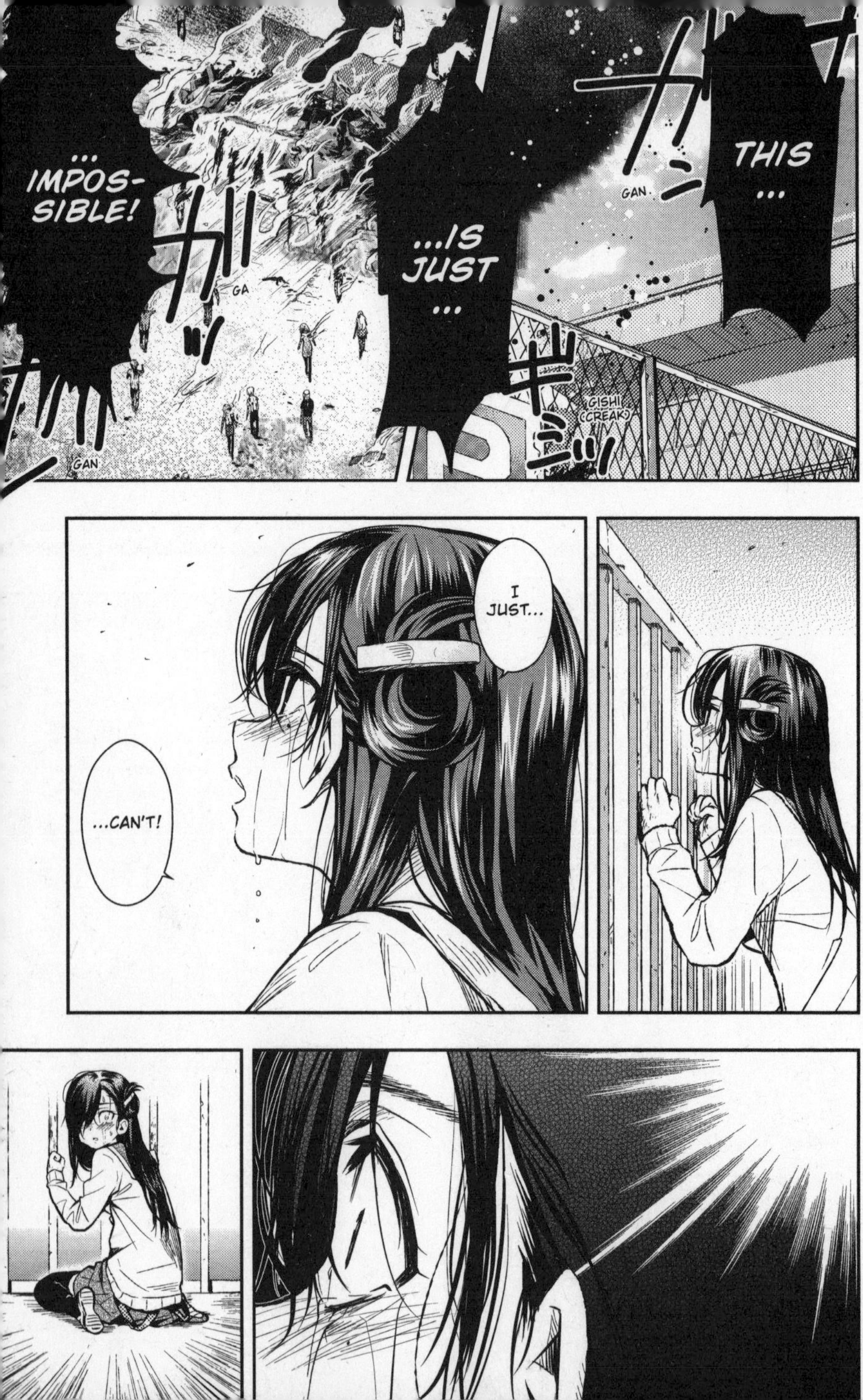
THIS ...
GAN
...IS JUST ...
GISHI (CREAK)
... IMPOSSIBLE!
GA
GAN
I JUST...
...CAN'T!

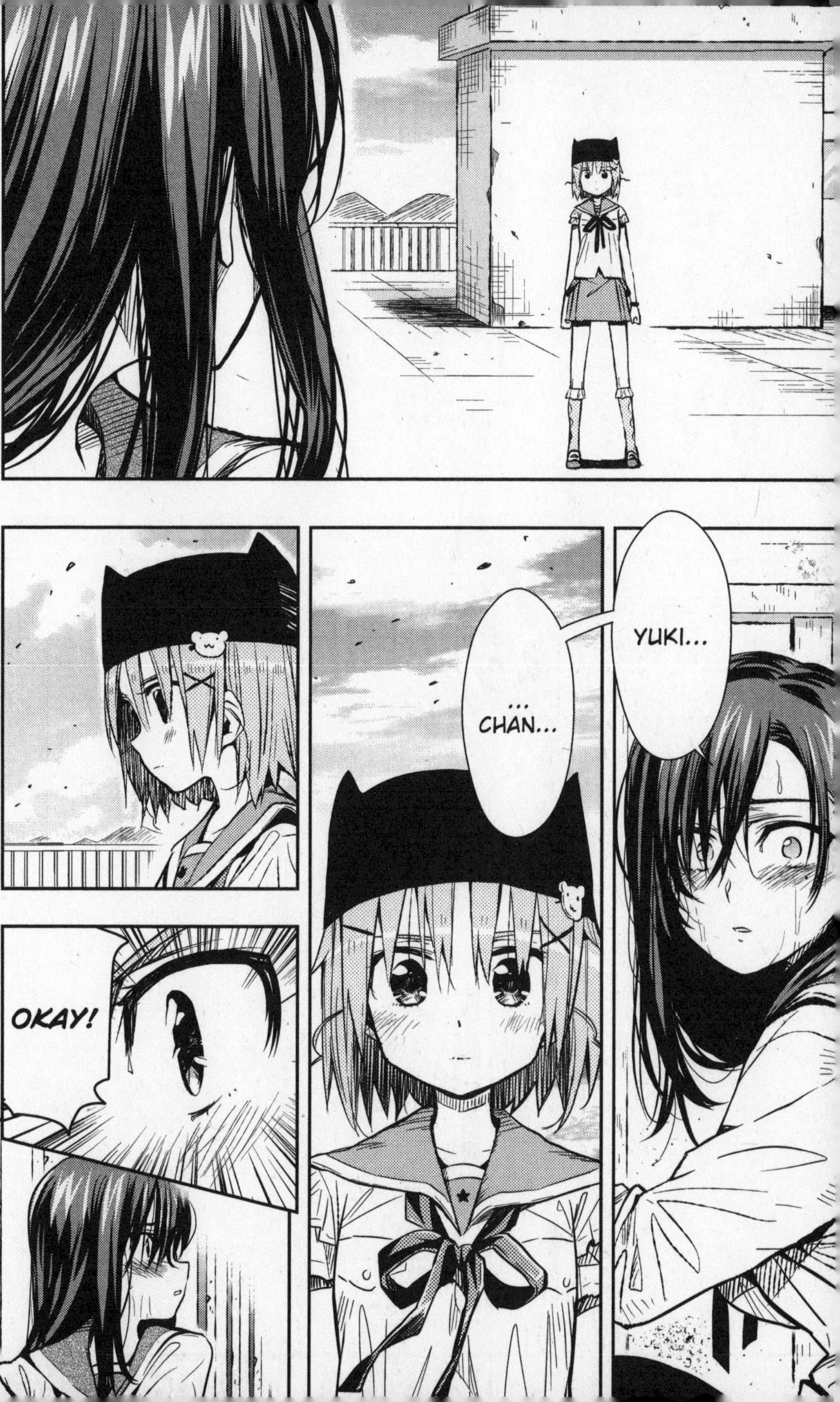
YUKI...
... CHAN...
OKAY!

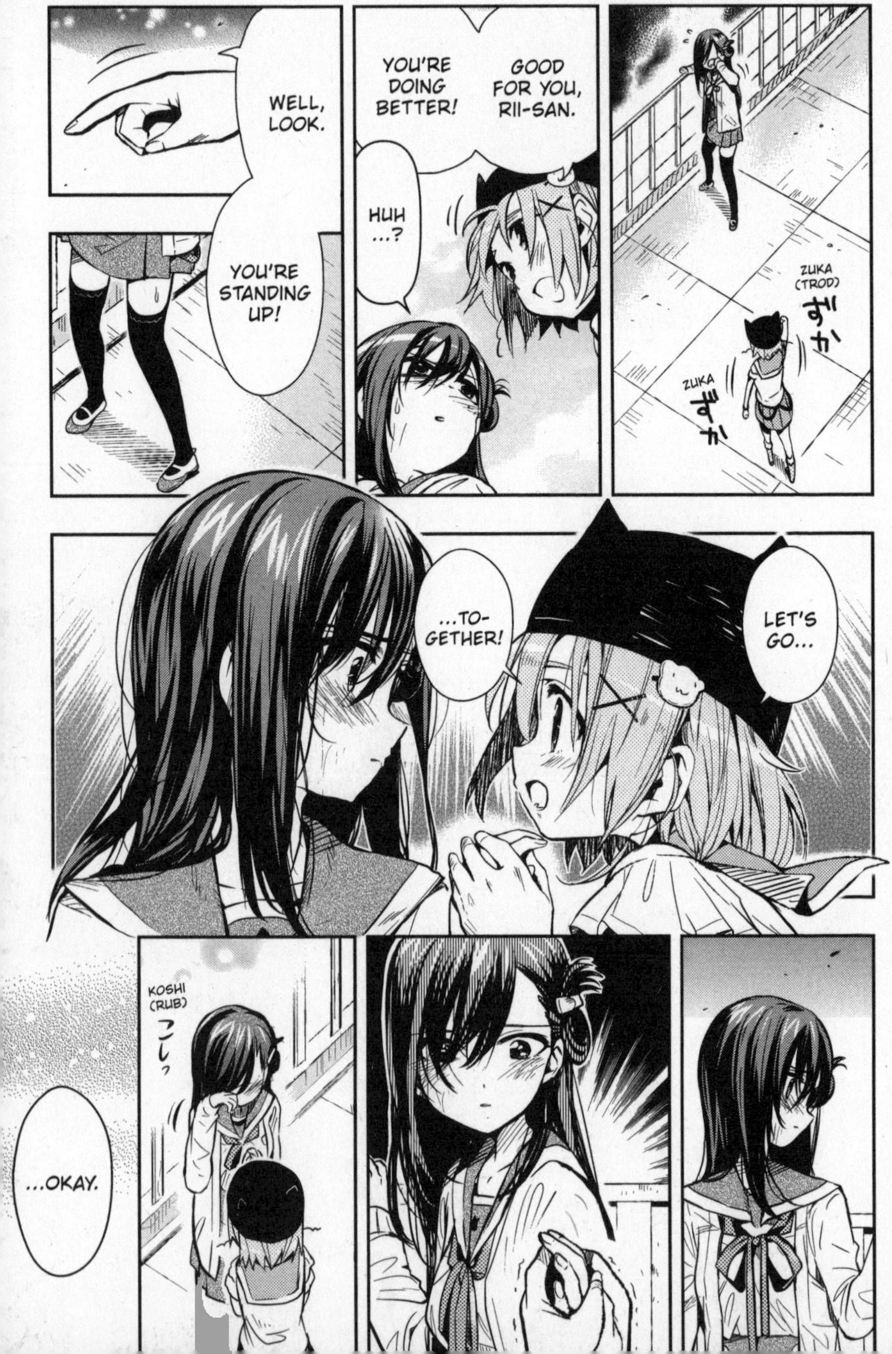
ZUKA (TROD)
ずか
ZUKA
ずか
GOOD FOR YOU, RII-SAN.
YOU'RE DOING BETTER!
HUH ...?
WELL, LOOK.
YOU'RE STANDING UP!
LET'S GO...
...TO-GETHER!
KOSHI (RUB)
こしっ
...OKAY.

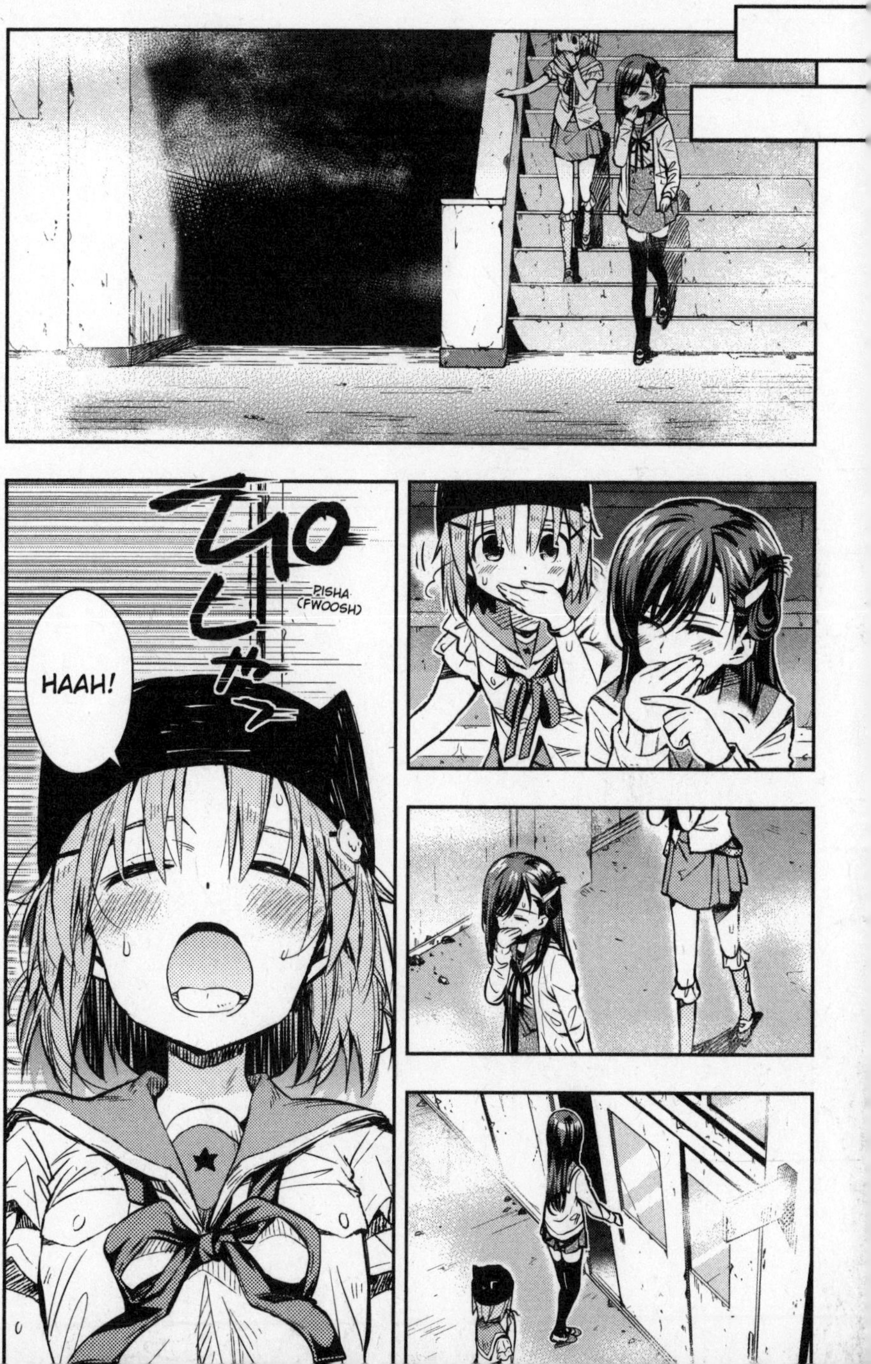
PISHA (FWOOSH)
HAAH!

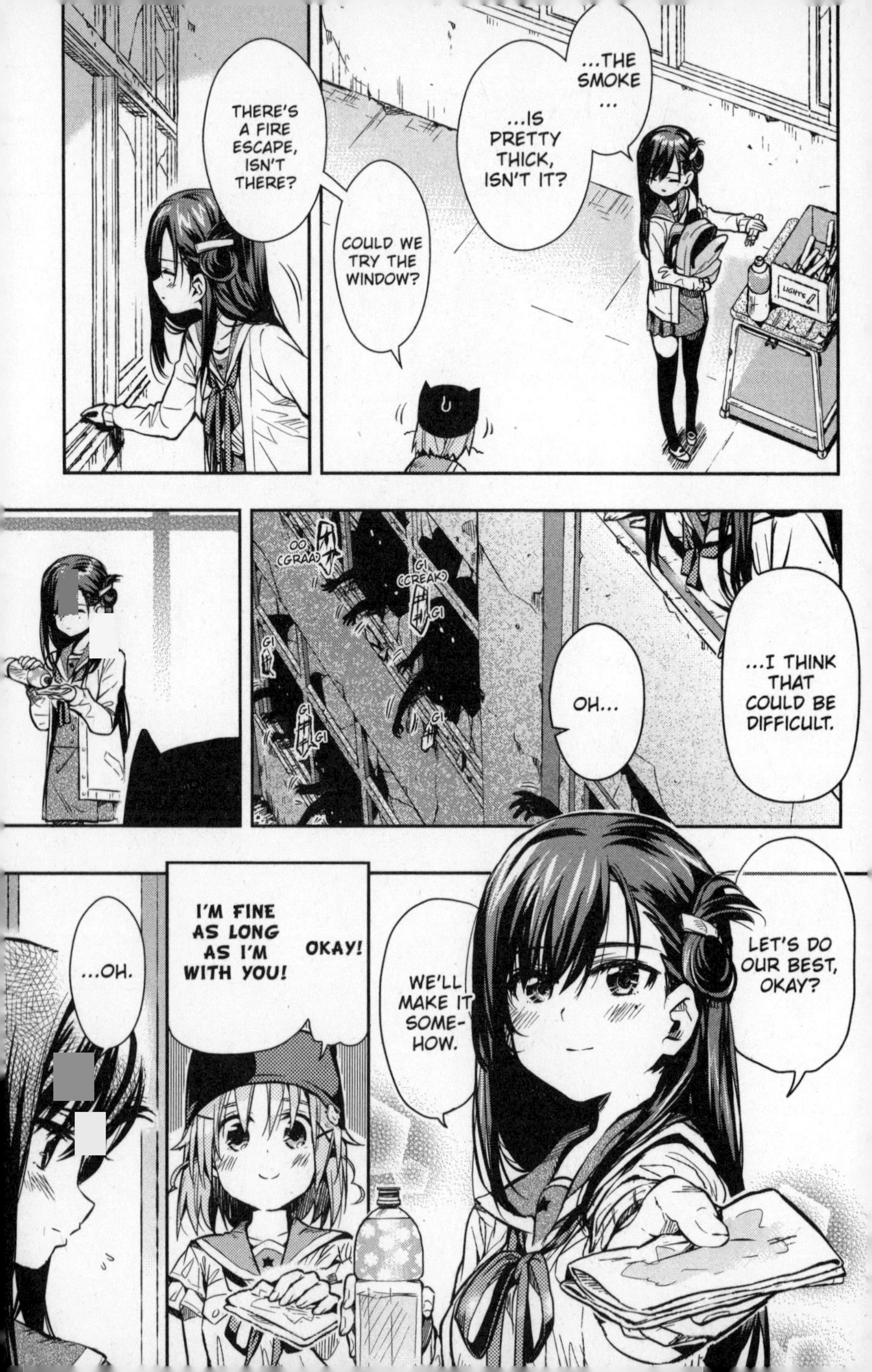
...THE SMOKE ...
...IS PRETTY THICK, ISN'T IT?
COULD WE TRY THE WINDOW?
THERE'S A FIRE ESCAPE, ISN'T THERE?
...I THINK THAT COULD BE DIFFICULT.
OH...
GI (CREAK)
GI
OO (GRAA)
GI
GI
GI
GI
LET'S DO OUR BEST, OKAY?
WE'LL MAKE IT SOME-HOW.
OKAY!
I'M FINE AS LONG AS I'M WITH YOU!
...OH.

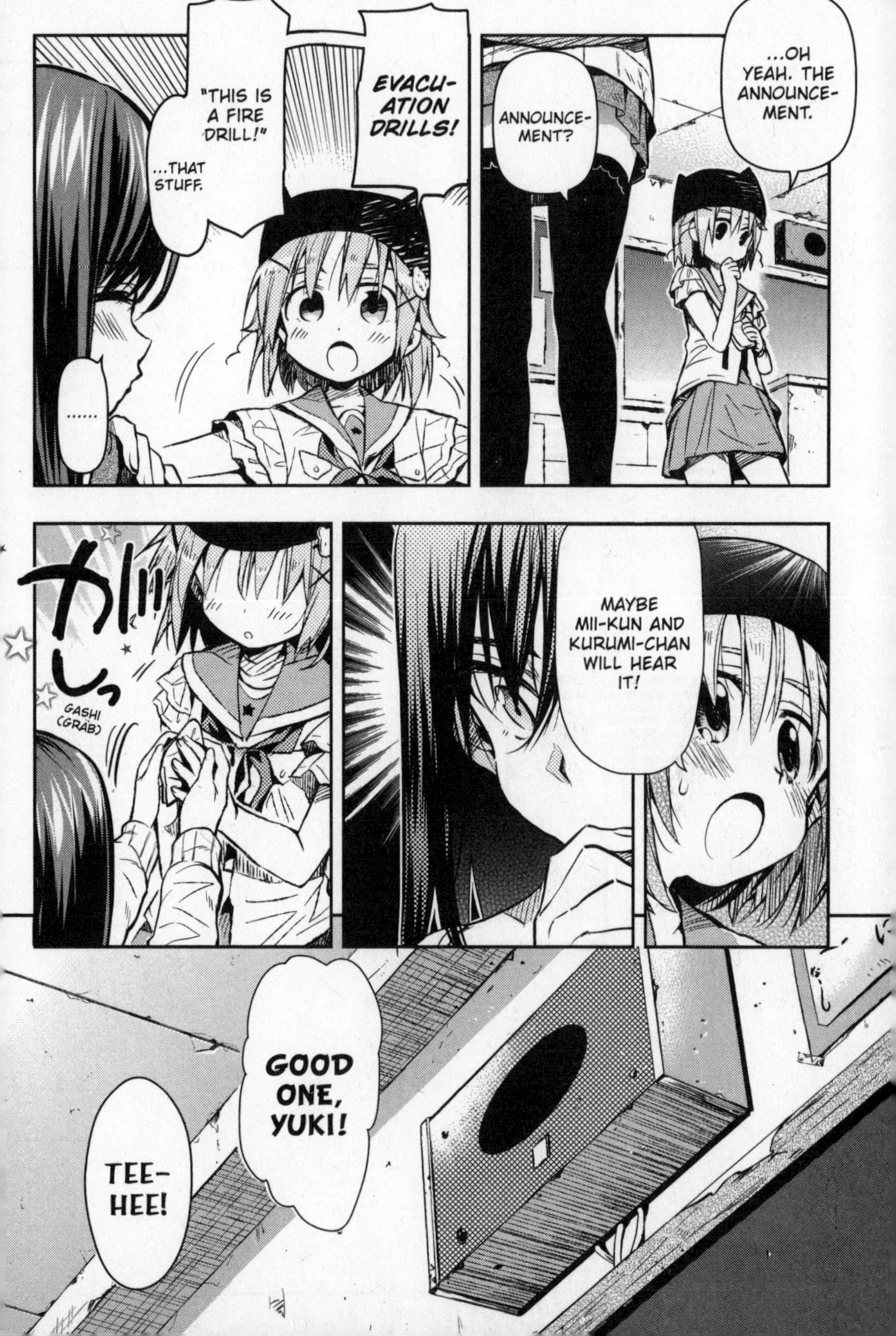
...OH YEAH. THE ANNOUNCEMENT.
ANNOUNCEMENT?
EVACUATION DRILLS!
"THIS IS A FIRE DRILL!"
...THAT STUFF.
......
MAYBE MII-KUN AND KURUMI-CHAN WILL HEAR IT!
GASHI (GRAB)
GOOD ONE, YUKI!
TEE-HEE!

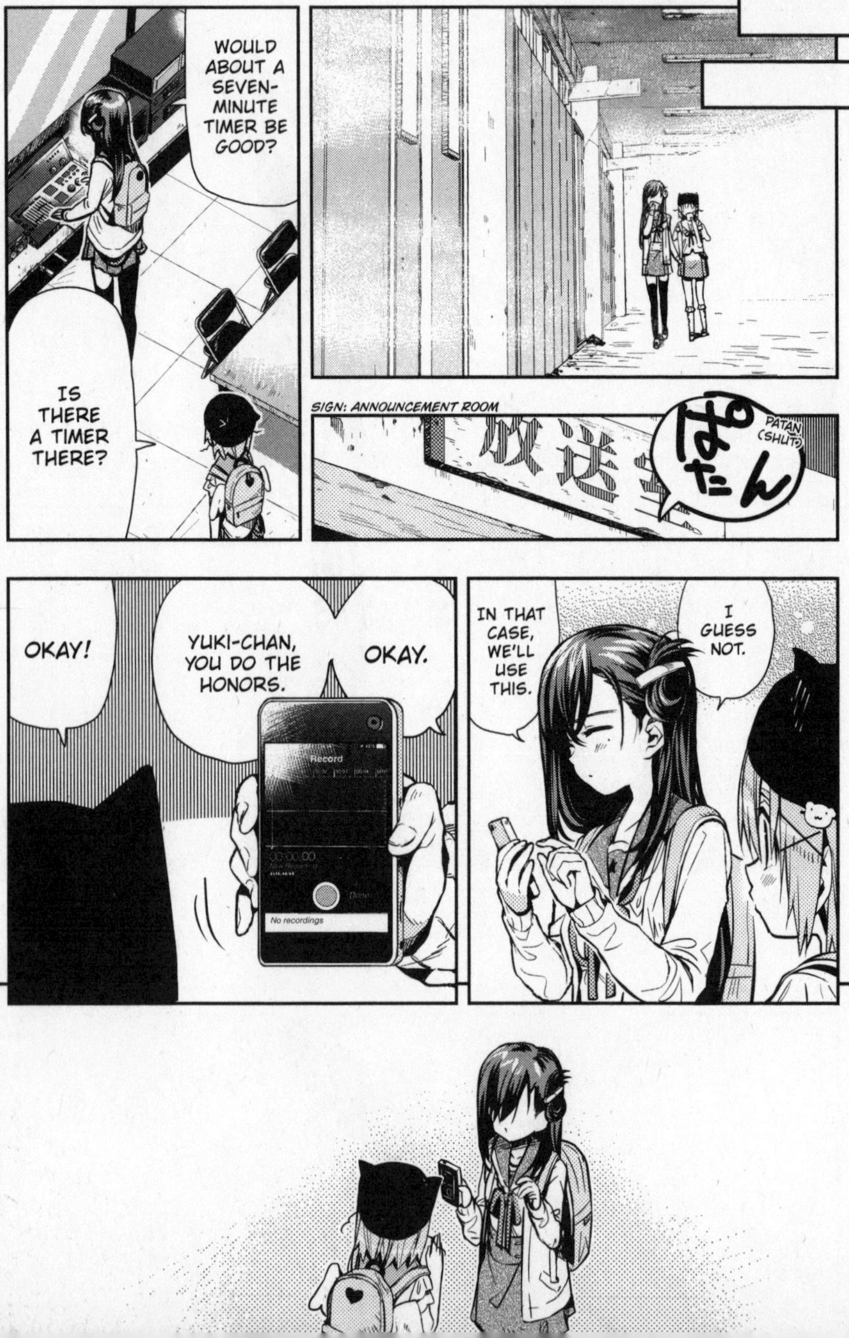
SIGN: ANNOUNCEMENT ROOM
ぱたん
PATAN (SHUT)
WOULD ABOUT A SEVEN-MINUTE TIMER BE GOOD?
IS THERE A TIMER THERE?
I GUESS NOT.
IN THAT CASE, WE'LL USE THIS.
YUKI-CHAN, YOU DO THE HONORS.
OKAY.
OKAY!
Record
Done
No recordings

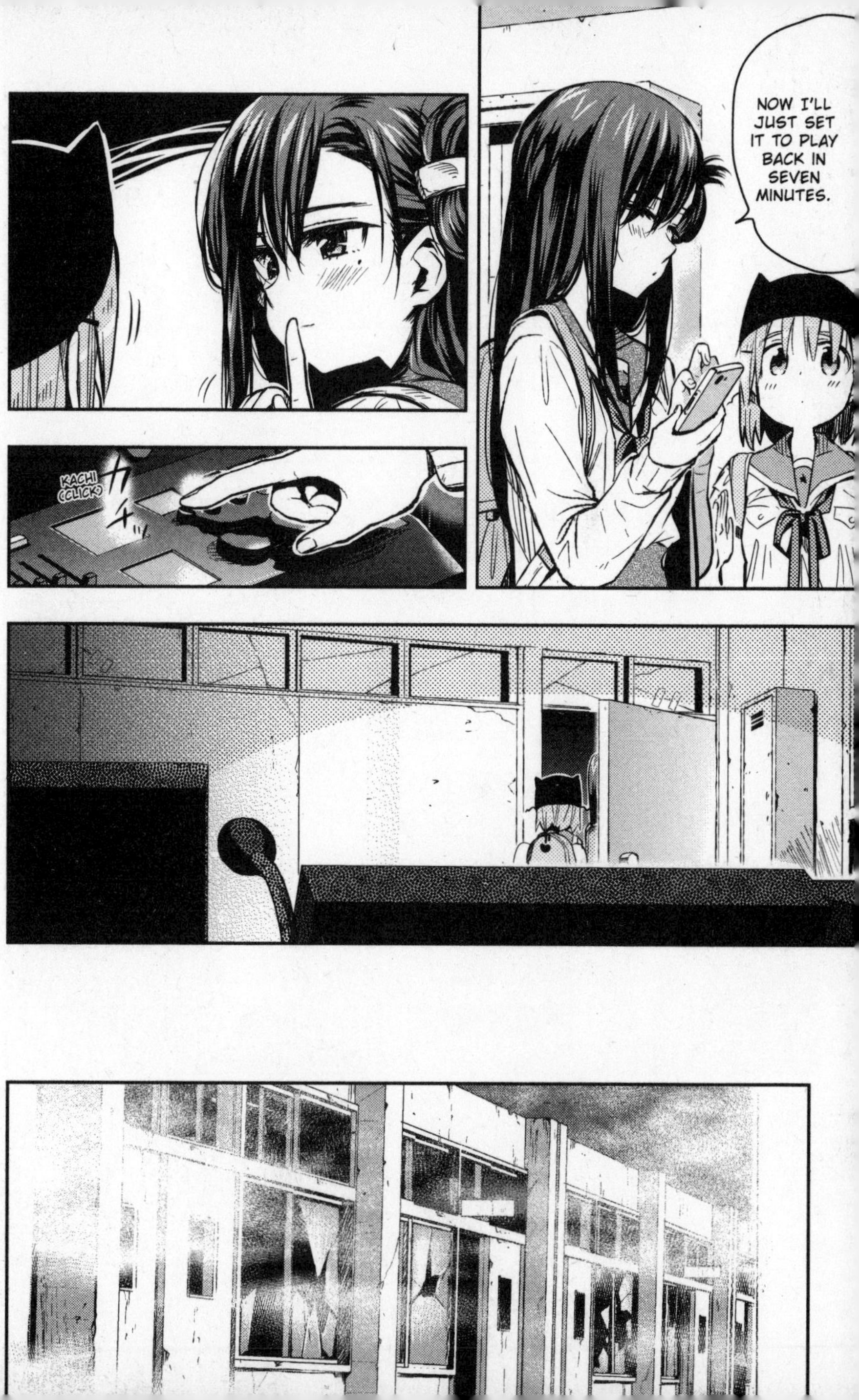
NOW I'LL JUST SET IT TO PLAY BACK IN SEVEN MINUTES.
KACHI (CLICK)

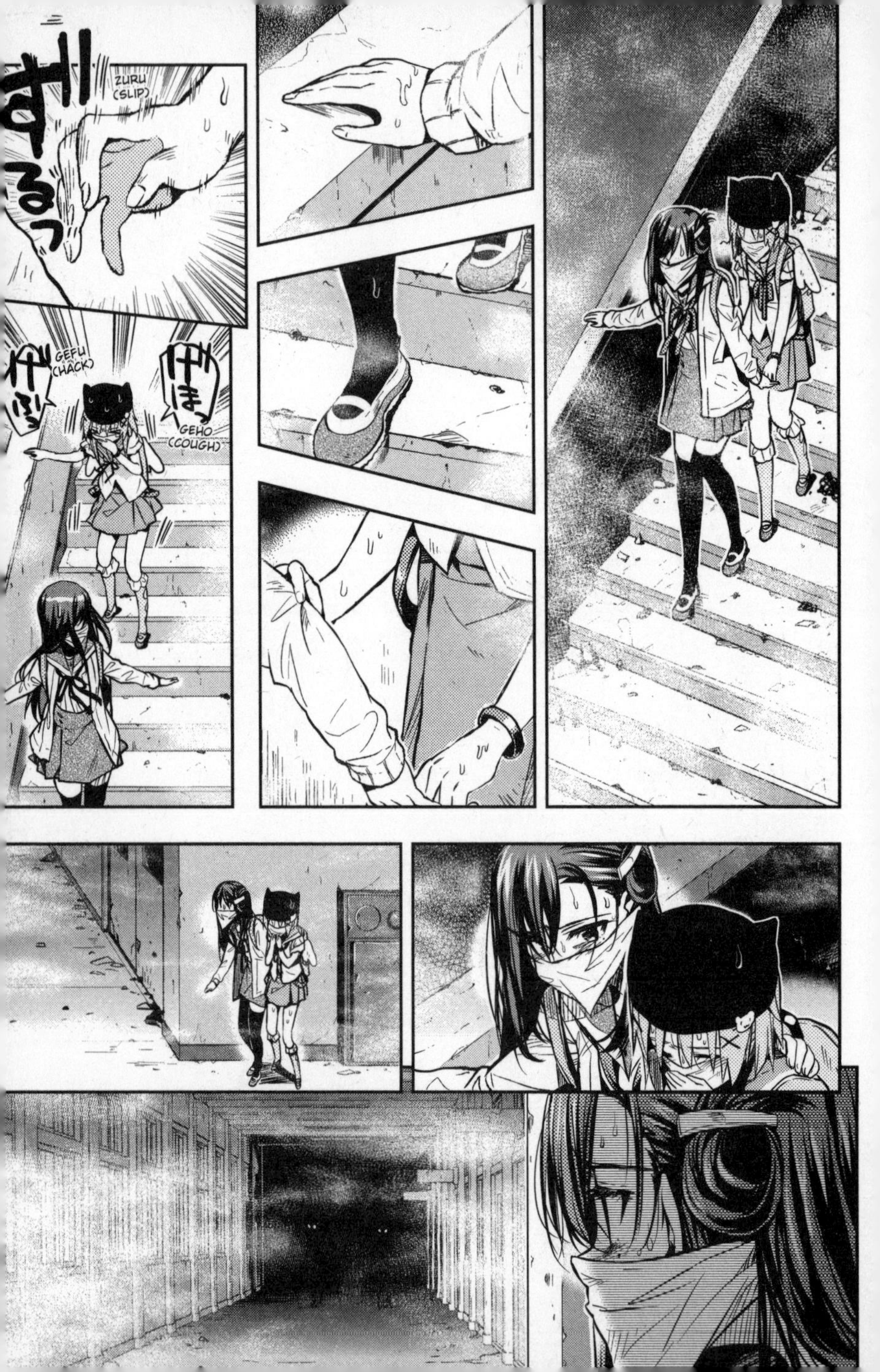
ずるっ
ZURU (SLIP)
げほっ
GEHO (COUGH)
げふっ
GEFU (HACK)

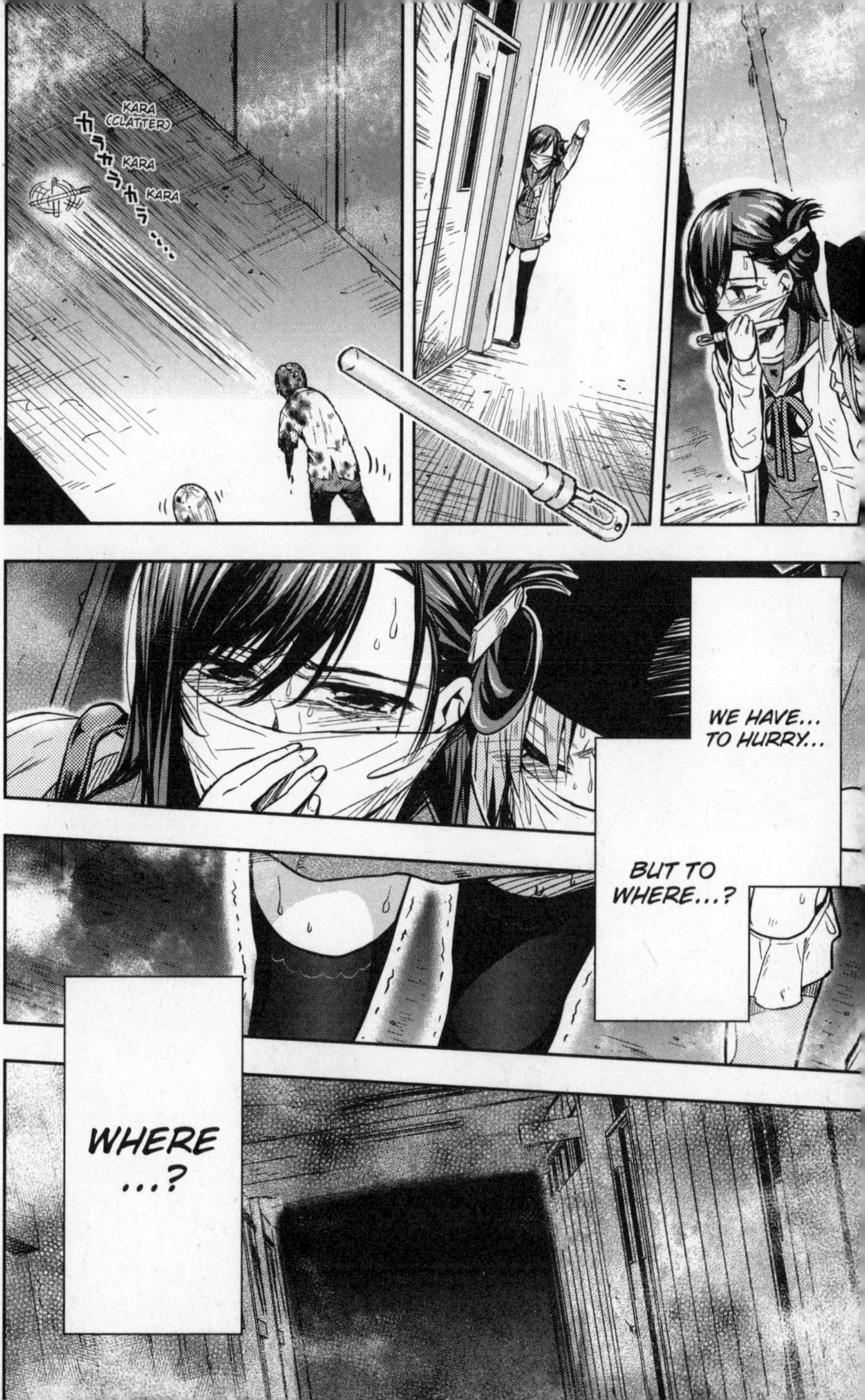
KARA (CLATTER)
カラカラカラ…
KARA
KARA
WE HAVE… TO HURRY…
BUT TO WHERE…?
WHERE …?

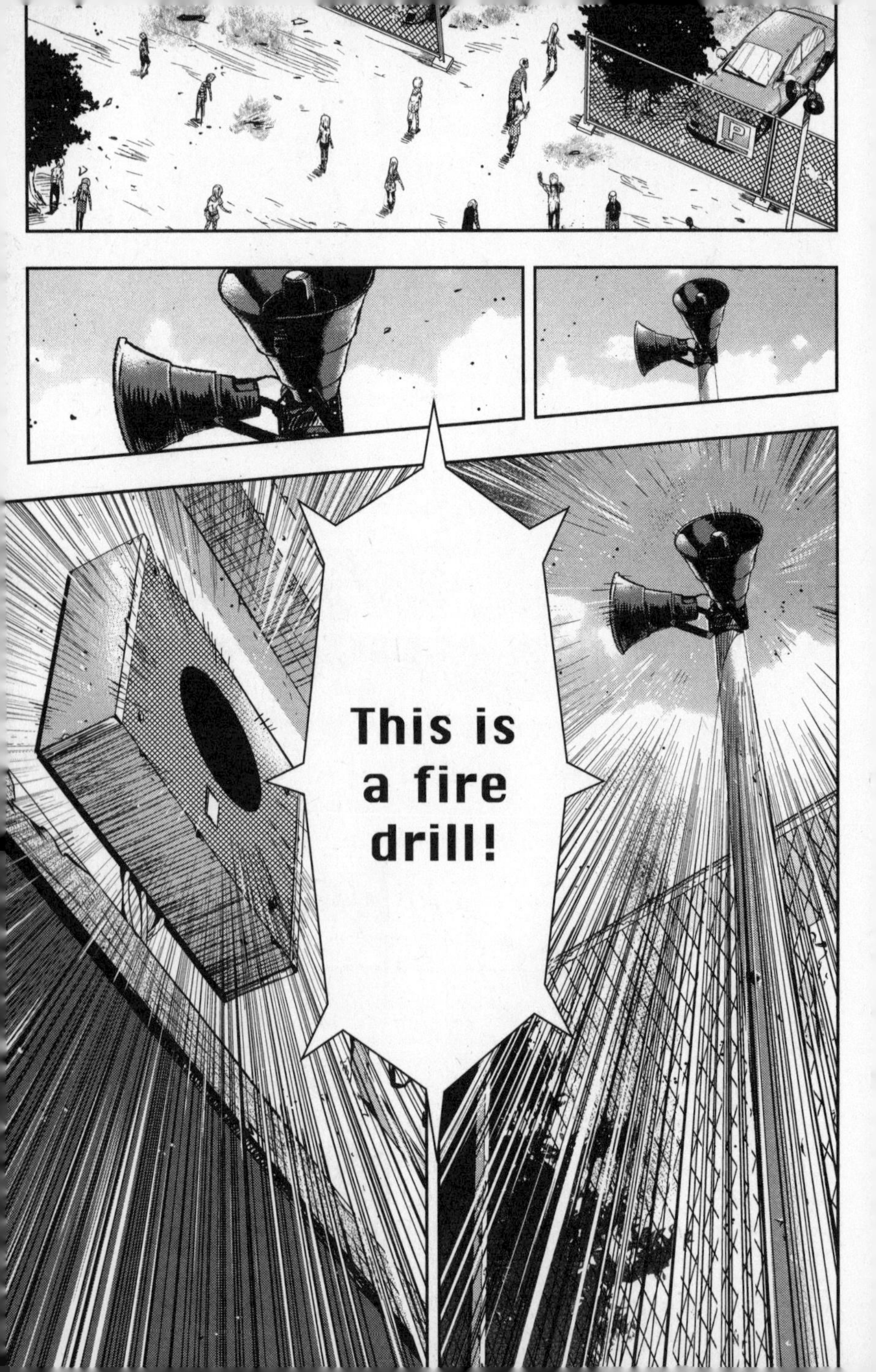
This is a fire drill!

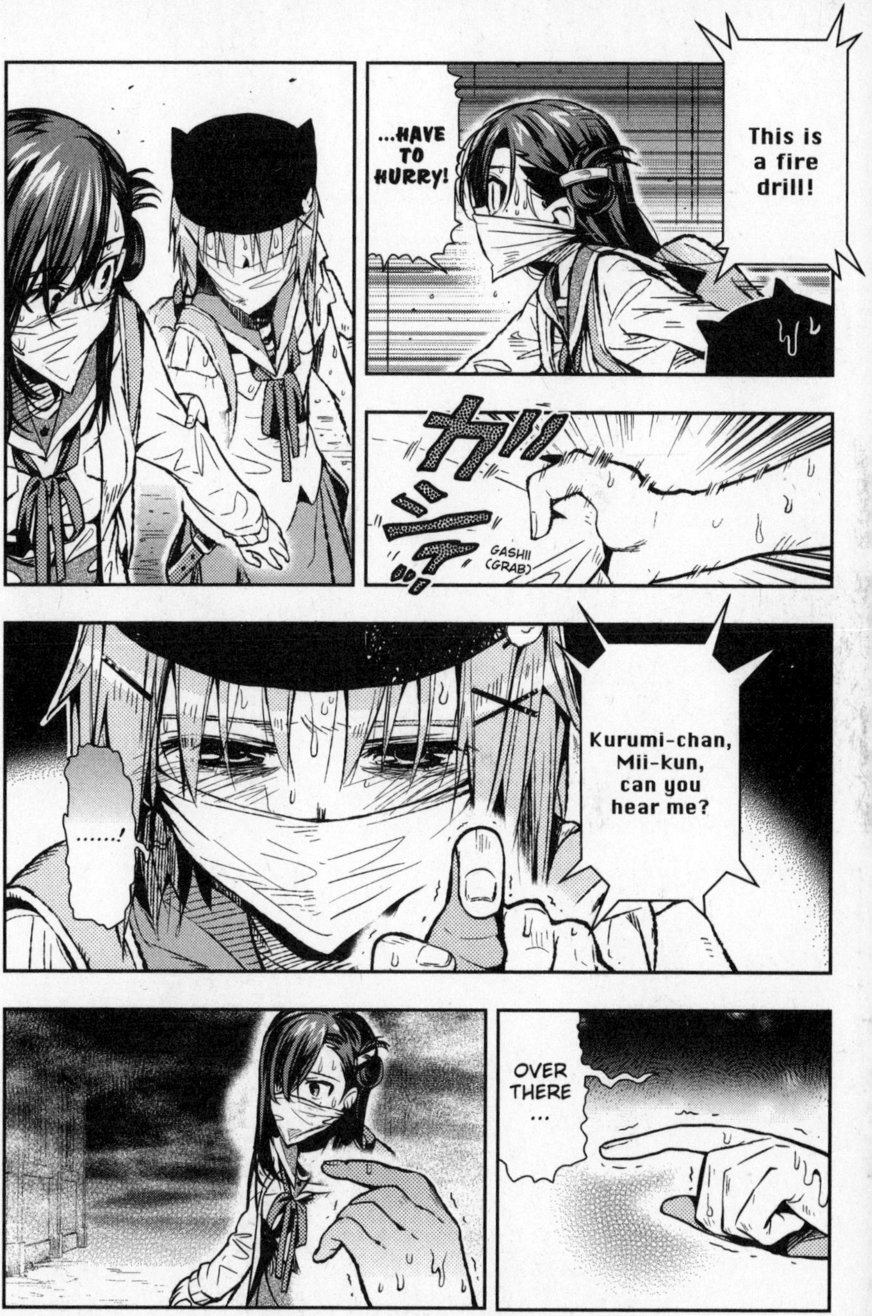
This is a fire drill!
...HAVE TO HURRY!
GASHII (GRAB)
Kurumi-chan, Mii-kun, can you hear me?
......!
OVER THERE ...

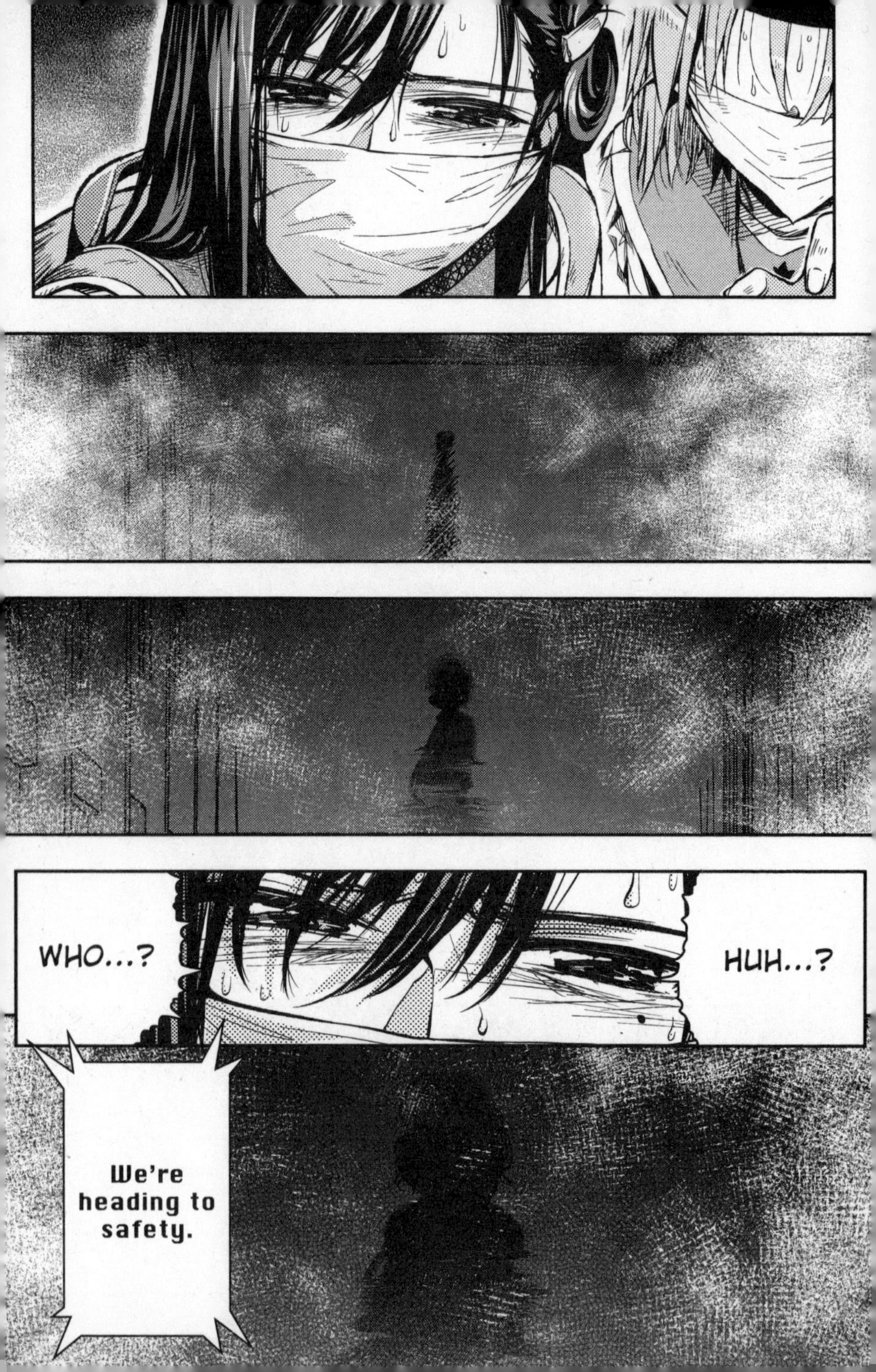
HUH...?
WHO...?
We're heading to safety.

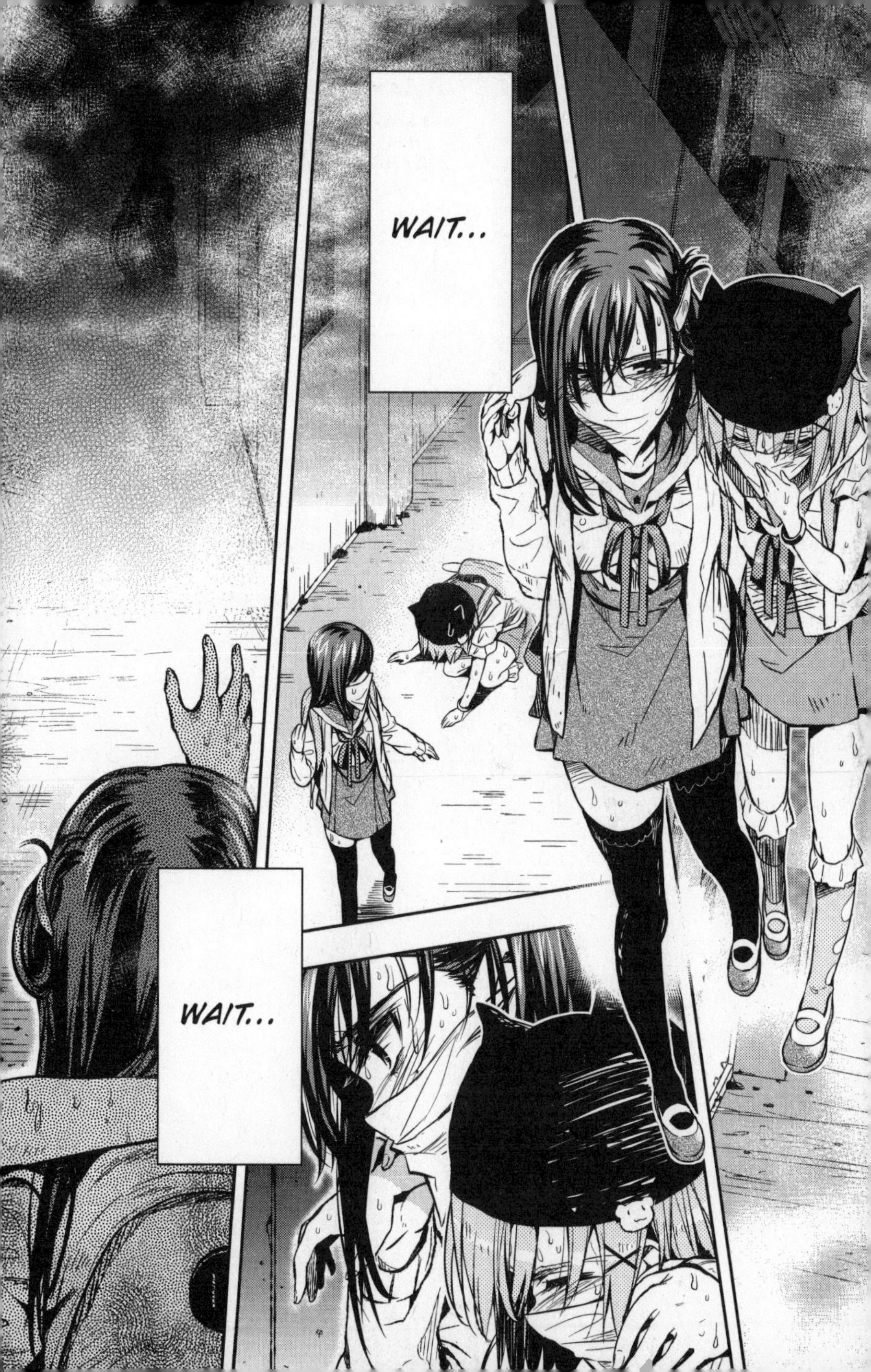
WAIT...
WAIT...

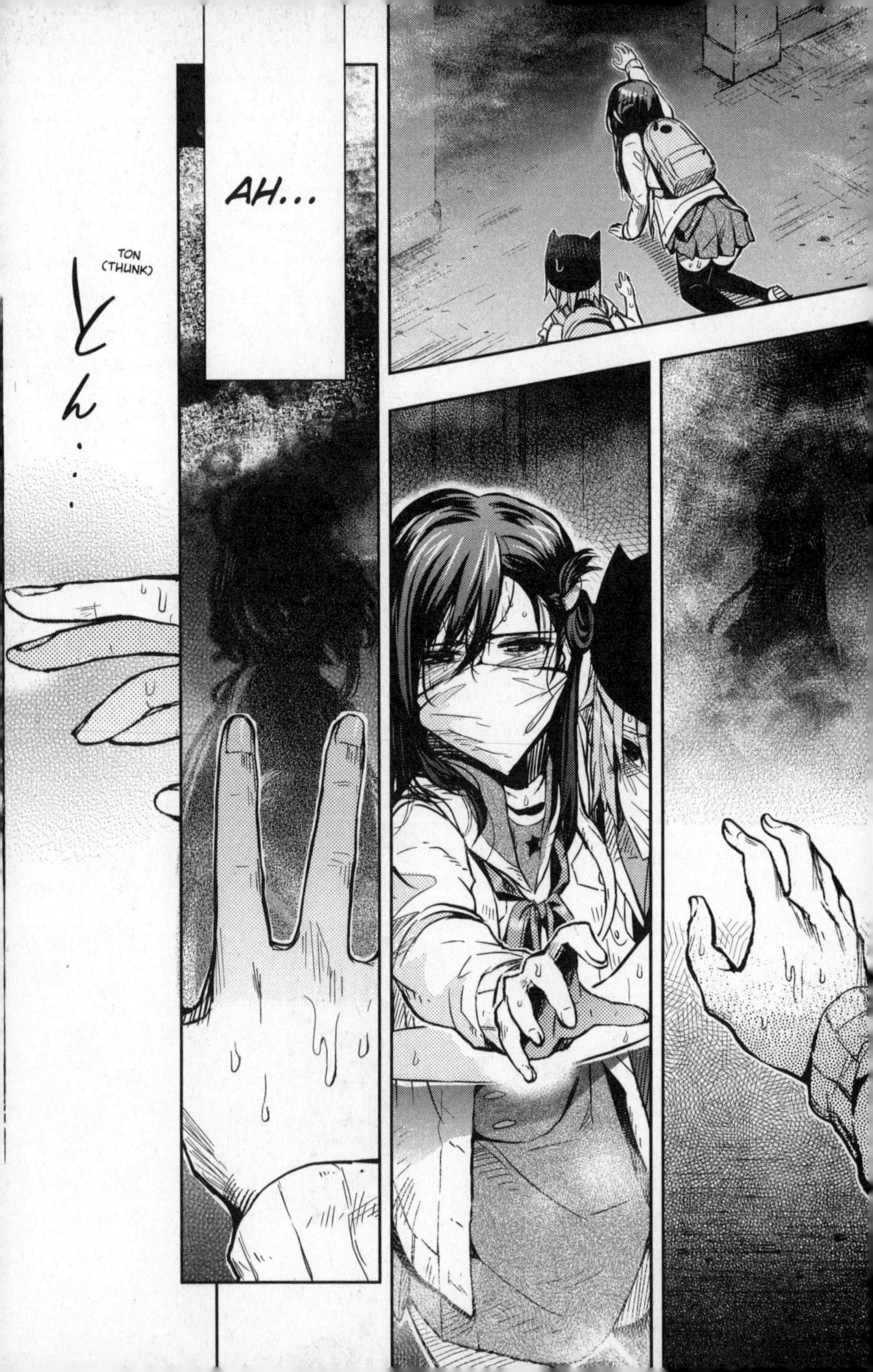
AH...
TON (THUNK)
とん...

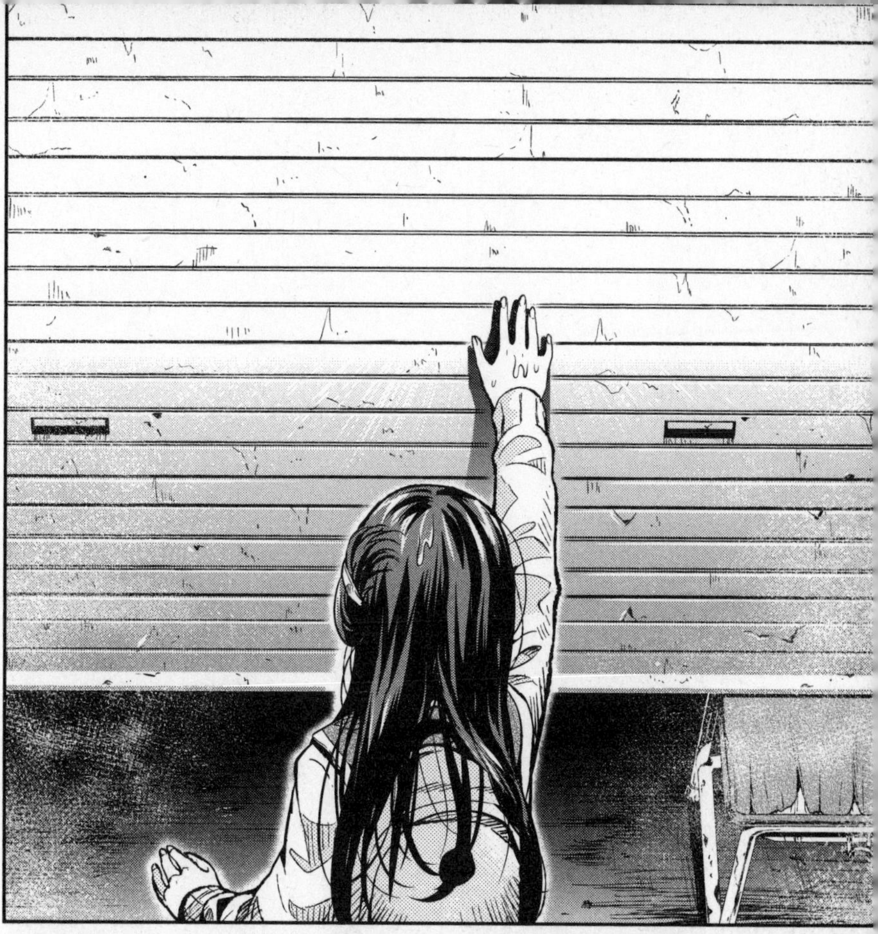
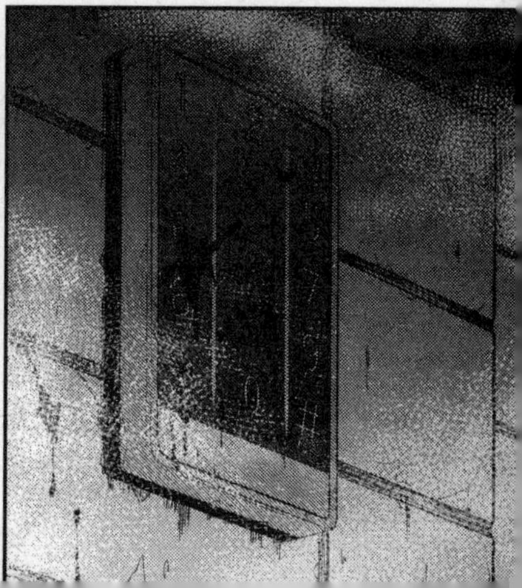
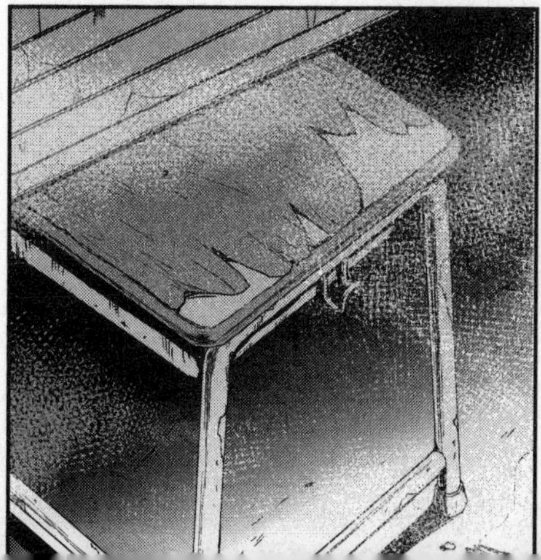

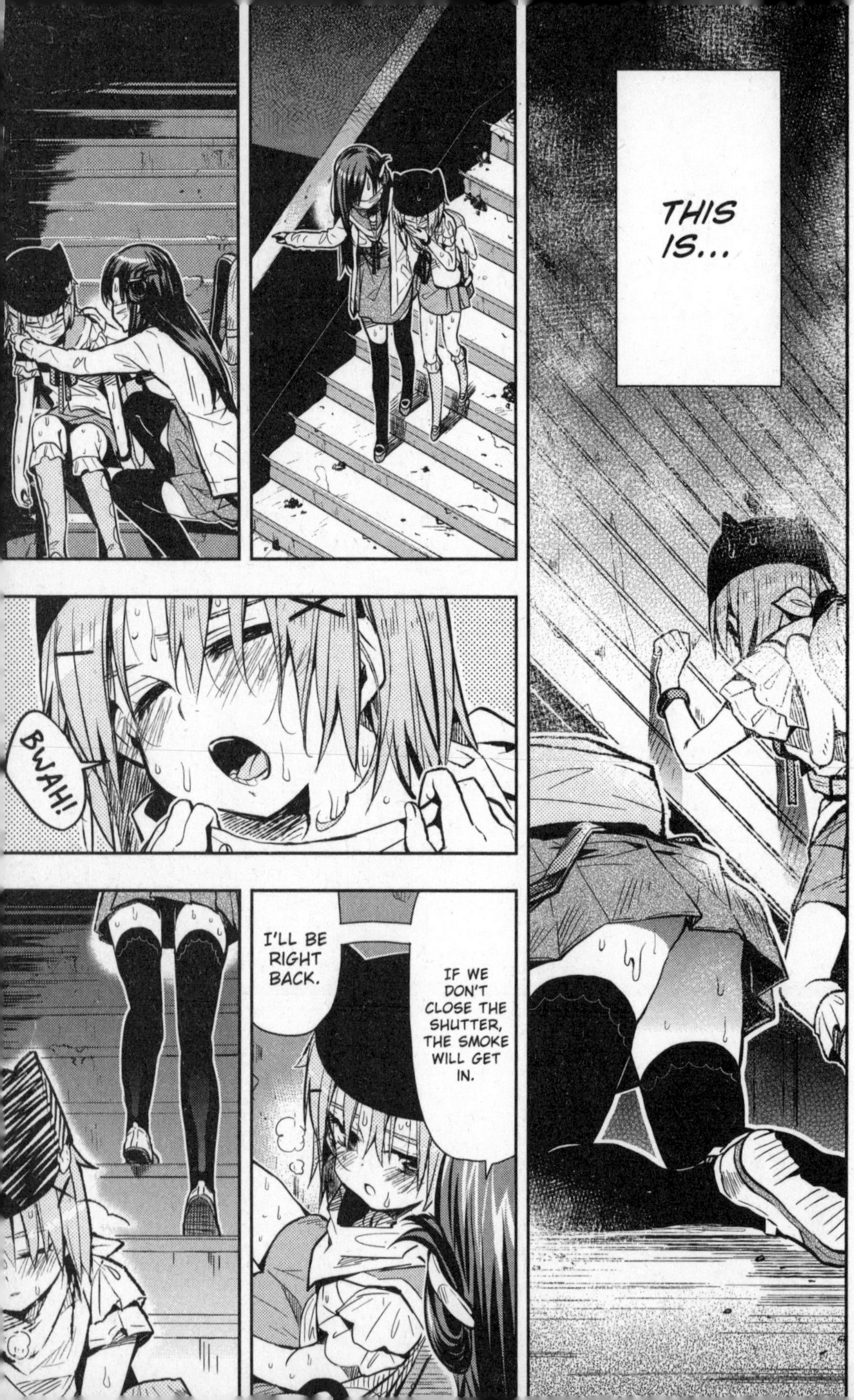
THIS IS...
BWAH!
IF WE DON'T CLOSE THE SHUTTER, THE SMOKE WILL GET IN.
I'LL BE RIGHT BACK.

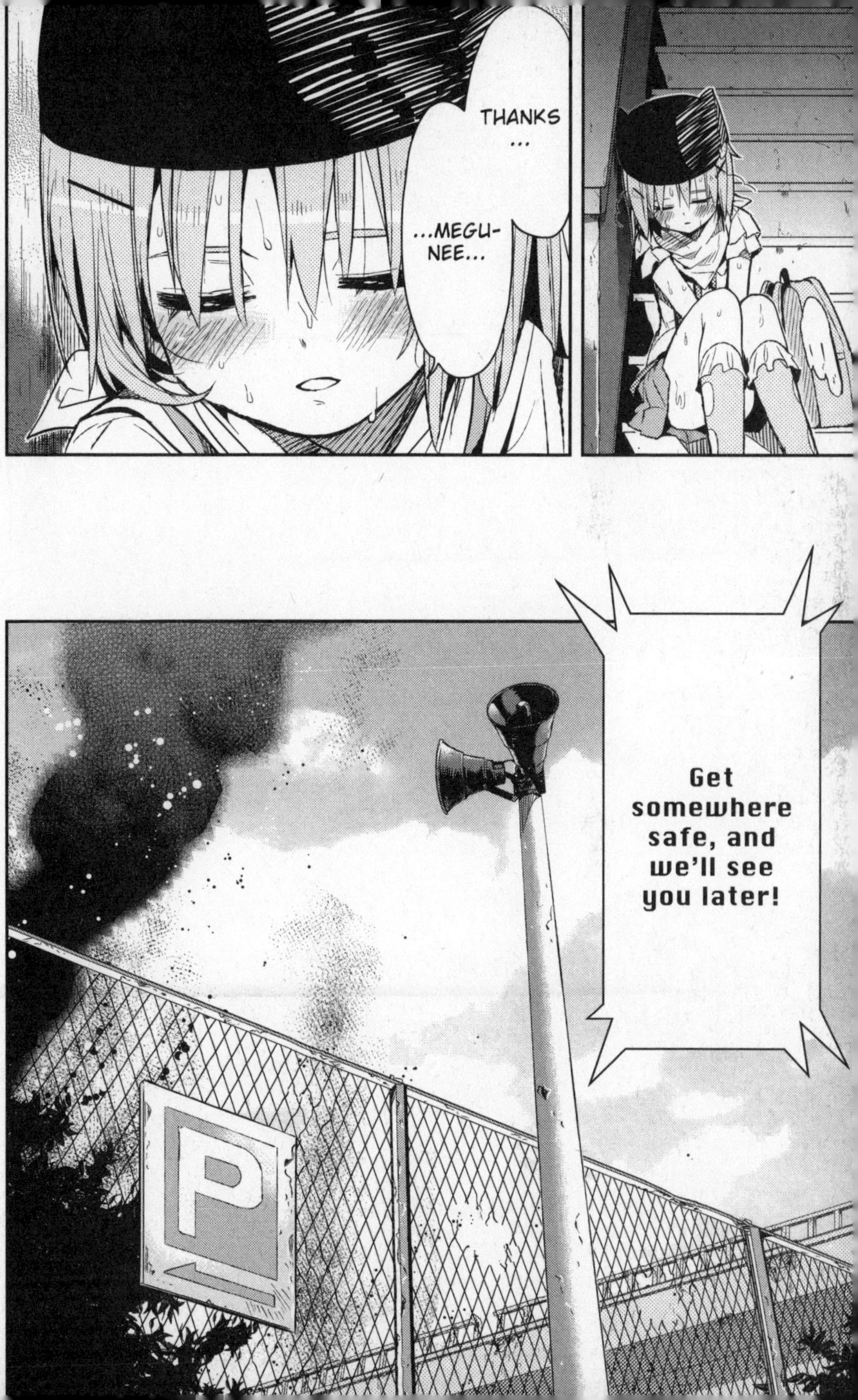
THANKS ...
...MEGU-NEE...
Get somewhere safe, and we'll see you later!

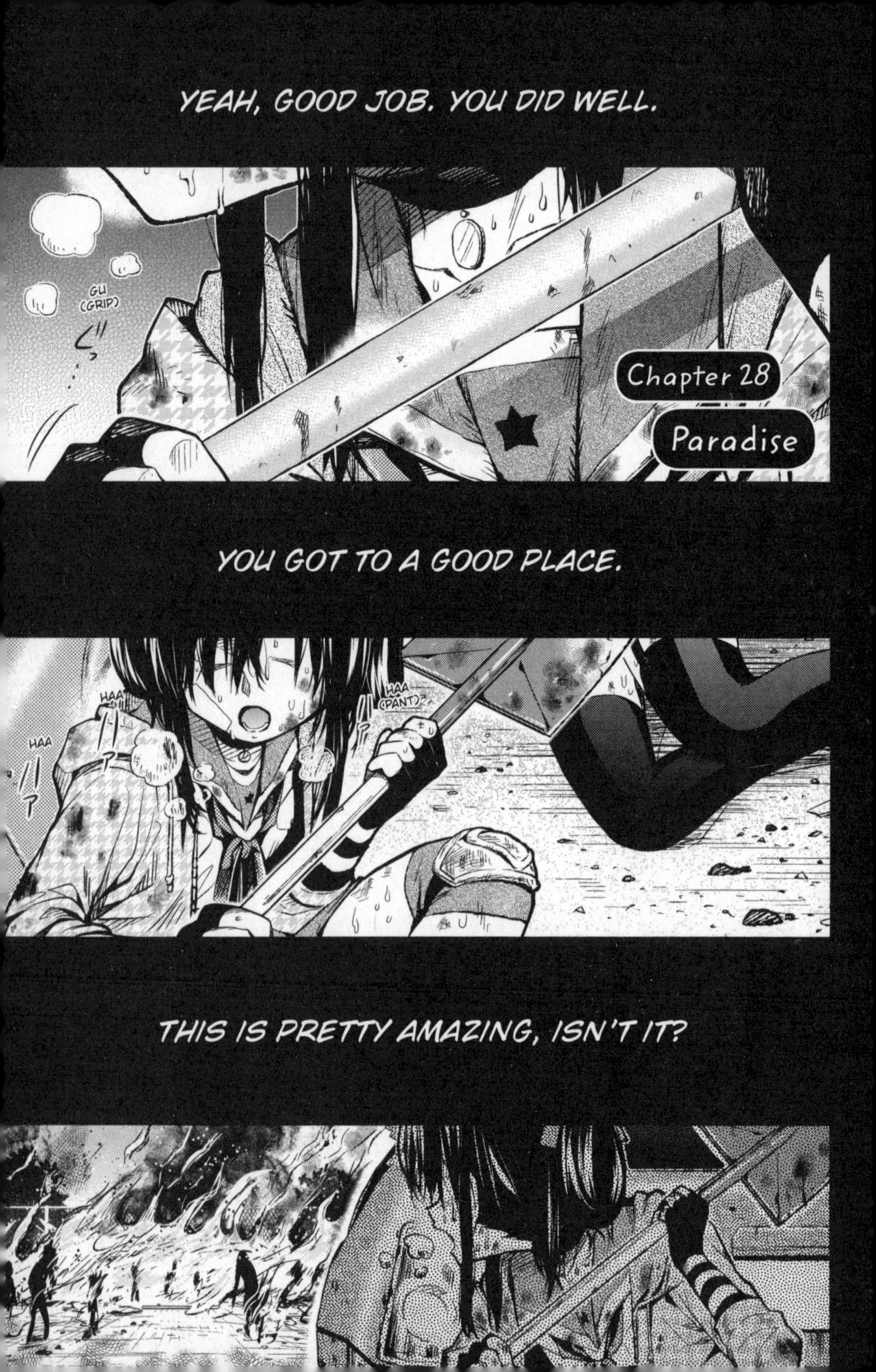
YEAH, GOOD JOB. YOU DID WELL.
GU (GRIP)
Chapter 28
Paradise
YOU GOT TO A GOOD PLACE.
HAA (PANT)
HAA
HAA
THIS IS PRETTY AMAZING, ISN'T IT?

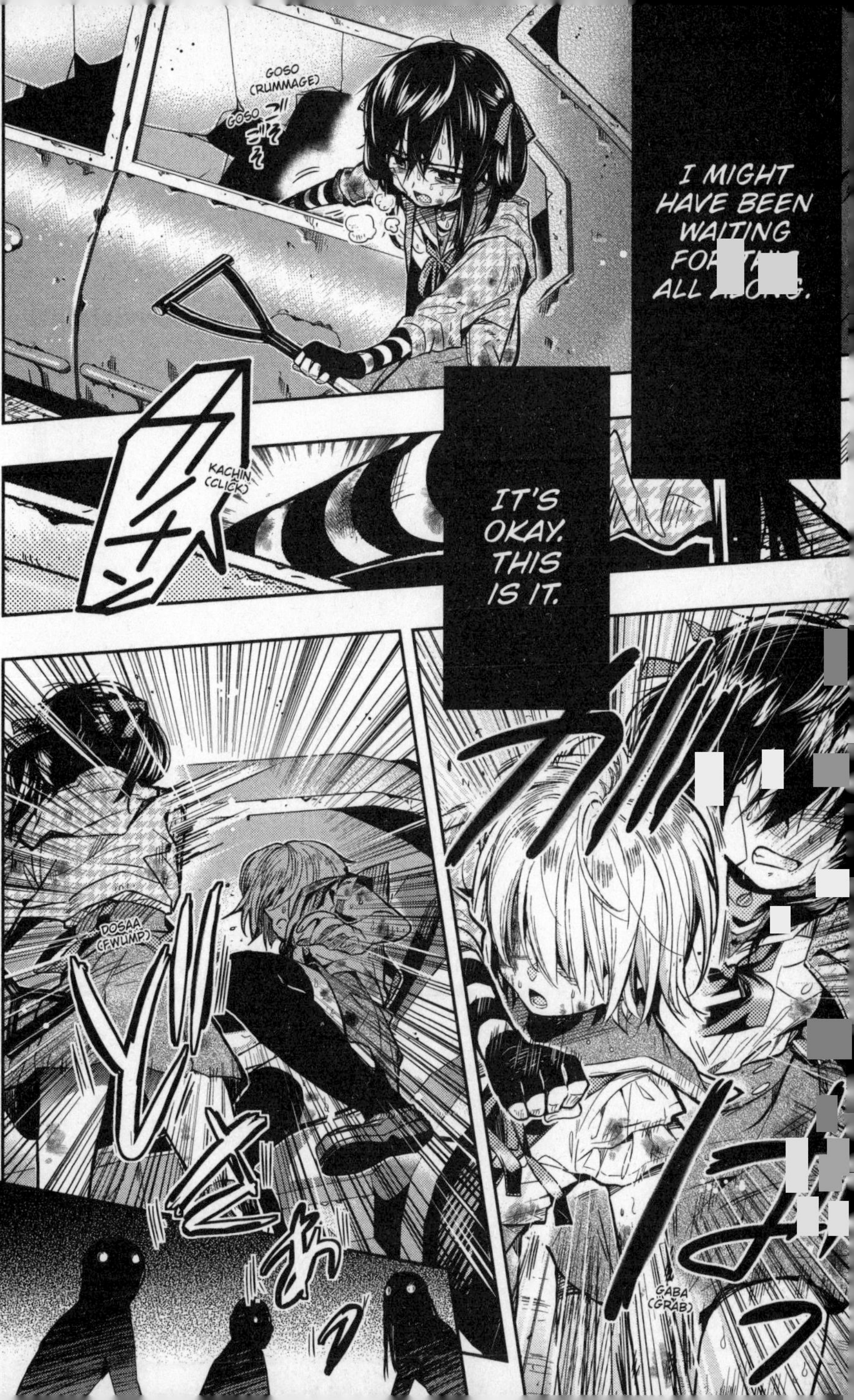
I MIGHT HAVE BEEN WAITING
GOSO (RUMMAGE)
GOSO
IT'S OKAY. THIS IS IT.
KACHIN (CLICK)
GABA (GRAB)
DOSAA (FWUMP)

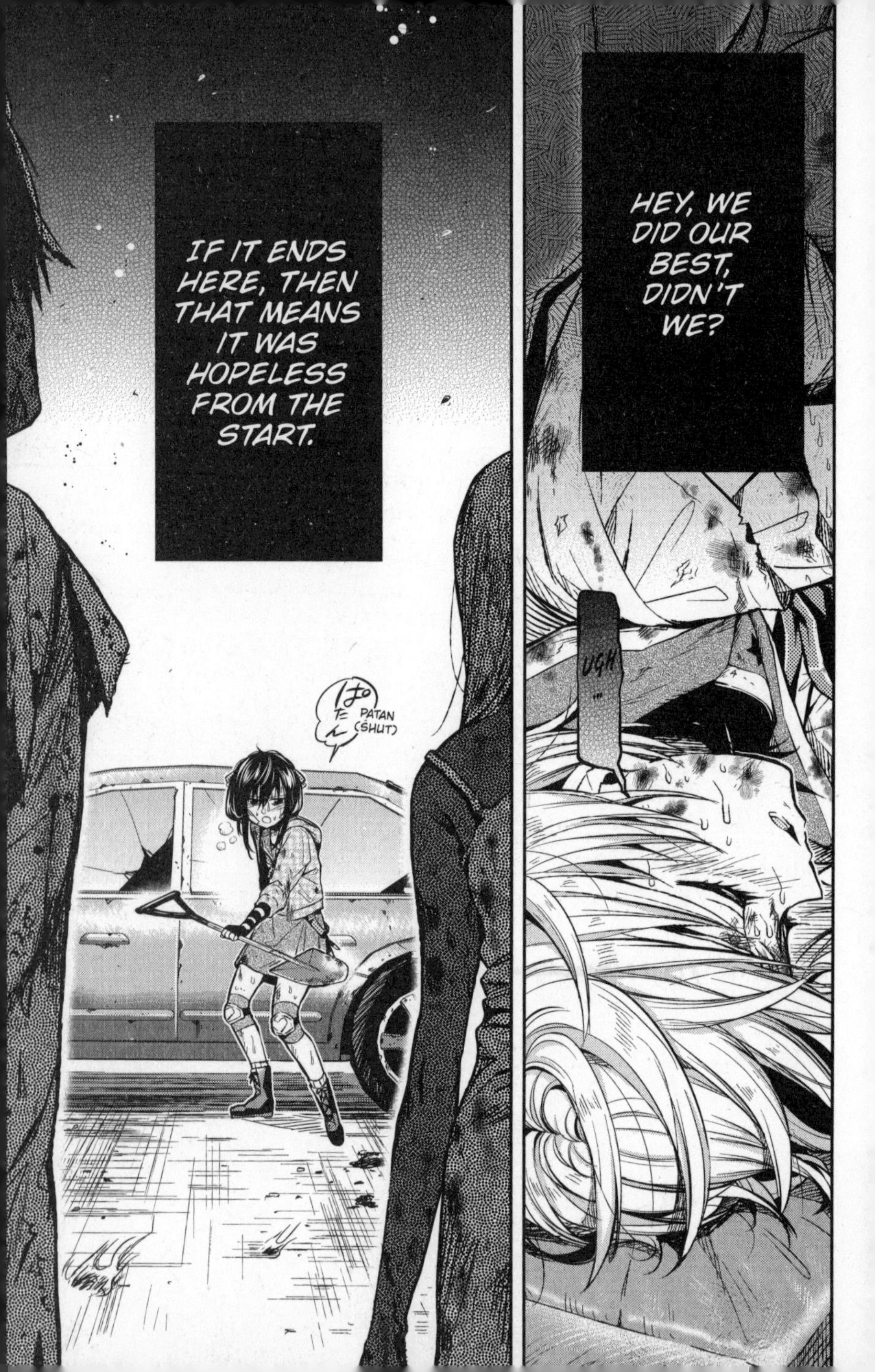
HEY, WE DID OUR BEST, DIDN'T WE?
UGH...
IF IT ENDS HERE, THEN THAT MEANS IT WAS HOPELESS FROM THE START.
ぱたん
PATAN (SHUT)

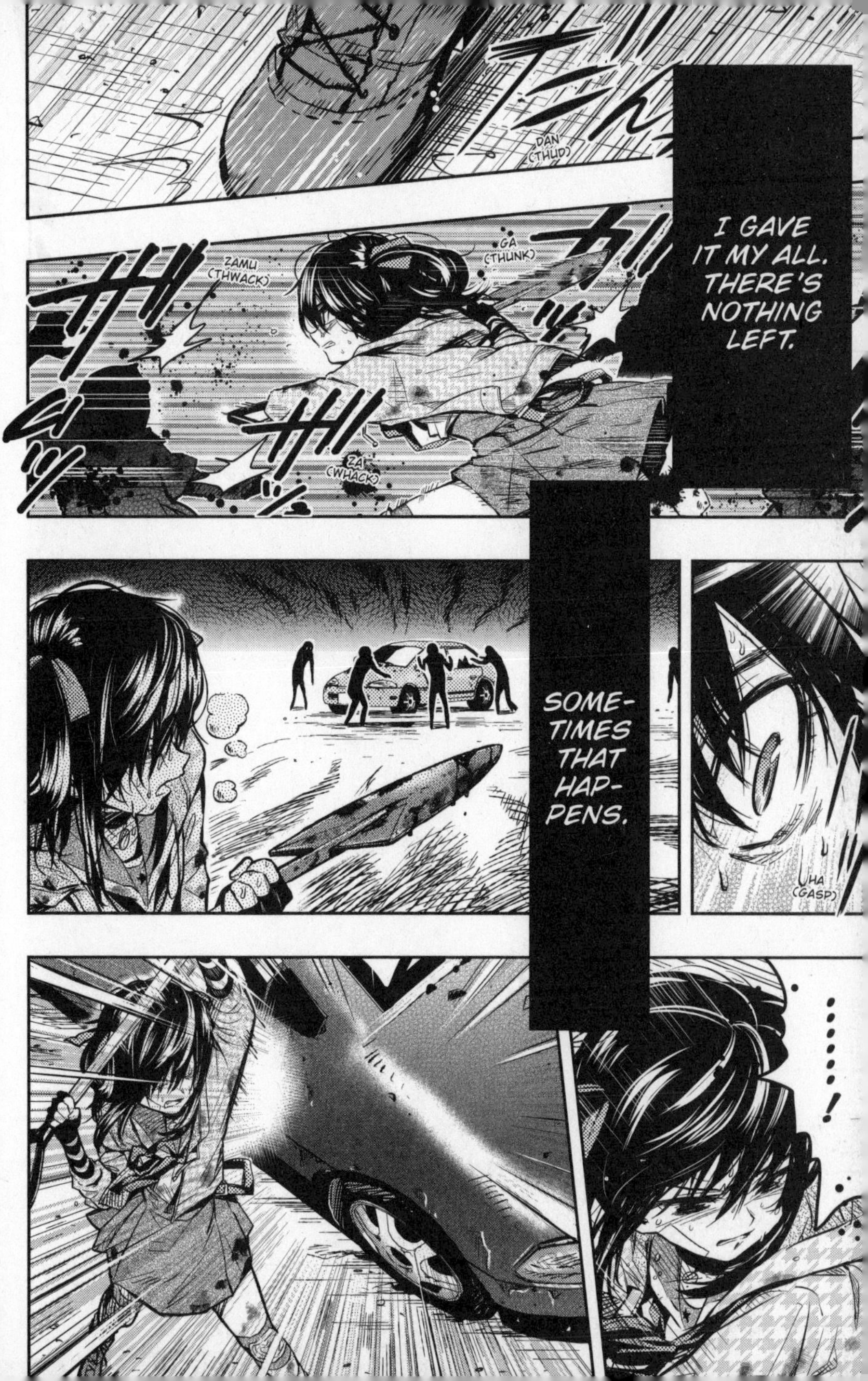

DAN (THUD)
I GAVE IT MY ALL. THERE'S NOTHING LEFT.
GA (THUNK)
ZAMU (THWACK)
ZA (WHACK)
HA (GASP)
SOME-TIMES THAT HAP-PENS.
......!

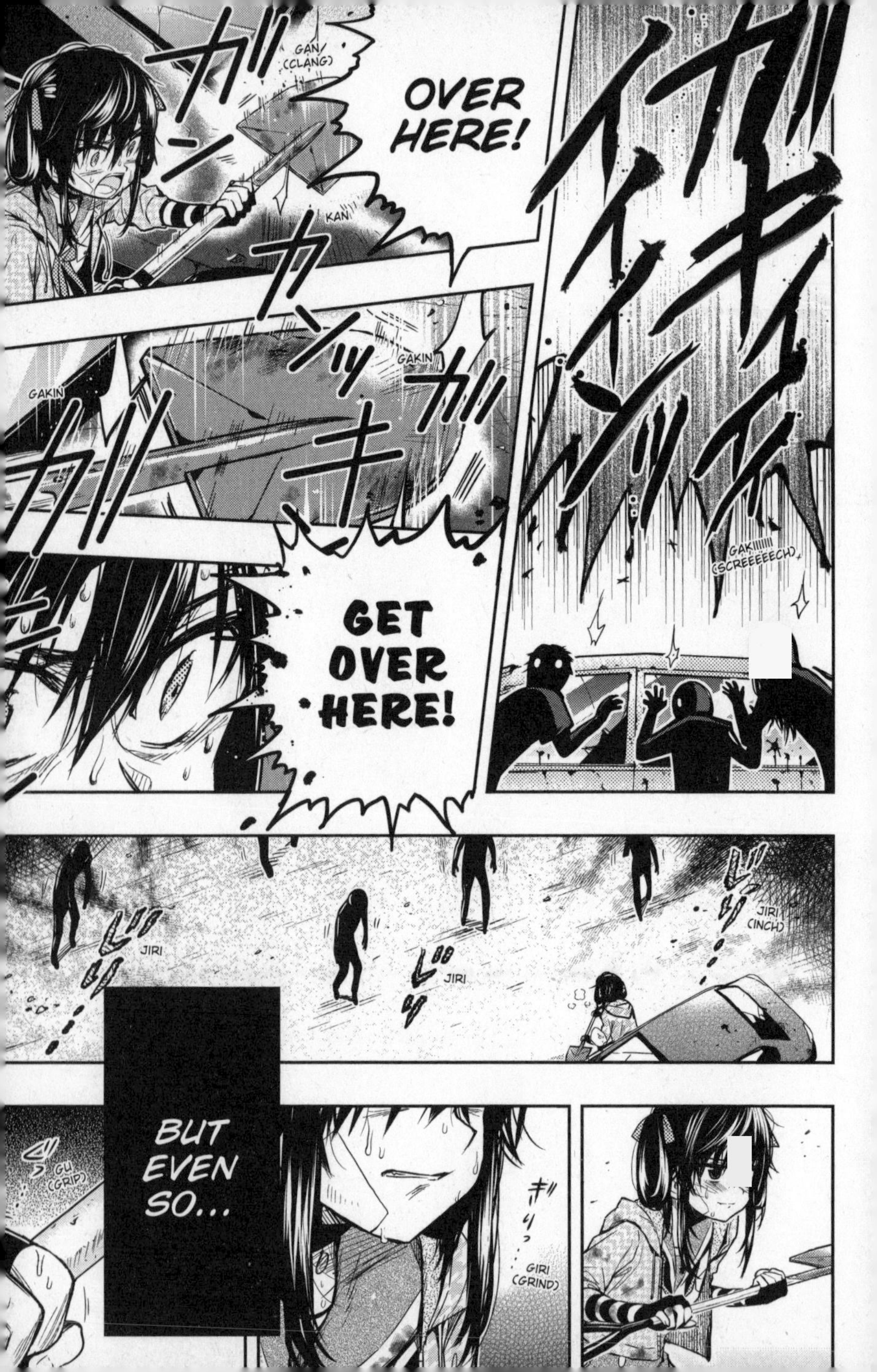
GAKIIIIII
(SCREEEEECH)
OVER HERE!
GAN/
(CLANG)
KAN
GAKIN
GAKIN
GET OVER HERE!
JIRI
(INCH)
JIRI
JIRI
GIRI
(GRIND)
BUT EVEN SO...
GU
(GRIP)

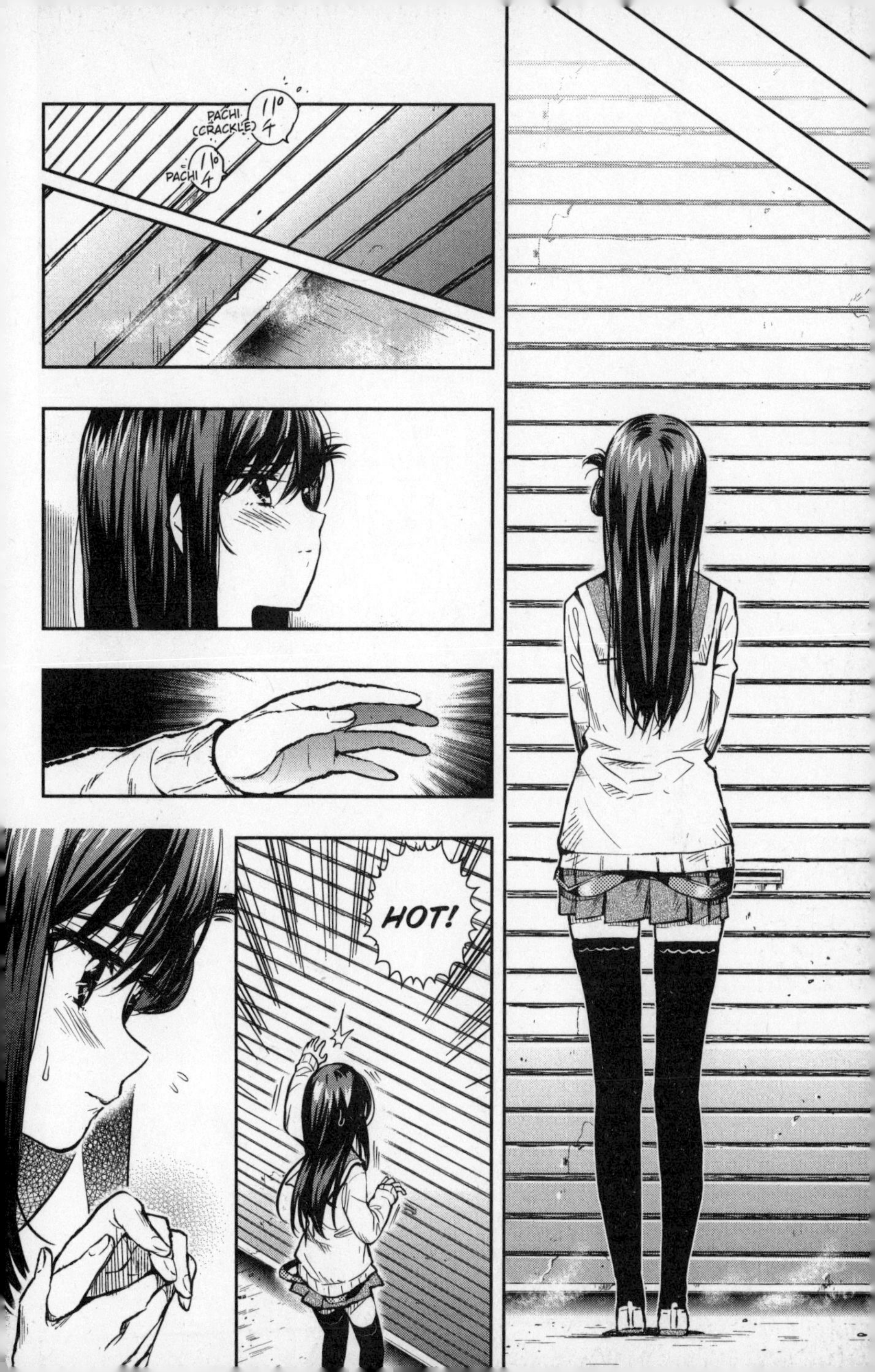
PACHI (CRACKLE)
PACHI
HOT!

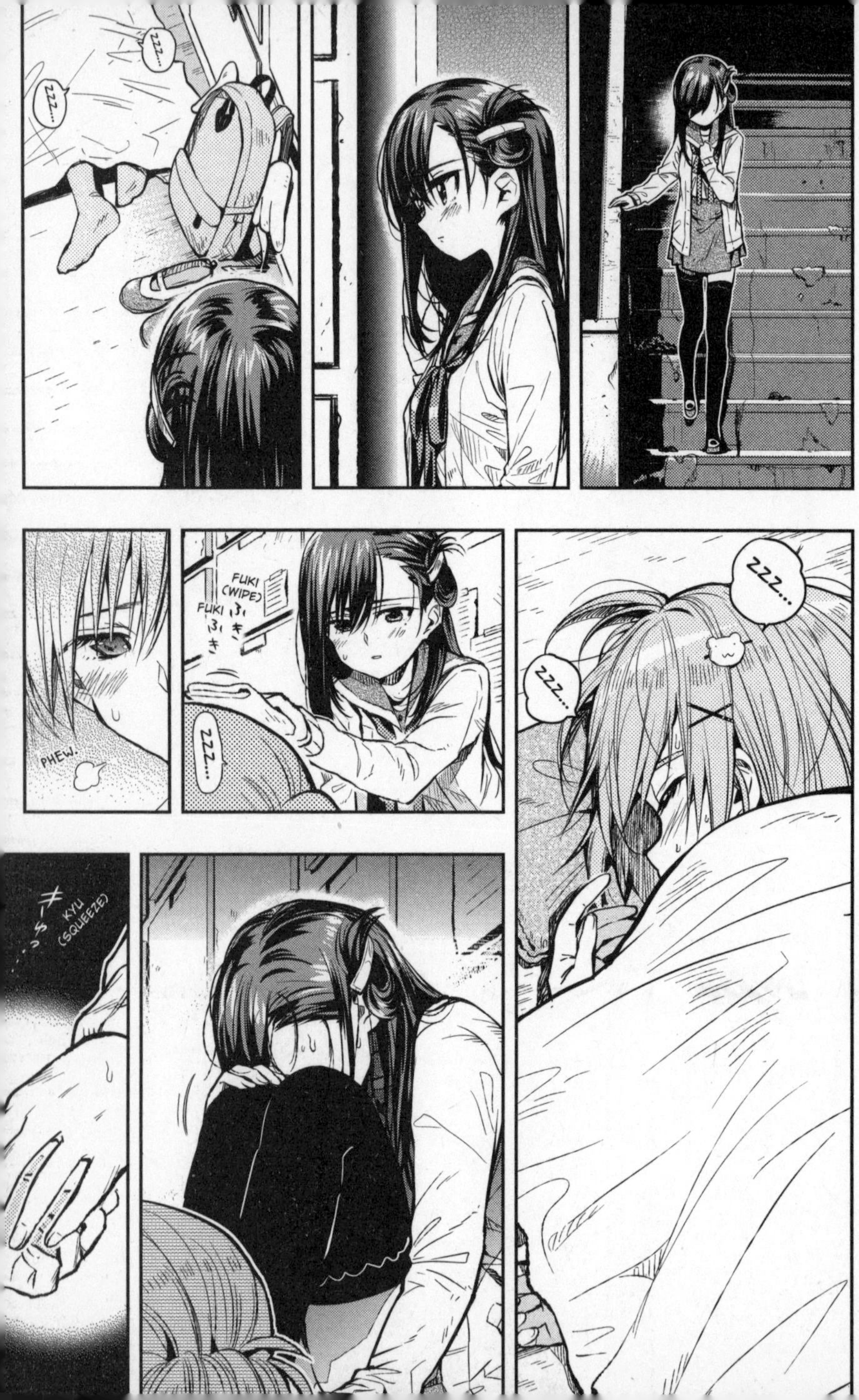
ZZZ...
ZZZ...
ZZZ...
ZZZ...
FUKI (WIPE)
FUKI
ふきふき
ZZZ...
PHEW.
KYU (SQUEEZE)

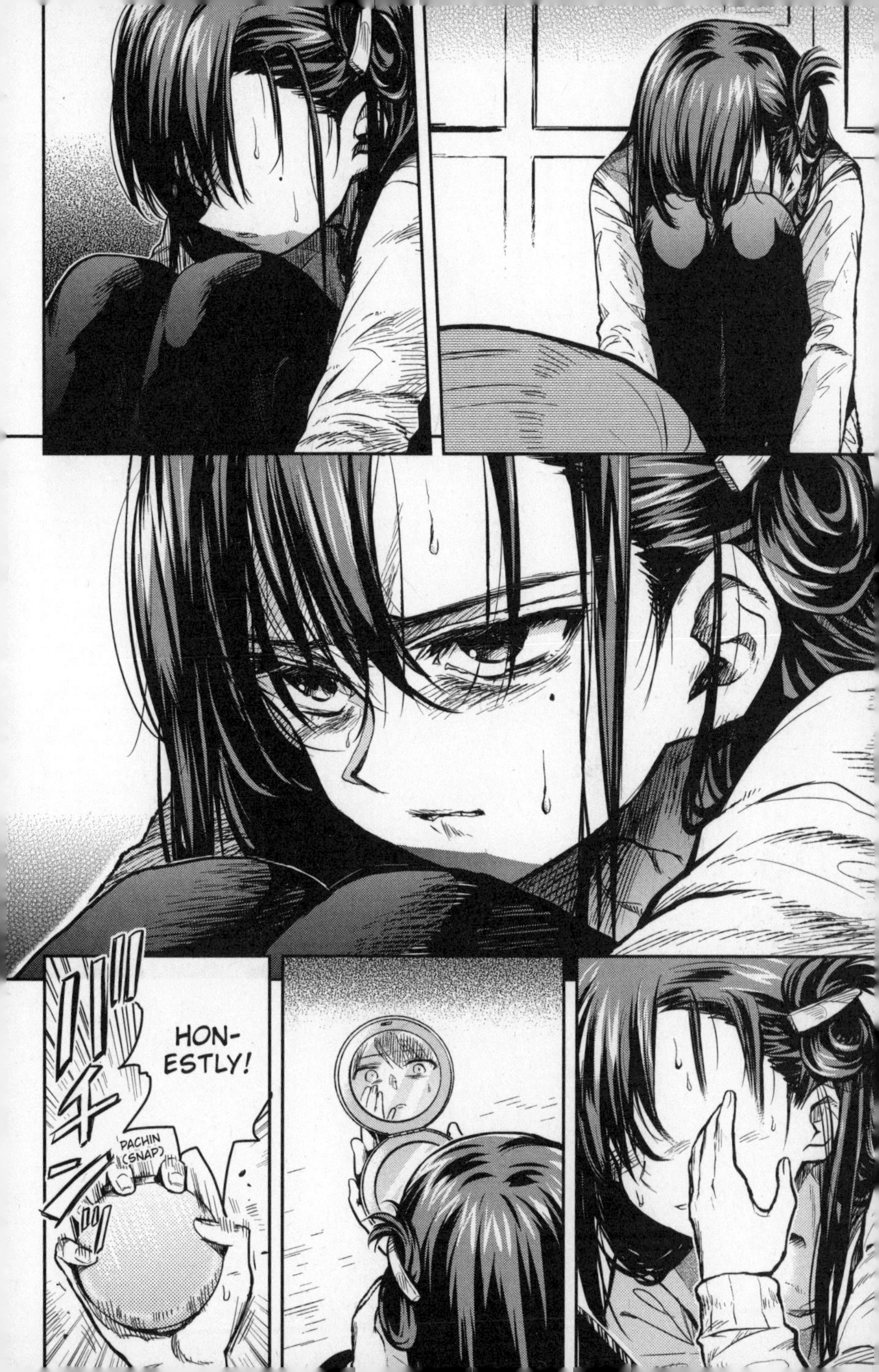
HON-
ESTLY!
PACHIN
(SNAP)

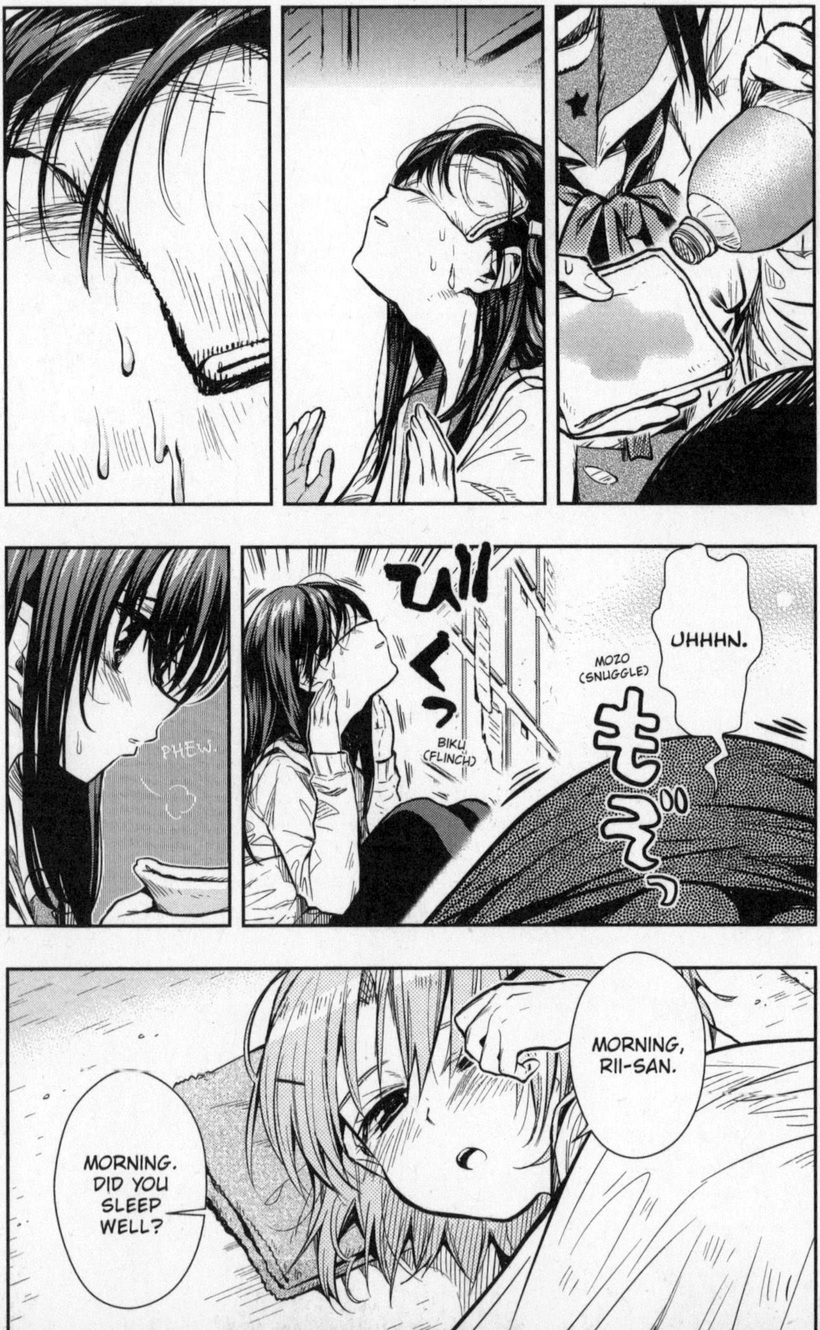
UHHHN.
もぞっ
MOZO (SNUGGLE)
びくっ
BIKU (FLINCH)
PHEW.
MORNING, RII-SAN.
MORNING. DID YOU SLEEP WELL?

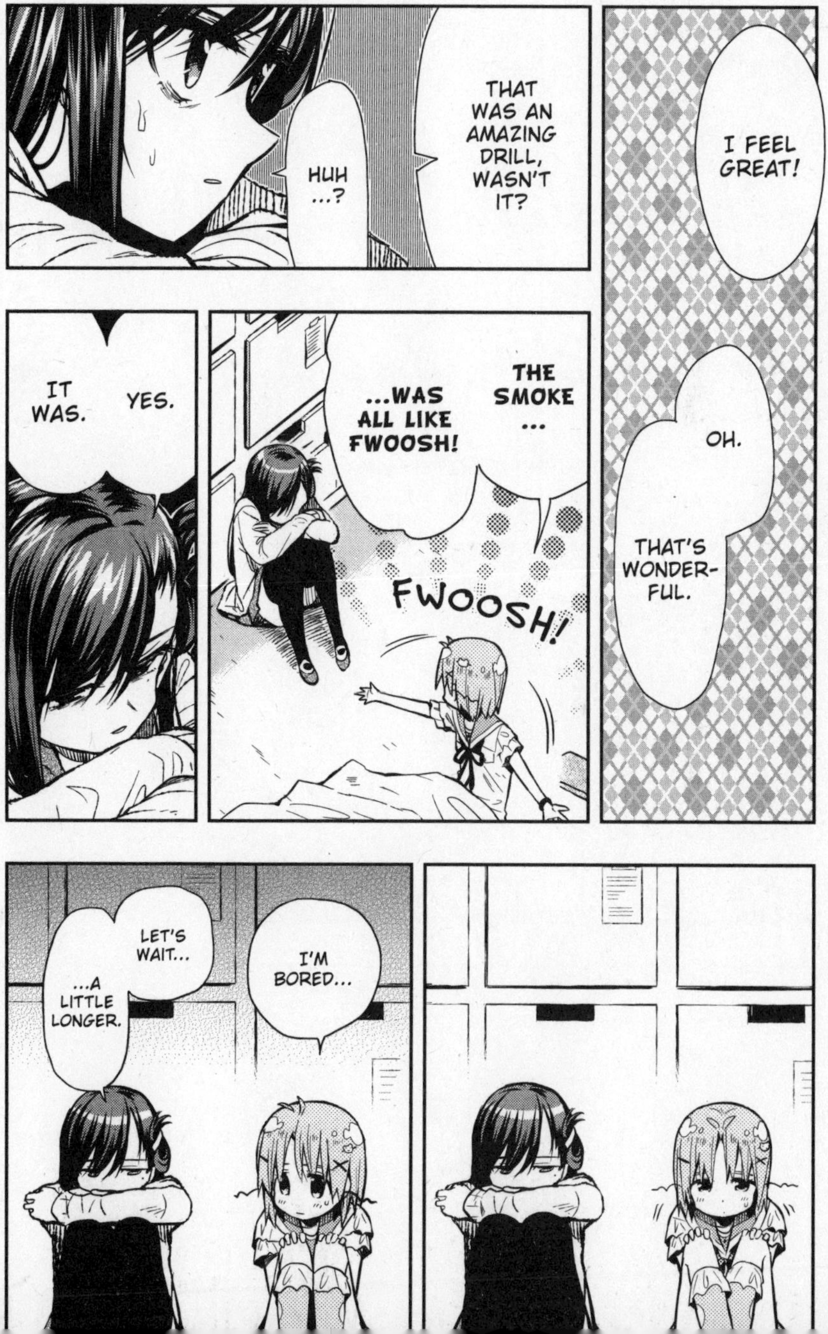
I FEEL GREAT!
OH.
THAT'S WONDER-FUL.
THAT WAS AN AMAZING DRILL, WASN'T IT?
HUH ...?
THE SMOKE ...
...WAS ALL LIKE FWOOSH!
FWOOSH!
YES.
IT WAS.
I'M BORED...
LET'S WAIT...
...A LITTLE LONGER.

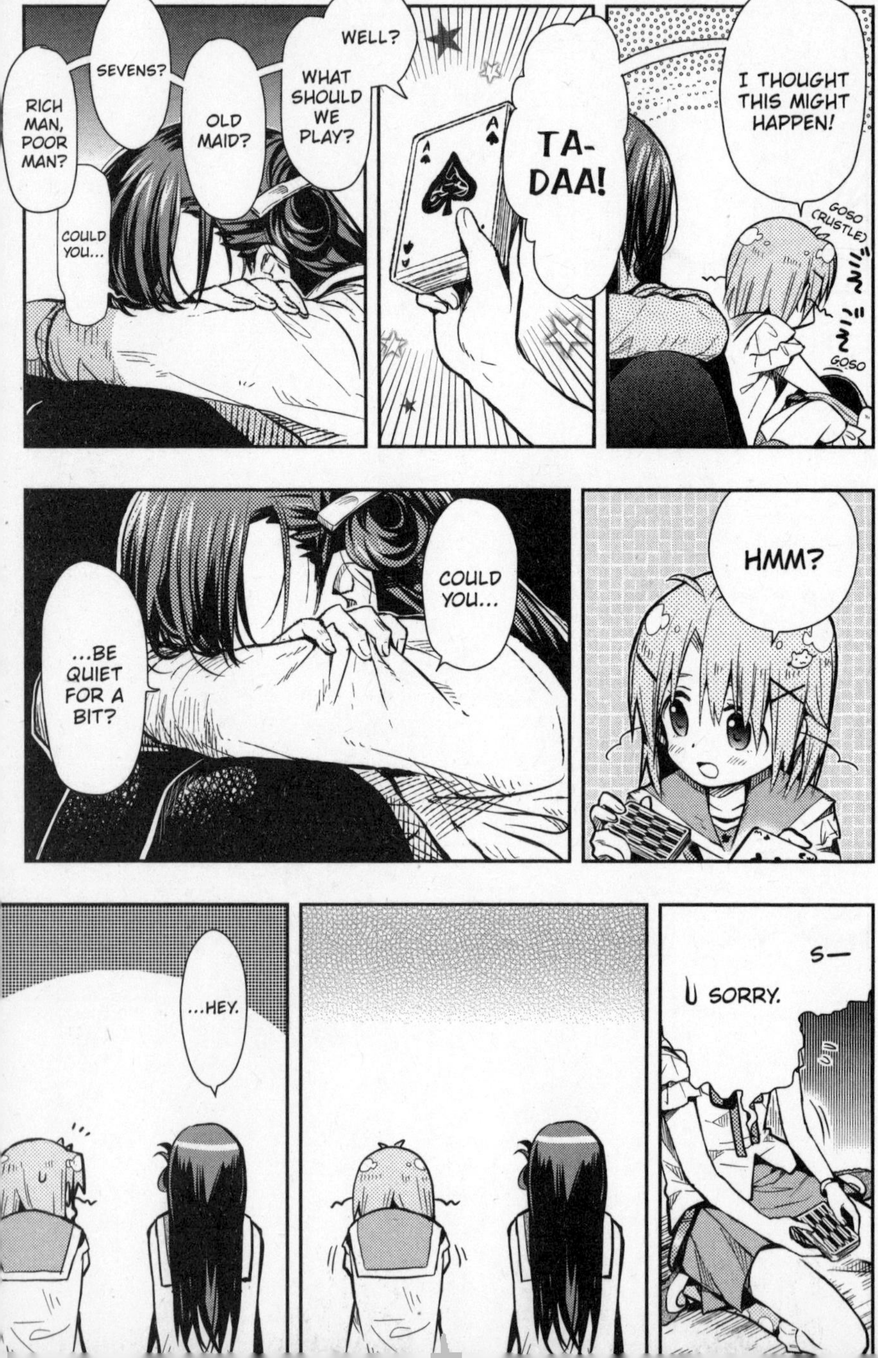
I THOUGHT THIS MIGHT HAPPEN!
GOSO (RUSTLE)
GOSO
TA-DAA!
WELL?
WHAT SHOULD WE PLAY?
OLD MAID?
SEVENS?
RICH MAN, POOR MAN?
COULD YOU...
HMM?
COULD YOU...
...BE QUIET FOR A BIT?
S—
SORRY.
...HEY.

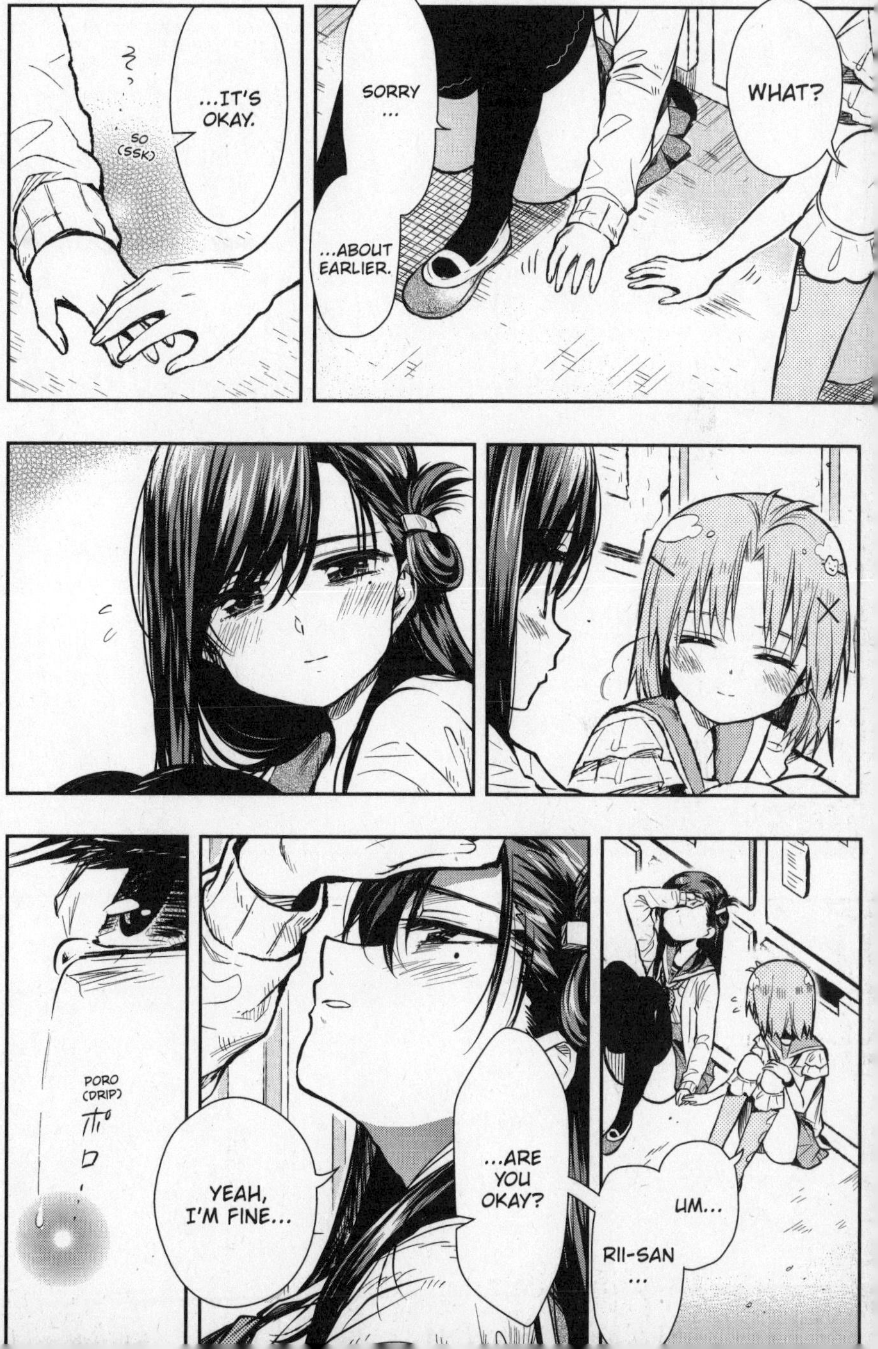
WHAT?
SORRY ...
...ABOUT EARLIER.
SO (SSK)
...IT'S OKAY.
UM...
RII-SAN ...
...ARE YOU OKAY?
YEAH, I'M FINE...
PORO (DRIP)

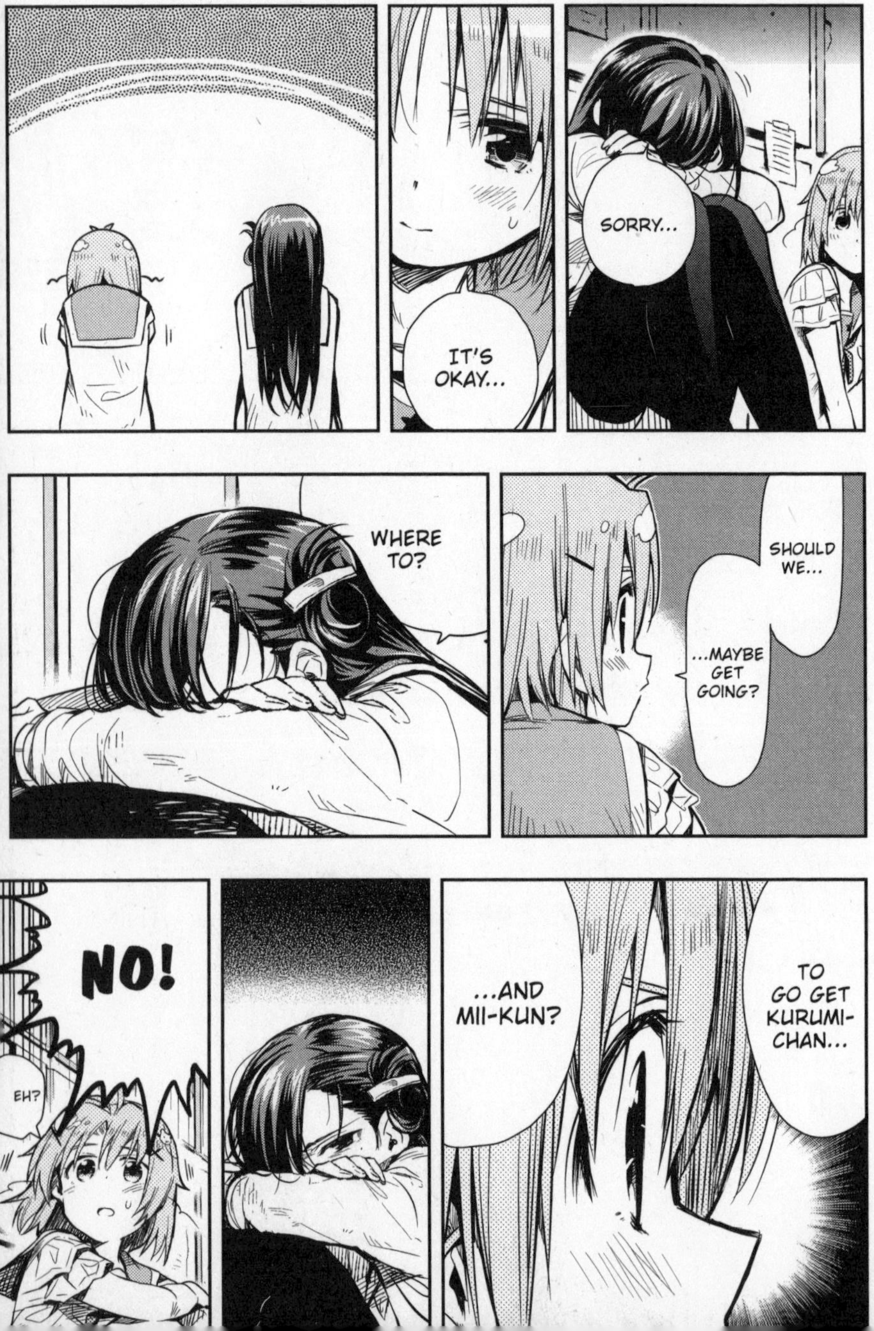
SORRY...
IT'S OKAY...
SHOULD WE...
...MAYBE GET GOING?
WHERE TO?
TO GO GET KURUMI-CHAN...
...AND MII-KUN?
NO!
EH?

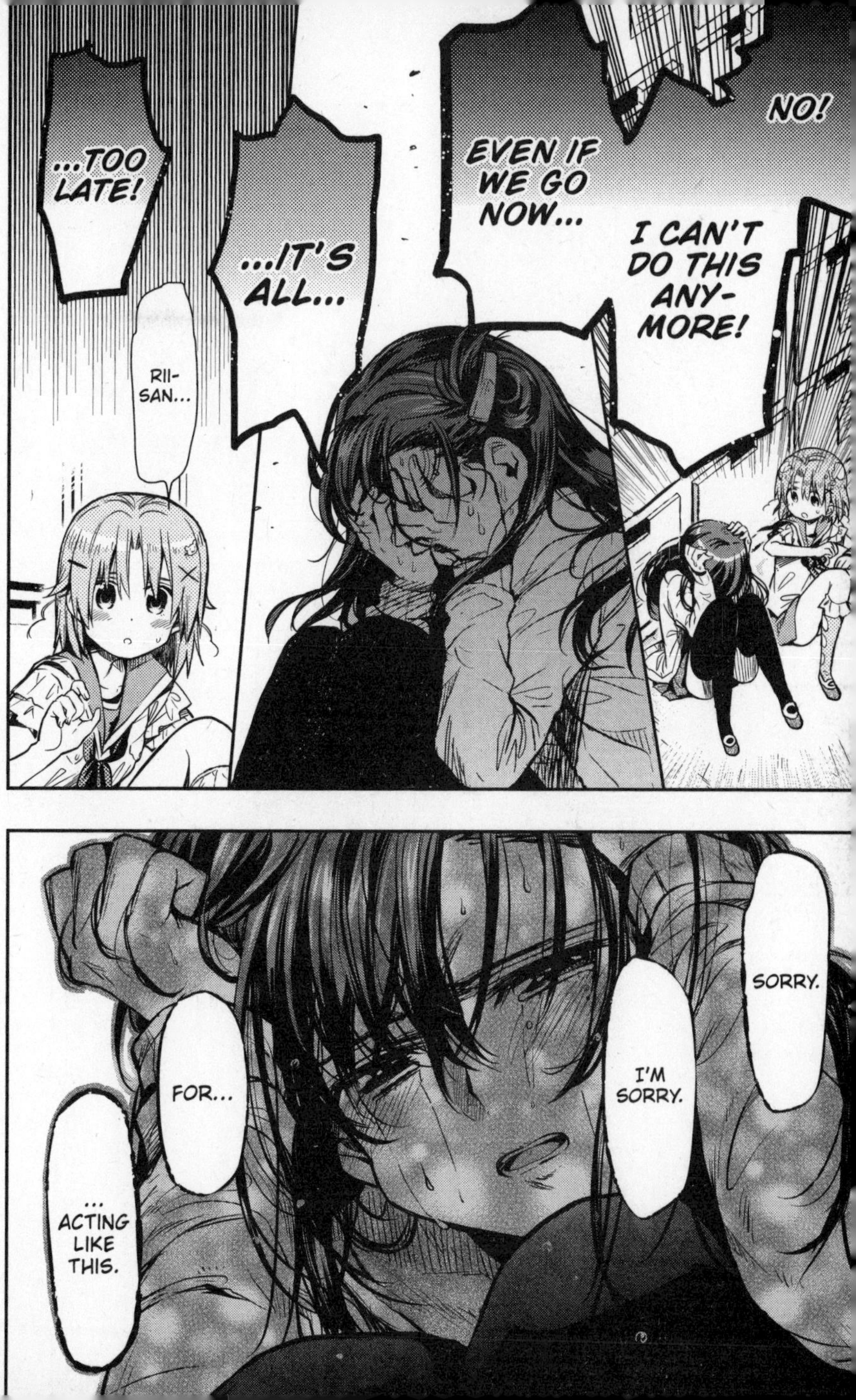
NO!
I CAN'T DO THIS ANYMORE!
EVEN IF WE GO NOW...
...IT'S ALL...
...TOO LATE!
RII-SAN...
SORRY.
I'M SORRY.
FOR...
... ACTING LIKE THIS.

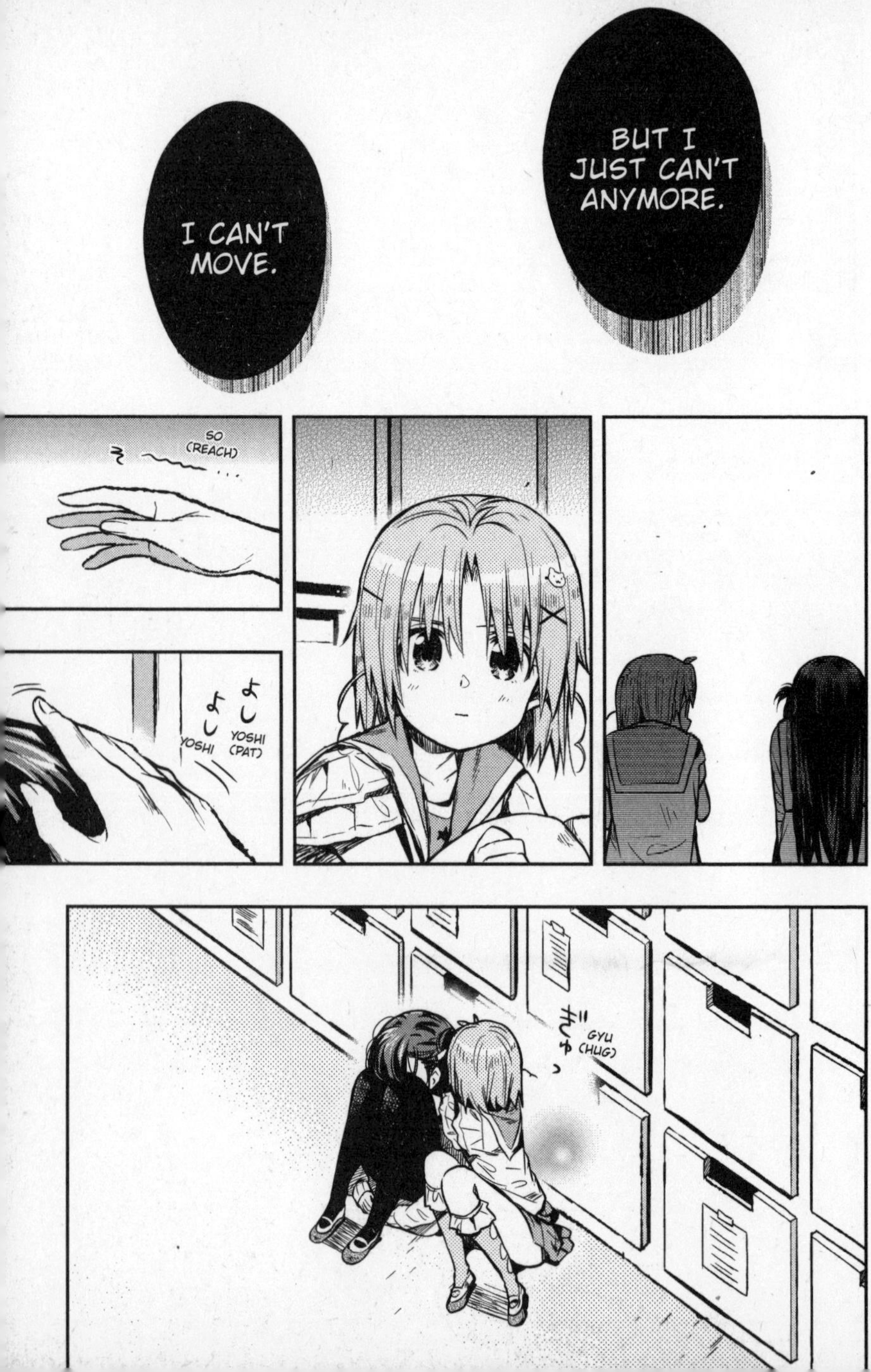
BUT I JUST CAN'T ANYMORE.
I CAN'T MOVE.
そ
SO (REACH)
よし よし
YOSHI YOSHI (PAT)
ぎゅ
GYU (HUG)

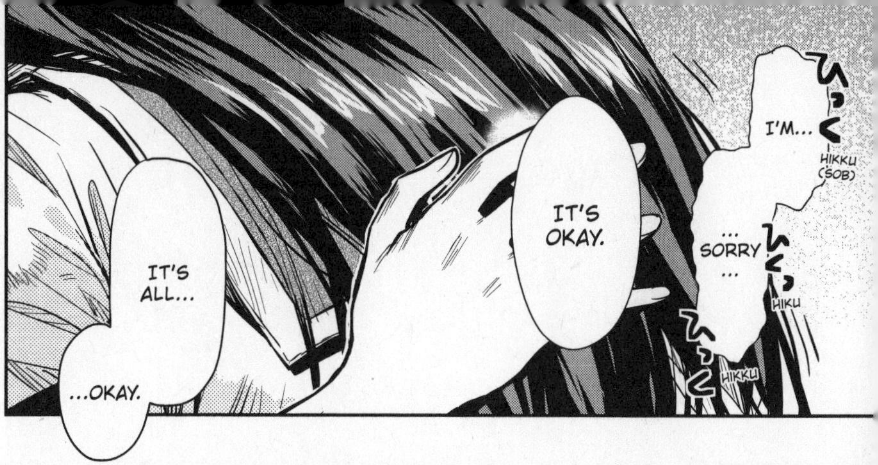

I'M...
ひっく
HIKKU (SOB)
...SORRY...
ひくっ
HIKU
ひっく
HIKKU
IT'S OKAY.
IT'S ALL...
...OKAY.

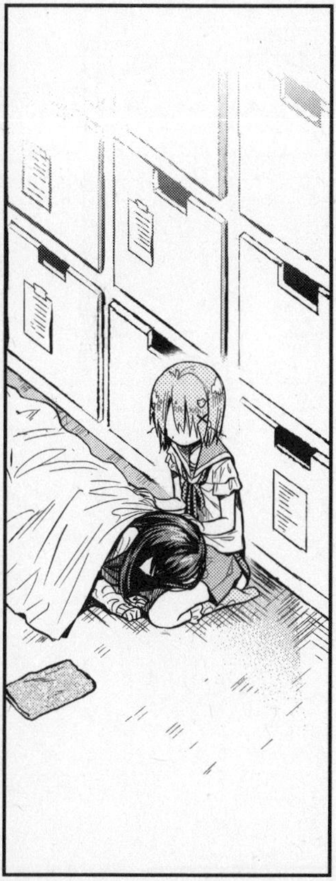
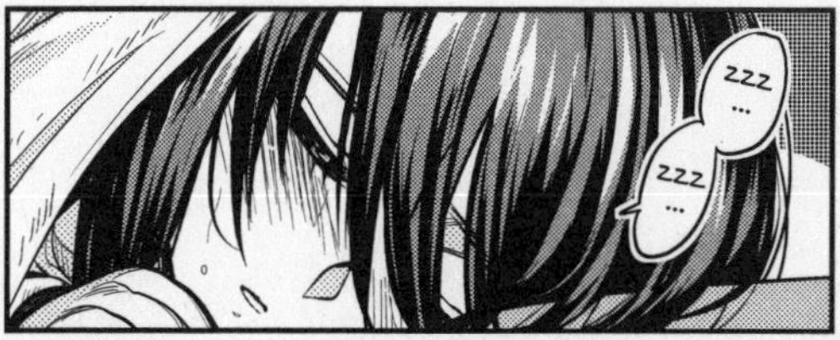

ZZZ...
ZZZ...

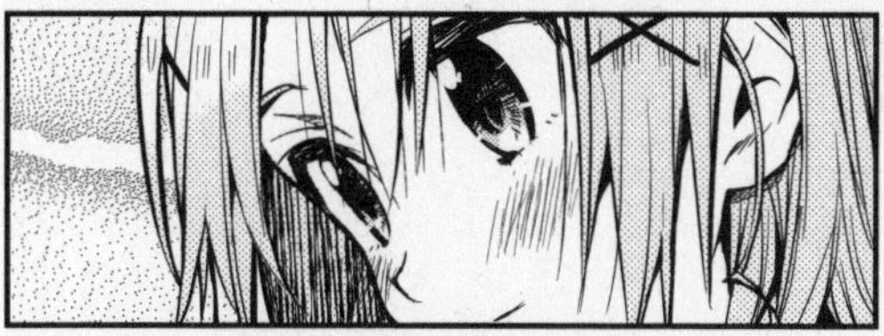
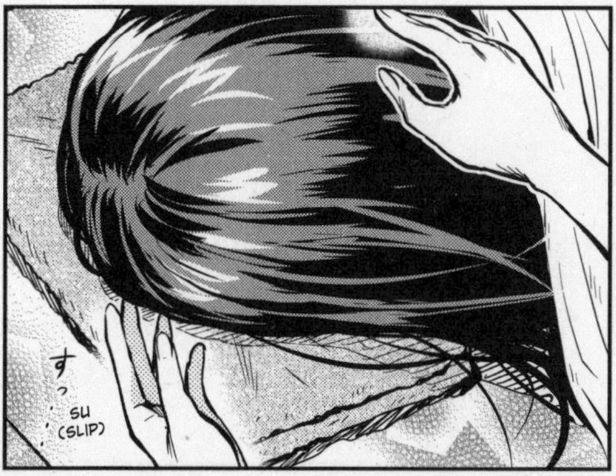

すっ
SU (SLIP)

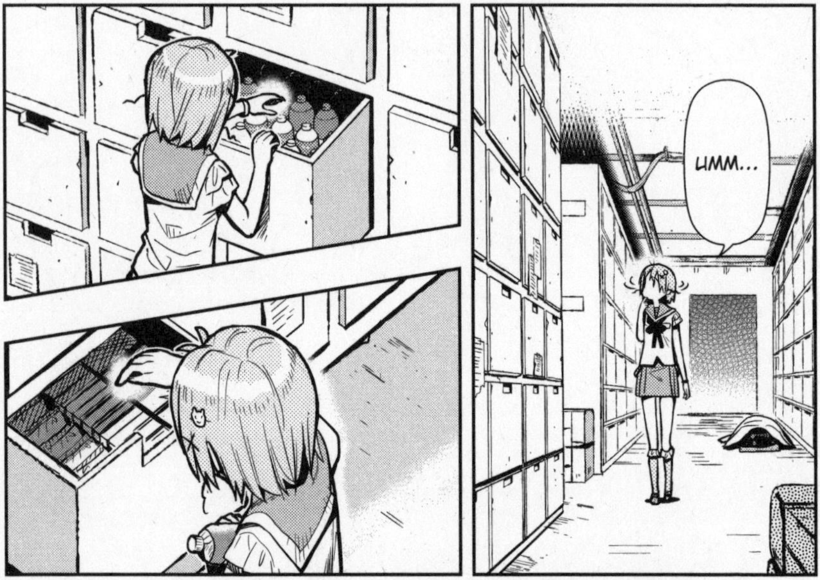
UMM...

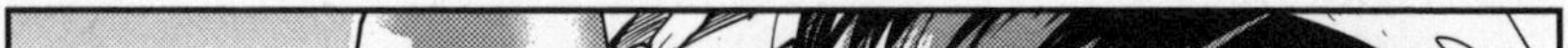
ちょっと行ってきます
ゆっくり休んでね.
ゆき
CHOCOLATE
ミルク
MILK CHOCOLATE

NOTE: I'M GOING OUT FOR A BIT. YOU JUST REST. —YUKI

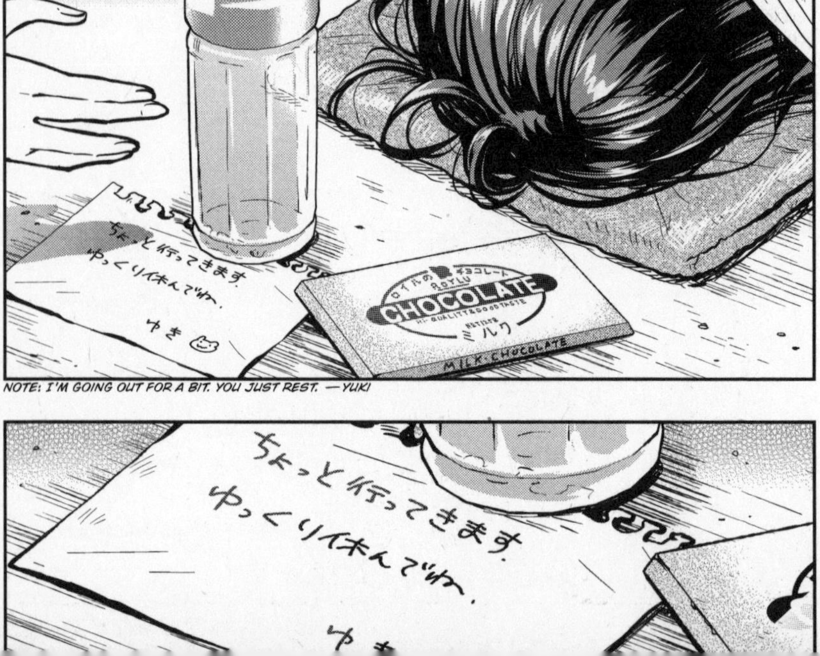
ちょっと行ってきます.
ゆっくり休んでね.

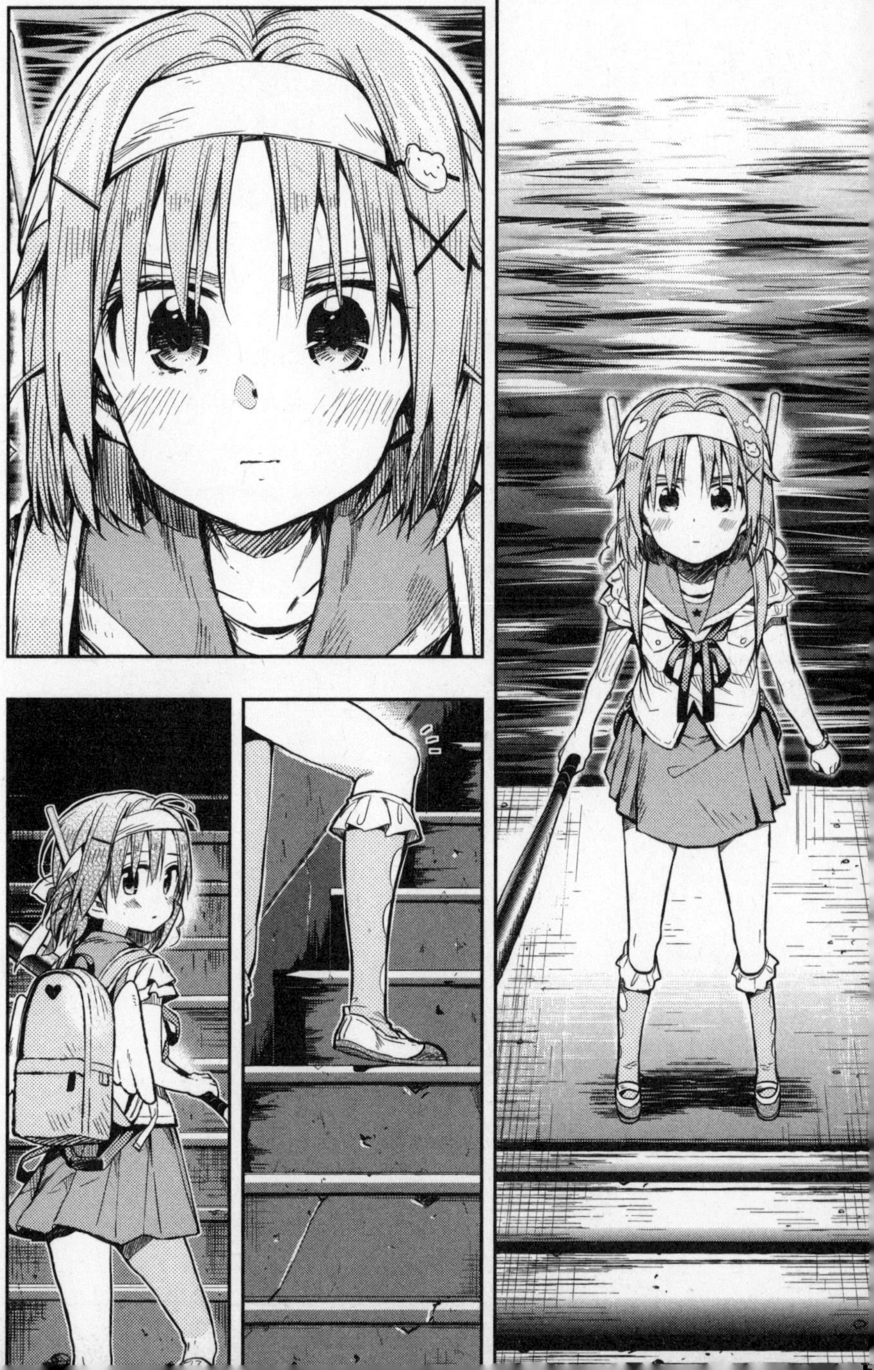

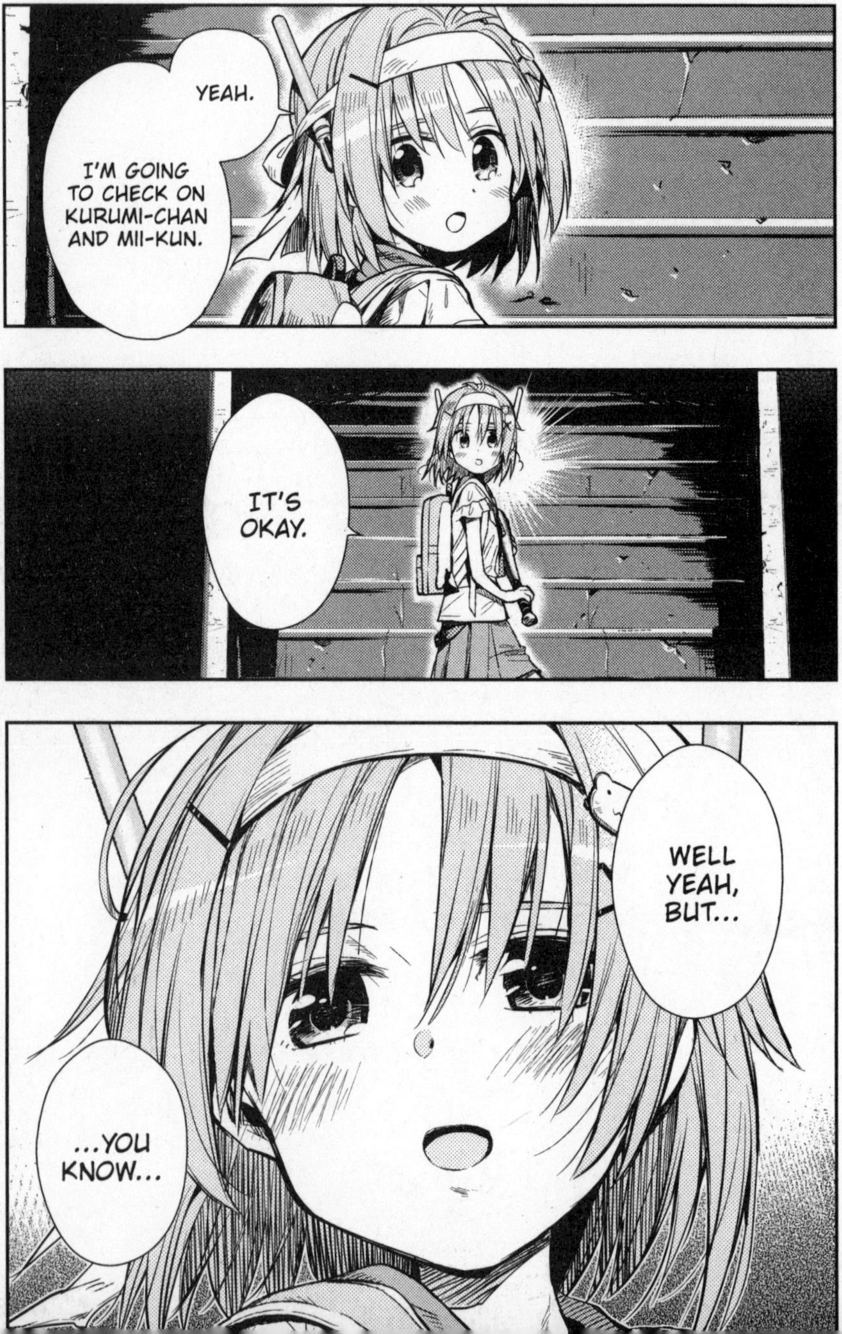
YEAH.
I'M GOING TO CHECK ON KURUMI-CHAN AND MII-KUN.
IT'S OKAY.
WELL YEAH, BUT...
...YOU KNOW...

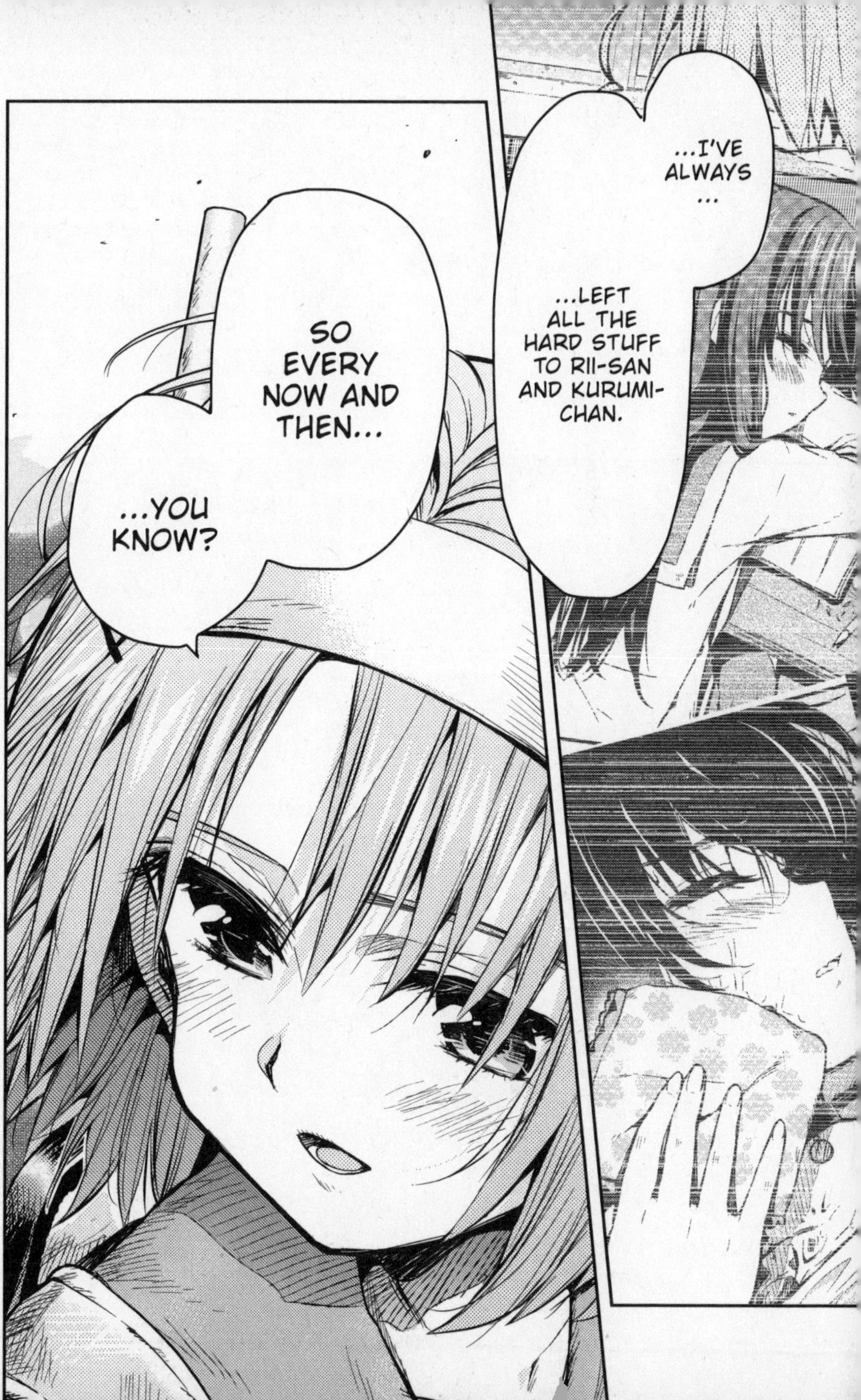
...I'VE ALWAYS ...
...LEFT ALL THE HARD STUFF TO RII-SAN AND KURUMI-CHAN.
SO EVERY NOW AND THEN...
...YOU KNOW?

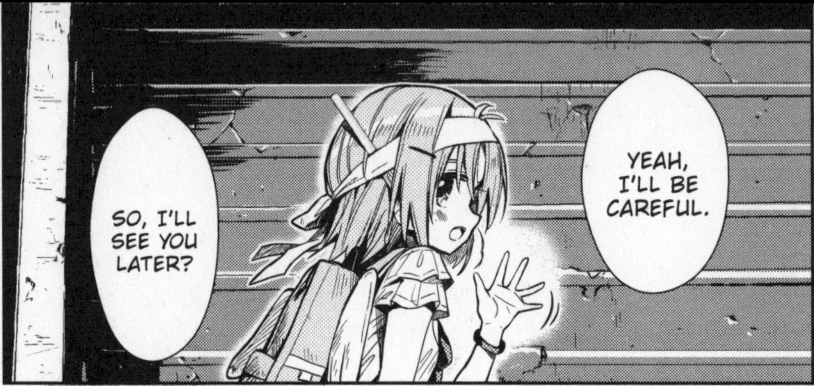
YEAH, I'LL BE CAREFUL.
SO, I'LL SEE YOU LATER?
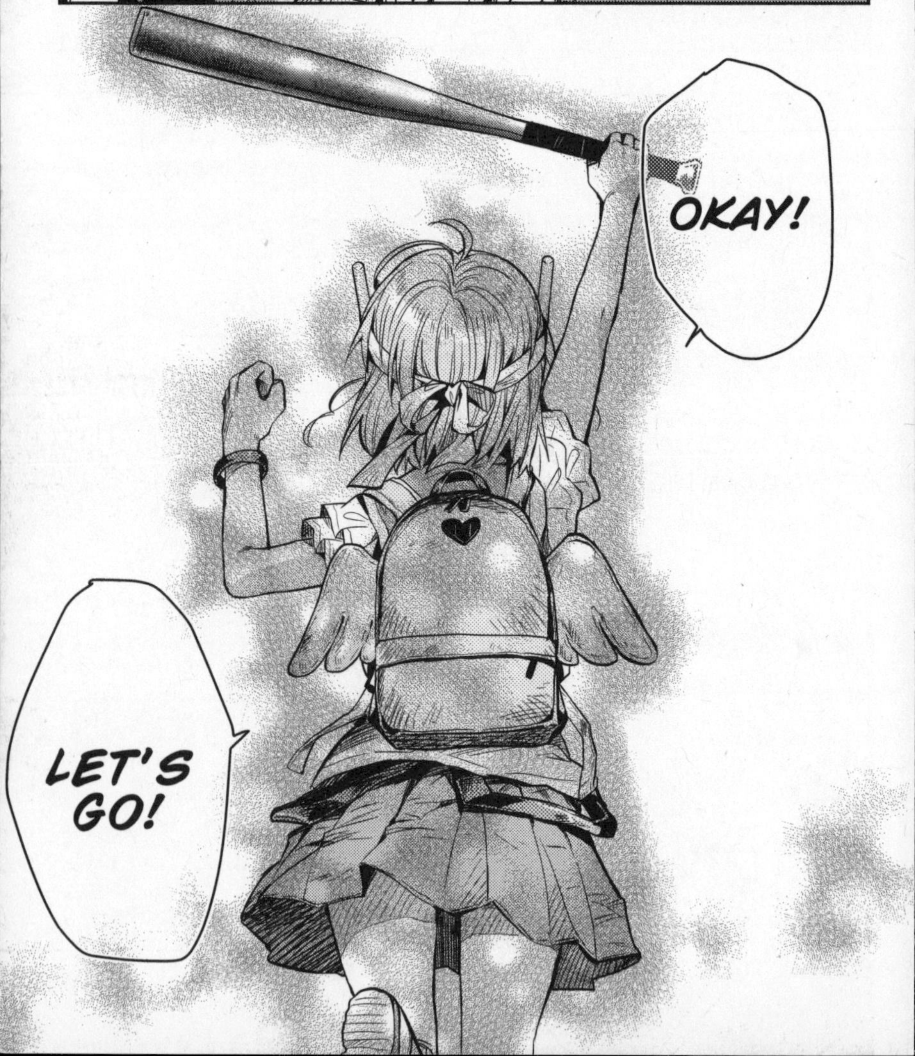
OKAY!
LET'S GO!

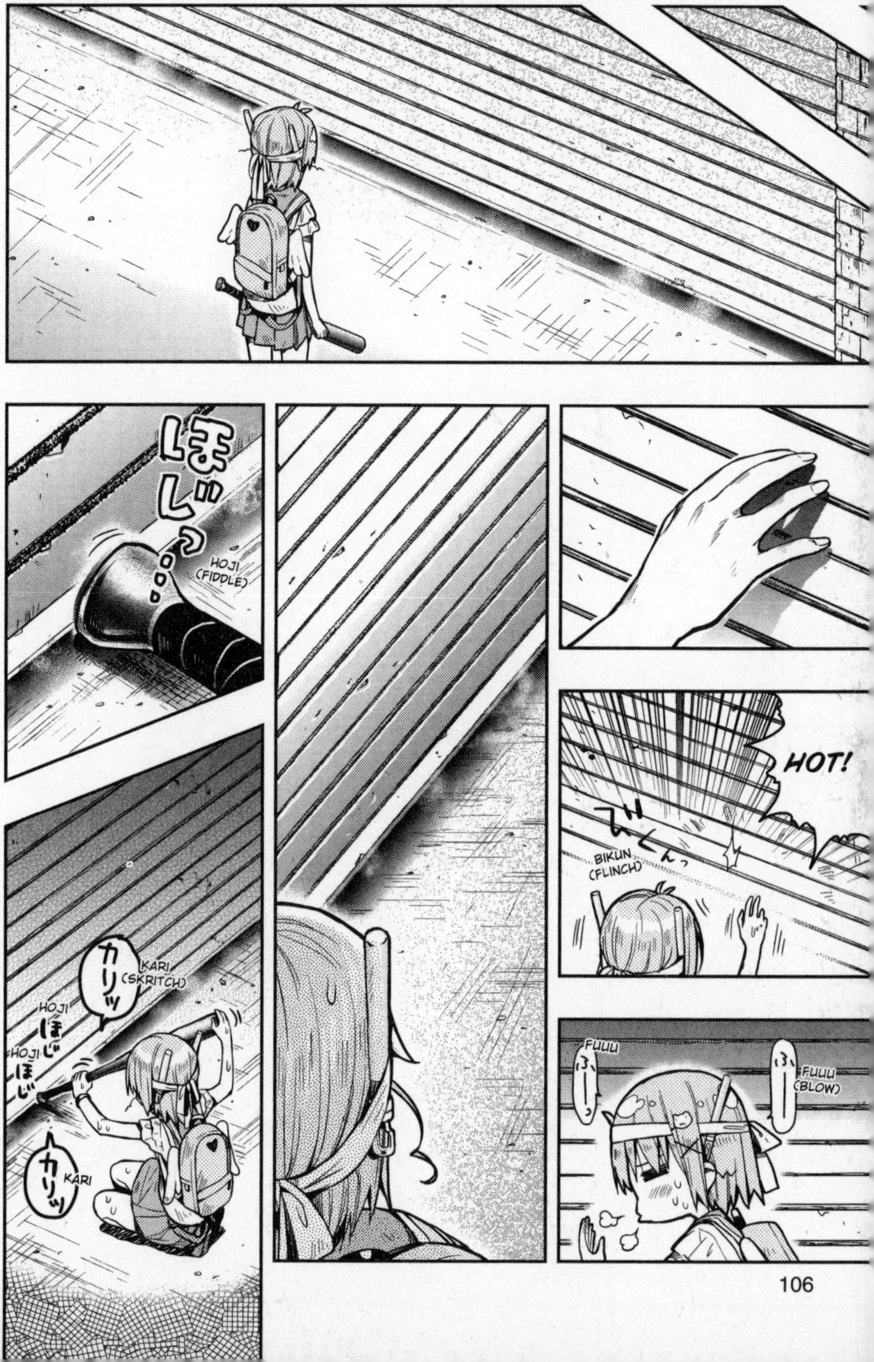
HOT!
びくんっ
BIKUN (FLINCH)
ふー…っ
FUUU (BLOW)
ふーーっ
FUUU
ほじっ…
HOJI (FIDDLE)
カリッ
KARI (SKRITCH)
ほじ
HOJI
ほじ
HOJI
カリッ
KARI

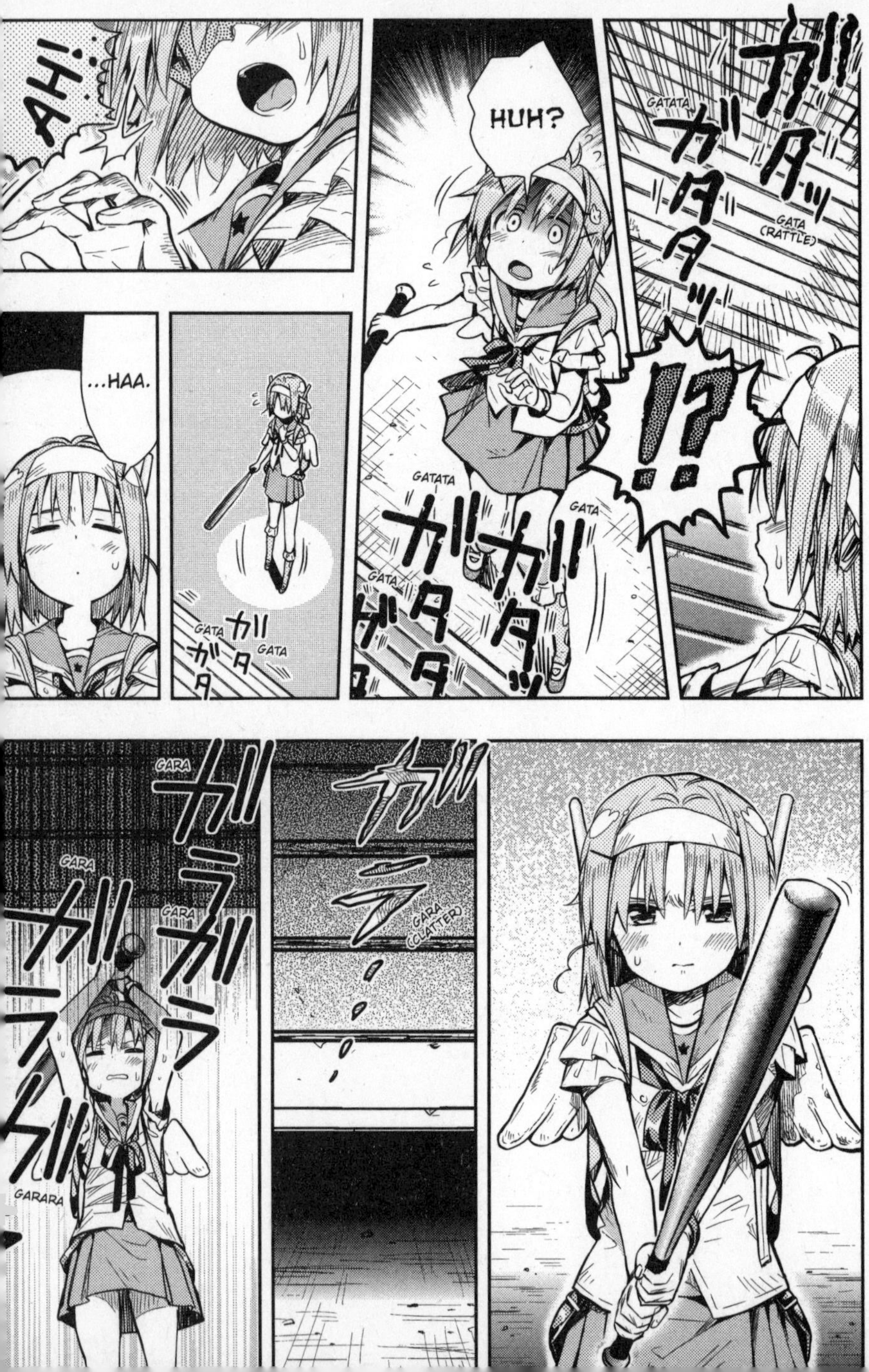
GATATA
GATA (RATTLE)
!?
HUH?
GATATA
GATA
GATA
AH!
GATA
GATA
...HAA.
GARA (CLATTER)
GARA
GARA
GARA
GARARA

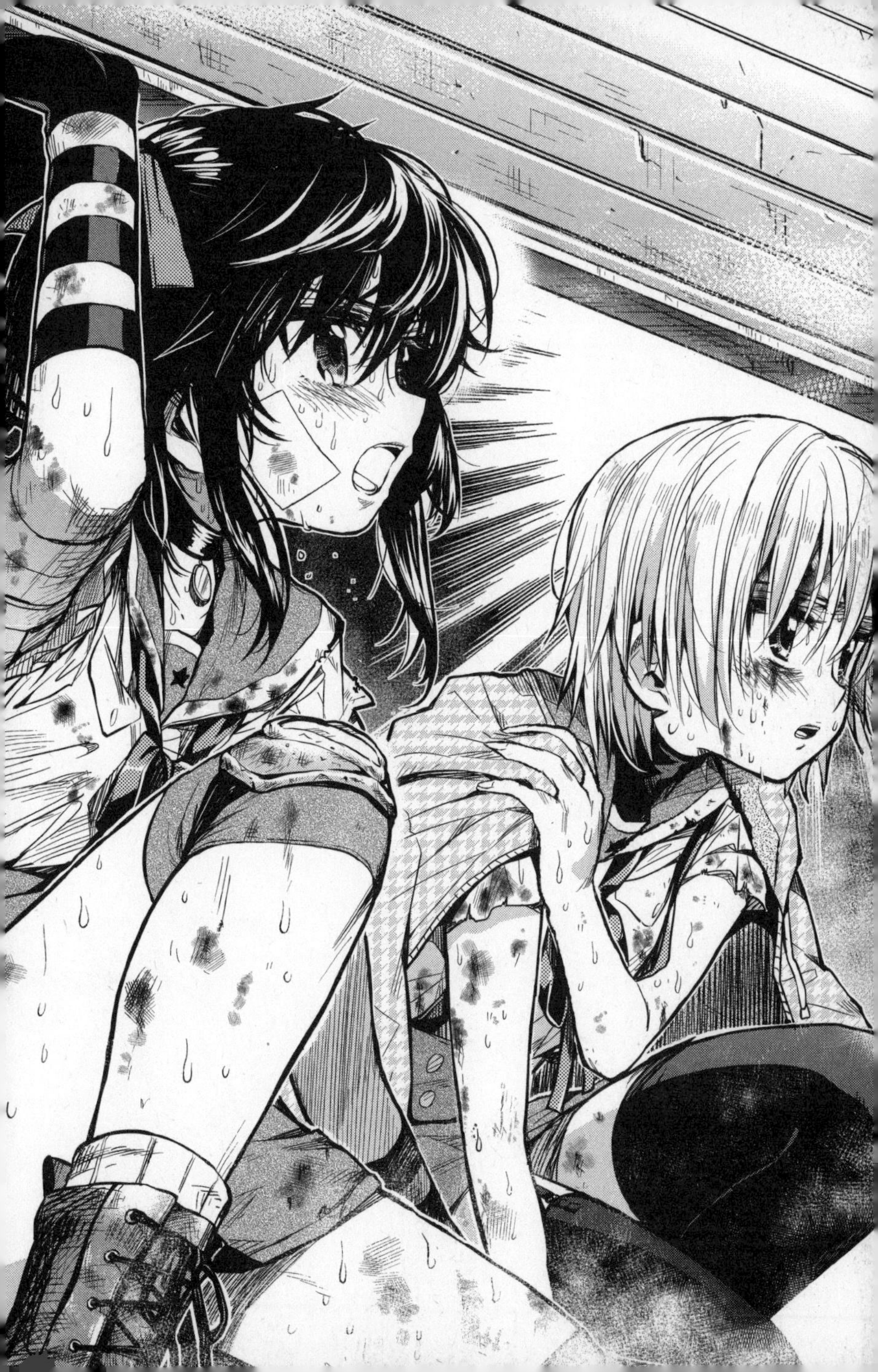

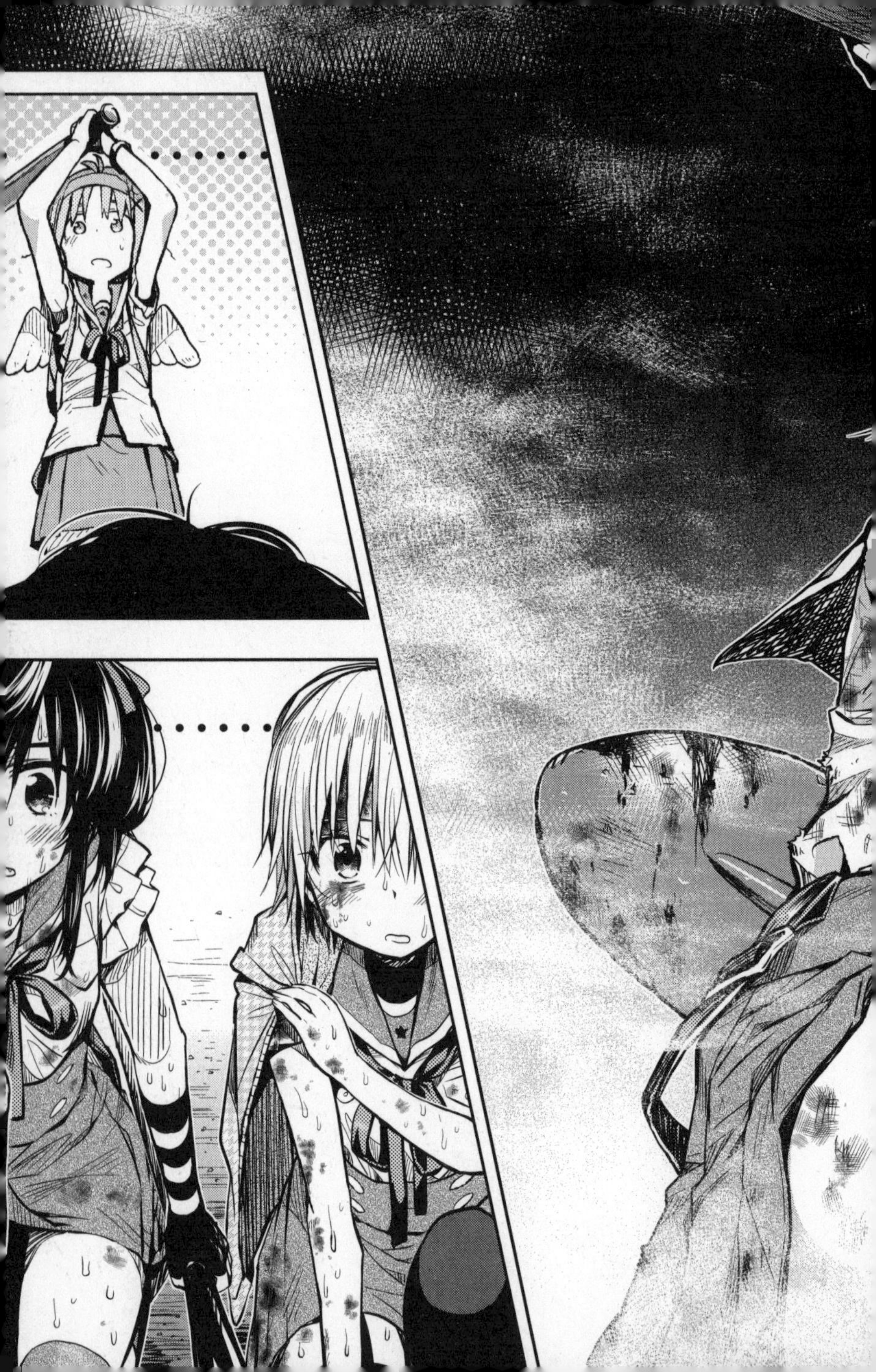
……
……

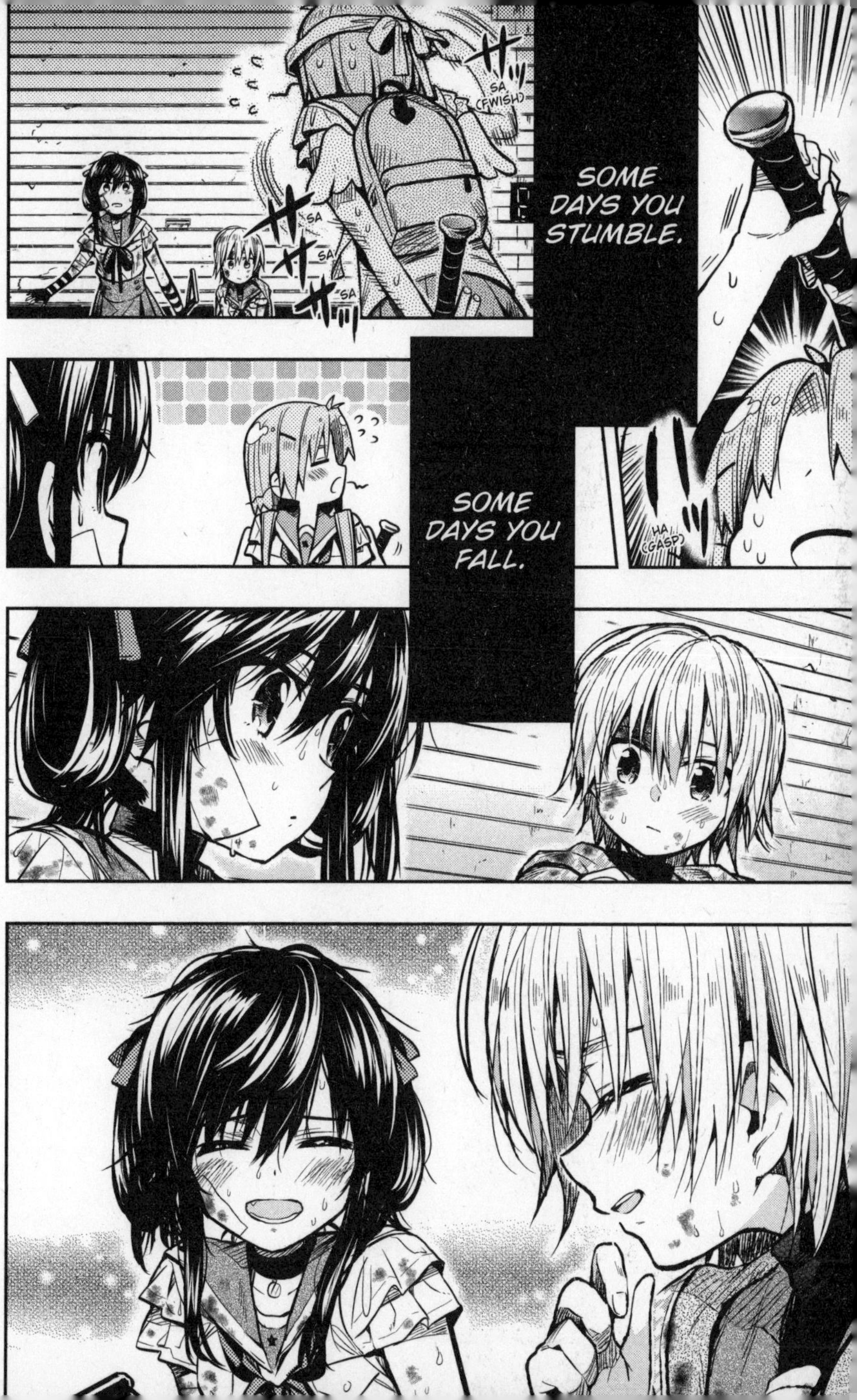
HA (GASP)
SOME DAYS YOU STUMBLE.
SA (FWISH)
SA
SA
SA
SOME DAYS YOU FALL.

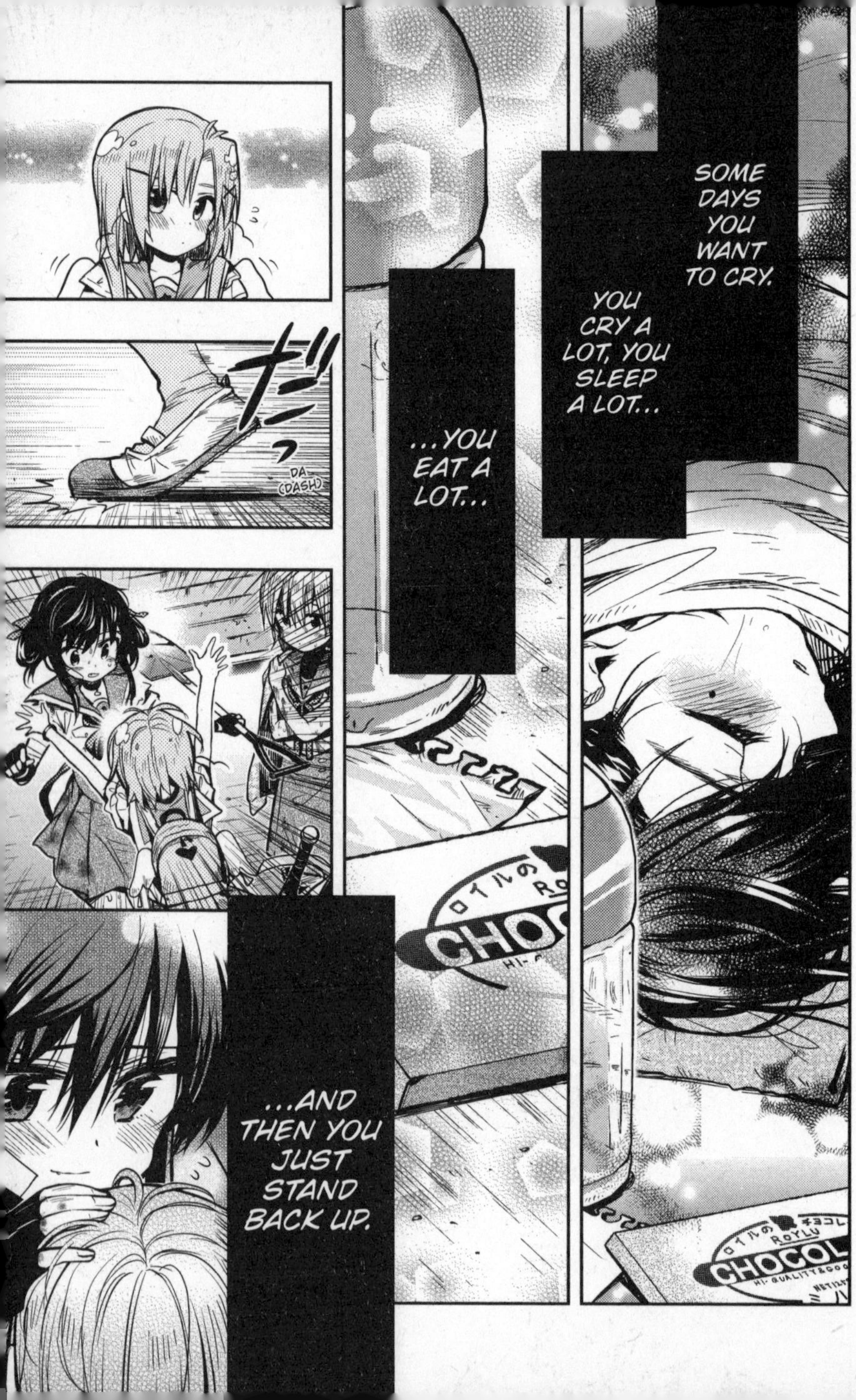
SOME DAYS YOU WANT TO CRY.
YOU CRY A LOT, YOU SLEEP A LOT...
...YOU EAT A LOT...
DA (DASH)
...AND THEN YOU JUST STAND BACK UP.

UNTIL THE DAY
YOU EVENTUALLY...

...STOP BREATHING—

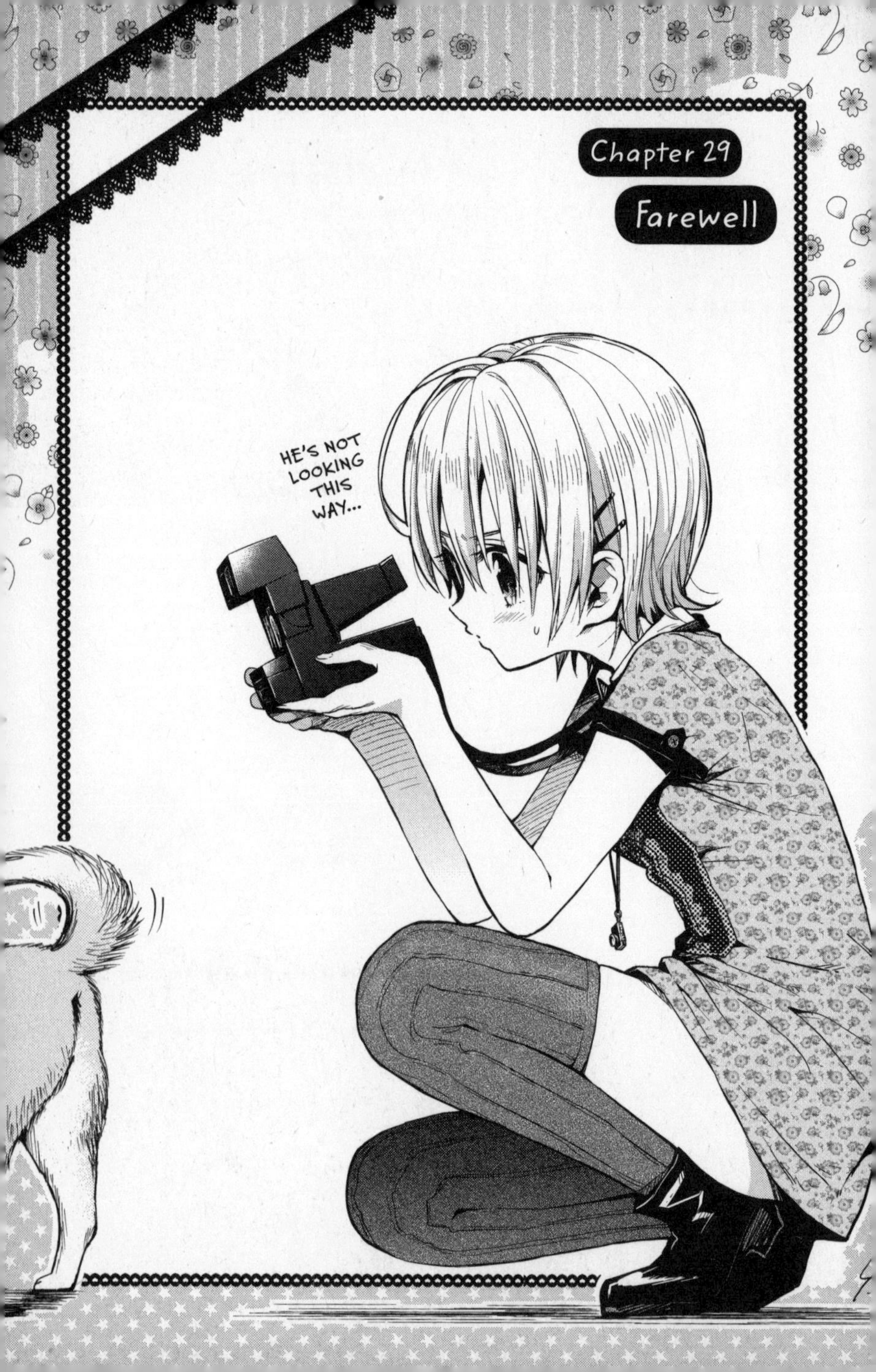

Chapter 29
Farewell
HE'S NOT LOOKING THIS WAY...

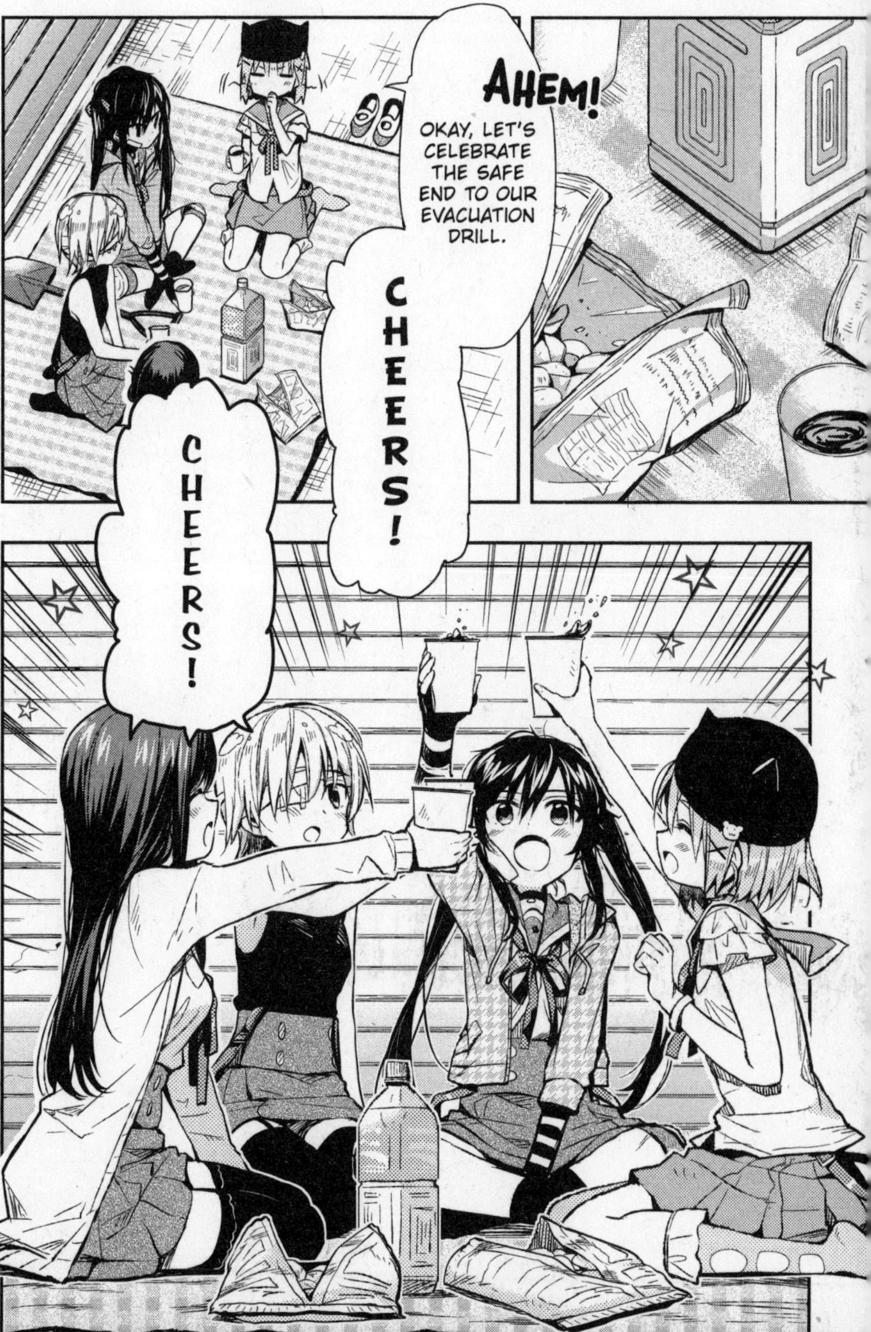
AHEM!
OKAY, LET'S CELEBRATE THE SAFE END TO OUR EVACUATION DRILL.
CHEERS!
CHEERS!

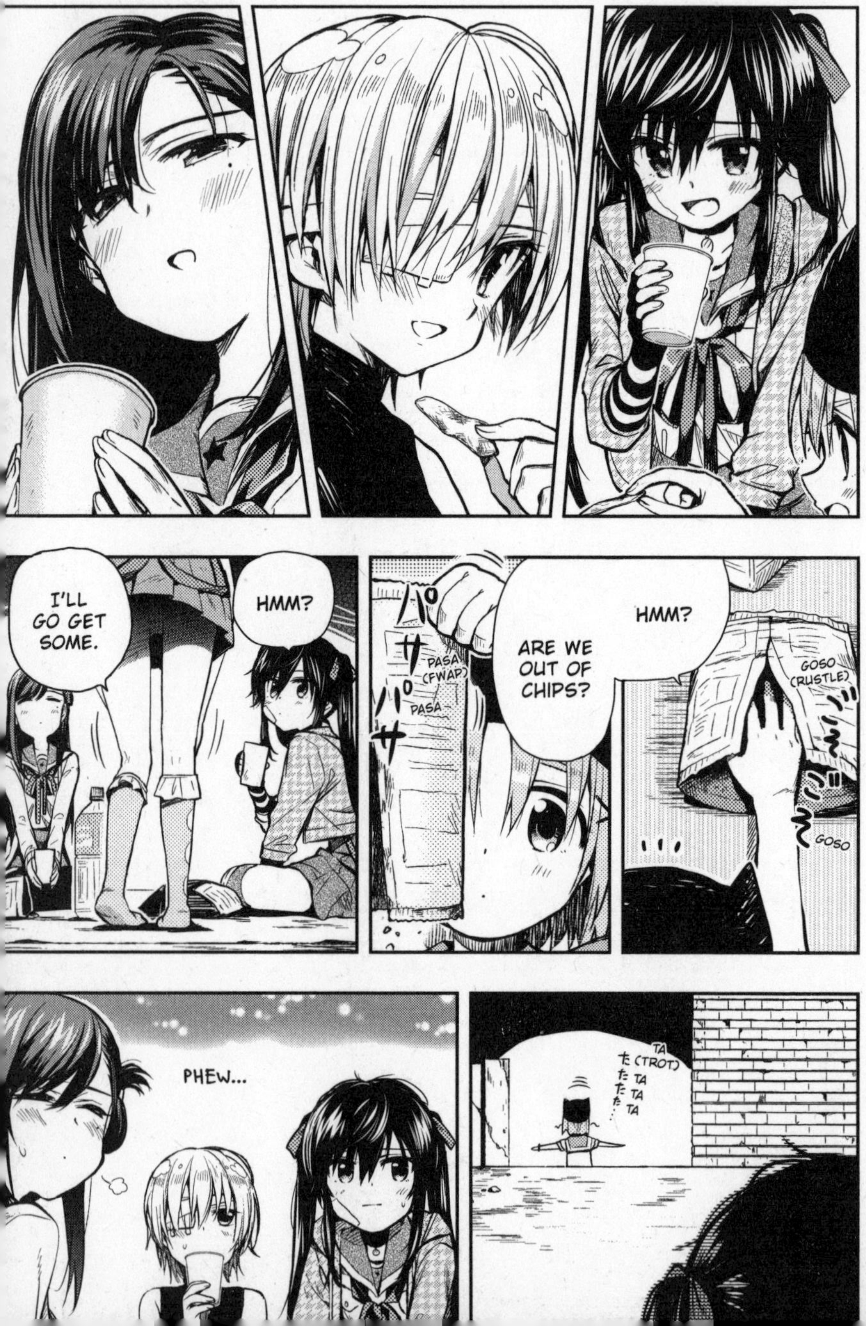

ゴソ
GOSO
(RUSTLE)
ゴソ
GOSO
HMM?
ARE WE OUT OF CHIPS?
パサ
PASA
(FWAP)
パサ
PASA
HMM?
I'LL GO GET SOME.
たたたた...
TA
(TROT)
TA
TA
TA
PHEW...

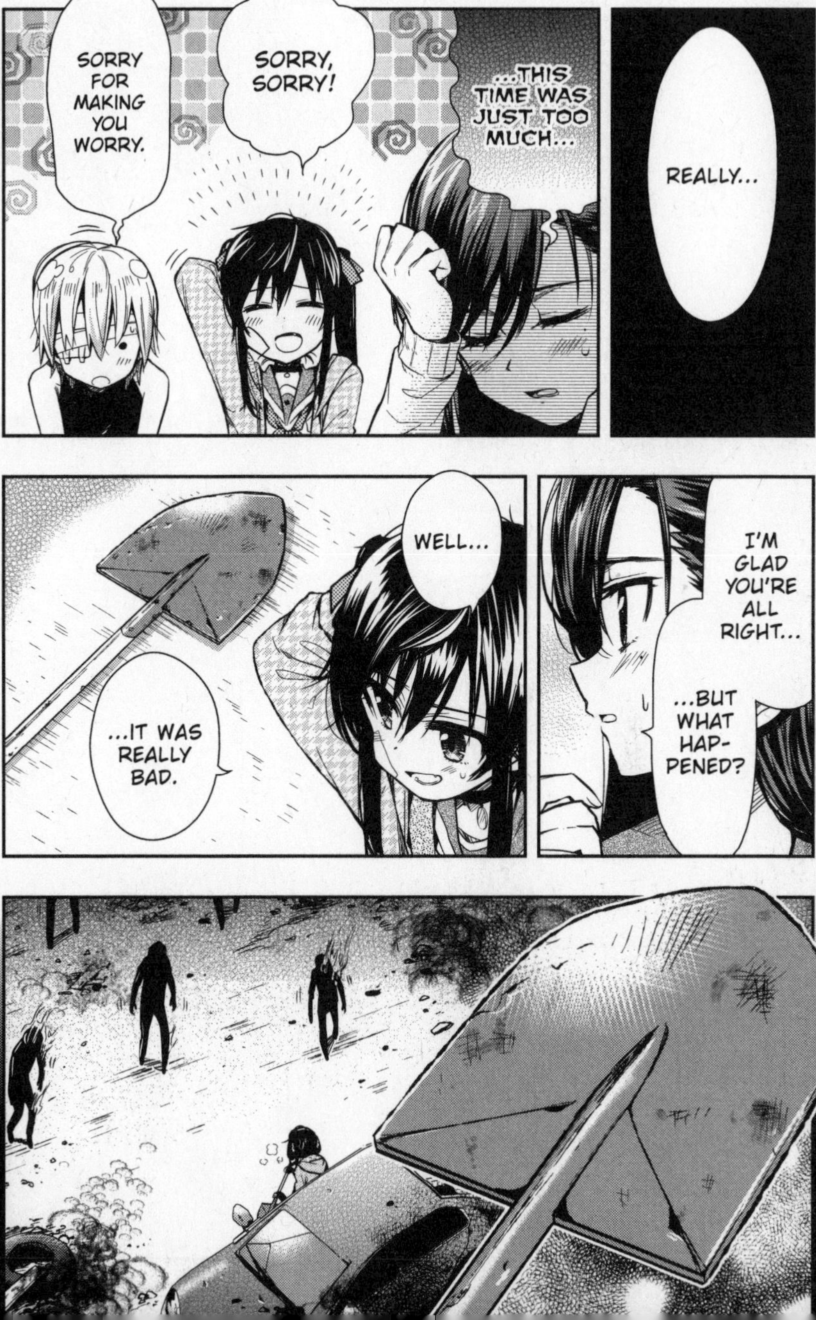
REALLY...
...THIS TIME WAS JUST TOO MUCH...
SORRY, SORRY!
SORRY FOR MAKING YOU WORRY.
I'M GLAD YOU'RE ALL RIGHT...
...BUT WHAT HAP-PENED?
WELL...
...IT WAS REALLY BAD.

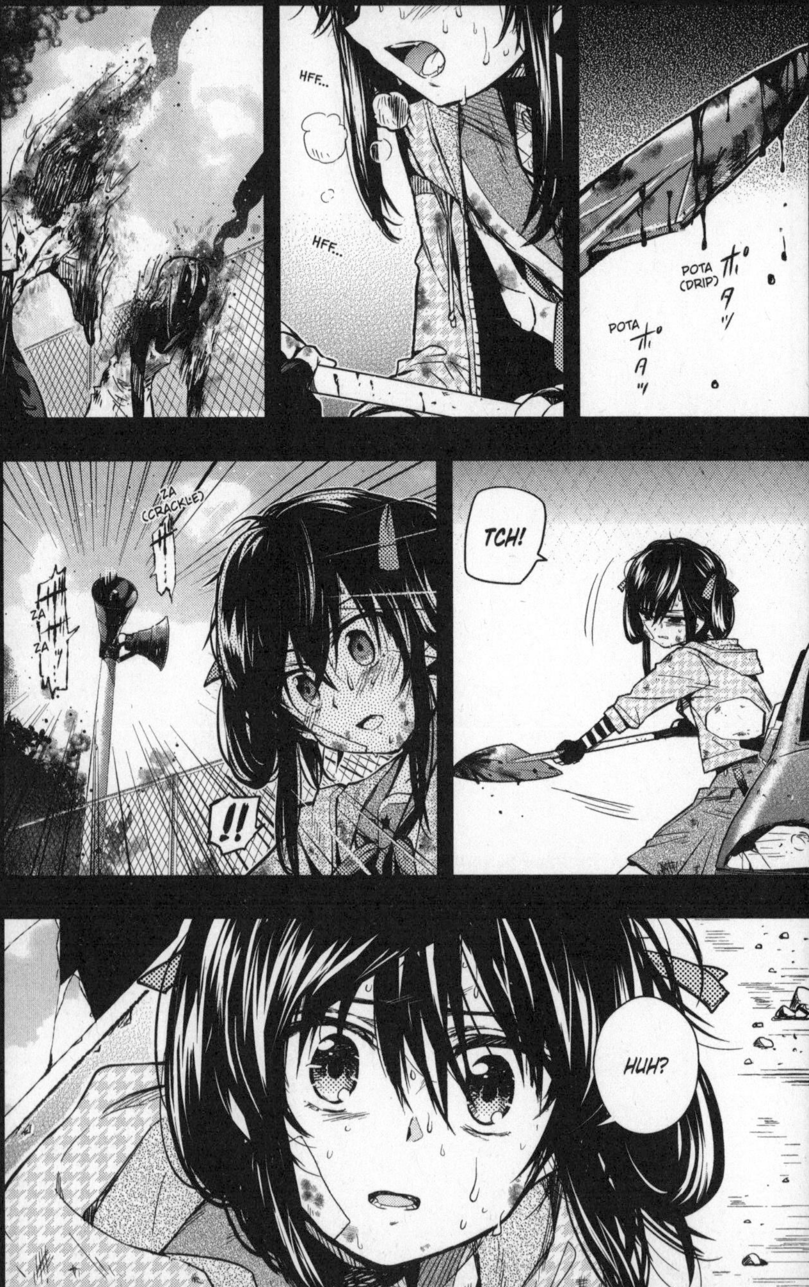
POTA (DRIP)
ポタッ
POTA
ポタッ
HFF...
HFF...
TCH!
ZA (CRACKLE)
ZA
ZA
!!
HUH?

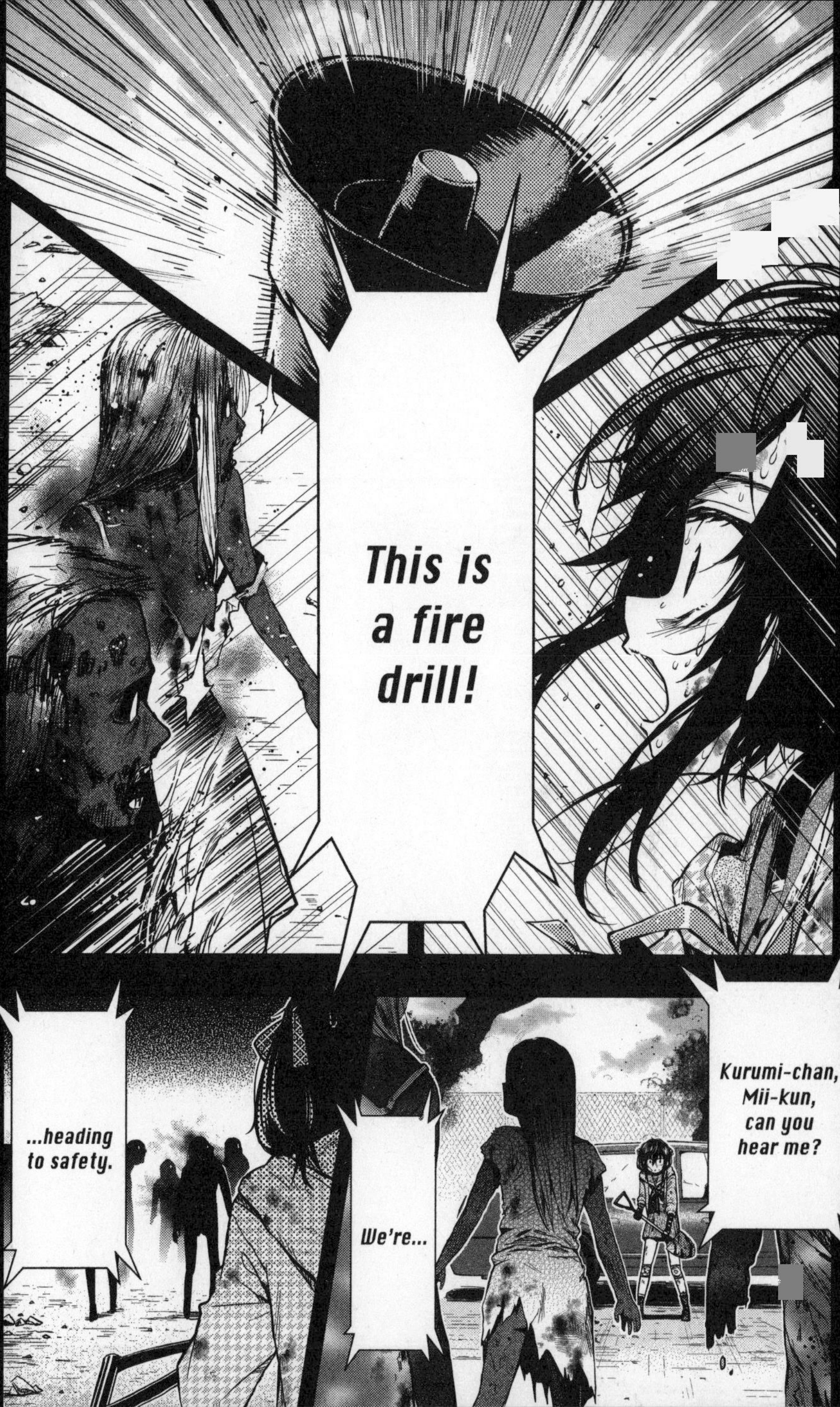
This is a fire drill!
Kurumi-chan, Mii-kun, can you hear me?
We're...
...heading to safety.

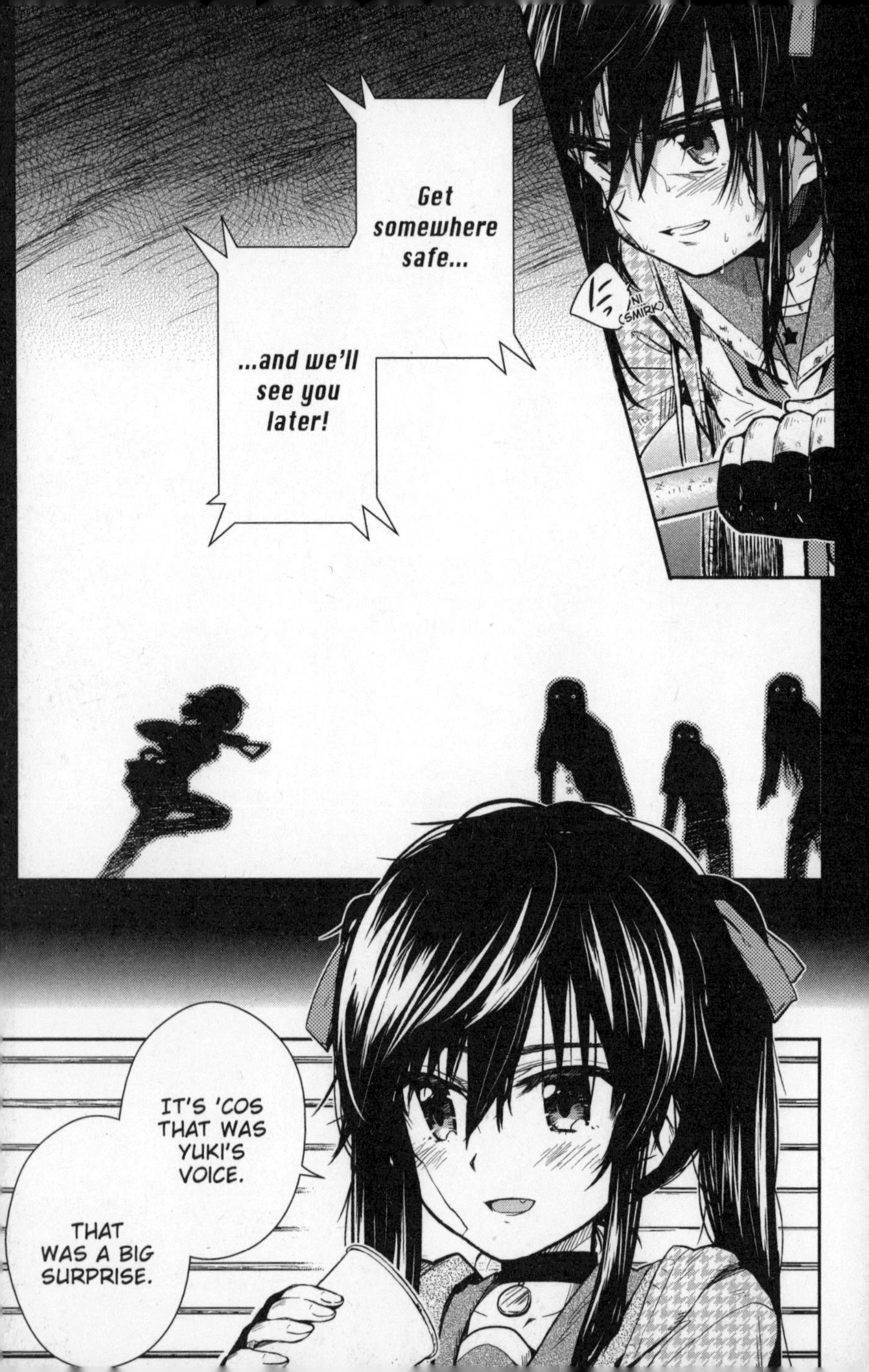
NI (SMIRK)
Get somewhere safe...
...and we'll see you later!
IT'S 'COS THAT WAS YUKI'S VOICE.
THAT WAS A BIG SURPRISE.

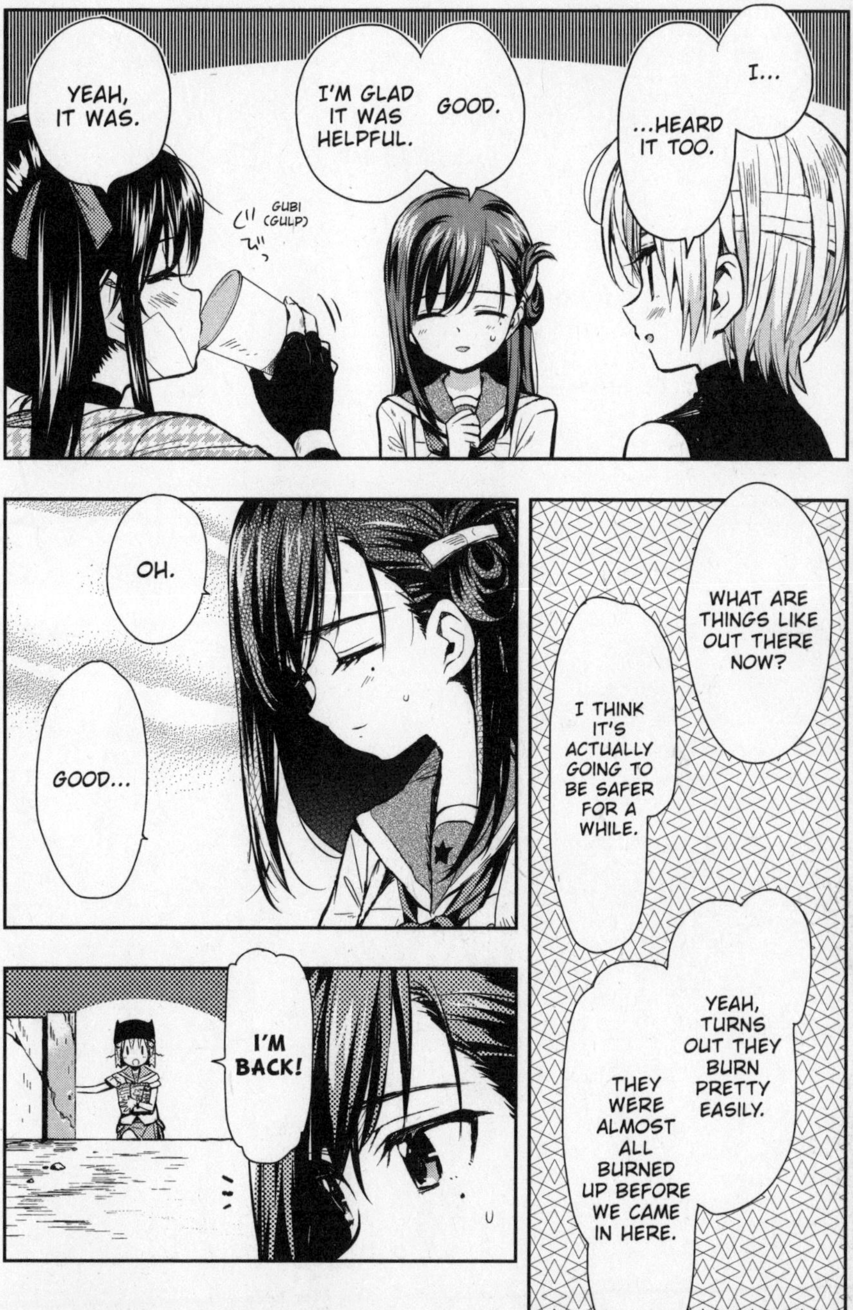
I...
...HEARD IT TOO.
GOOD.
I'M GLAD IT WAS HELPFUL.
GUBI (GULP)
YEAH, IT WAS.
WHAT ARE THINGS LIKE OUT THERE NOW?
I THINK IT'S ACTUALLY GOING TO BE SAFER FOR A WHILE.
YEAH, TURNS OUT THEY BURN PRETTY EASILY.
THEY WERE ALMOST ALL BURNED UP BEFORE WE CAME IN HERE.
OH.
GOOD...
I'M BACK!

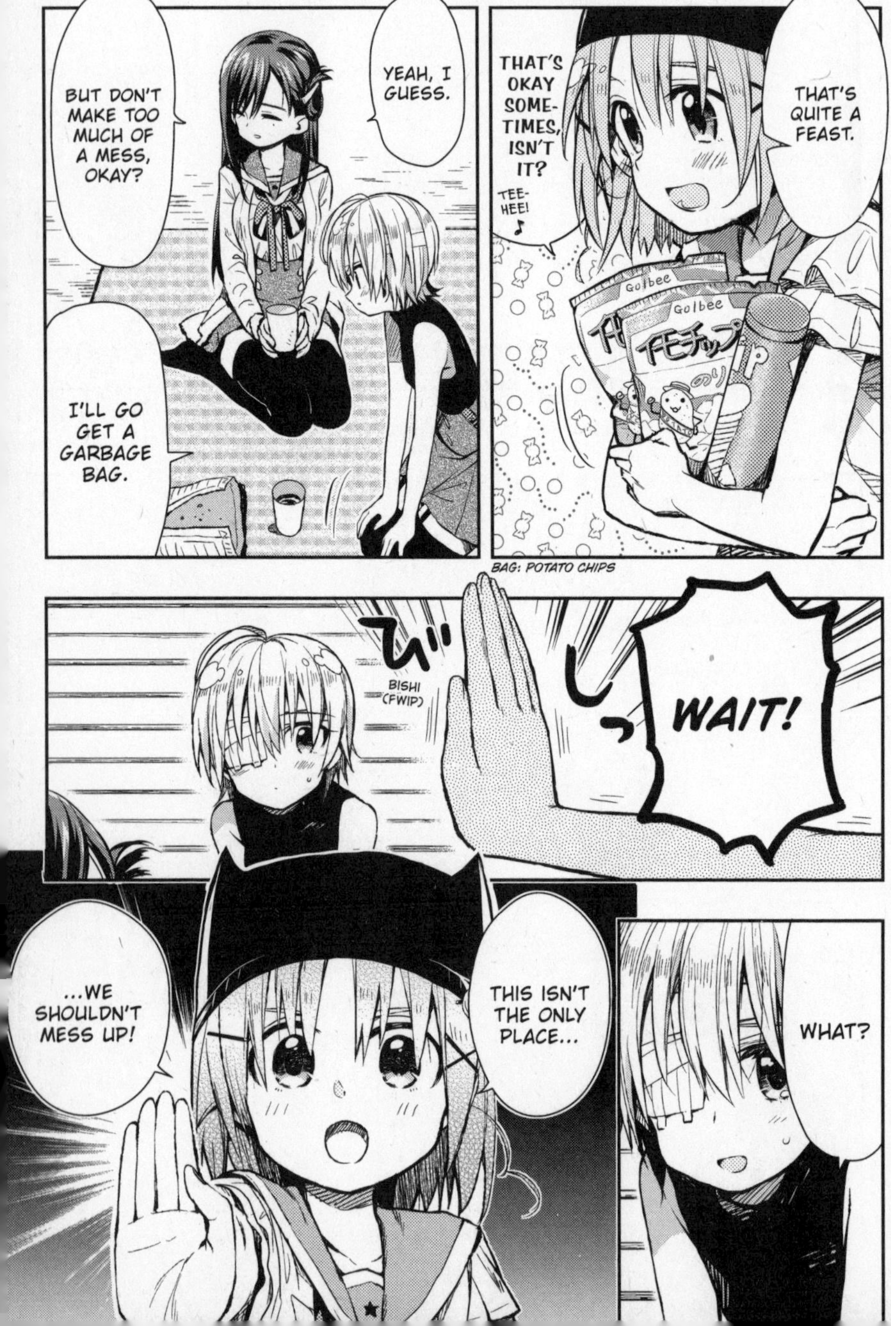
THAT'S QUITE A FEAST.
THAT'S OKAY SOMETIMES, ISN'T IT?
TEE-HEE! ♪
BAG: POTATO CHIPS
YEAH, I GUESS.
BUT DON'T MAKE TOO MUCH OF A MESS, OKAY?
I'LL GO GET A GARBAGE BAG.
WAIT!
BISHI (FWIP)
WHAT?
THIS ISN'T THE ONLY PLACE...
...WE SHOULDN'T MESS UP!

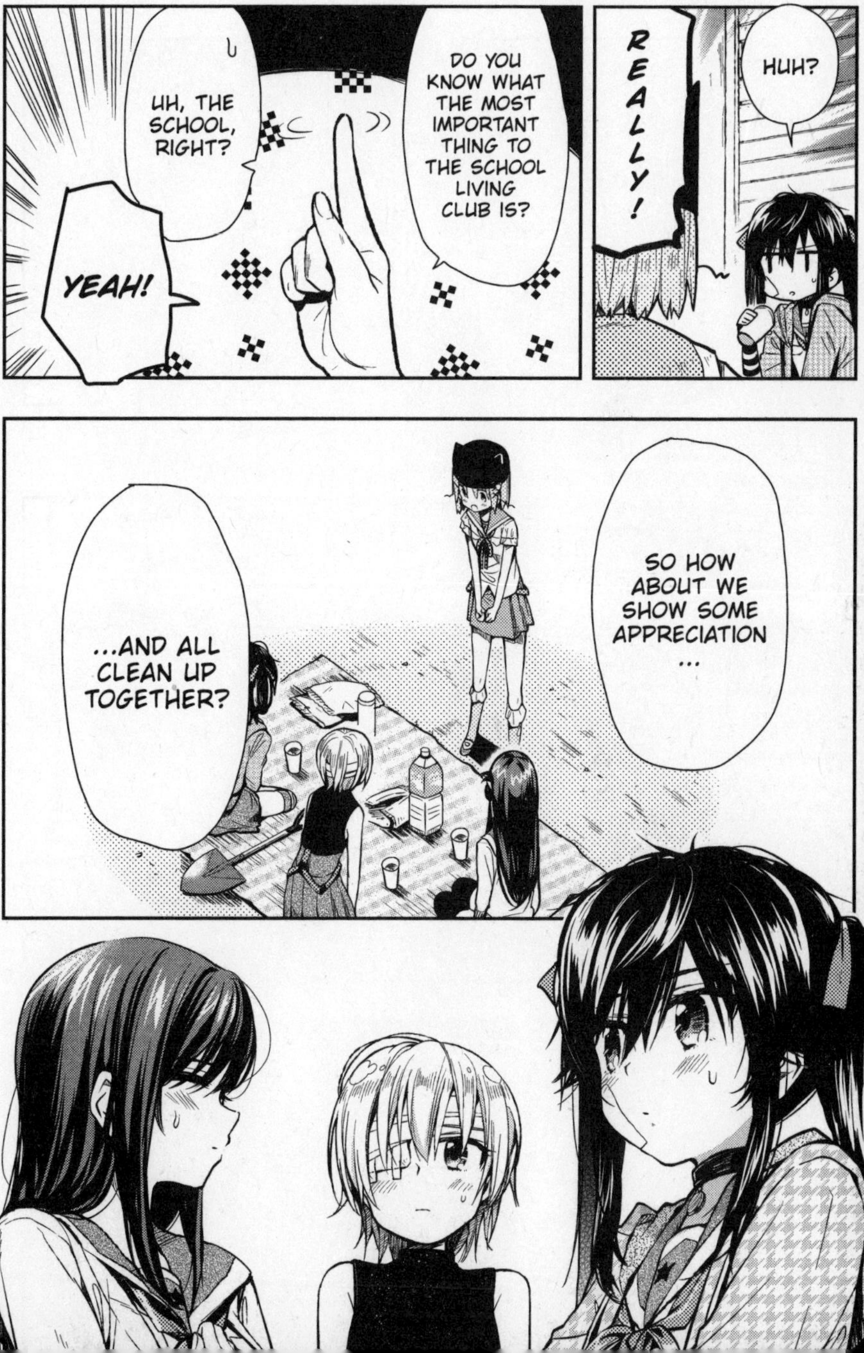
HUH?
REALLY!
DO YOU KNOW WHAT THE MOST IMPORTANT THING TO THE SCHOOL LIVING CLUB IS?
UH, THE SCHOOL, RIGHT?
YEAH!
SO HOW ABOUT WE SHOW SOME APPRECIATION...
...AND ALL CLEAN UP TOGETHER?

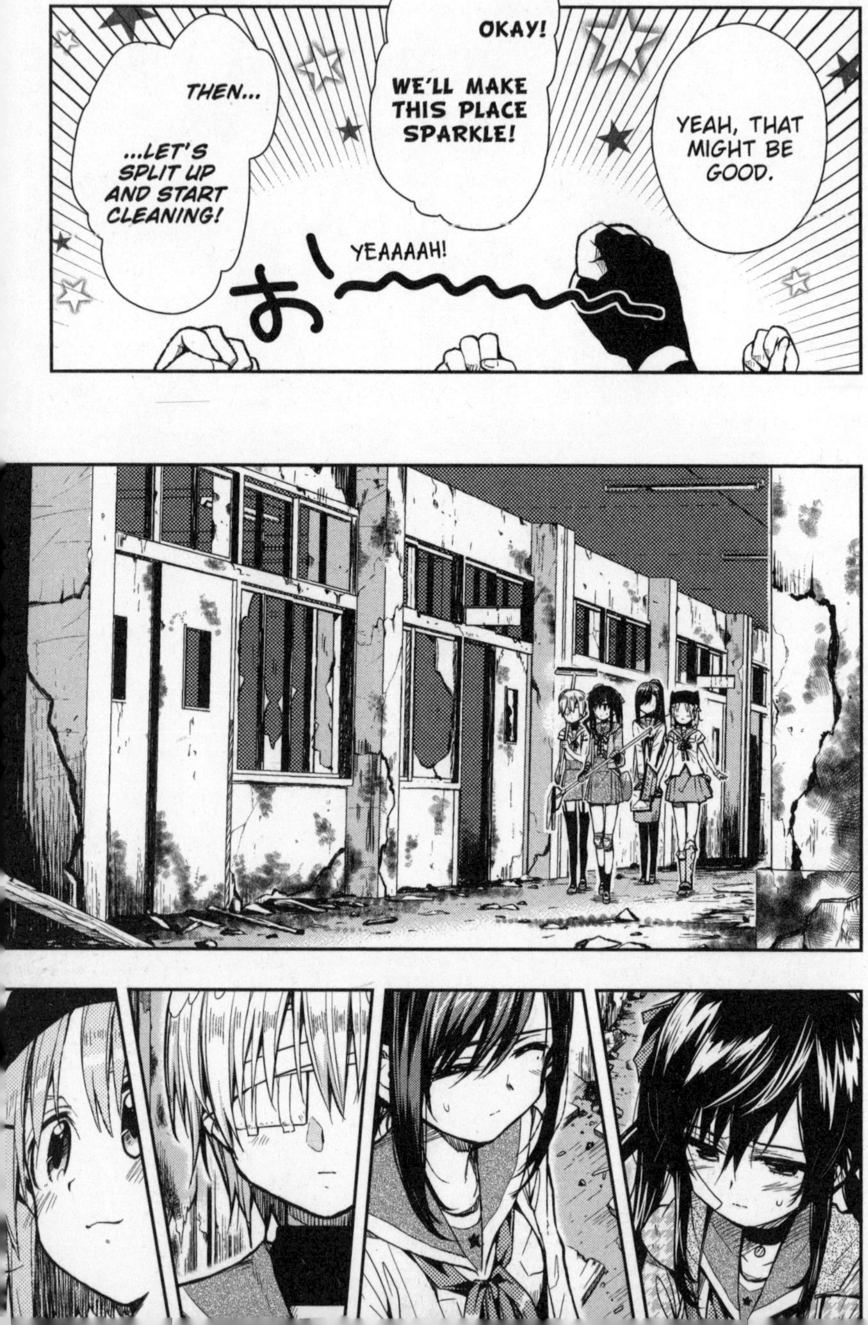
YEAH, THAT MIGHT BE GOOD.
OKAY!
WE'LL MAKE THIS PLACE SPARKLE!
THEN...
...LET'S SPLIT UP AND START CLEANING!
YEAAAAH!
お〜

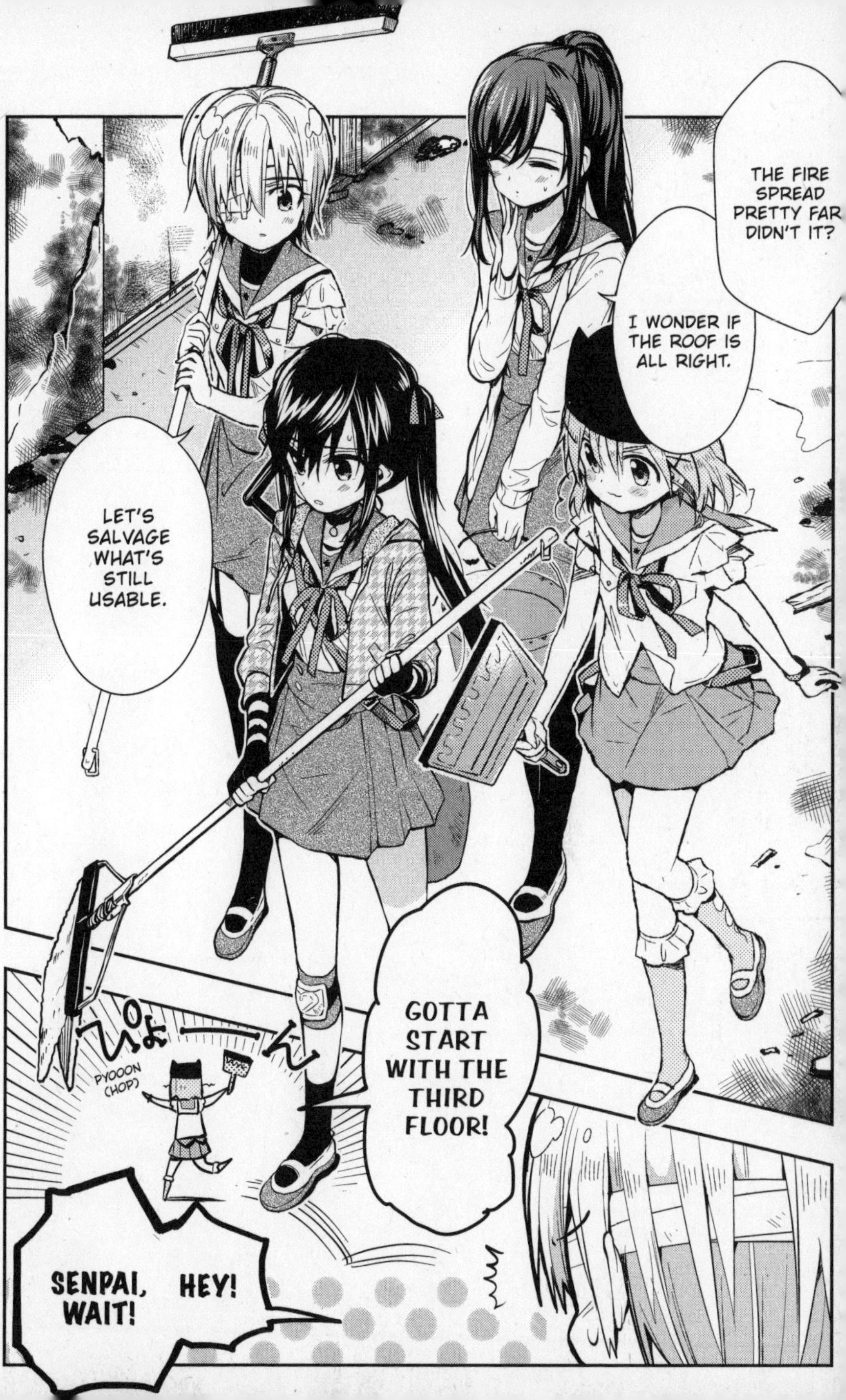
THE FIRE SPREAD PRETTY FAR DIDN'T IT?
I WONDER IF THE ROOF IS ALL RIGHT.
LET'S SALVAGE WHAT'S STILL USABLE.
GOTTA START WITH THE THIRD FLOOR!
ぴょーーん
PYOOON (HOP)
HEY!
SENPAI, WAIT!

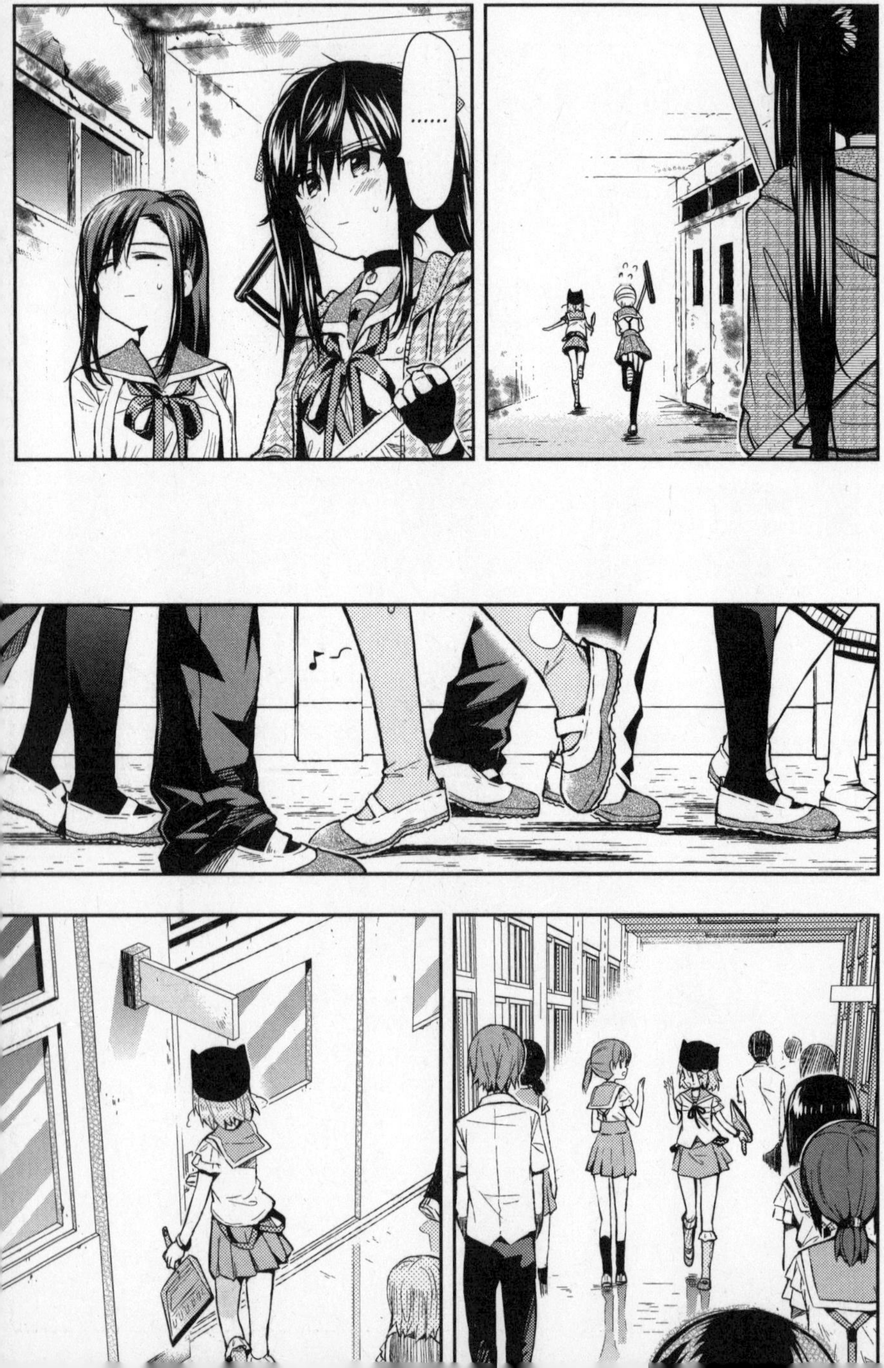
......

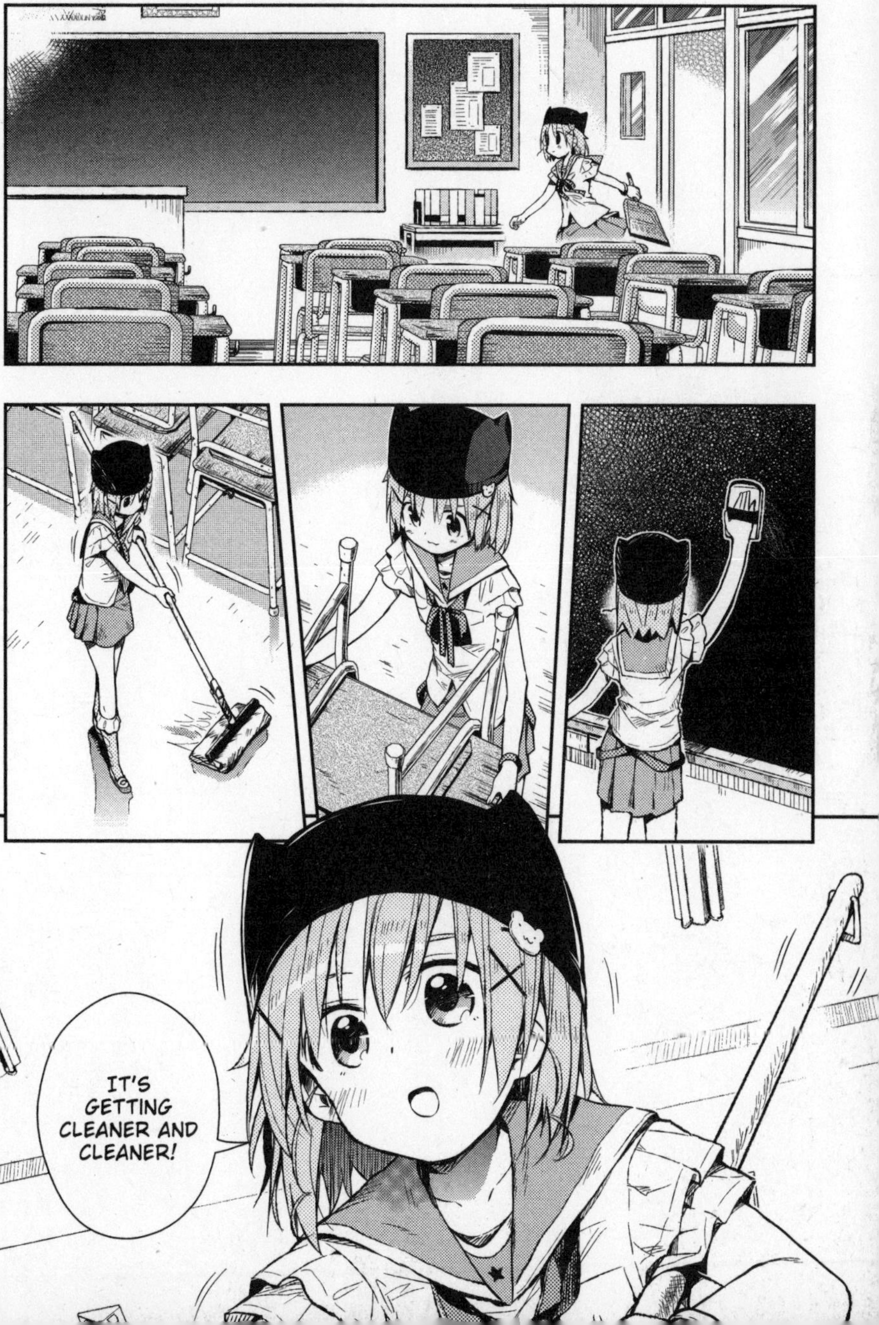
IT'S GETTING CLEANER AND CLEANER!

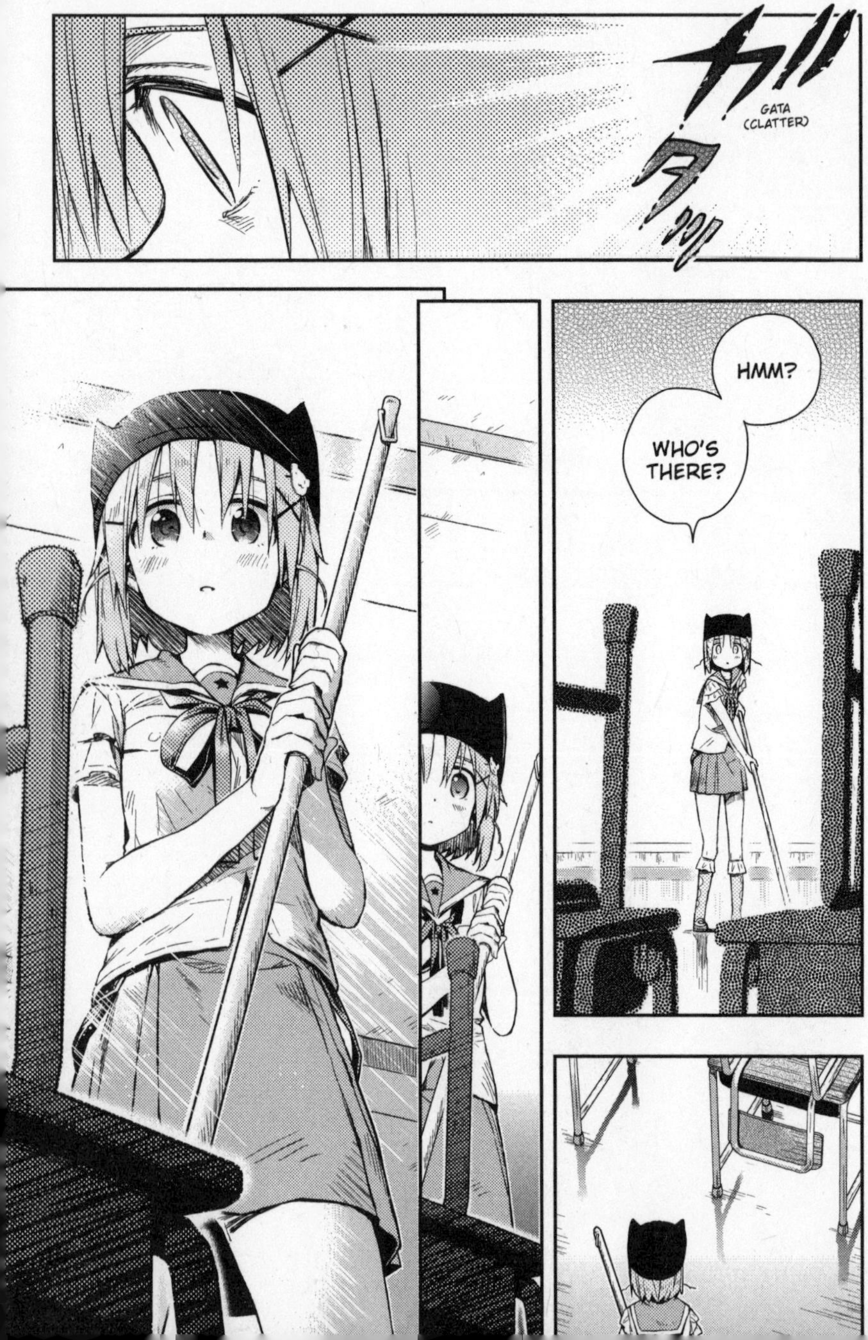
ガタッ
GATA (CLATTER)
HMM?
WHO'S THERE?

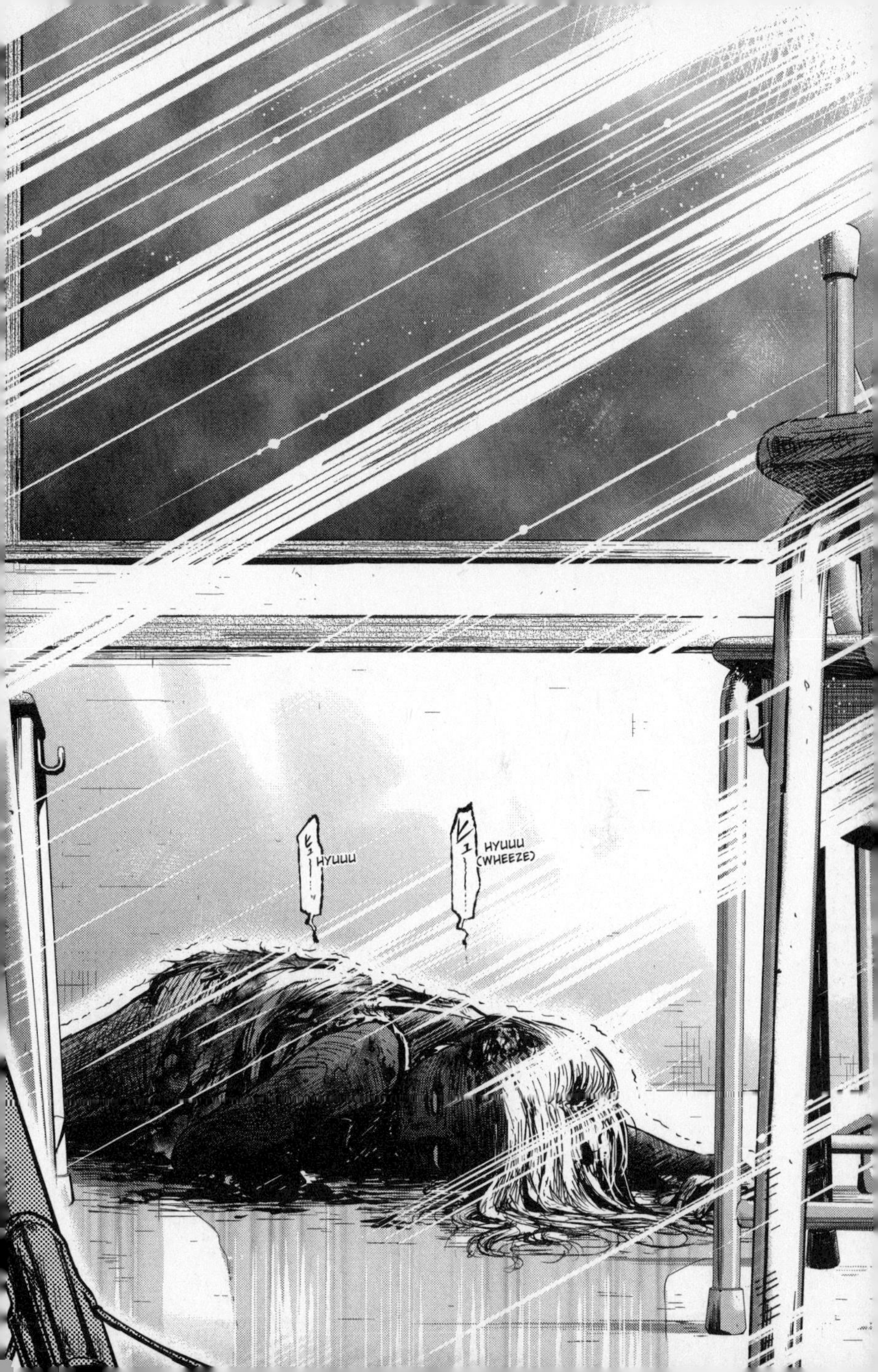
HYUUU
(WHEEZE)
HYUUU

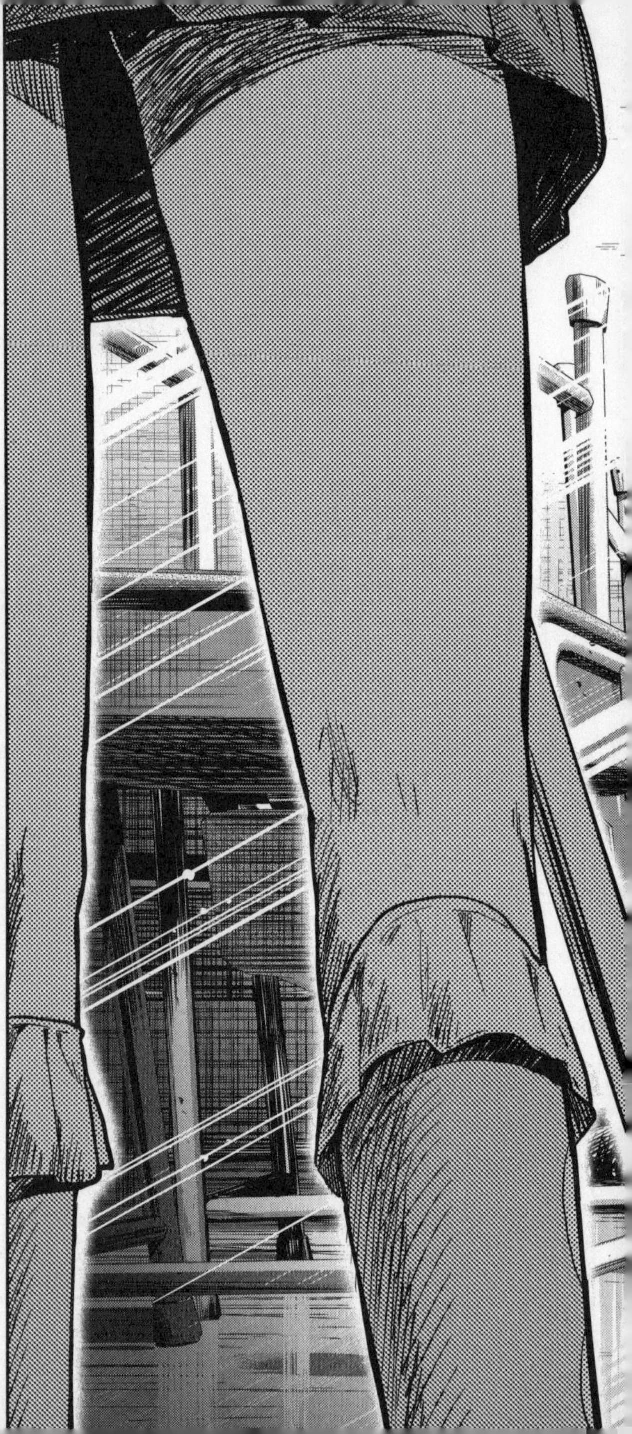
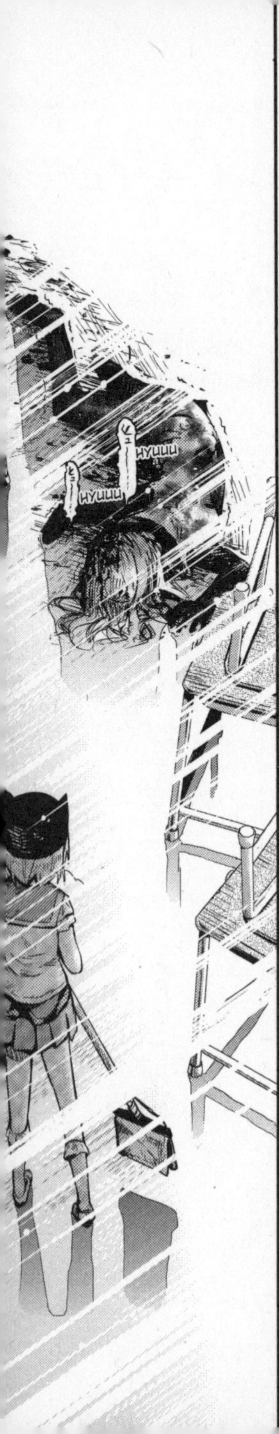
HYUUU
HYUUU

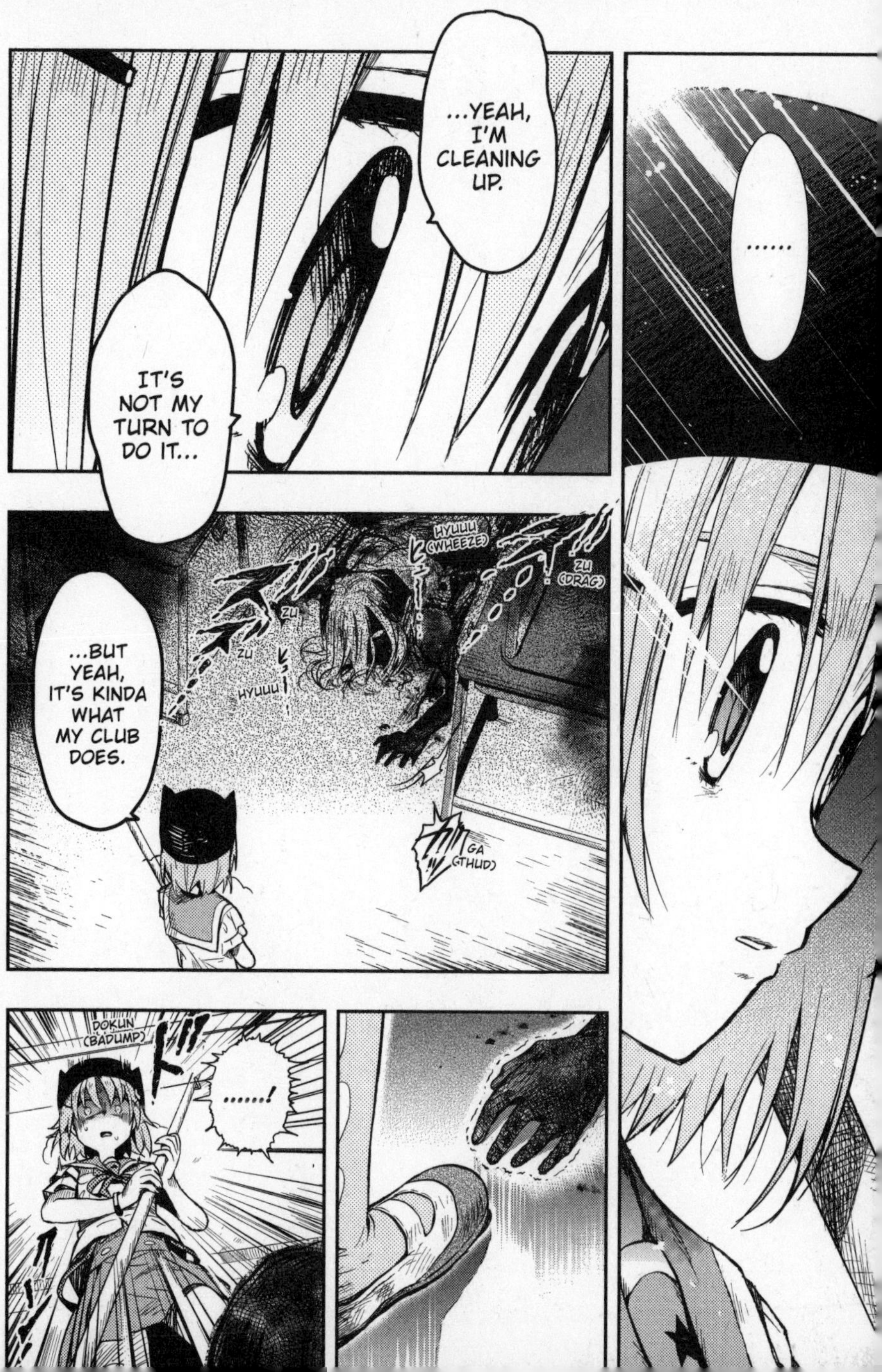
......
...YEAH, I'M CLEANING UP.
IT'S NOT MY TURN TO DO IT...
HYUUU (WHEEZE)
ZU (DRAG)
ZU
ZU
HYUUU
...BUT YEAH, IT'S KINDA WHAT MY CLUB DOES.
GA (THUD)
DOKUN (BADUMP)
......!

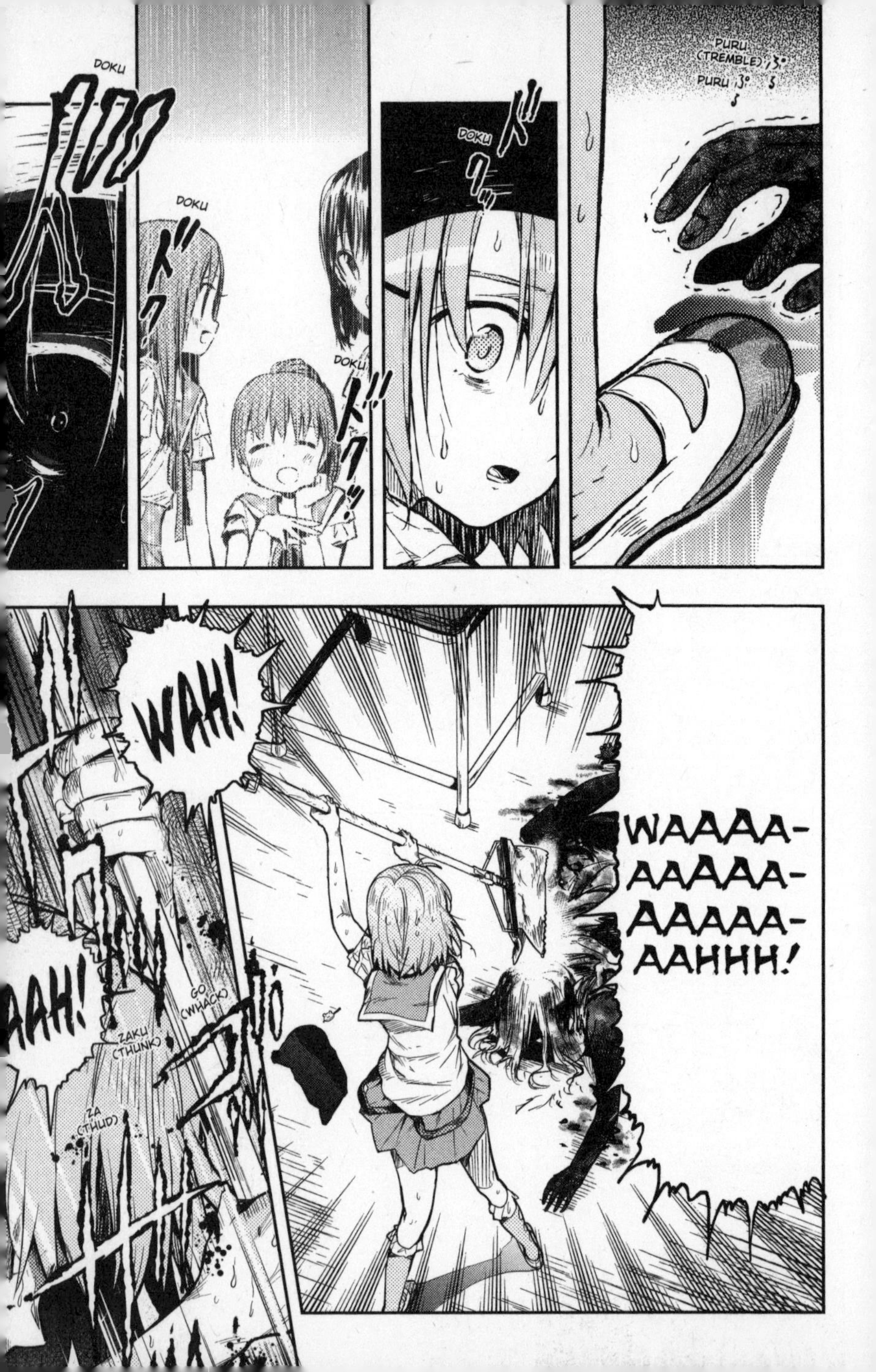

PURU (TREMBLE)
PURU
DOKU
DOKU
DOKU
DOKU
WAAAA-AAAAA-AAAAA-AAHHH!
WAH!
GO (WHACK)
ZAKU (THUNK)
ZA (THUD)
AAH!

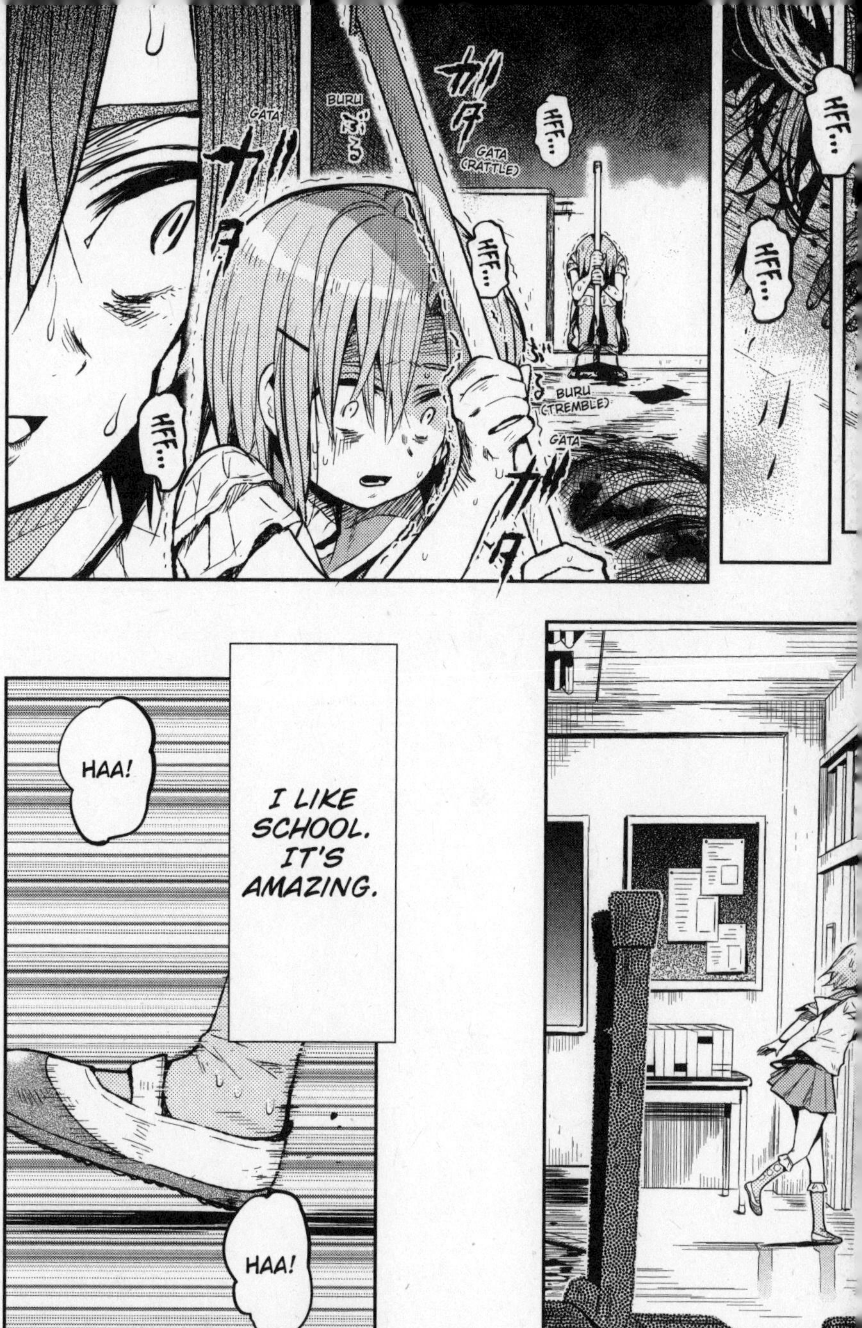
HFF...
HFF...
GATA (RATTLE)
HFF...
BURU
GATA
HFF...
BURU (TREMBLE)
GATA
HFF...
I LIKE SCHOOL. IT'S AMAZING.
HAA!
HAA!

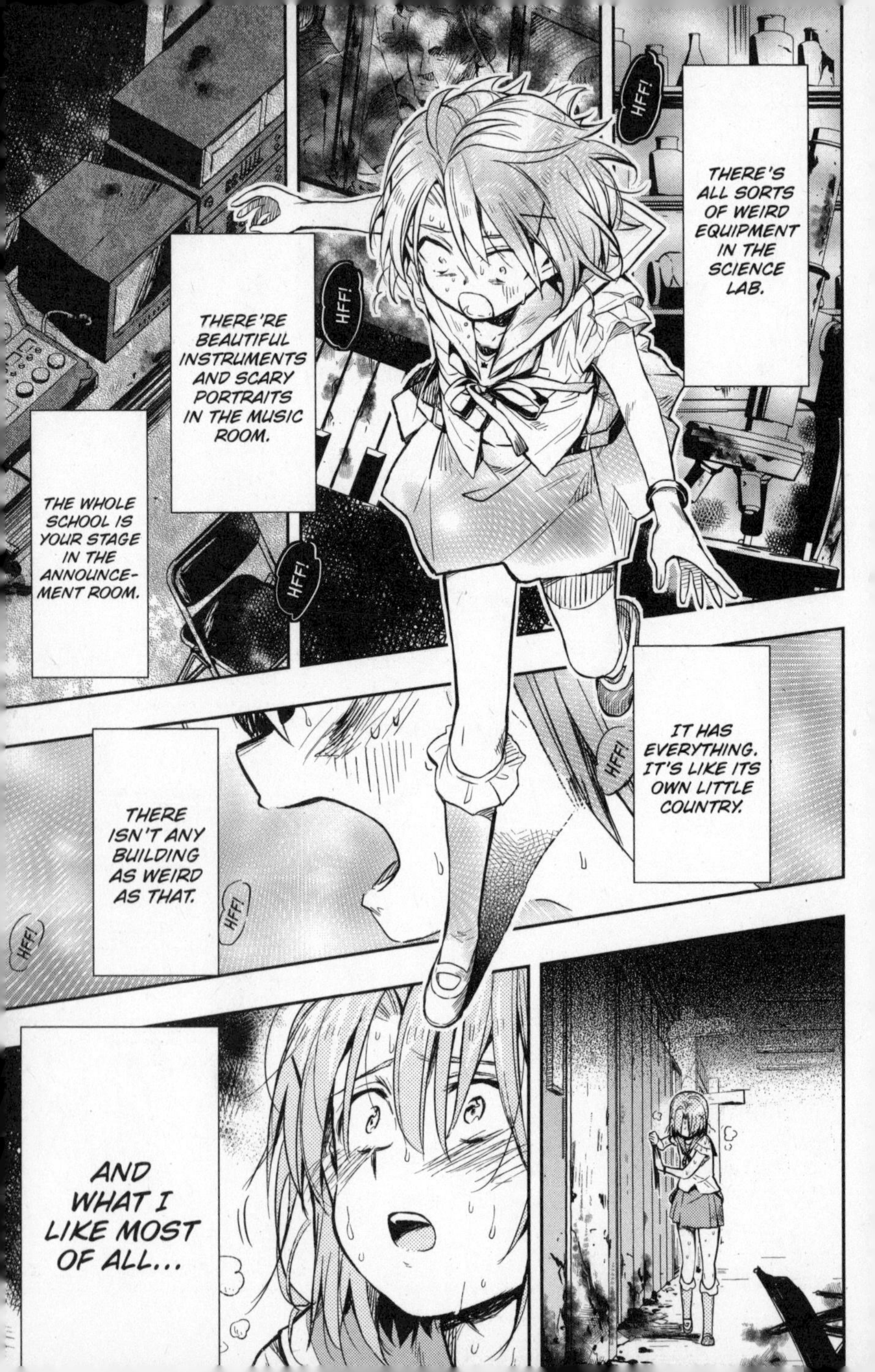
HFF!
THERE'S ALL SORTS OF WEIRD EQUIPMENT IN THE SCIENCE LAB.
HFF!
THERE'RE BEAUTIFUL INSTRUMENTS AND SCARY PORTRAITS IN THE MUSIC ROOM.
HFF!
THE WHOLE SCHOOL IS YOUR STAGE IN THE ANNOUNCE-MENT ROOM.
HFF!
IT HAS EVERYTHING. IT'S LIKE ITS OWN LITTLE COUNTRY.
THERE ISN'T ANY BUILDING AS WEIRD AS THAT.
HFF!
HFF!
AND WHAT I LIKE MOST OF ALL...

SIGN: STUDENT COUNCIL / PAPER ON TOP: SCHOOL LIVING

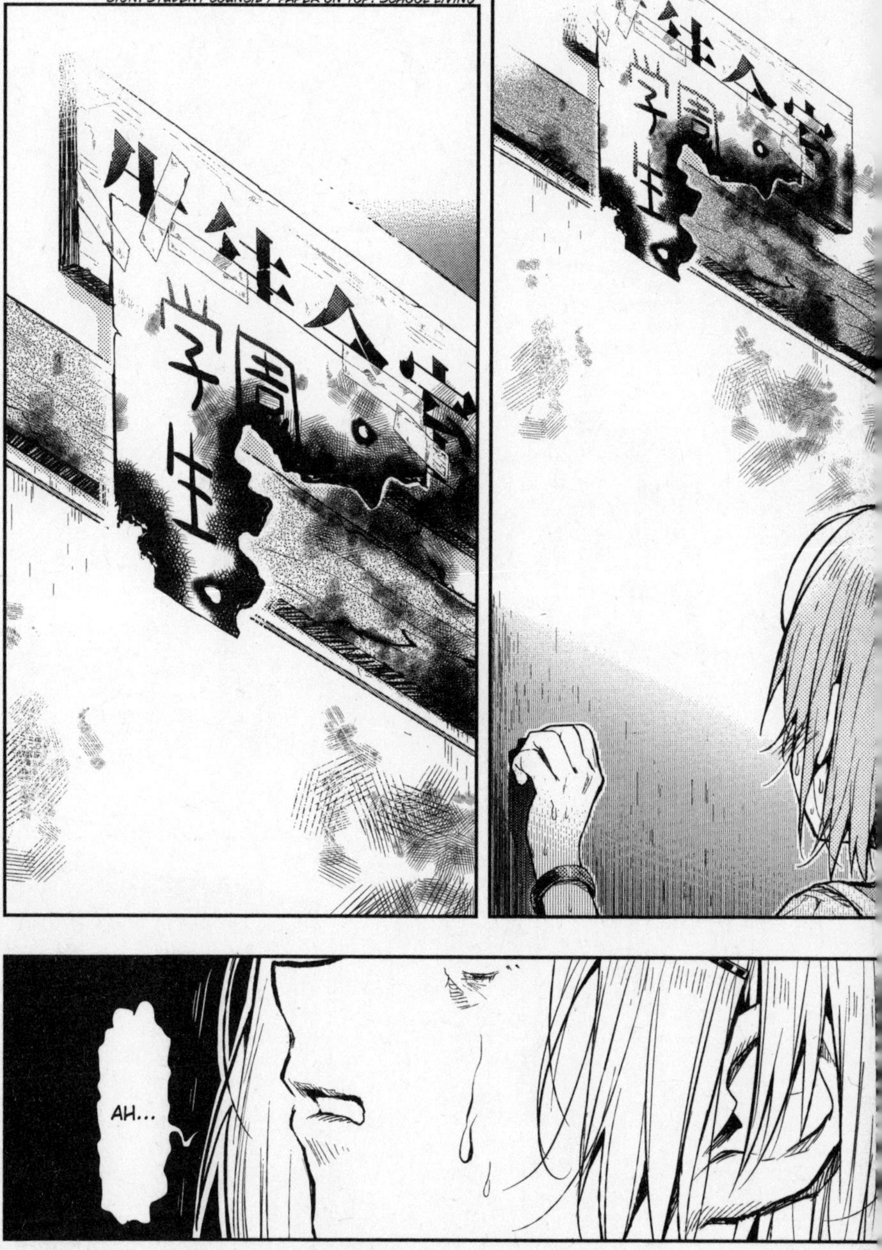
AH...

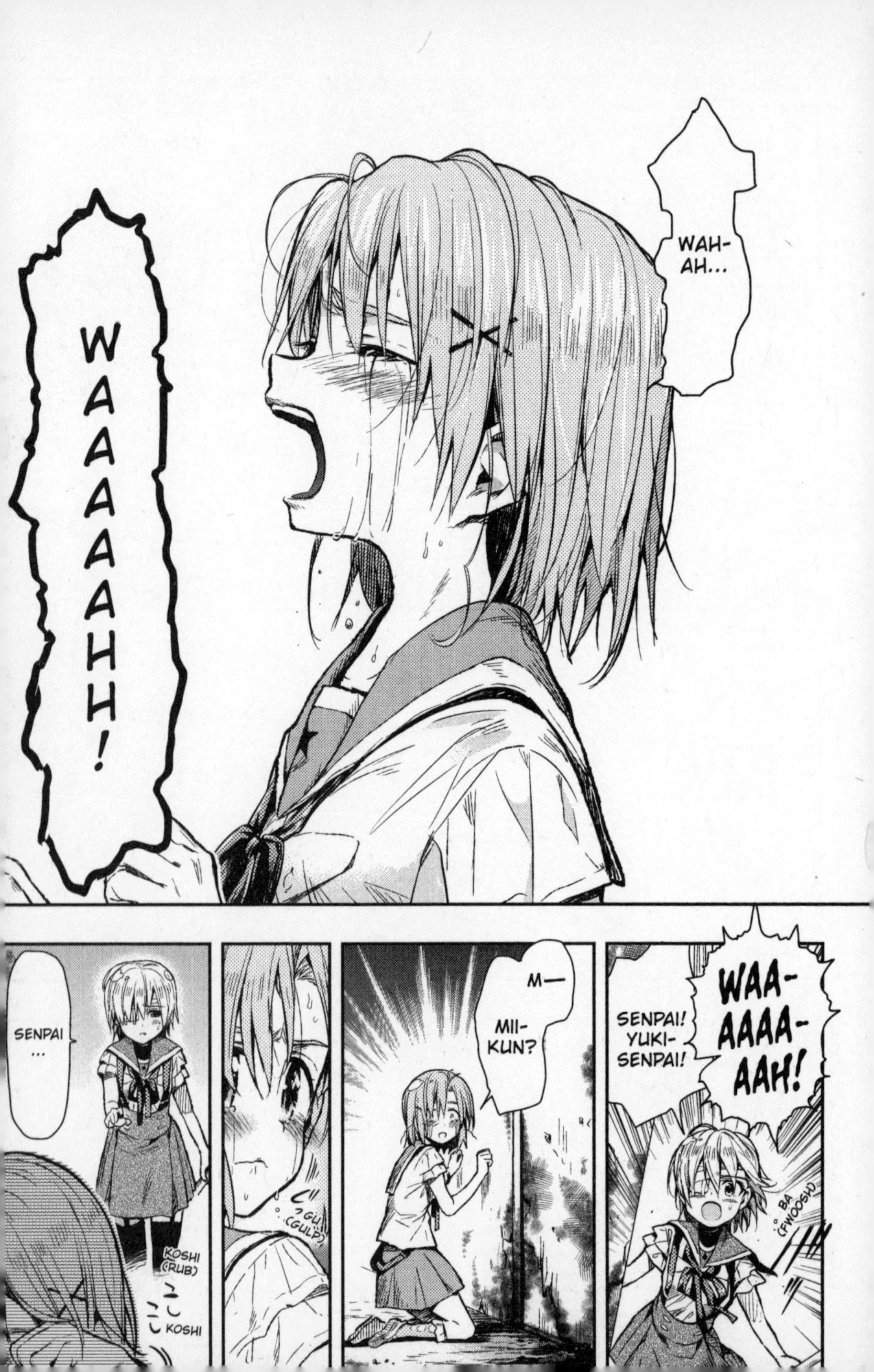
WAH-AH...
WAAAAAHH!
WAA-AAAA-AAH!
SENPAI! YUKI-SENPAI!
BA (FWOOSH)
M— MII-KUN?
GU (GULP)
SENPAI ...
KOSHI (RUB)
KOSHI

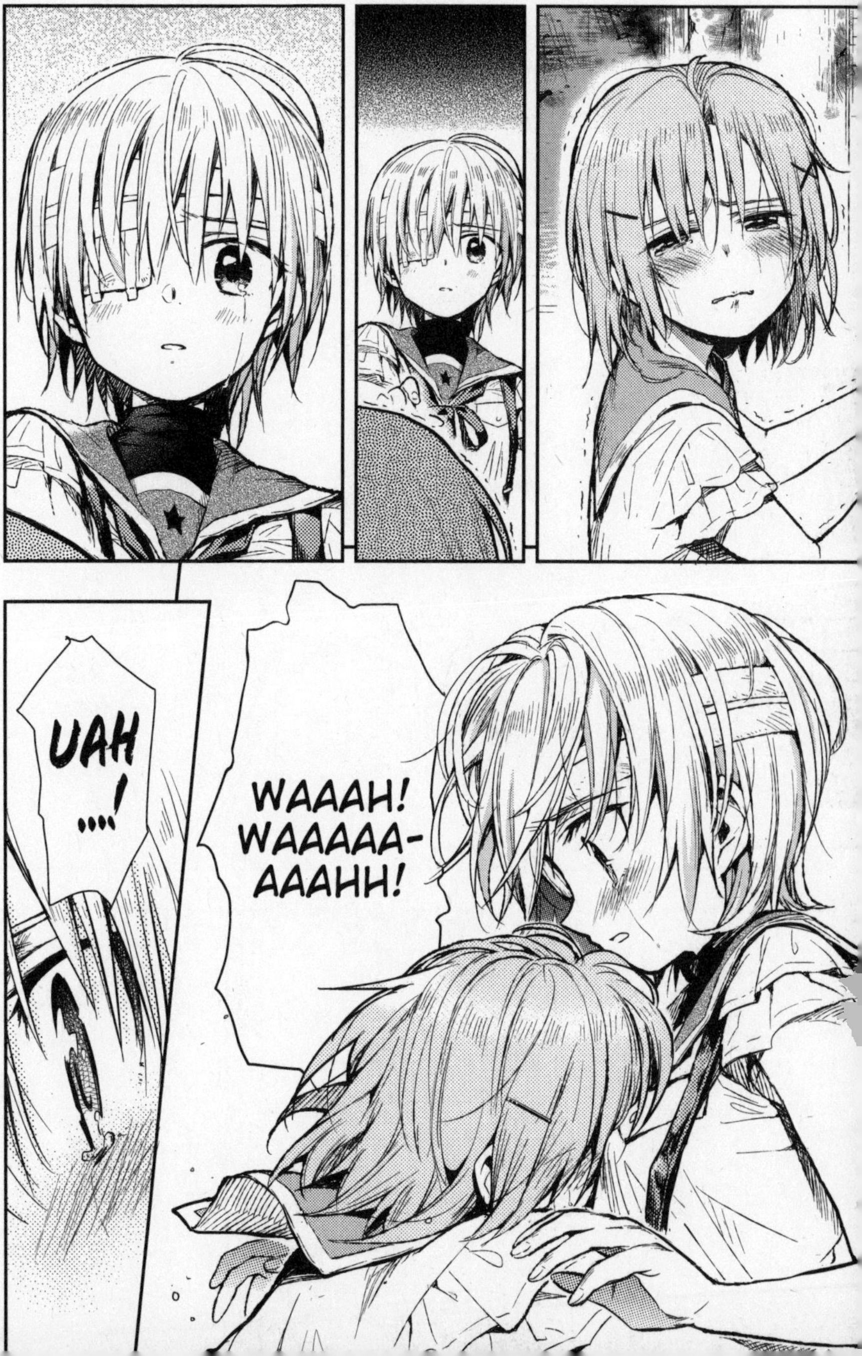
WAAAH! WAAAAA-AAAHH!
UAH ....!

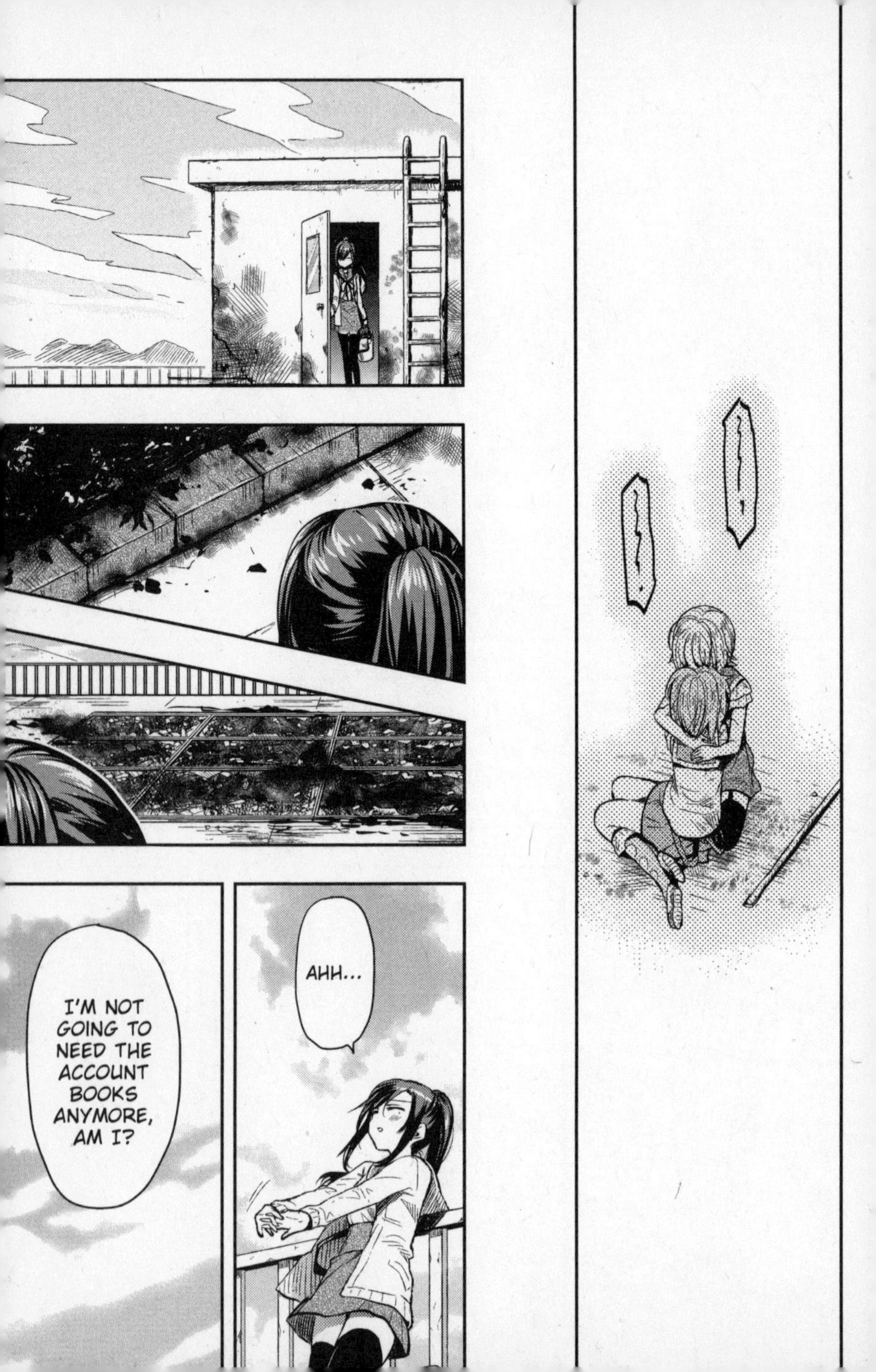
AHH...
I'M NOT GOING TO NEED THE ACCOUNT BOOKS ANYMORE, AM I?

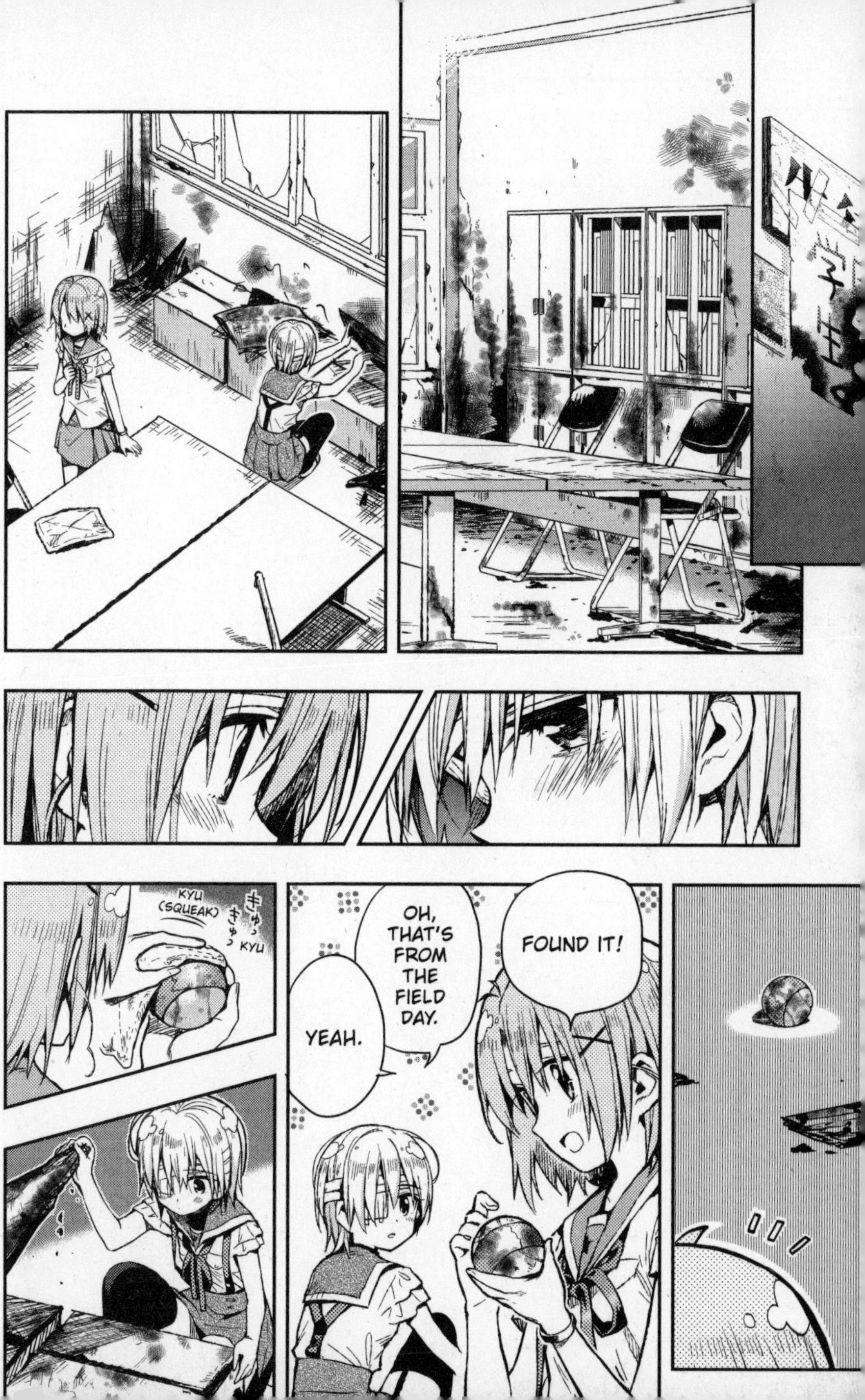
FOUND IT!
OH, THAT'S FROM THE FIELD DAY.
YEAH.
きゅっ きゅっ
KYU (SQUEAK) KYU

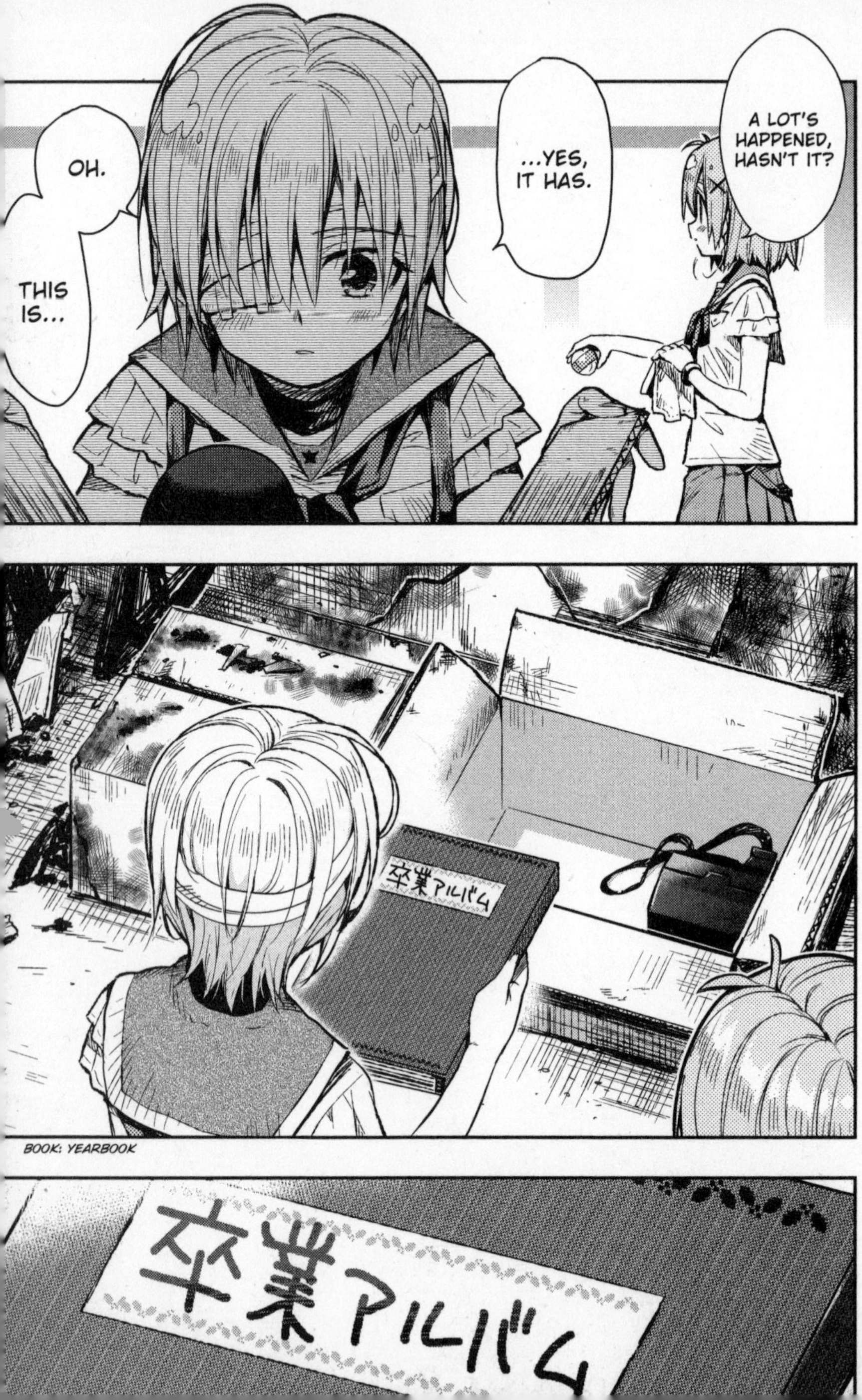
A LOT'S HAPPENED, HASN'T IT?
...YES, IT HAS.
OH.
THIS IS...
卒業アルバム
BOOK: YEARBOOK
卒業アルバム

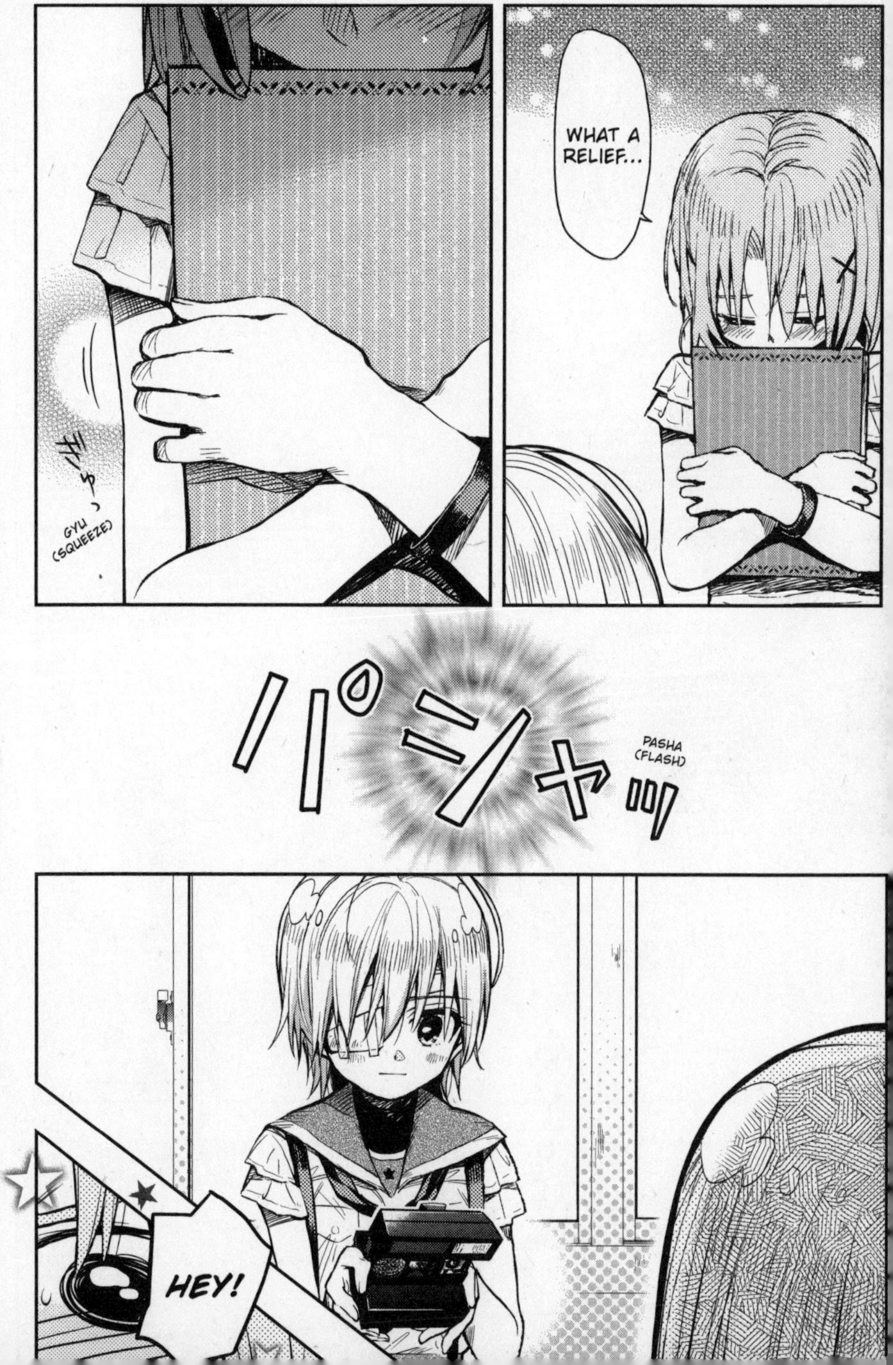
WHAT A RELIEF...
ぎゅっ
GYU (SQUEEZE)
パシャッ
PASHA (FLASH)
HEY!

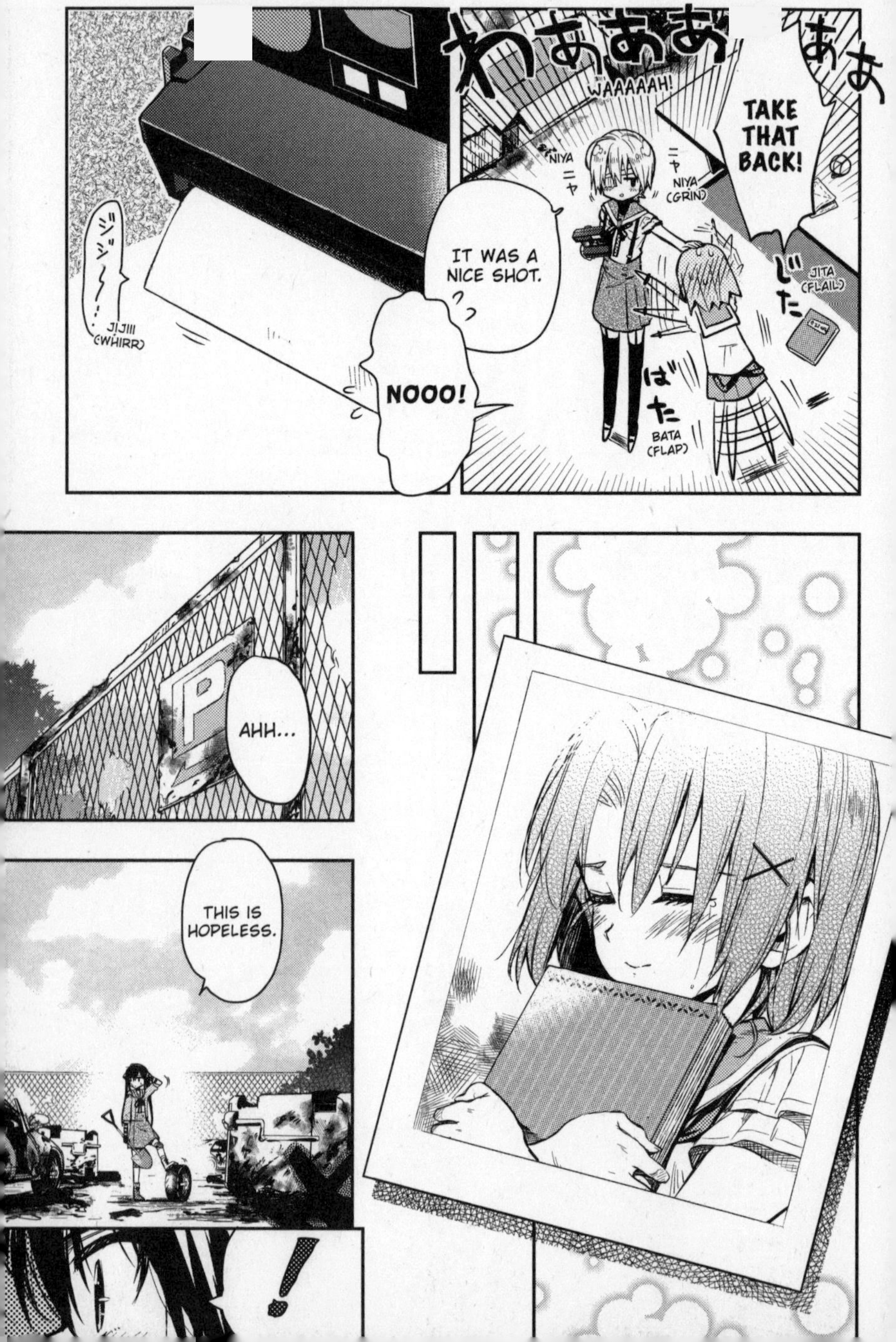

わあああ
ああ
WAAAAAH!
TAKE THAT BACK!
ニャ
NIYA (GRIN)
NIYA
ニャ
IT WAS A NICE SHOT.
じた
JITA (FLAIL)
ばた
BATA (FLAP)
NOOO!
ジジジ
JIJIII (WHIRR)
AHH...
THIS IS HOPELESS.
!

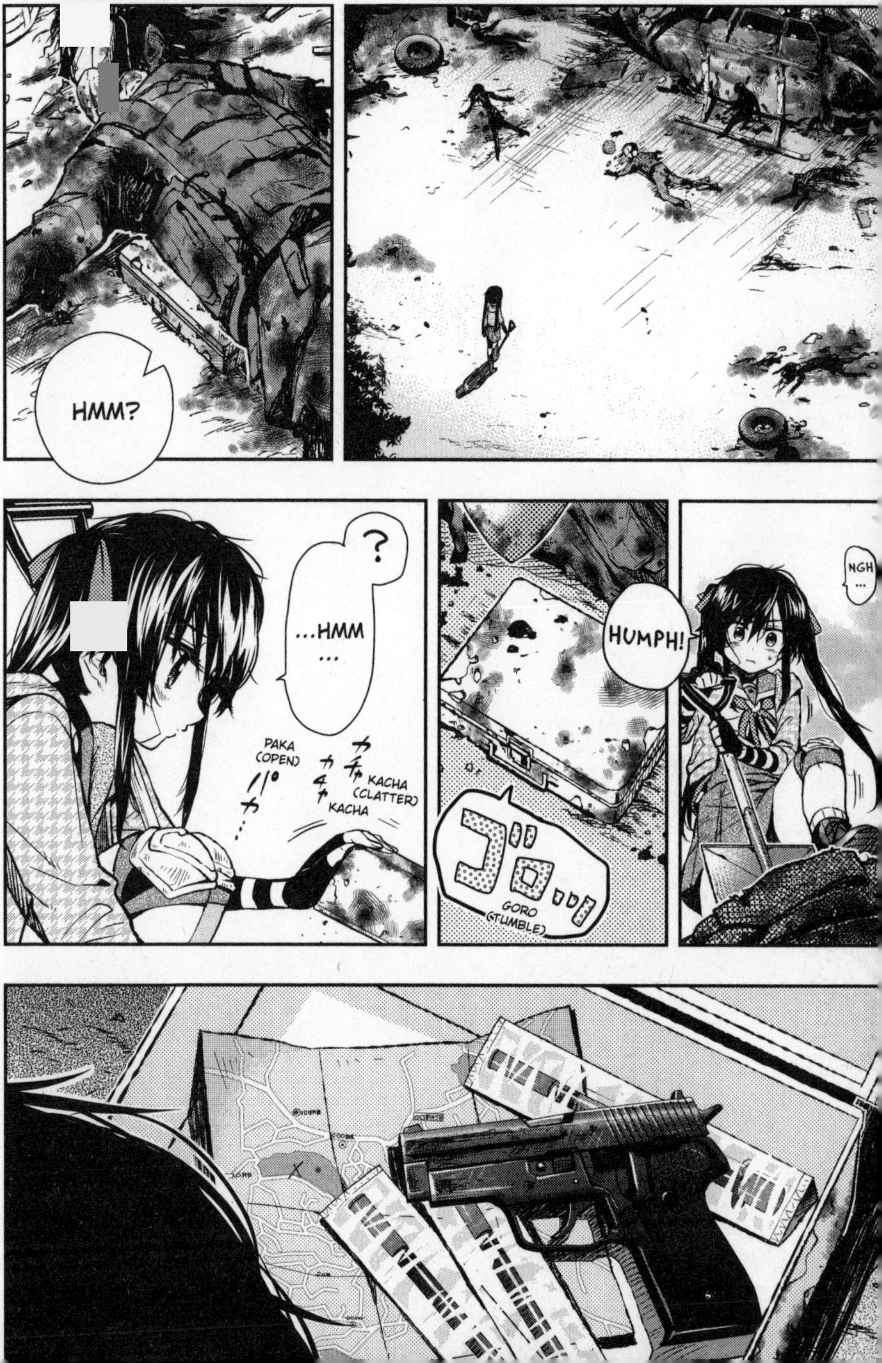
HMM?
NGH ...
HUMPH!
ゴロッ!!
GORO (TUMBLE)
?
...HMM ...
カチャ
KACHA (CLATTER)
カチャ
KACHA
パカ...
PAKA (OPEN)

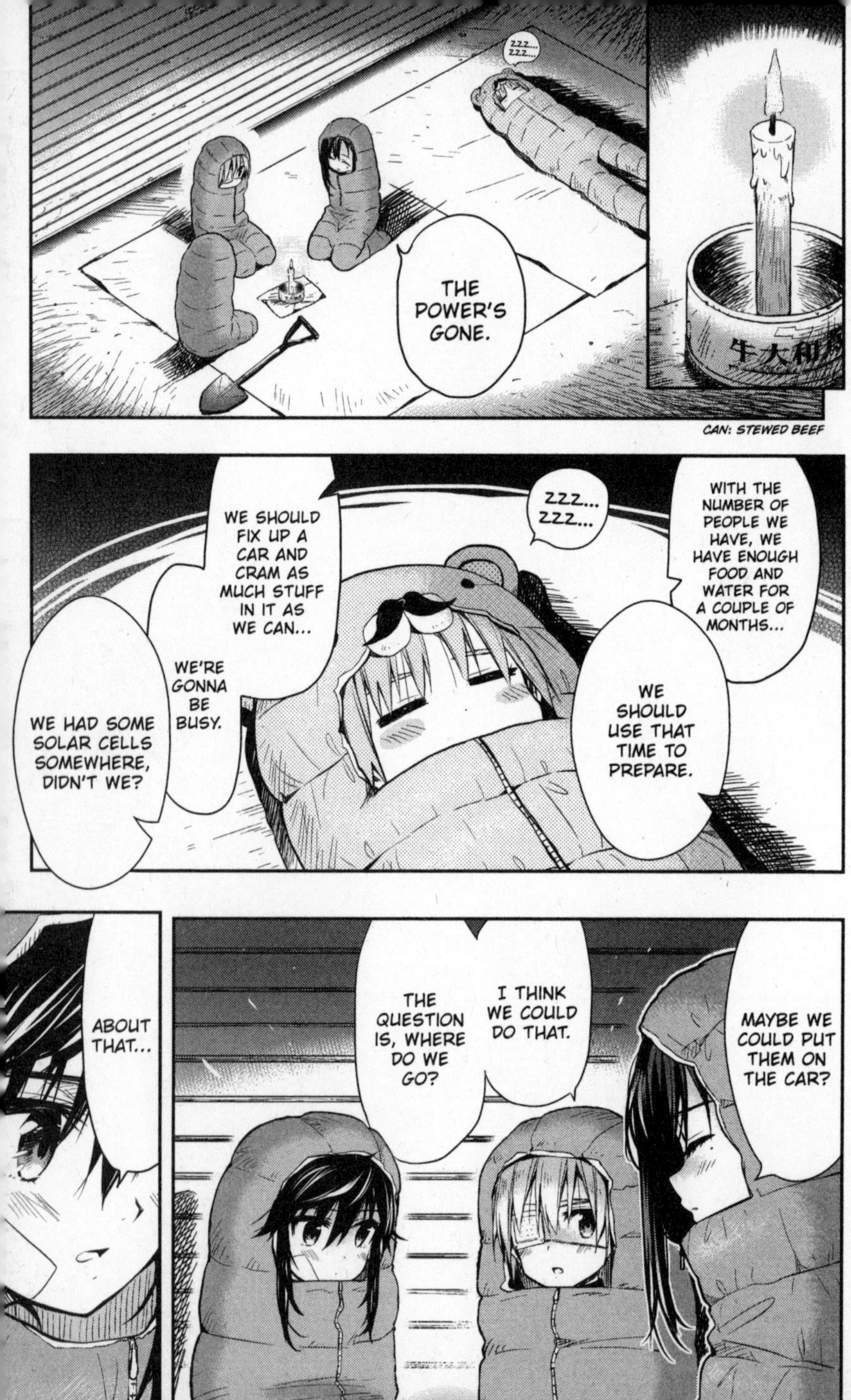
ZZZ... ZZZ...
THE POWER'S GONE.
CAN: STEWED BEEF
WITH THE NUMBER OF PEOPLE WE HAVE, WE HAVE ENOUGH FOOD AND WATER FOR A COUPLE OF MONTHS...
ZZZ... ZZZ...
WE SHOULD USE THAT TIME TO PREPARE.
WE SHOULD FIX UP A CAR AND CRAM AS MUCH STUFF IN IT AS WE CAN...
WE'RE GONNA BE BUSY.
WE HAD SOME SOLAR CELLS SOMEWHERE, DIDN'T WE?
MAYBE WE COULD PUT THEM ON THE CAR?
I THINK WE COULD DO THAT.
THE QUESTION IS, WHERE DO WE GO?
ABOUT THAT...

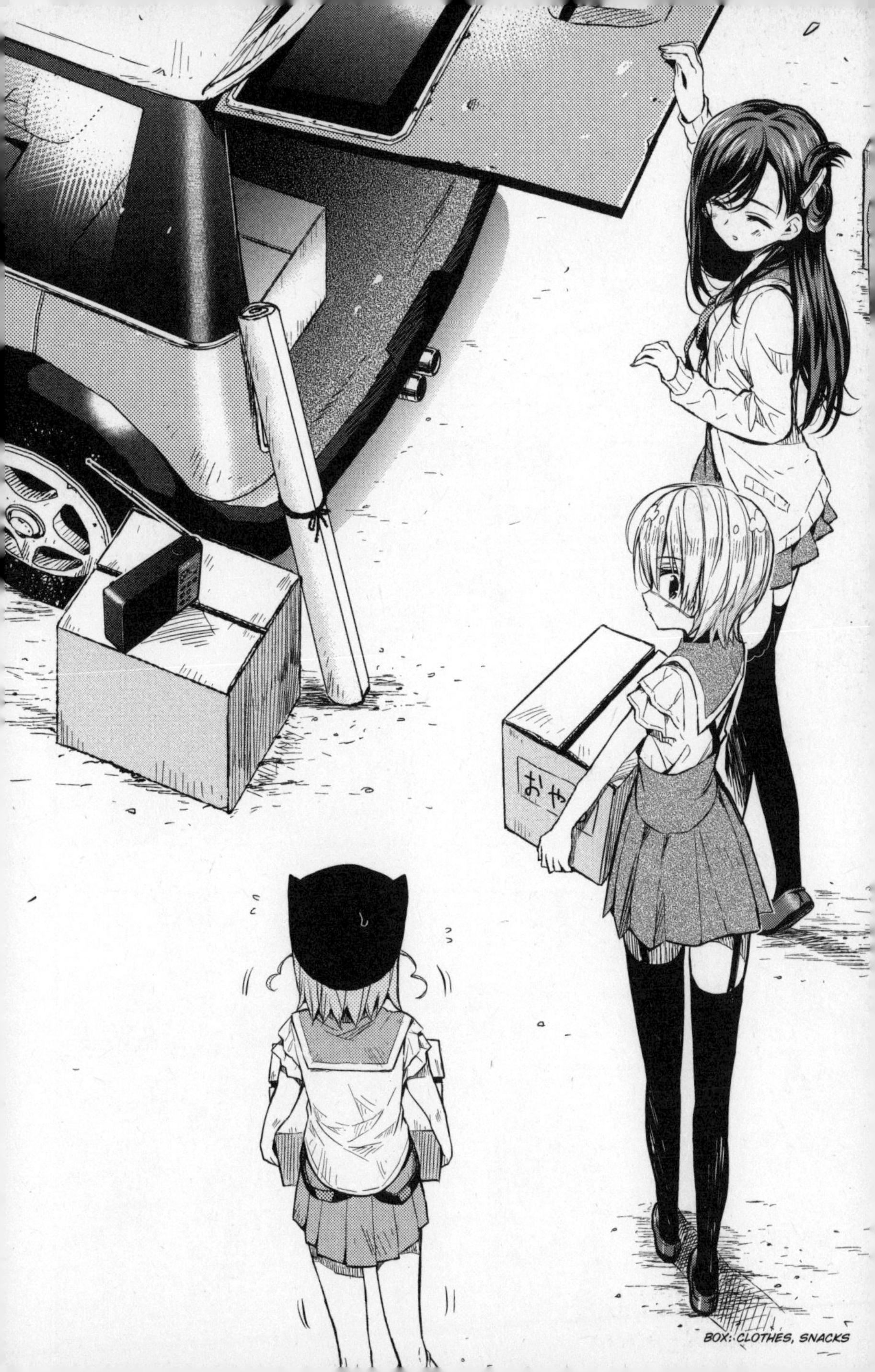
おや
BOX: CLOTHES, SNACKS

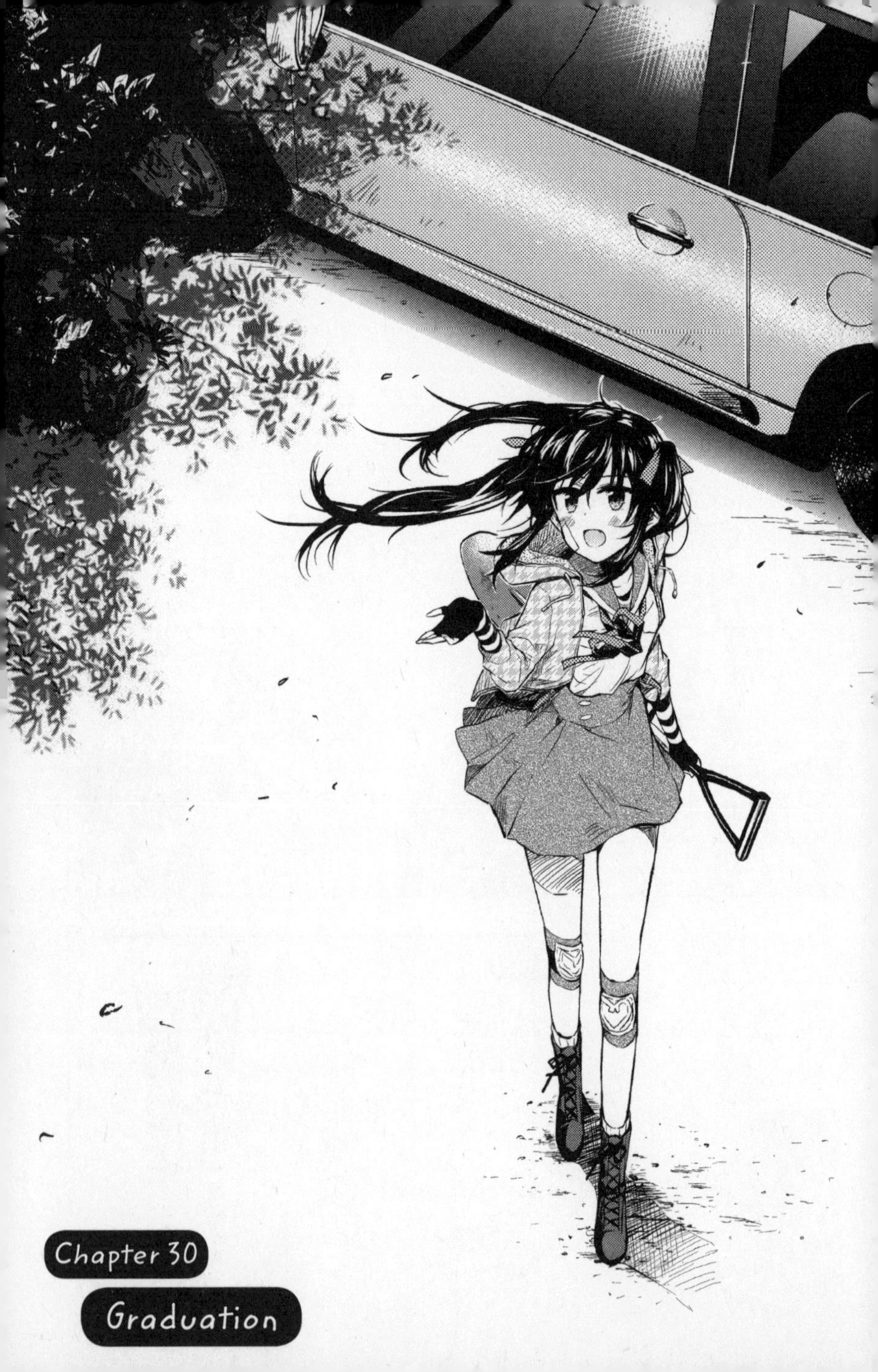
Chapter 30
Graduation

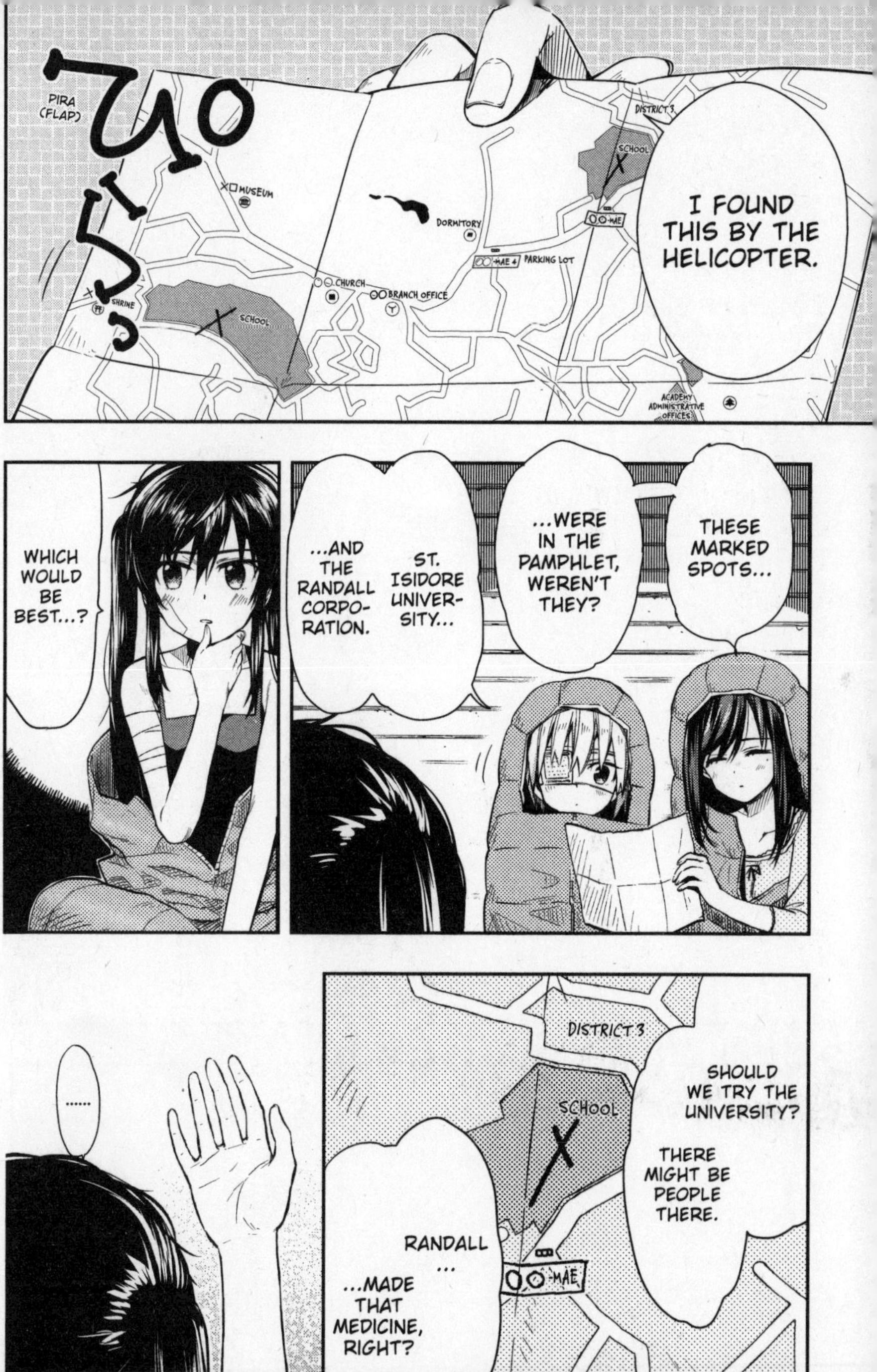
I FOUND THIS BY THE HELICOPTER.
DISTRICT 3
SCHOOL
○○-MAE
DORMITORY
○○-MAE
PARKING LOT
MUSEUM
○○ CHURCH
○○ BRANCH OFFICE
SHRINE
SCHOOL
ACADEMY ADMINISTRATIVE OFFICES
PIRA (FLAP)
ぴらっ
THESE MARKED SPOTS...
...WERE IN THE PAMPHLET, WEREN'T THEY?
ST. ISIDORE UNIVERSITY...
...AND THE RANDALL CORPORATION.
WHICH WOULD BE BEST...?
DISTRICT 3
SHOULD WE TRY THE UNIVERSITY?
THERE MIGHT BE PEOPLE THERE.
SCHOOL
○○-MAE
RANDALL...
...MADE THAT MEDICINE, RIGHT?
......

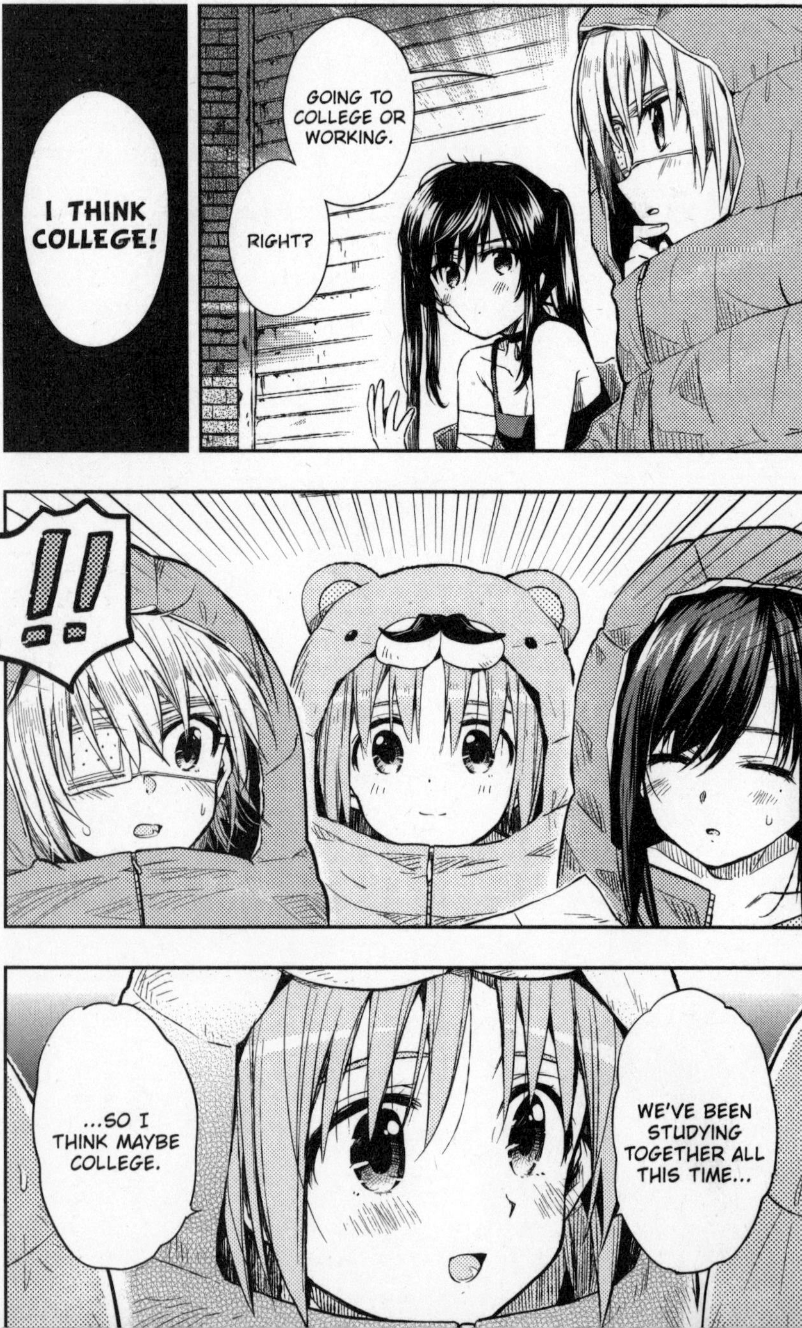
GOING TO COLLEGE OR WORKING.
RIGHT?
I THINK COLLEGE!
!!
WE'VE BEEN STUDYING TOGETHER ALL THIS TIME...
...SO I THINK MAYBE COLLEGE.

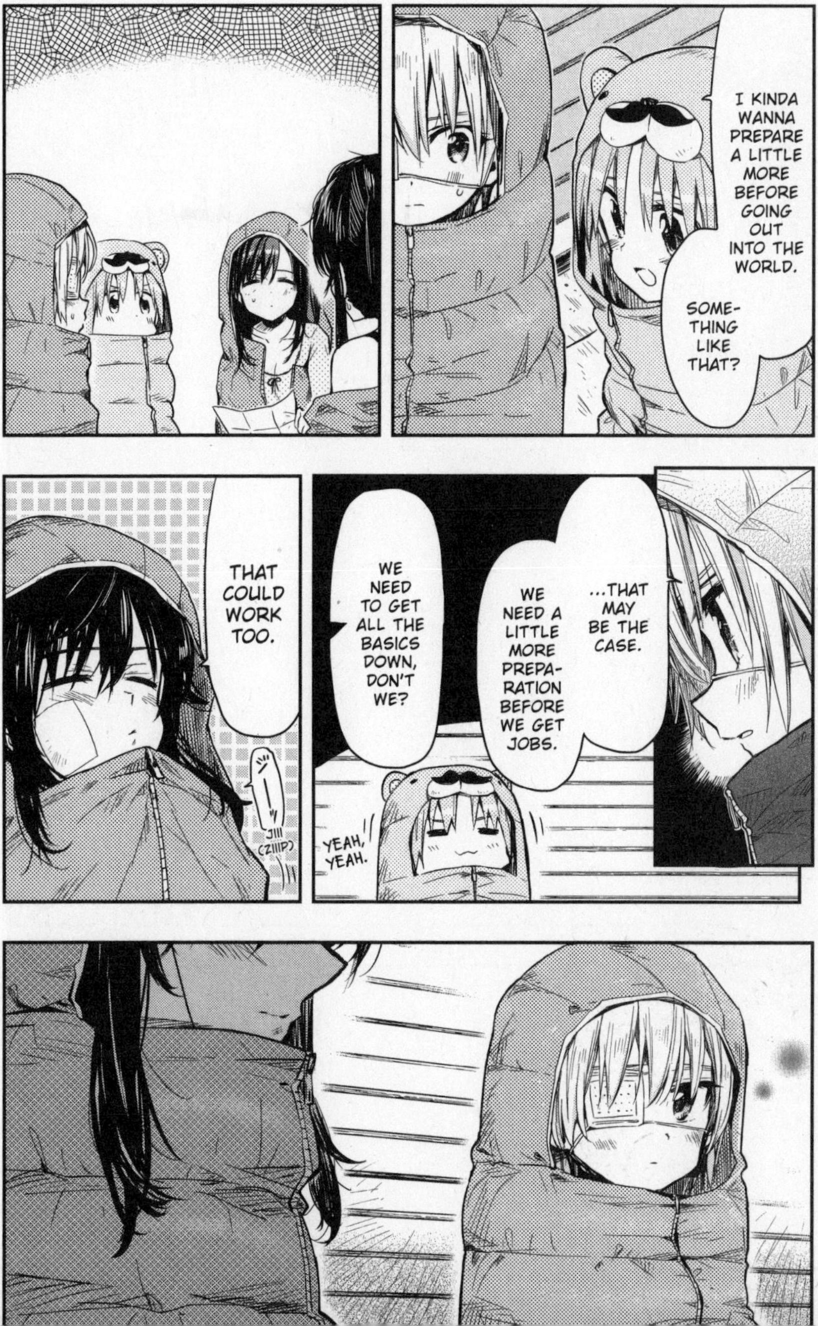
I KINDA WANNA PREPARE A LITTLE MORE BEFORE GOING OUT INTO THE WORLD.
SOME-THING LIKE THAT?
...THAT MAY BE THE CASE.
WE NEED A LITTLE MORE PREPA-RATION BEFORE WE GET JOBS.
WE NEED TO GET ALL THE BASICS DOWN, DON'T WE?
YEAH, YEAH.
THAT COULD WORK TOO.
JIII (ZIIIP)

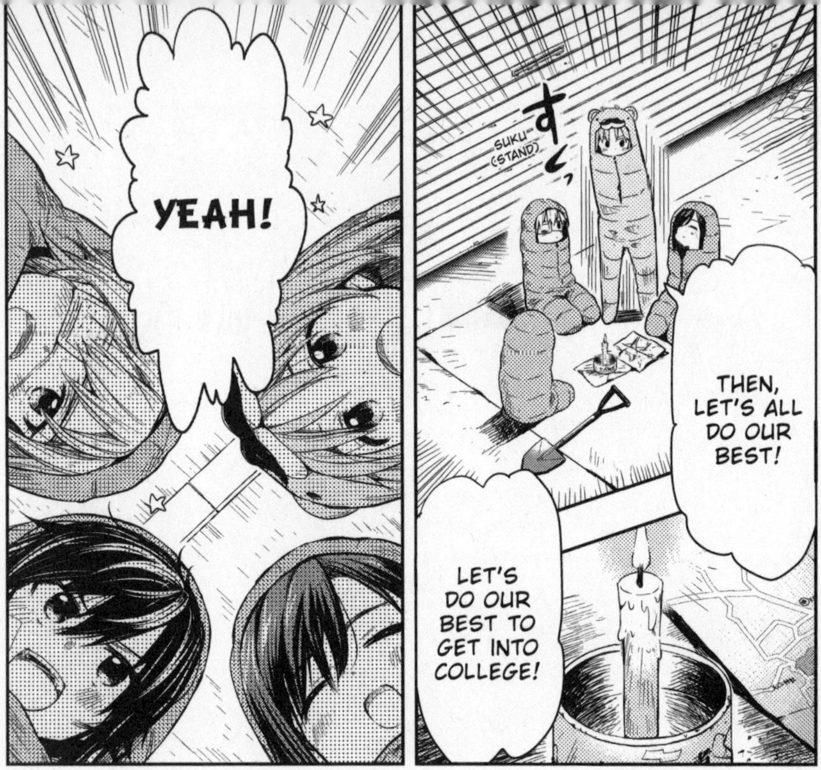

SUKU (STAND)
THEN, LET'S ALL DO OUR BEST!
LET'S DO OUR BEST TO GET INTO COLLEGE!
YEAH!

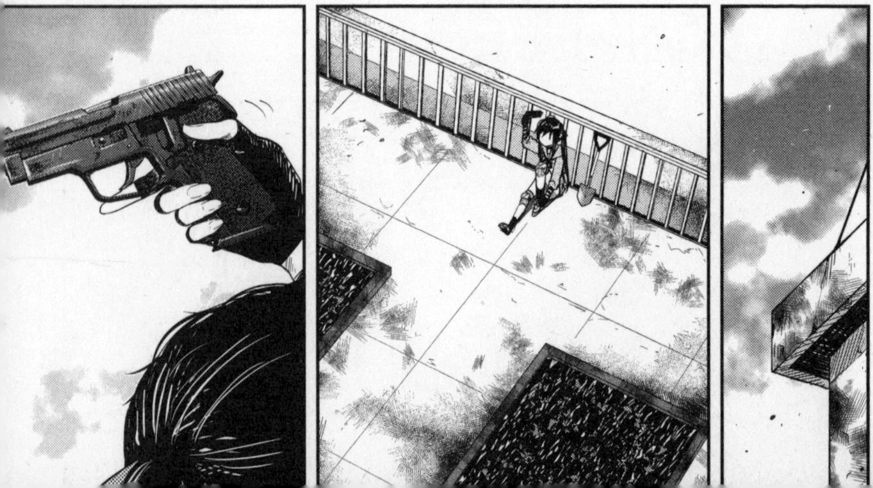

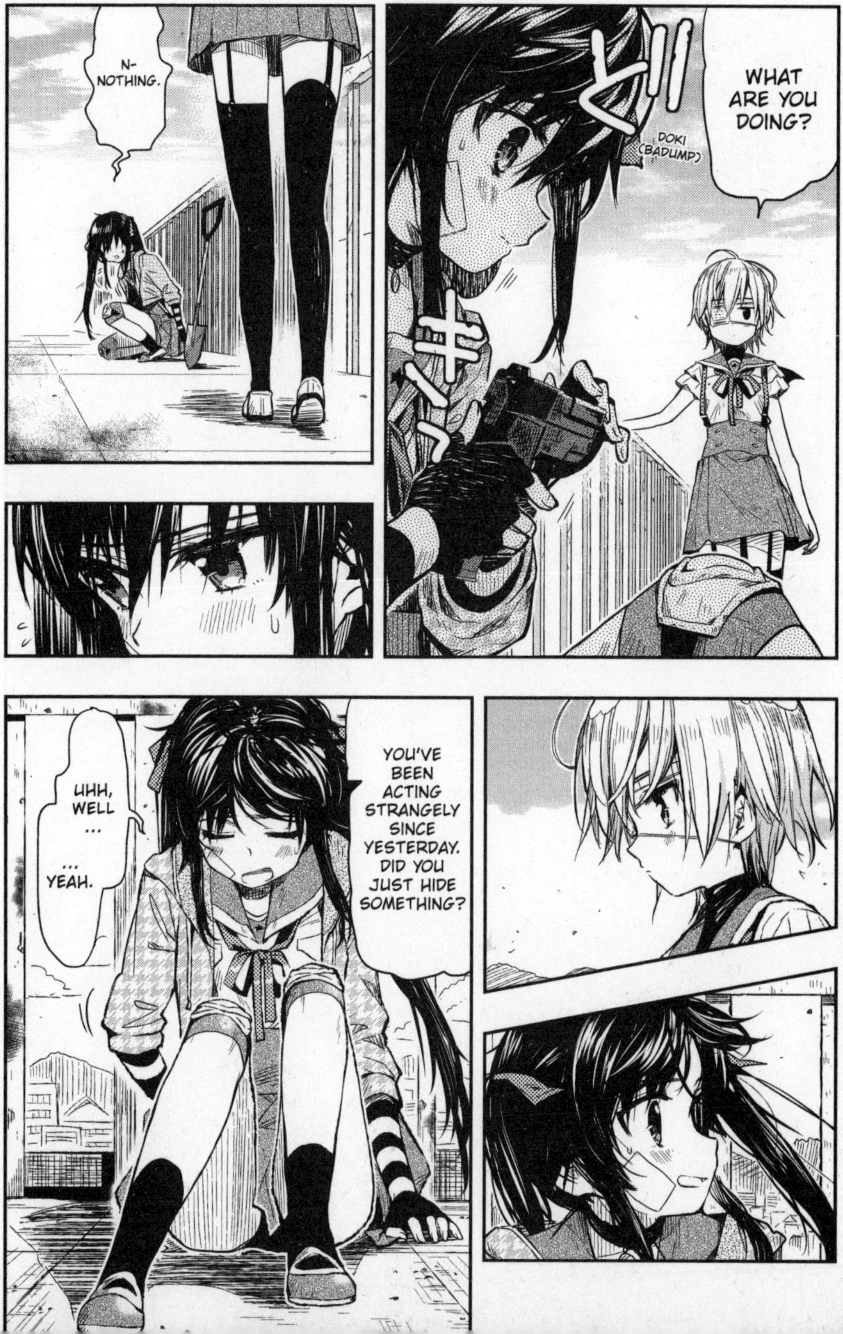
WHAT ARE YOU DOING?
DOKI (BADUMP)
N- NOTHING.
YOU'VE BEEN ACTING STRANGELY SINCE YESTERDAY. DID YOU JUST HIDE SOMETHING?
UHH, WELL ...
... YEAH.

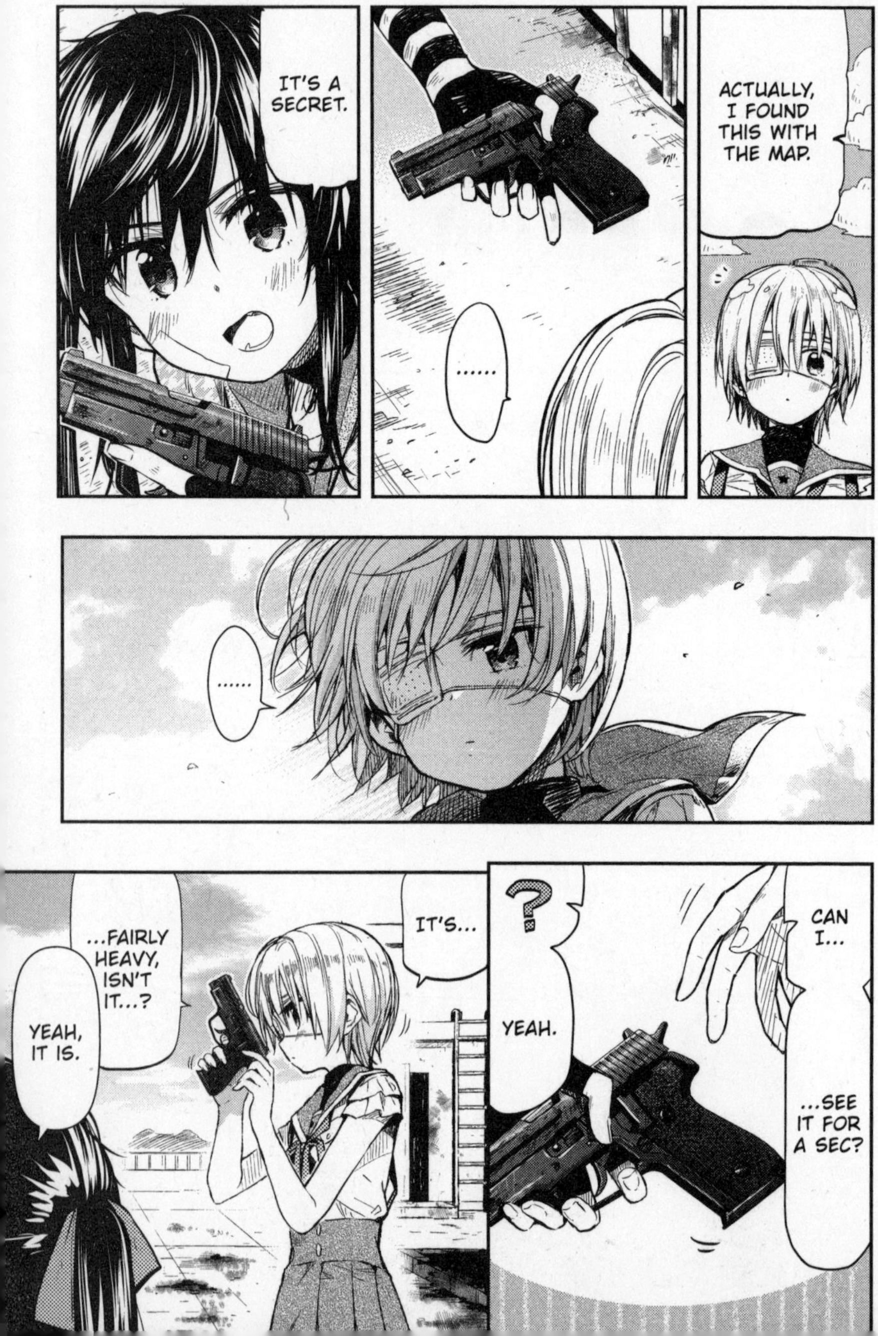
ACTUALLY, I FOUND THIS WITH THE MAP.
......
IT'S A SECRET.
......
CAN I...
?
...SEE IT FOR A SEC?
YEAH.
IT'S...
...FAIRLY HEAVY, ISN'T IT...?
YEAH, IT IS.

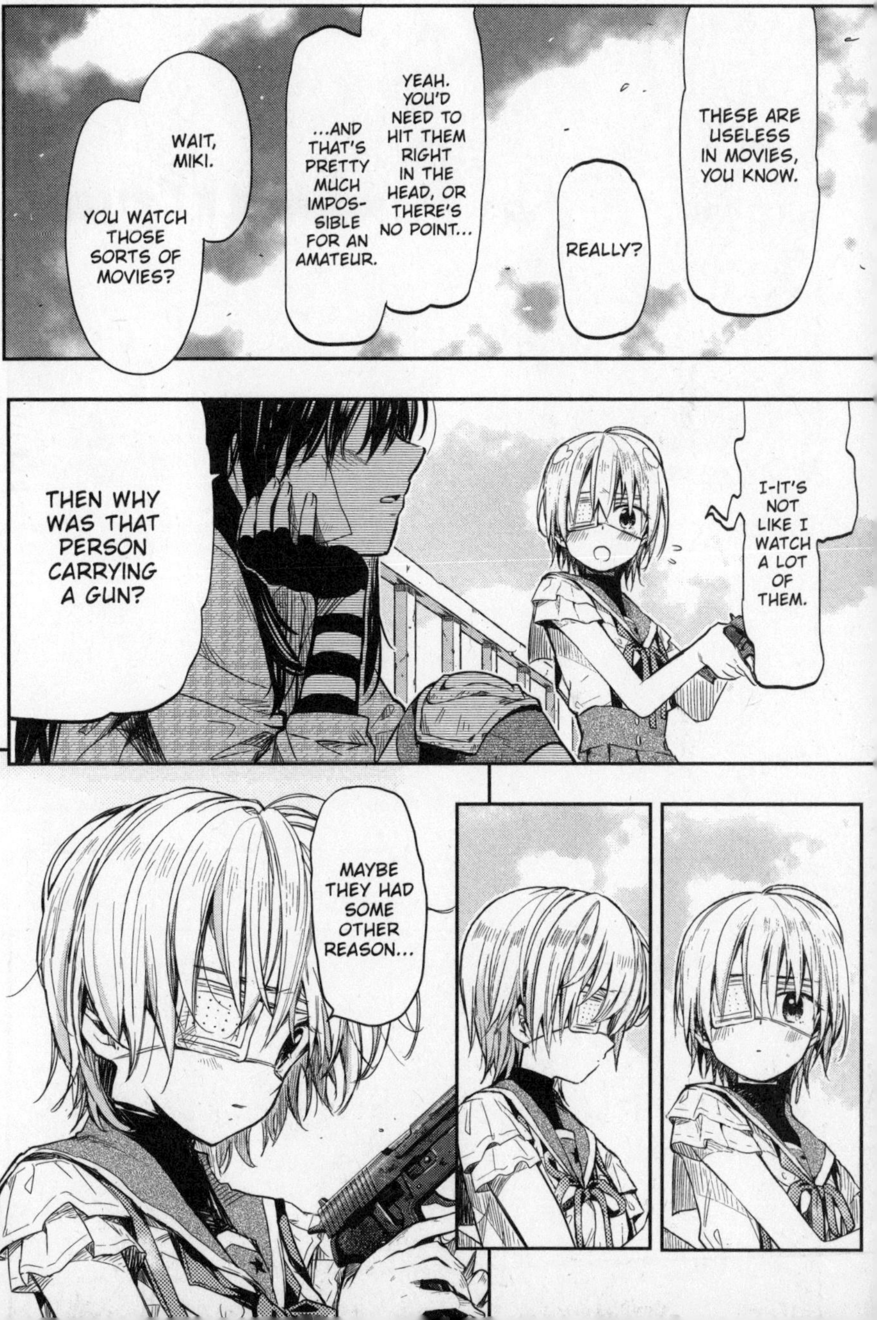
THESE ARE USELESS IN MOVIES, YOU KNOW.
REALLY?
YEAH. YOU'D NEED TO HIT THEM RIGHT IN THE HEAD, OR THERE'S NO POINT...
...AND THAT'S PRETTY MUCH IMPOS-SIBLE FOR AN AMATEUR.
WAIT, MIKI.
YOU WATCH THOSE SORTS OF MOVIES?
I-IT'S NOT LIKE I WATCH A LOT OF THEM.
THEN WHY WAS THAT PERSON CARRYING A GUN?
MAYBE THEY HAD SOME OTHER REASON...

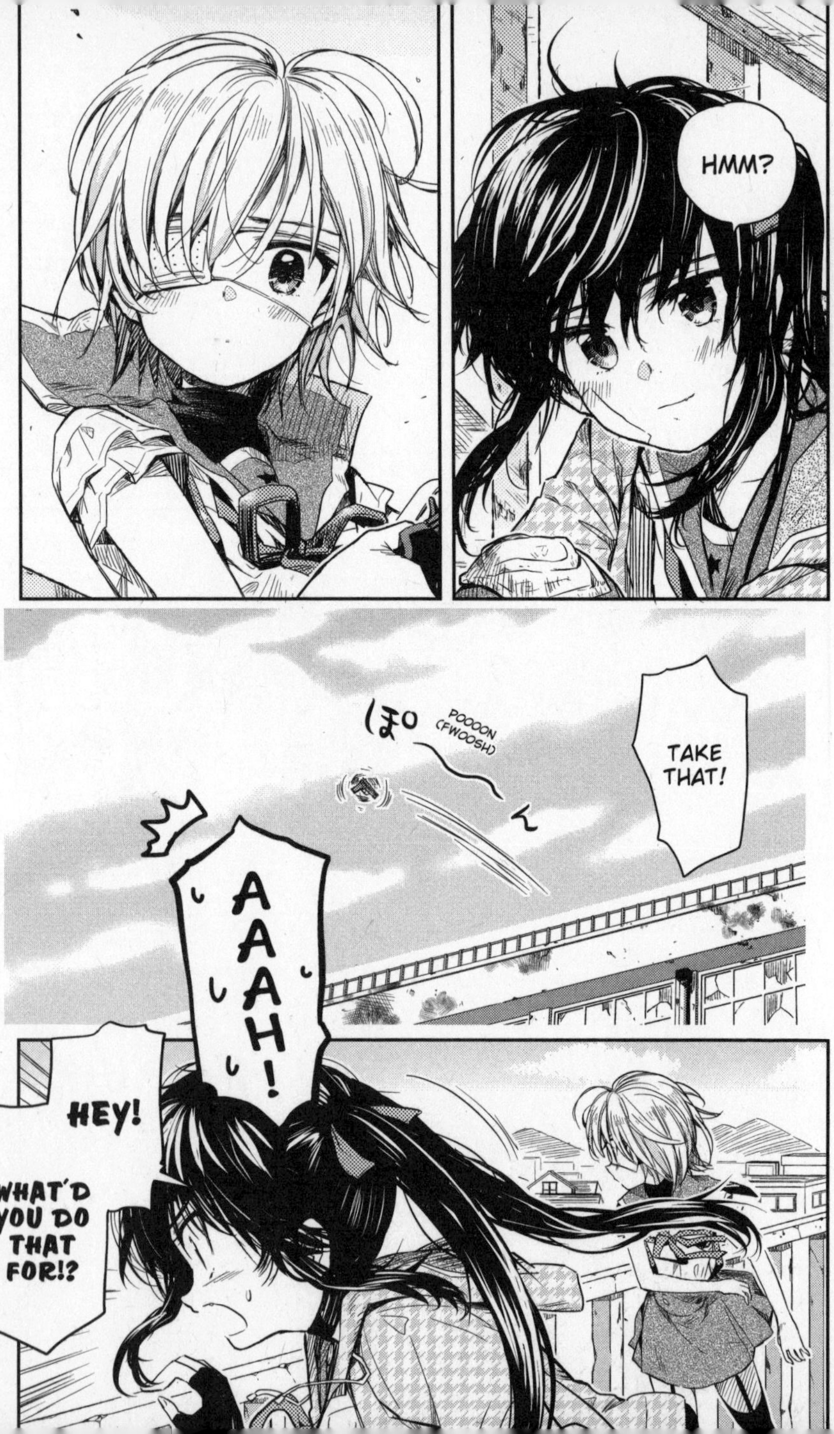
HMM?
TAKE THAT!
ほ
POOOON (FWOOSH)
ん
AAAAH!
HEY!
WHAT'D YOU DO THAT FOR!?

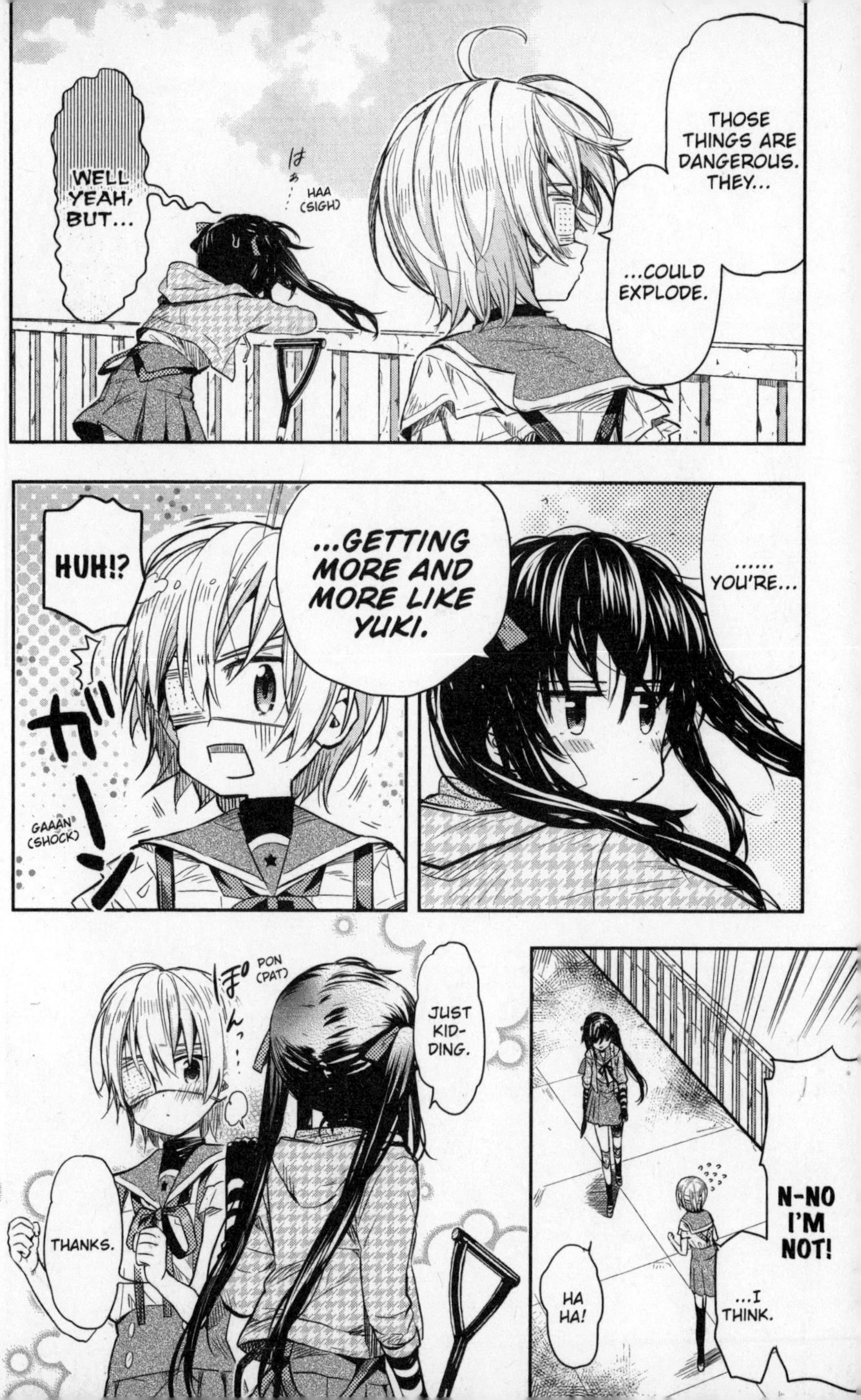
THOSE THINGS ARE DANGEROUS. THEY...
...COULD EXPLODE.
はぁ
HAA (SIGH)
WELL YEAH, BUT...
...... YOU'RE...
...GETTING MORE AND MORE LIKE YUKI.
HUH!?
ガーン
GAAAN (SHOCK)
N-NO I'M NOT!
...I THINK.
HA HA!
JUST KID-DING.
ぽんっ
PON (PAT)
THANKS.

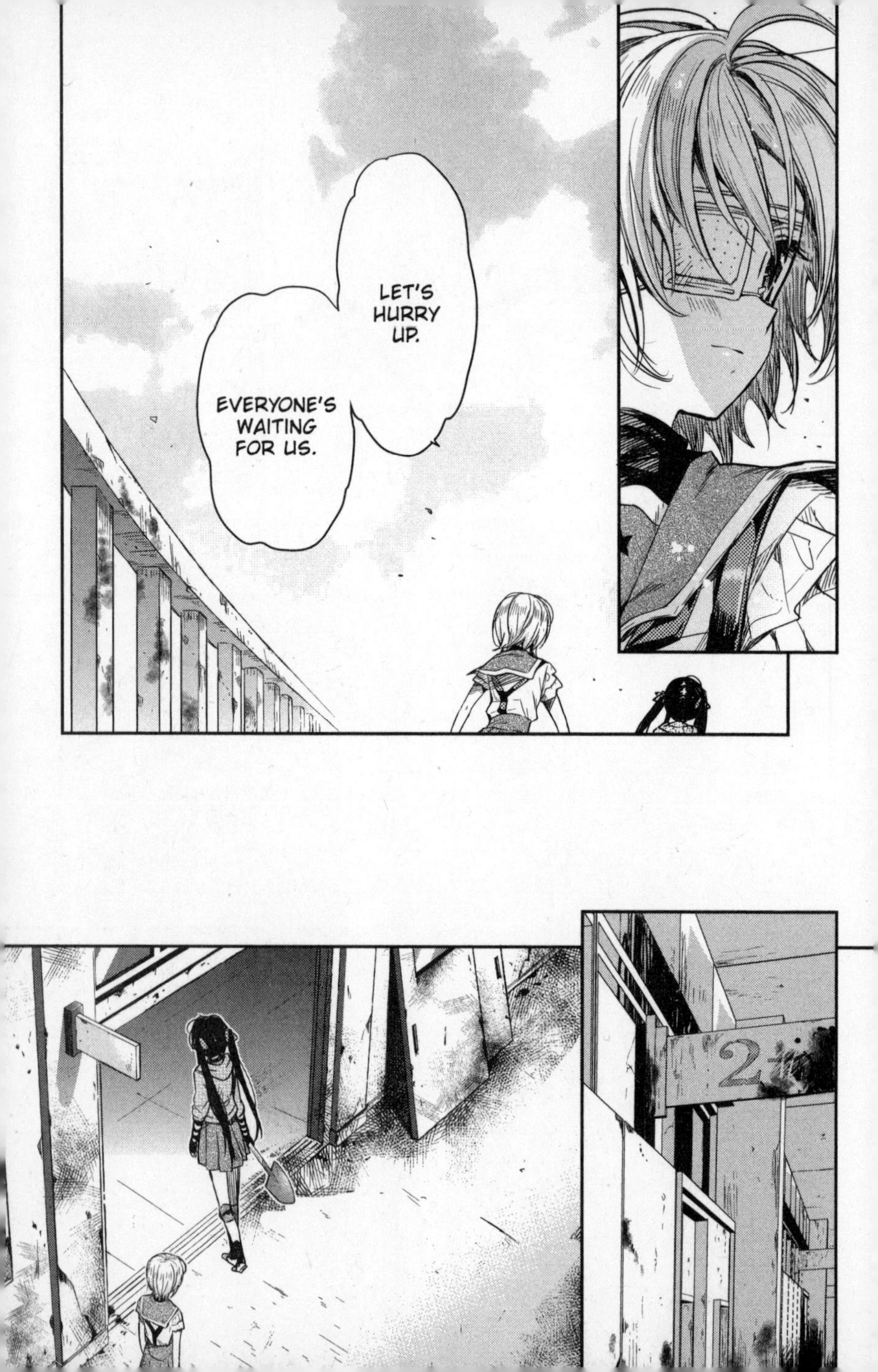
LET'S HURRY UP.
EVERYONE'S WAITING FOR US.

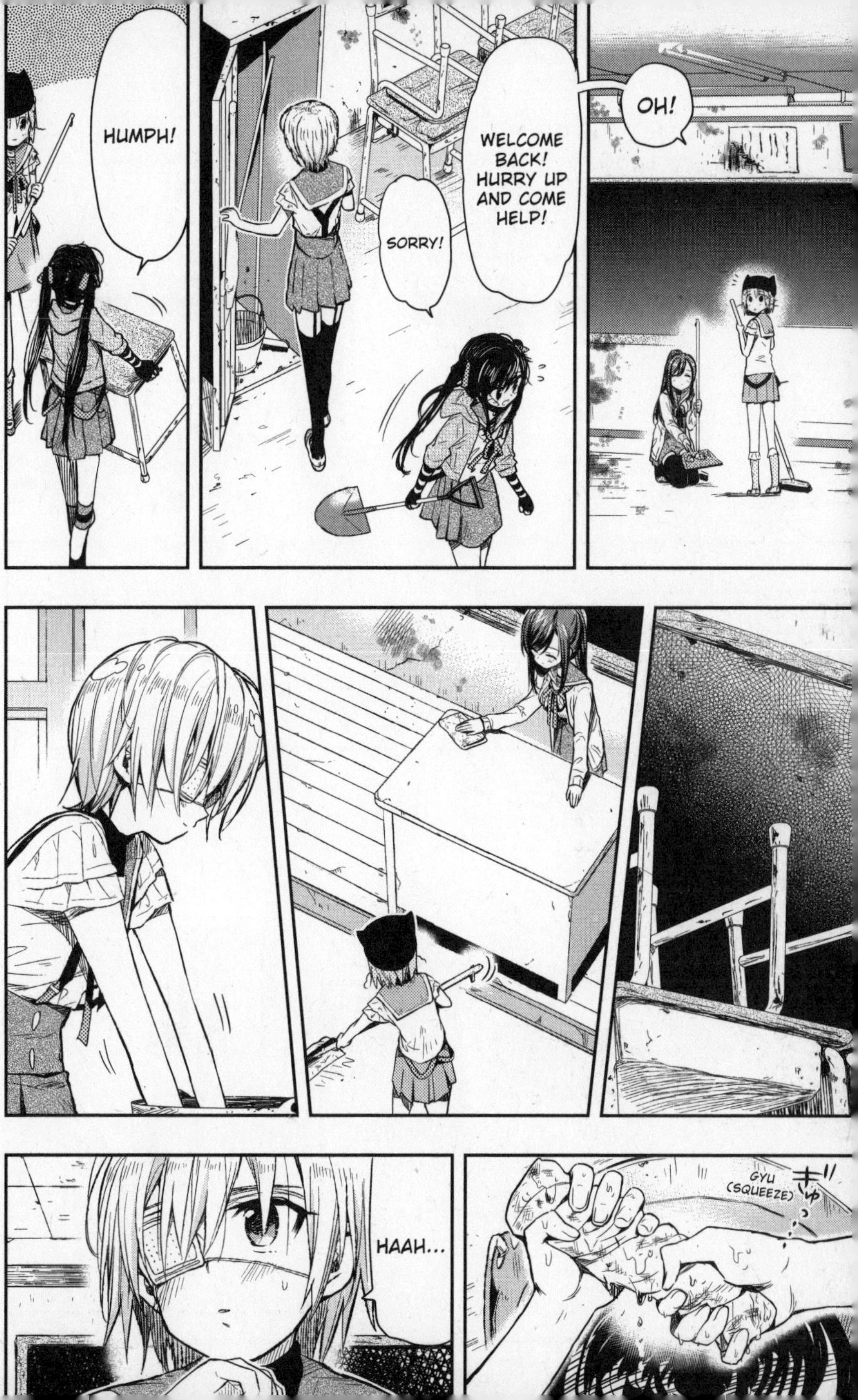
OH!
WELCOME BACK! HURRY UP AND COME HELP!
SORRY!
HUMPH!
GYU (SQUEEZE)
HAAH...

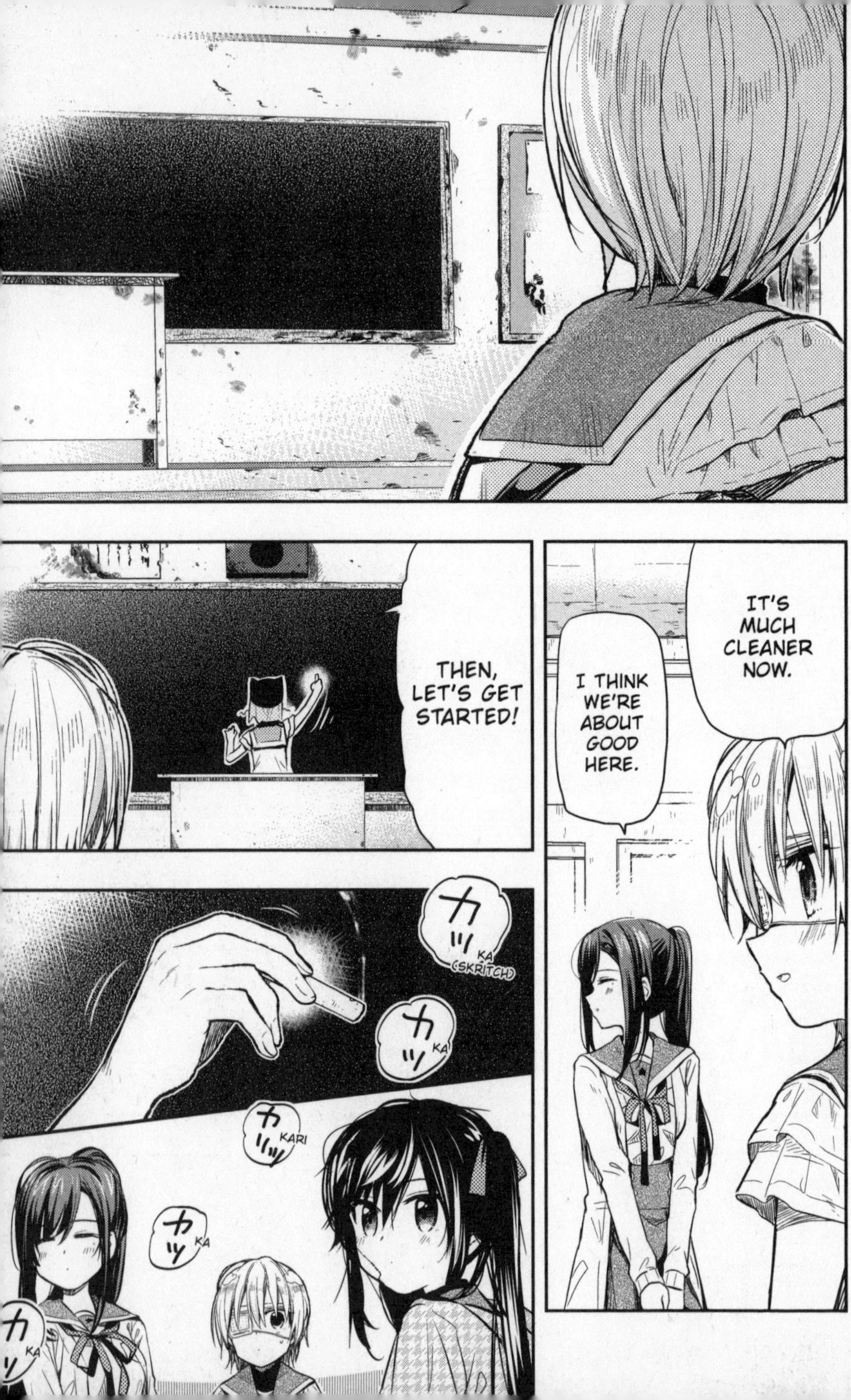
IT'S MUCH CLEANER NOW.
I THINK WE'RE ABOUT GOOD HERE.
THEN, LET'S GET STARTED!
カッ
KA (SKRITCH)
カッ
KA
カリッ
KARI
カッ
KA
カッ
KA

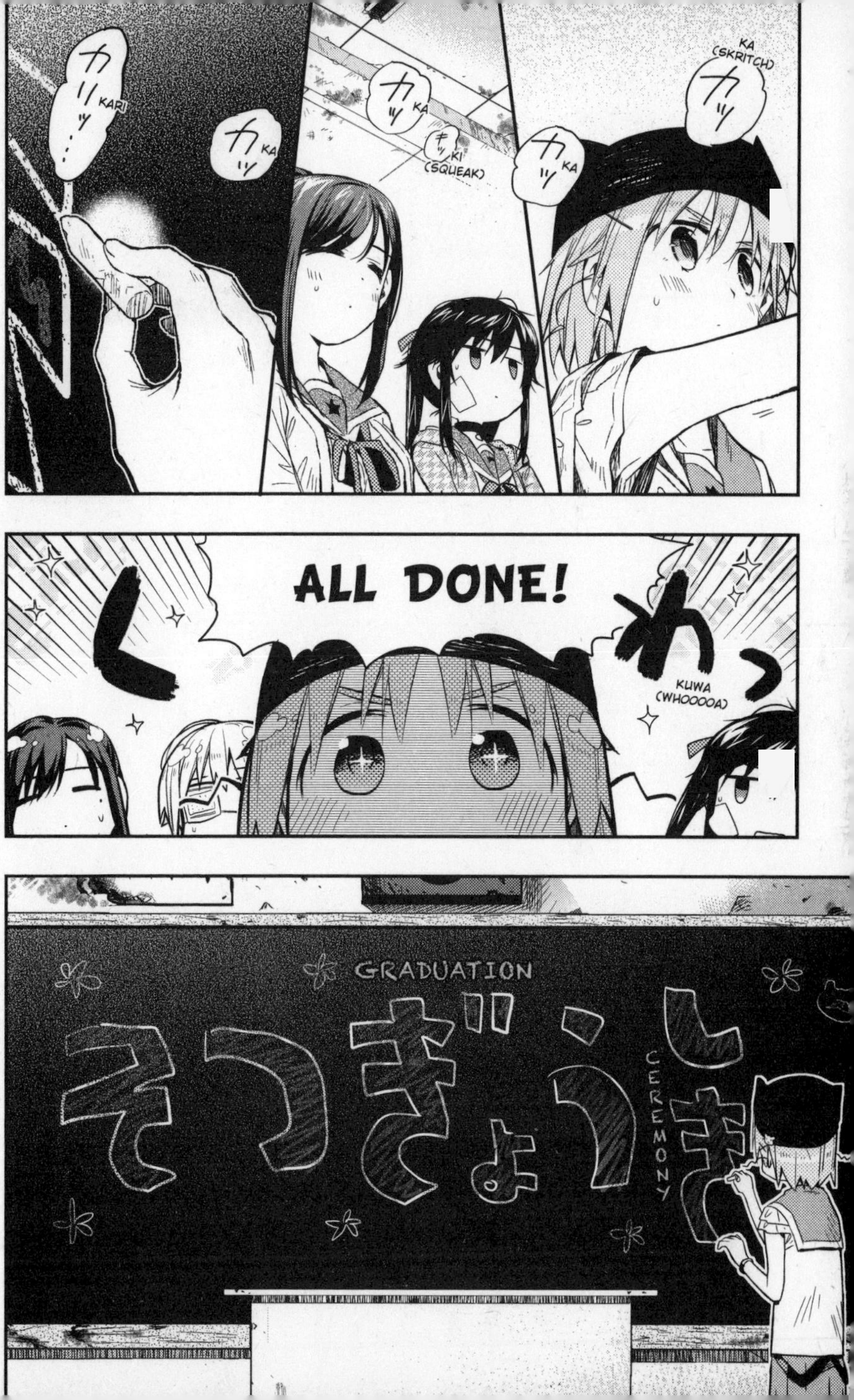
カッ
KA (SKRITCH)
カッ
KA
カッ
KA
キッ
KI (SQUEAK)
カリッ…
KARI
カッ
KA
ALL DONE!
くわっ
KUWA (WHOOOOA)
GRADUATION
そつぎょうしき
CEREMONY

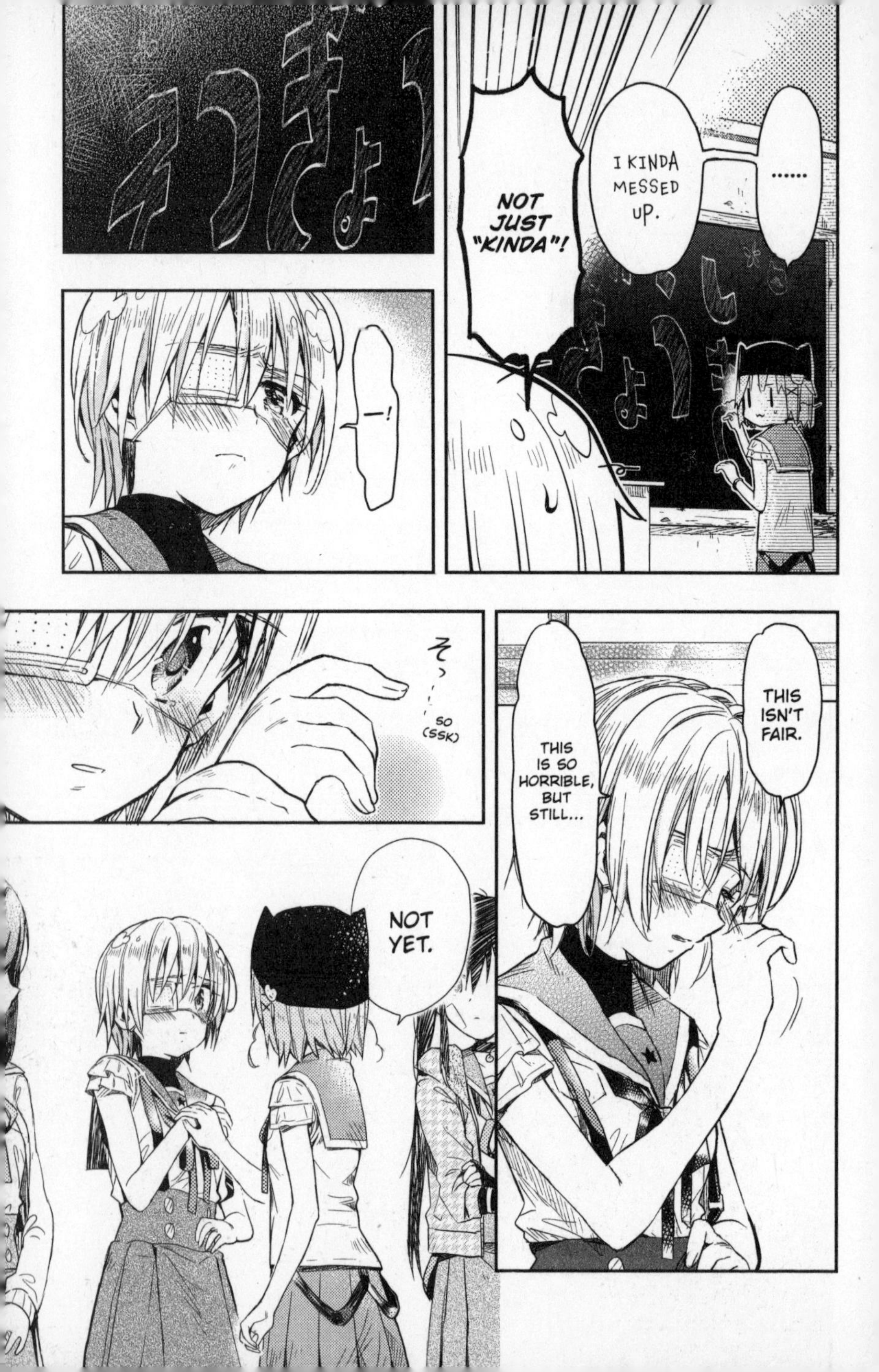
......
I KINDA MESSED UP.
NOT JUST "KINDA"!
—!
THIS ISN'T FAIR.
THIS IS SO HORRIBLE, BUT STILL...
SO (SSK)
NOT YET.

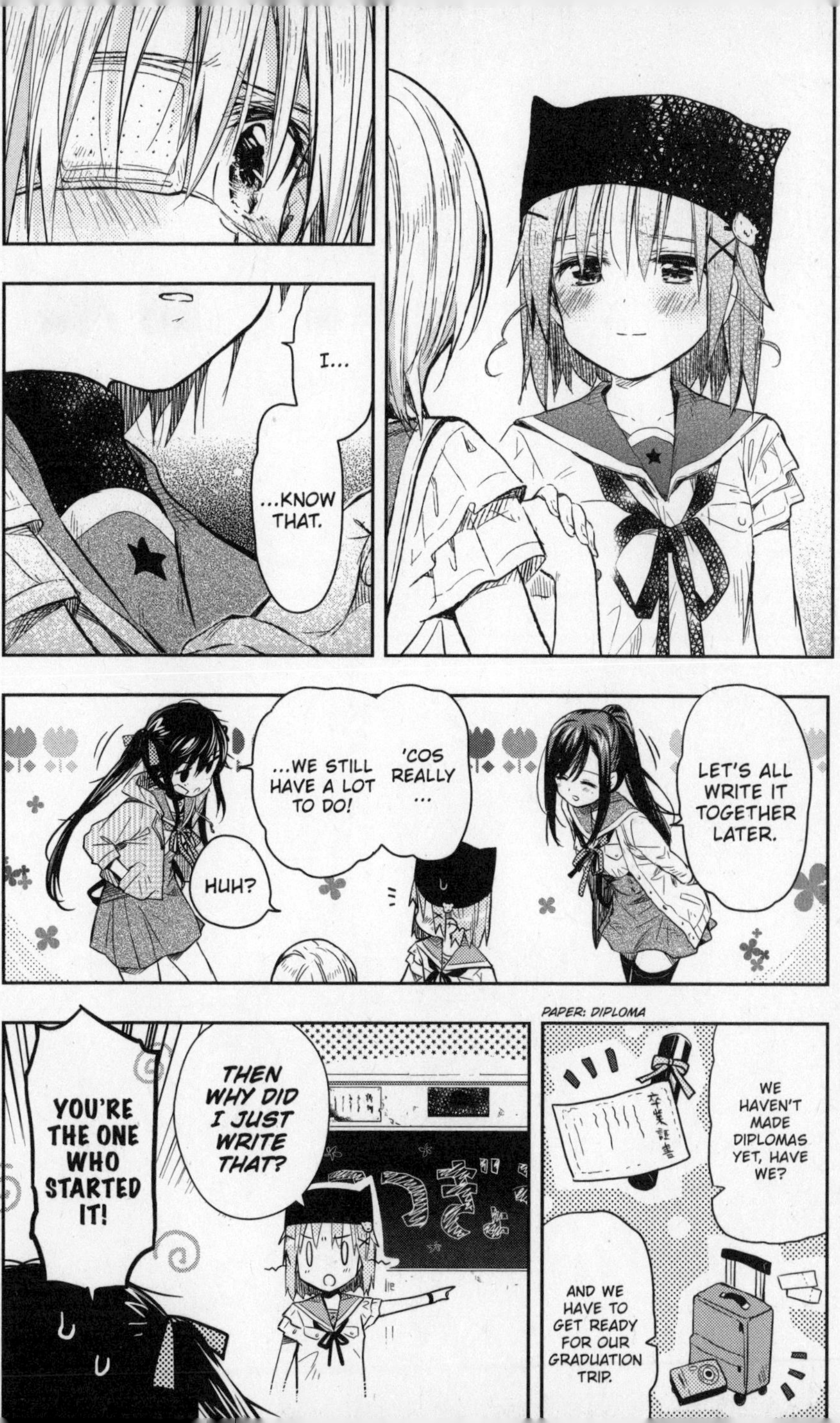
I...
...KNOW THAT.
LET'S ALL WRITE IT TOGETHER LATER.
'COS REALLY ...
...WE STILL HAVE A LOT TO DO!
HUH?
PAPER: DIPLOMA
WE HAVEN'T MADE DIPLOMAS YET, HAVE WE?
AND WE HAVE TO GET READY FOR OUR GRADUATION TRIP.
THEN WHY DID I JUST WRITE THAT?
YOU'RE THE ONE WHO STARTED IT!

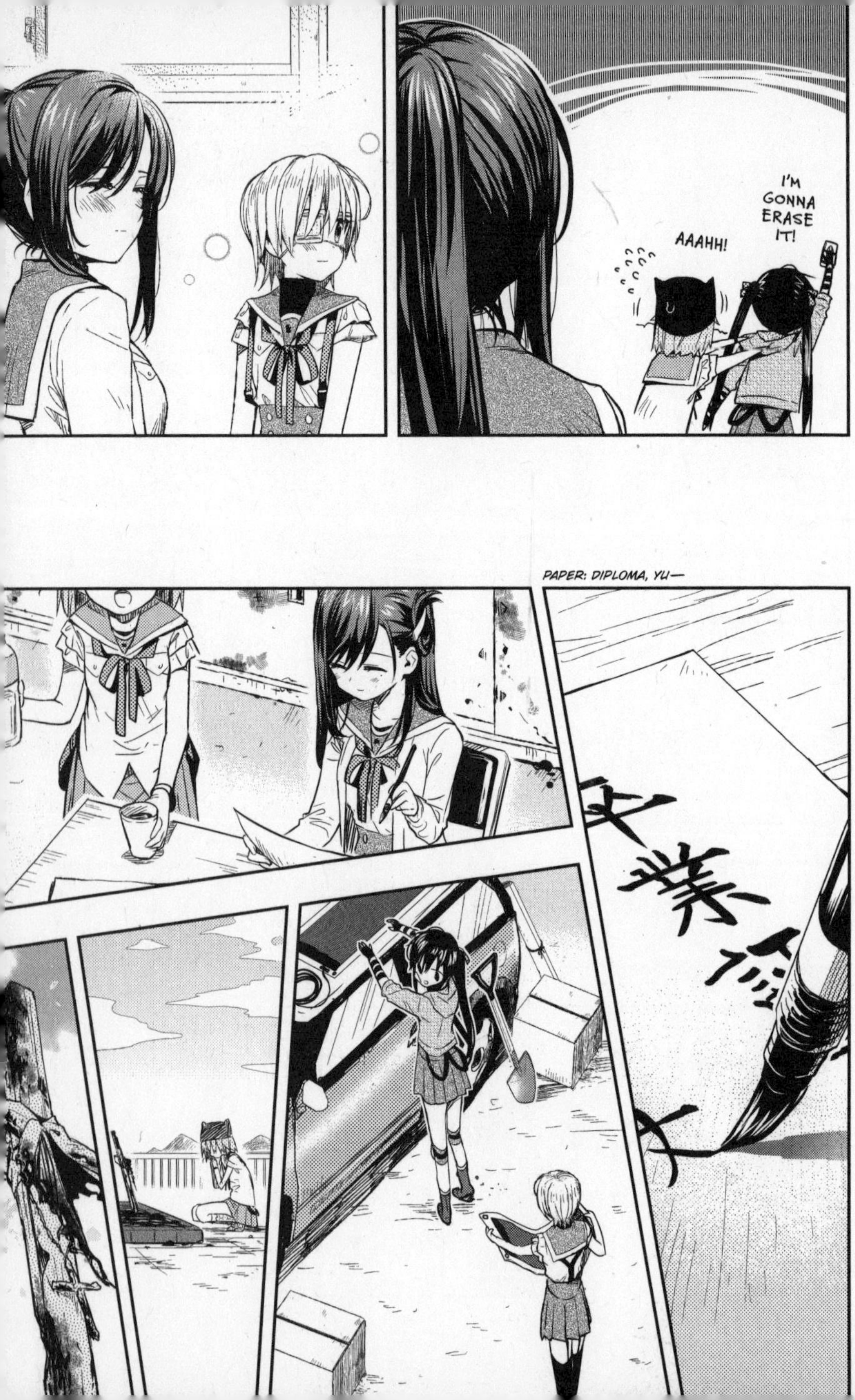
I'M GONNA ERASE IT!
AAAHH!
PAPER: DIPLOMA, YU—

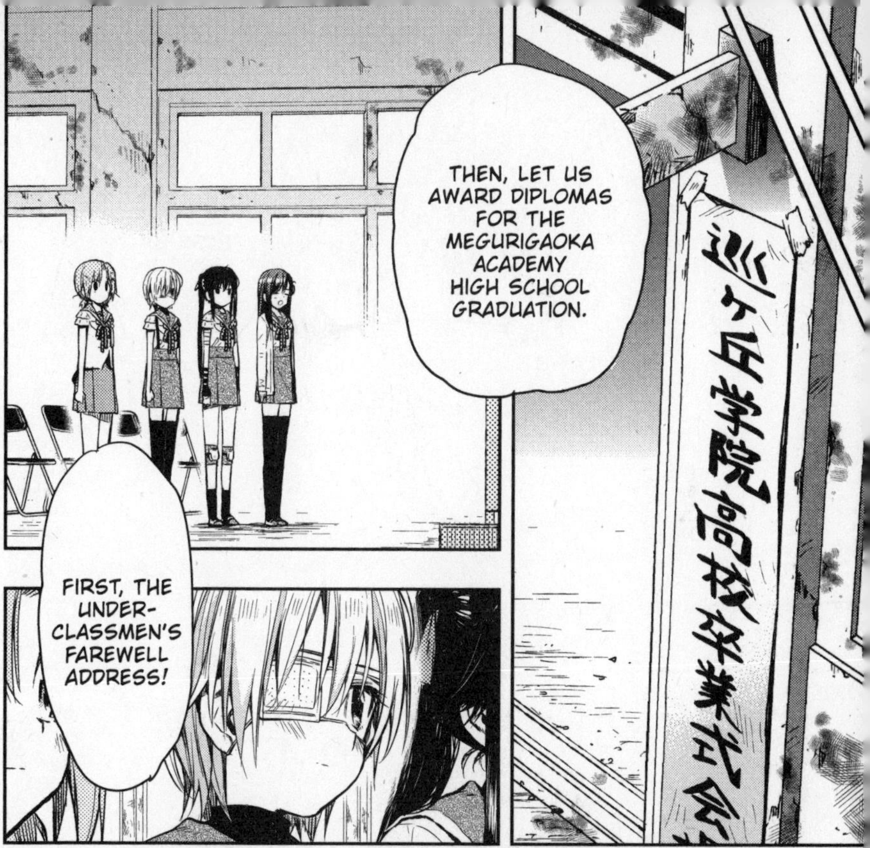

巡ヶ丘学院高校卒業式会
THEN, LET US AWARD DIPLOMAS FOR THE MEGURIGAOKA ACADEMY HIGH SCHOOL GRADUATION.
FIRST, THE UNDER-CLASSMEN'S FAREWELL ADDRESS!

SIGN: MEGURIGAOKA ACADEMY HIGH SCHOOL GRADUATION CEREMONY

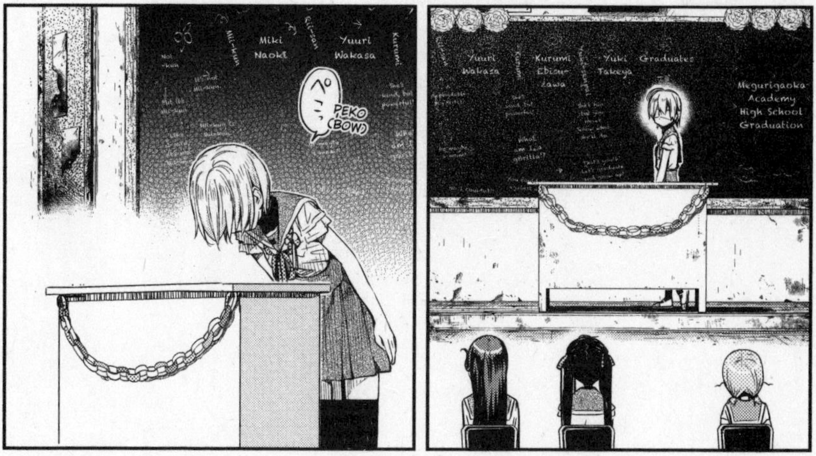

Yuuri Wakasa
Kurumi Ebisu-zawa
Yuki Takeya
Graduates
Megurigaoka Academy High School Graduation
Miki Naoki
Yuuri Wakasa
Kurumi
PEKO (BOW)

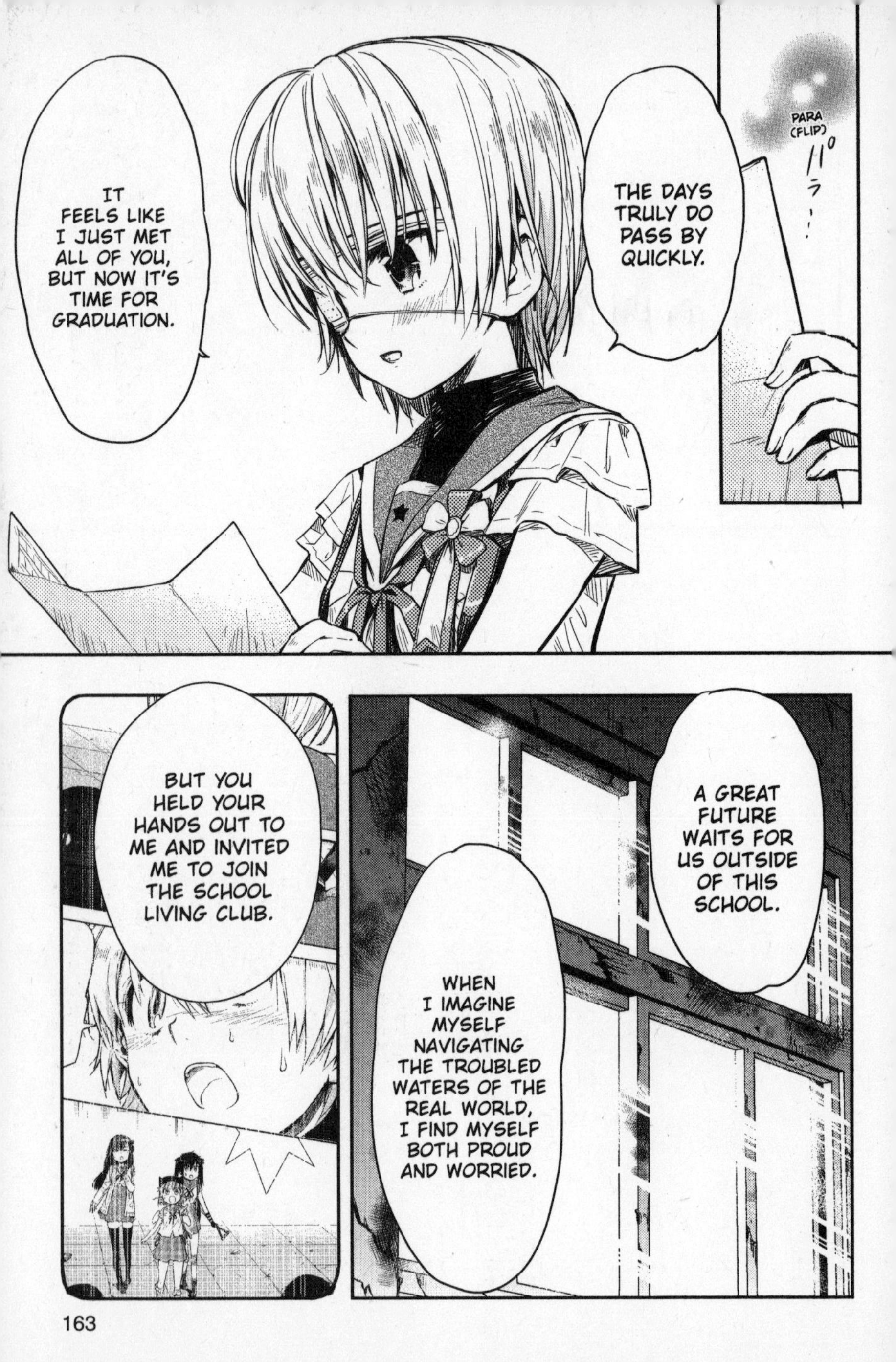
PARA (FLIP)
パラ…
THE DAYS TRULY DO PASS BY QUICKLY.
IT FEELS LIKE I JUST MET ALL OF YOU, BUT NOW IT'S TIME FOR GRADUATION.
A GREAT FUTURE WAITS FOR US OUTSIDE OF THIS SCHOOL.
WHEN I IMAGINE MYSELF NAVIGATING THE TROUBLED WATERS OF THE REAL WORLD, I FIND MYSELF BOTH PROUD AND WORRIED.
BUT YOU HELD YOUR HANDS OUT TO ME AND INVITED ME TO JOIN THE SCHOOL LIVING CLUB.

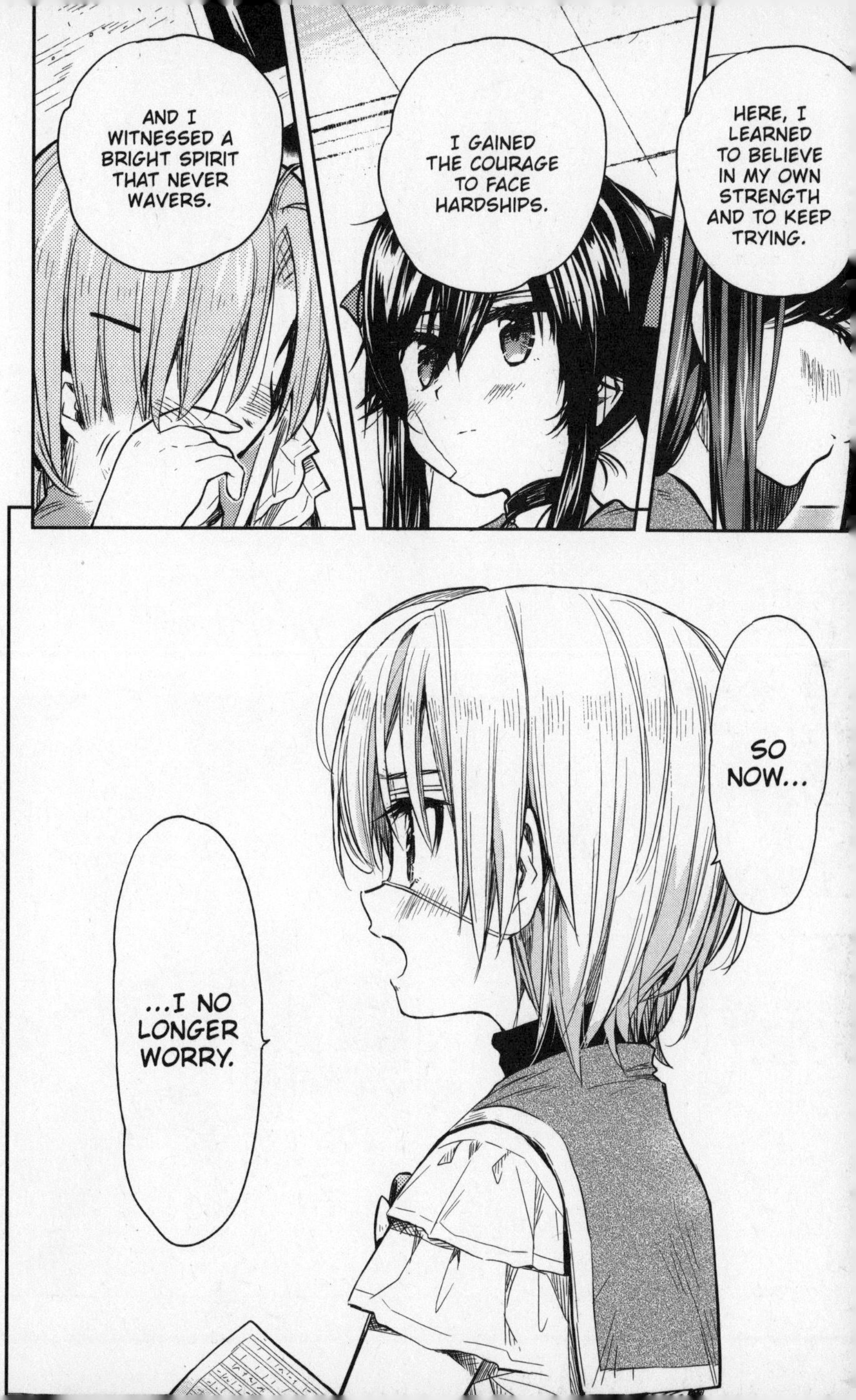
HERE, I LEARNED TO BELIEVE IN MY OWN STRENGTH AND TO KEEP TRYING.
I GAINED THE COURAGE TO FACE HARDSHIPS.
AND I WITNESSED A BRIGHT SPIRIT THAT NEVER WAVERS.
SO NOW...
...I NO LONGER WORRY.

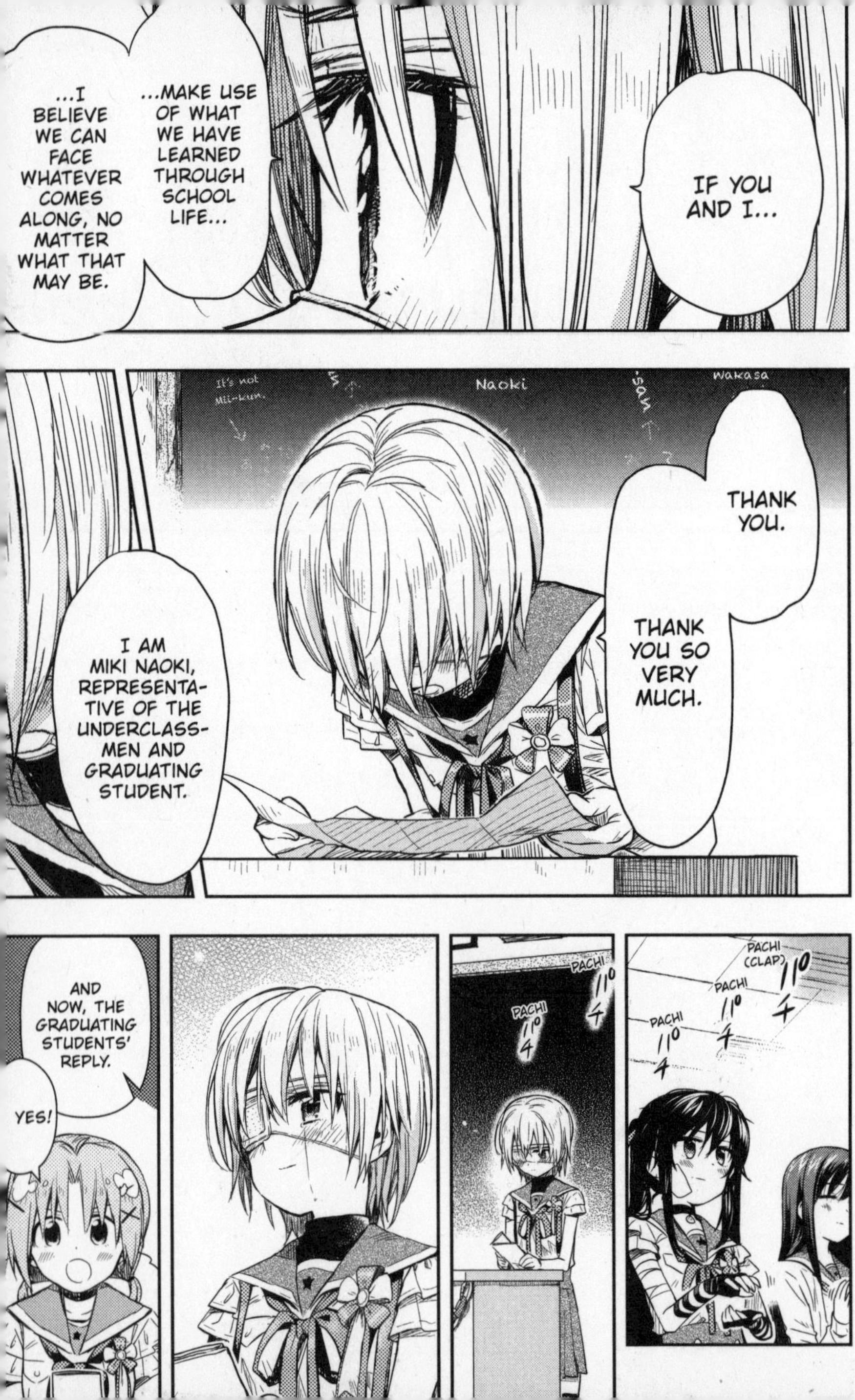
IF YOU AND I...
...MAKE USE OF WHAT WE HAVE LEARNED THROUGH SCHOOL LIFE...
...I BELIEVE WE CAN FACE WHATEVER COMES ALONG, NO MATTER WHAT THAT MAY BE.
Wakasa
-san
Naoki
It's not Mii-kun.
THANK YOU.
THANK YOU SO VERY MUCH.
I AM MIKI NAOKI, REPRESENTATIVE OF THE UNDERCLASSMEN AND GRADUATING STUDENT.
PACHI (CLAP)
PACHI
PACHI
PACHI
PACHI
AND NOW, THE GRADUATING STUDENTS' REPLY.
YES!

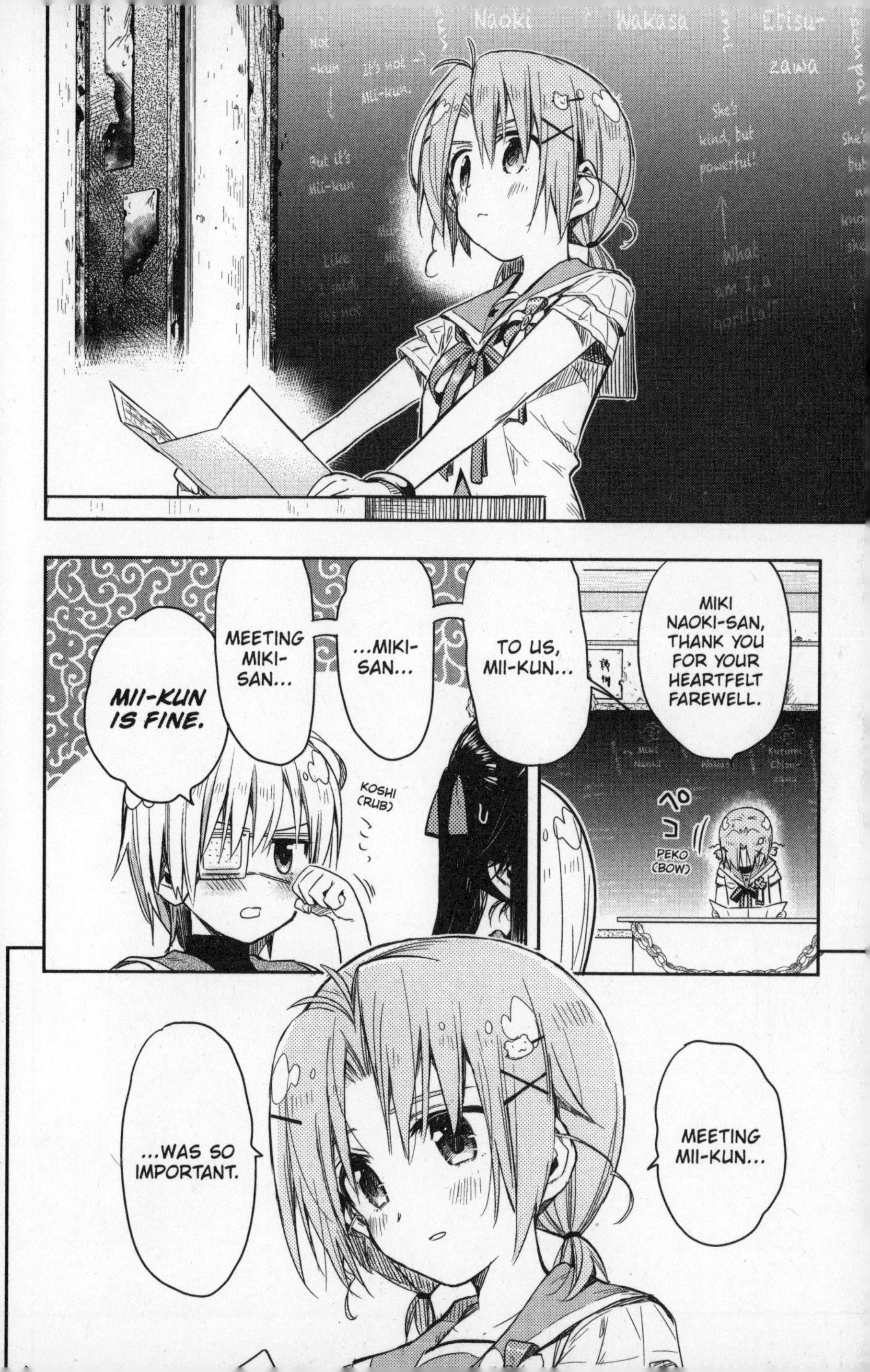

Naoki
Wakasa
Ebisu-zawa
not -kun
It's not Mii-kun.
But it's Mii-kun
Like I said, it's not
She's kind, but powerful!
What am I, a gorilla!?
MIKI NAOKI-SAN, THANK YOU FOR YOUR HEARTFELT FAREWELL.
Miki Naoki
Wakasa
Kurumi Ebisu-zawa
PEKO (BOW)
TO US, MII-KUN...
...MIKI-SAN...
MEETING MIKI-SAN...
KOSHI (RUB)
MII-KUN IS FINE.
MEETING MII-KUN...
...WAS SO IMPORTANT.

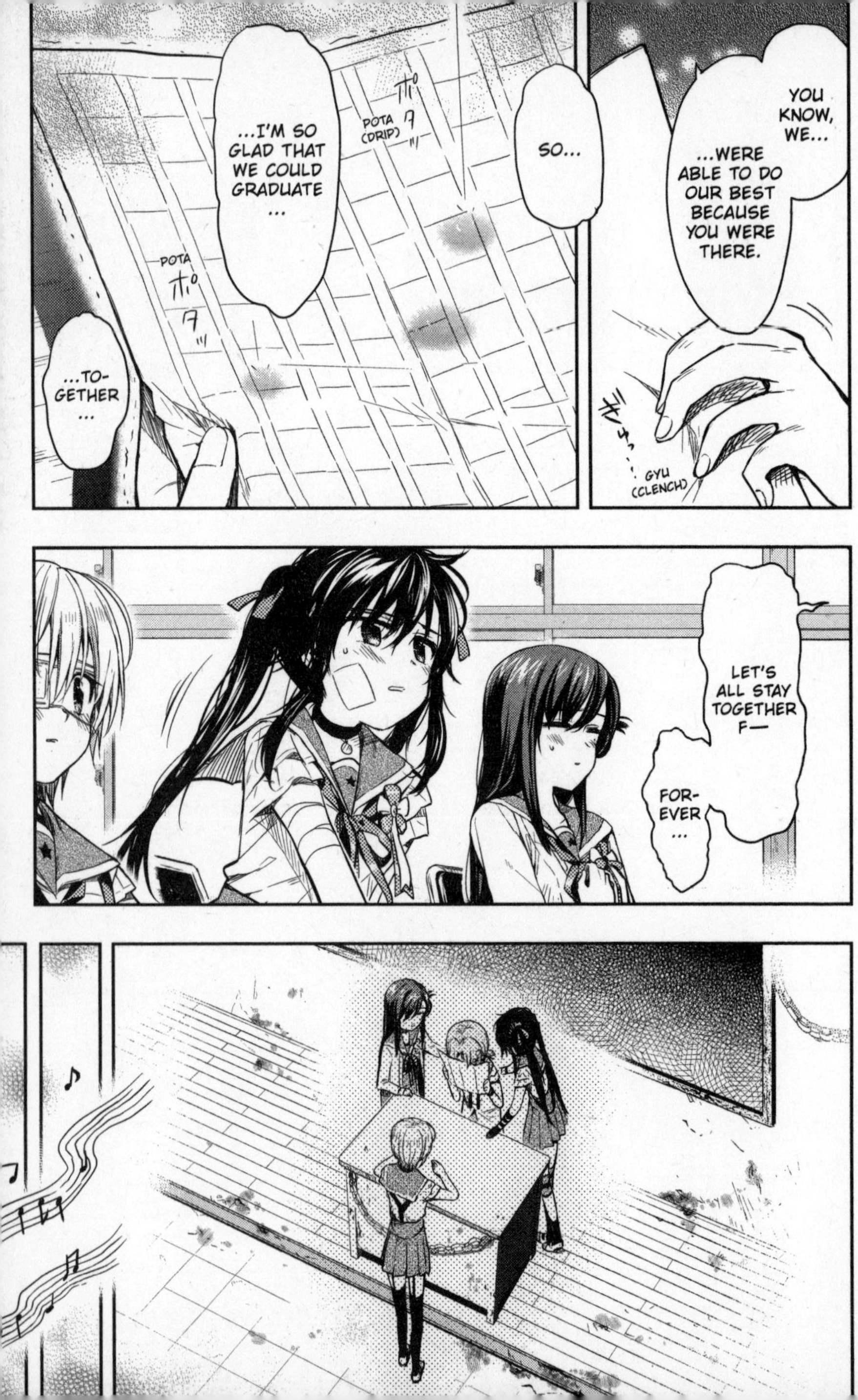
YOU KNOW, WE...
...WERE ABLE TO DO OUR BEST BECAUSE YOU WERE THERE.
GYU (CLENCH)
SO...
...I'M SO GLAD THAT WE COULD GRADUATE...
POTA (DRIP)
POTA
...TO-GETHER...
LET'S ALL STAY TOGETHER F—
FOR-EVER...

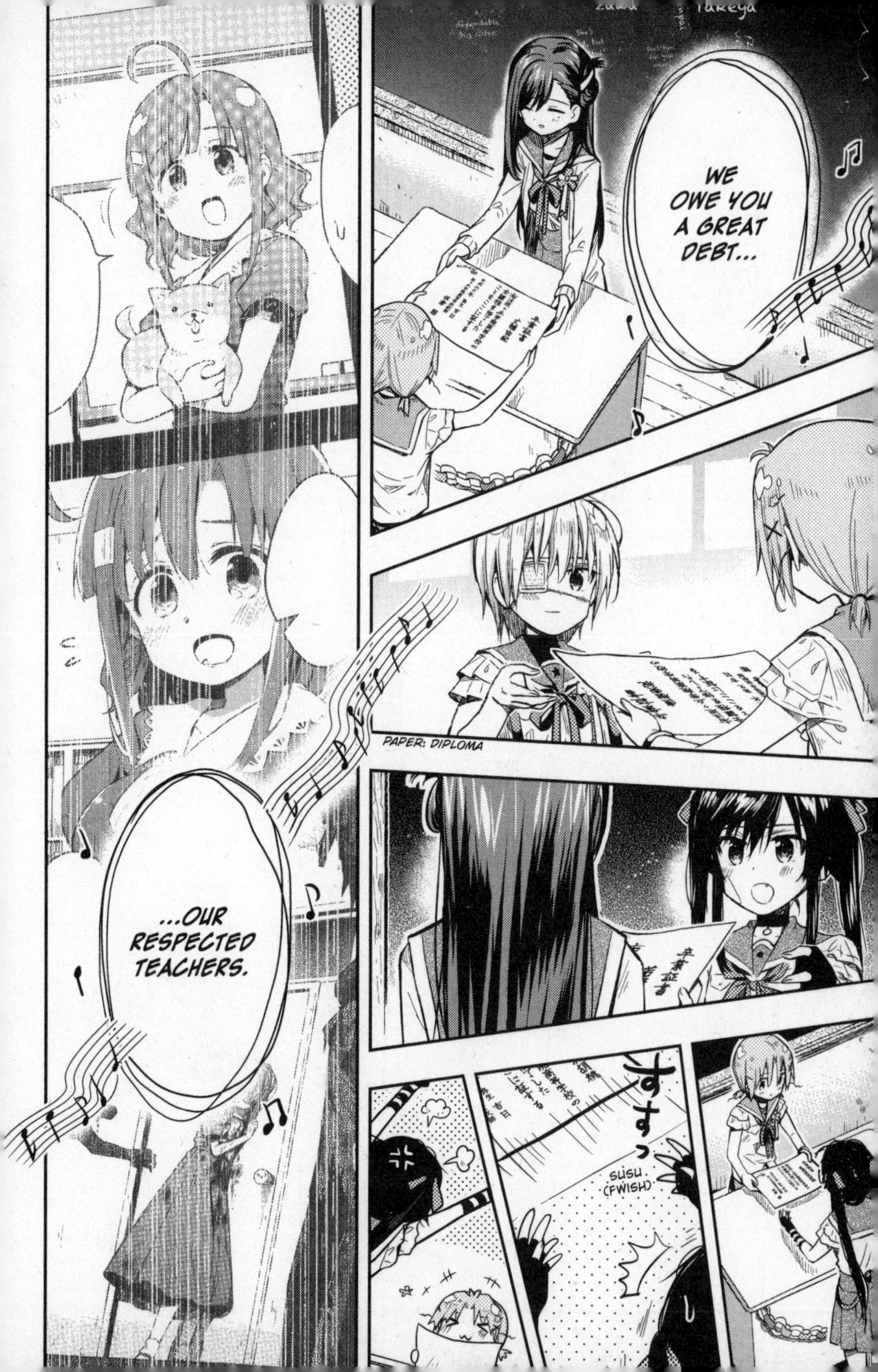
WE OWE YOU A GREAT DEBT...
PAPER: DIPLOMA
卒業証書
すすっ
SUSU (FWISH)
...OUR RESPECTED TEACHERS.

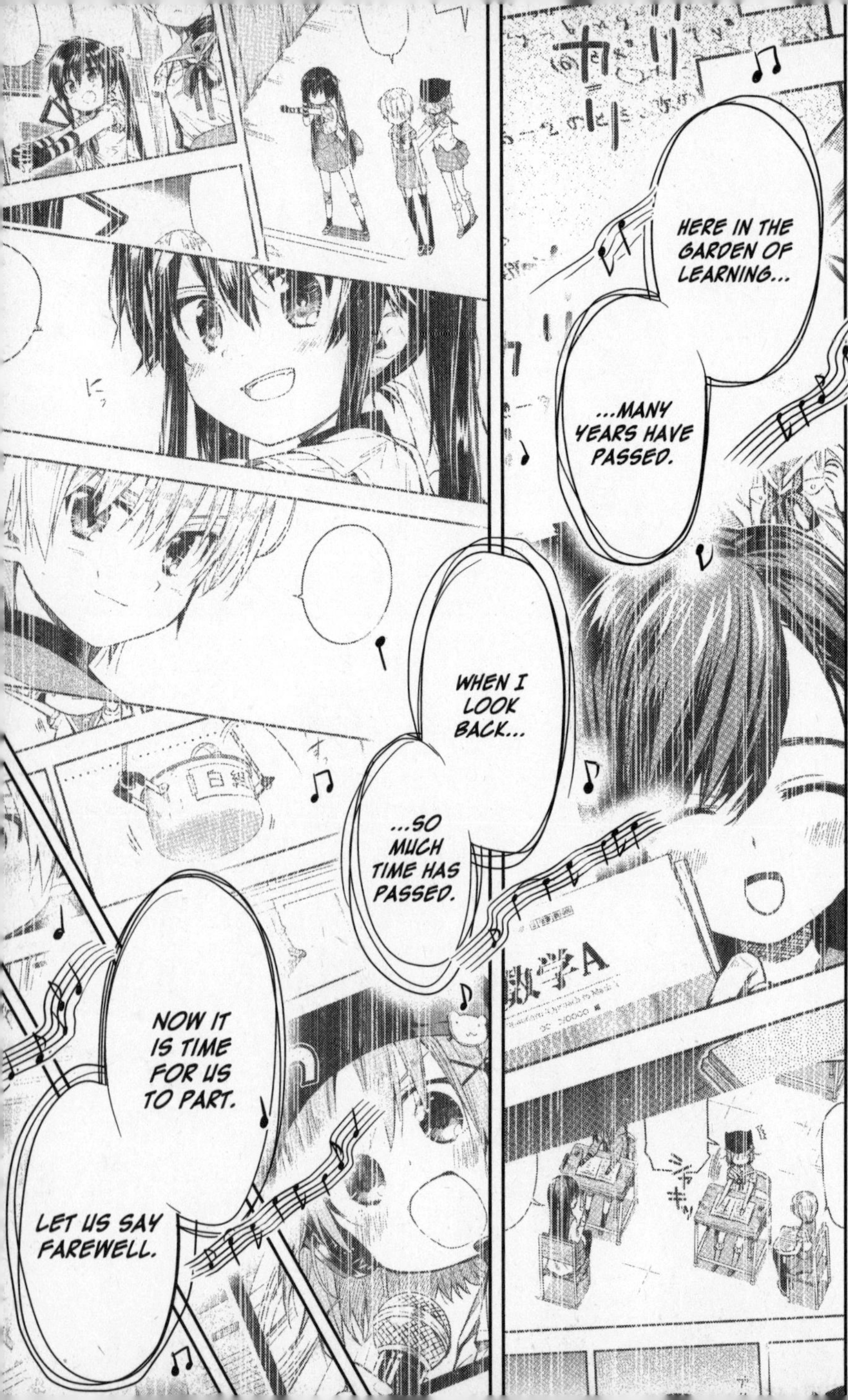
HERE IN THE GARDEN OF LEARNING...
...MANY YEARS HAVE PASSED.
数学A
WHEN I LOOK BACK...
...SO MUCH TIME HAS PASSED.
NOW IT IS TIME FOR US TO PART.
LET US SAY FAREWELL.

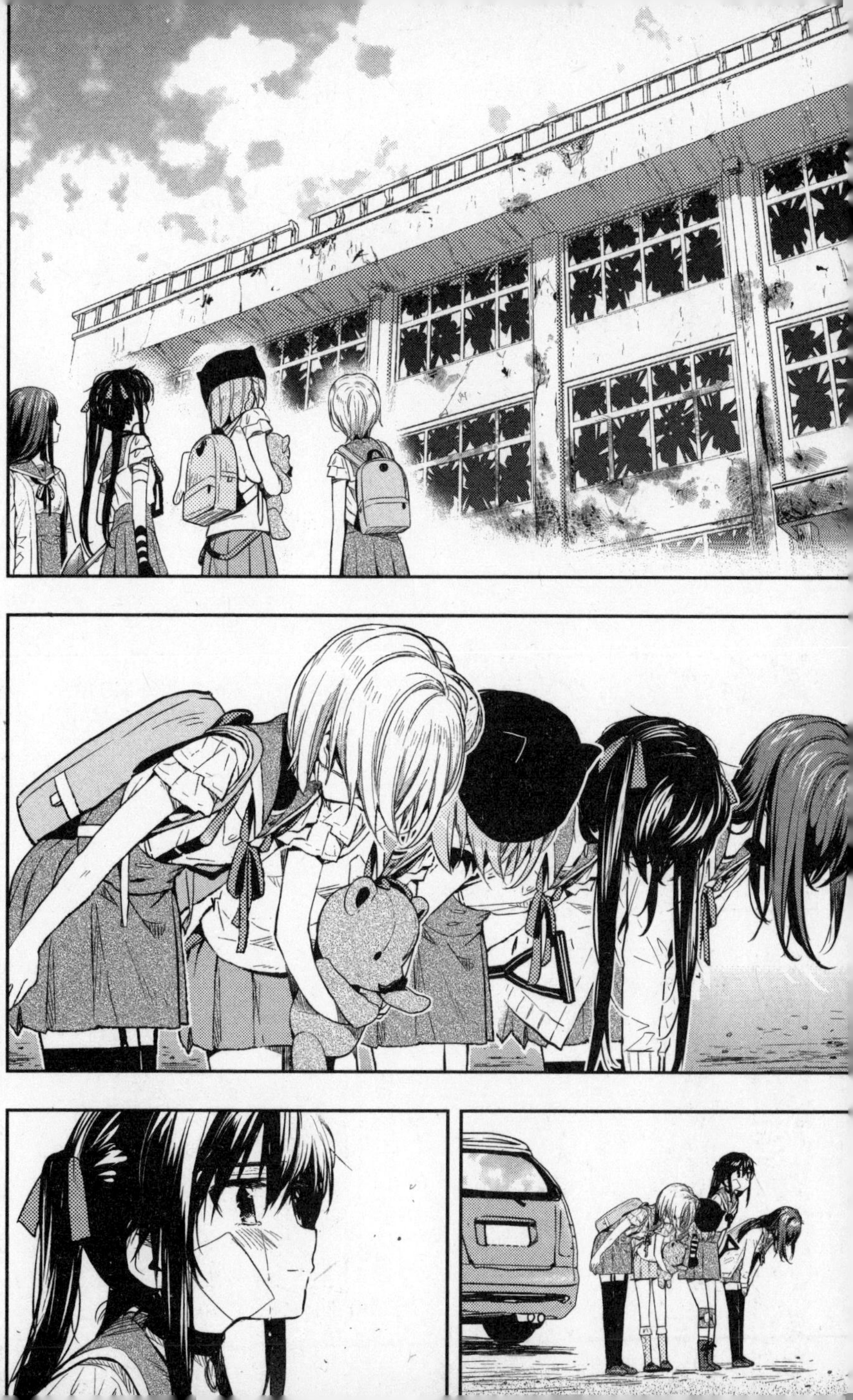

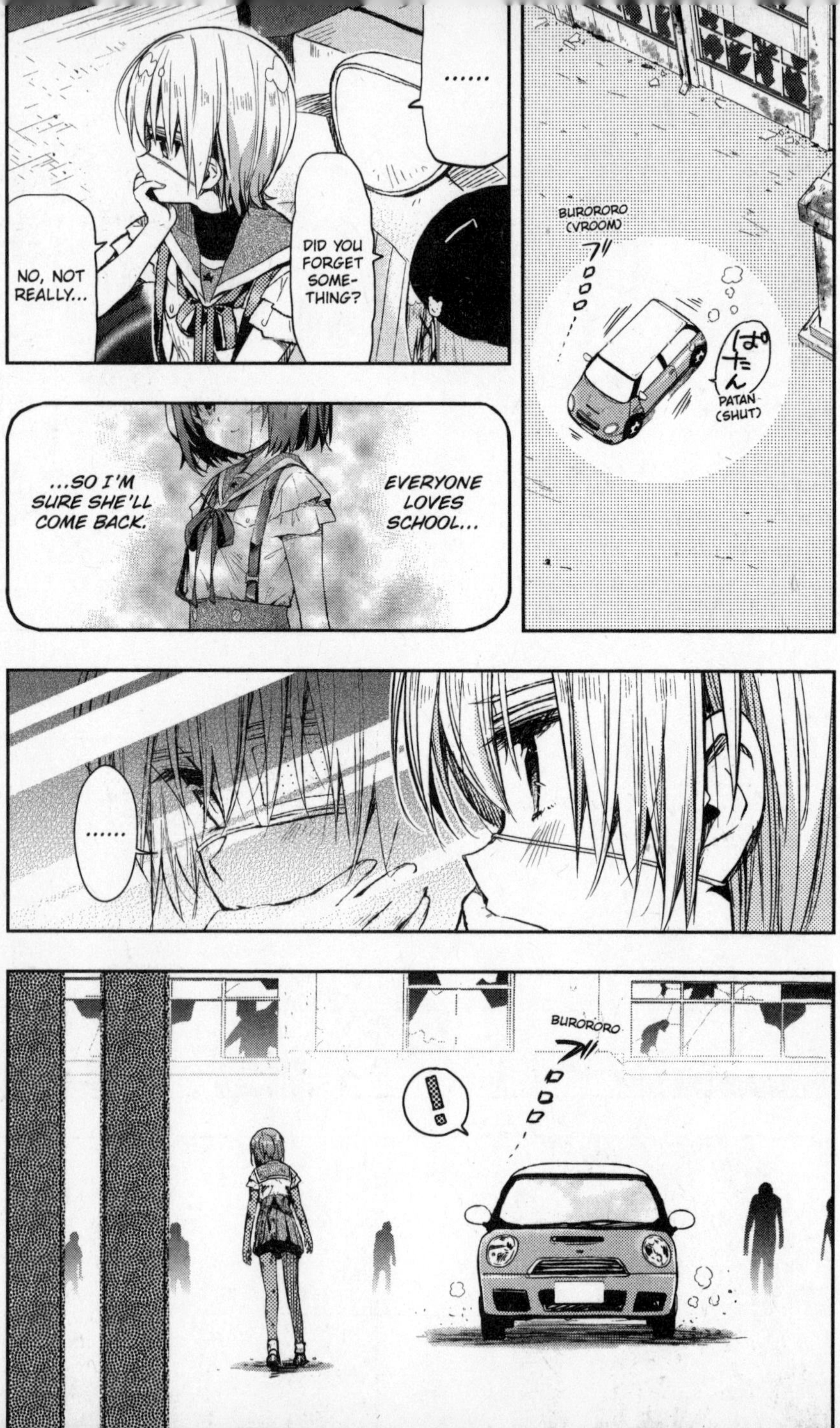
BURORORO (VROOM)
ブロロロ
ぱたん
PATAN (SHUT)
......
DID YOU FORGET SOMETHING?
NO, NOT REALLY...
EVERYONE LOVES SCHOOL...
...SO I'M SURE SHE'LL COME BACK.
......
BURORORO
ブロロロ
!!

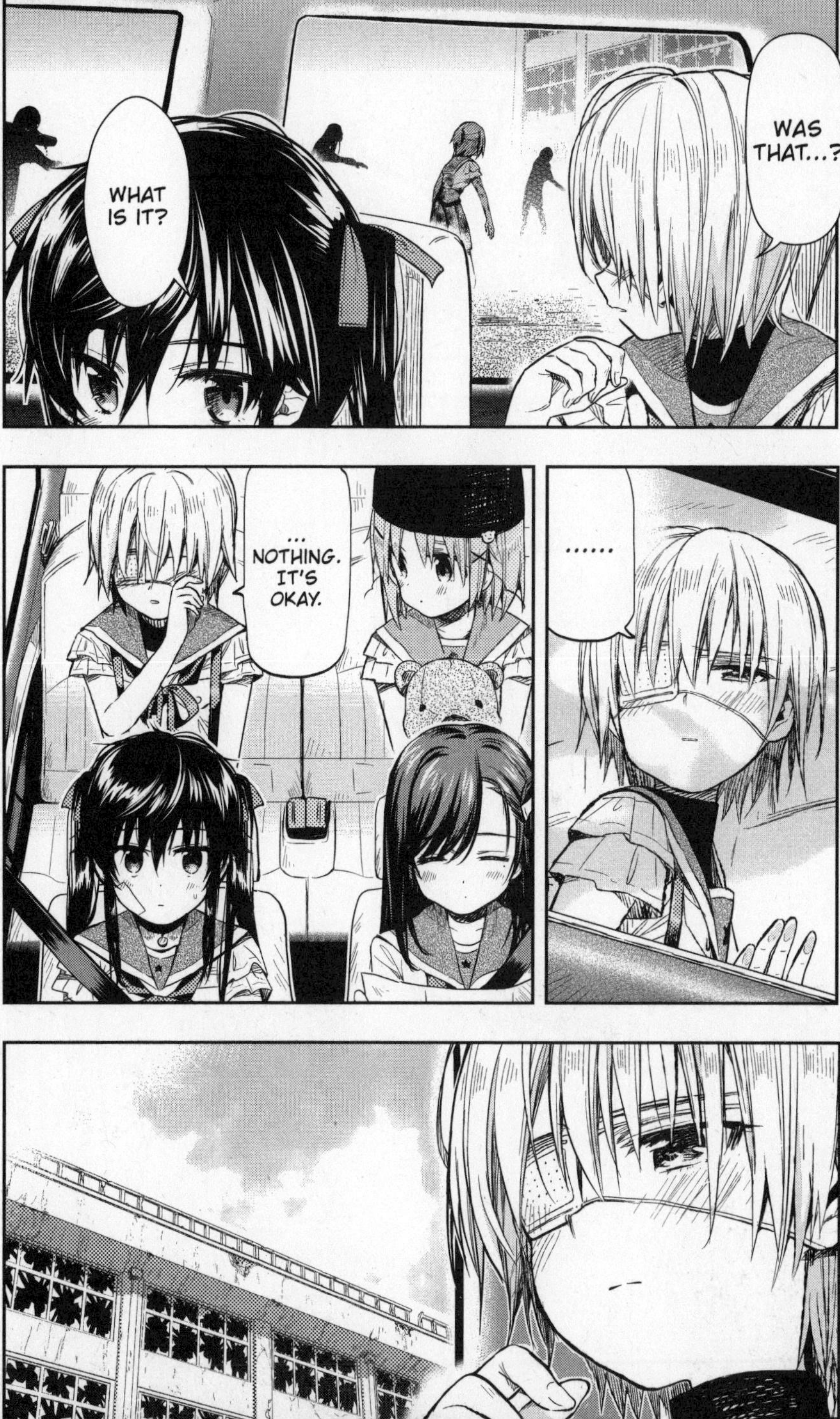
WAS THAT...?
WHAT IS IT?
......
... NOTHING. IT'S OKAY.

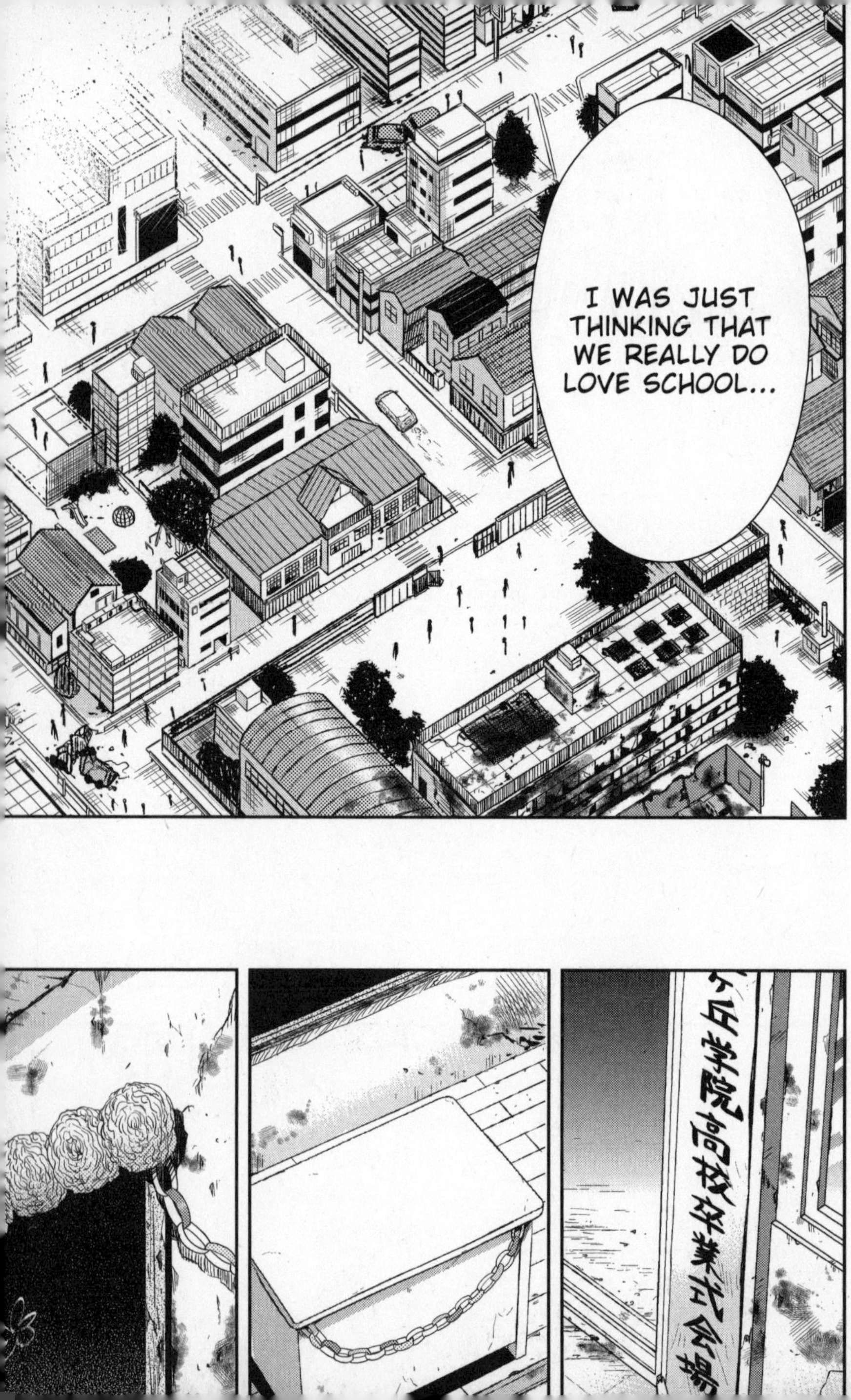
I WAS JUST THINKING THAT WE REALLY DO LOVE SCHOOL...
丘学院高校卒業式会場

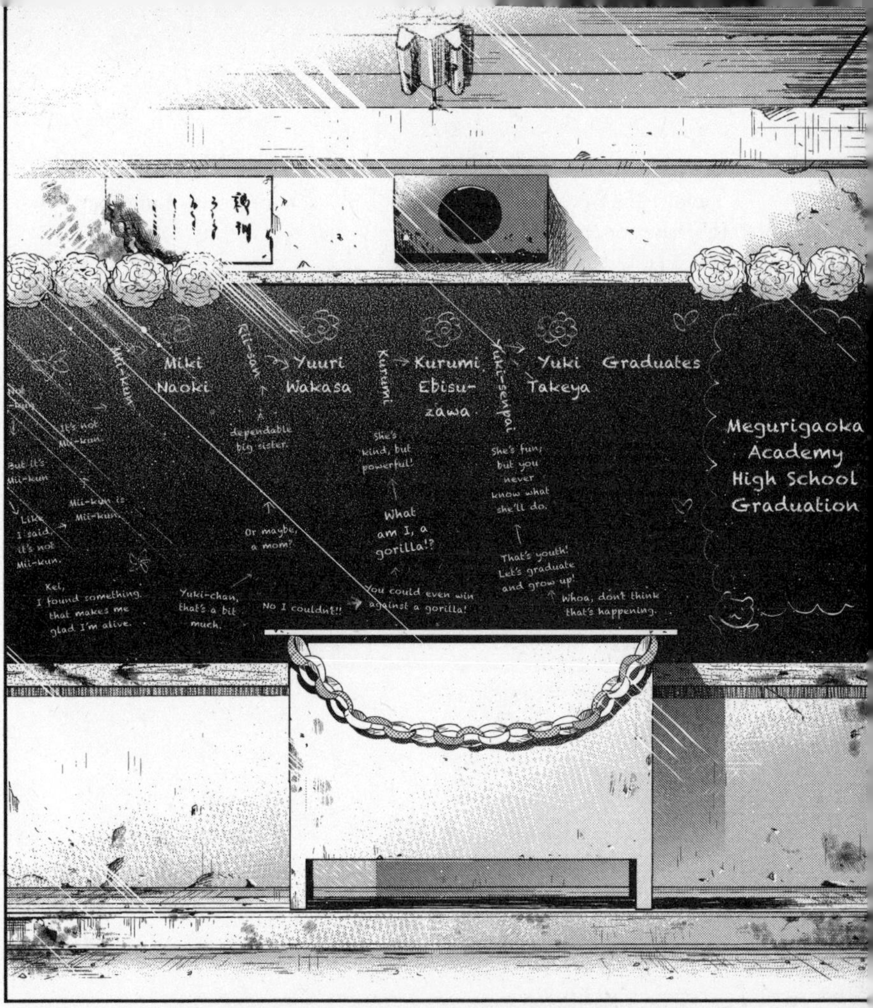

Meguirgaoka Academy High School Graduation
Graduates
Yuki Takeya
Yuki-senpai
She's fun, but you never know what she'll do.
That's youth! Let's graduate and grow up!
Whoa, don't think that's happening.
Kurumi Ebisu-zawa
Kurumi
She's kind, but powerful!
What am I, a gorilla!?
You could even win against a gorilla!
Yuuri Wakasa
Rii-san
dependable big sister.
Or maybe, a mom?
No I couldn't!!
Yuki-chan, that's a bit much.
Miki Naoki
Mii-kun
It's not Mii-kun.
But it's Mii-kun
Mii-kun is Mii-kun.
Like I said, it's not Mii-kun.
Kei, I found something that makes me glad I'm alive.

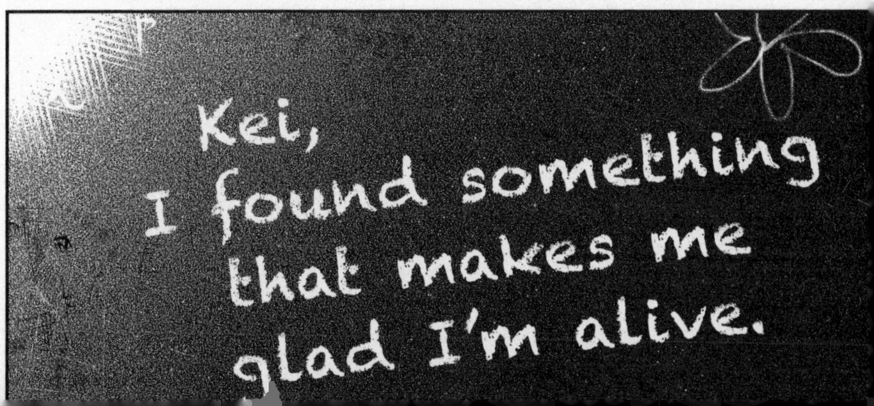

Kei, I found something that makes me glad I'm alive.

I have a lot of fun memories from my school years, but when I think back on how I felt back then, I get the feeling that I was fighting just to survive day to day.

Myself, myself with my friends, myself out in the world. I came up against all those inconsistencies and got mad, got sad, and felt despair.

I didn't have the power or authority to change anything, so I'm pretty sure I was always banging my head against a wall.

It's not like I had a particularly rough school life either. That time is just pretty much life and death.

I didn't realize it back then, but I made it through with the help of a lot of people.

To expand on that life or death time, Yuki and the girls have graduated in this volume.

The outside world is waiting for them, where new adventures and new possibilities stretch out in front of them.

Along with the anime adaptation, please do have high hopes for Yuki and the girls' new possibilities!

Thank you.

Norimitsu.

Kaiho

It's time to
start the
graduation
trip!!

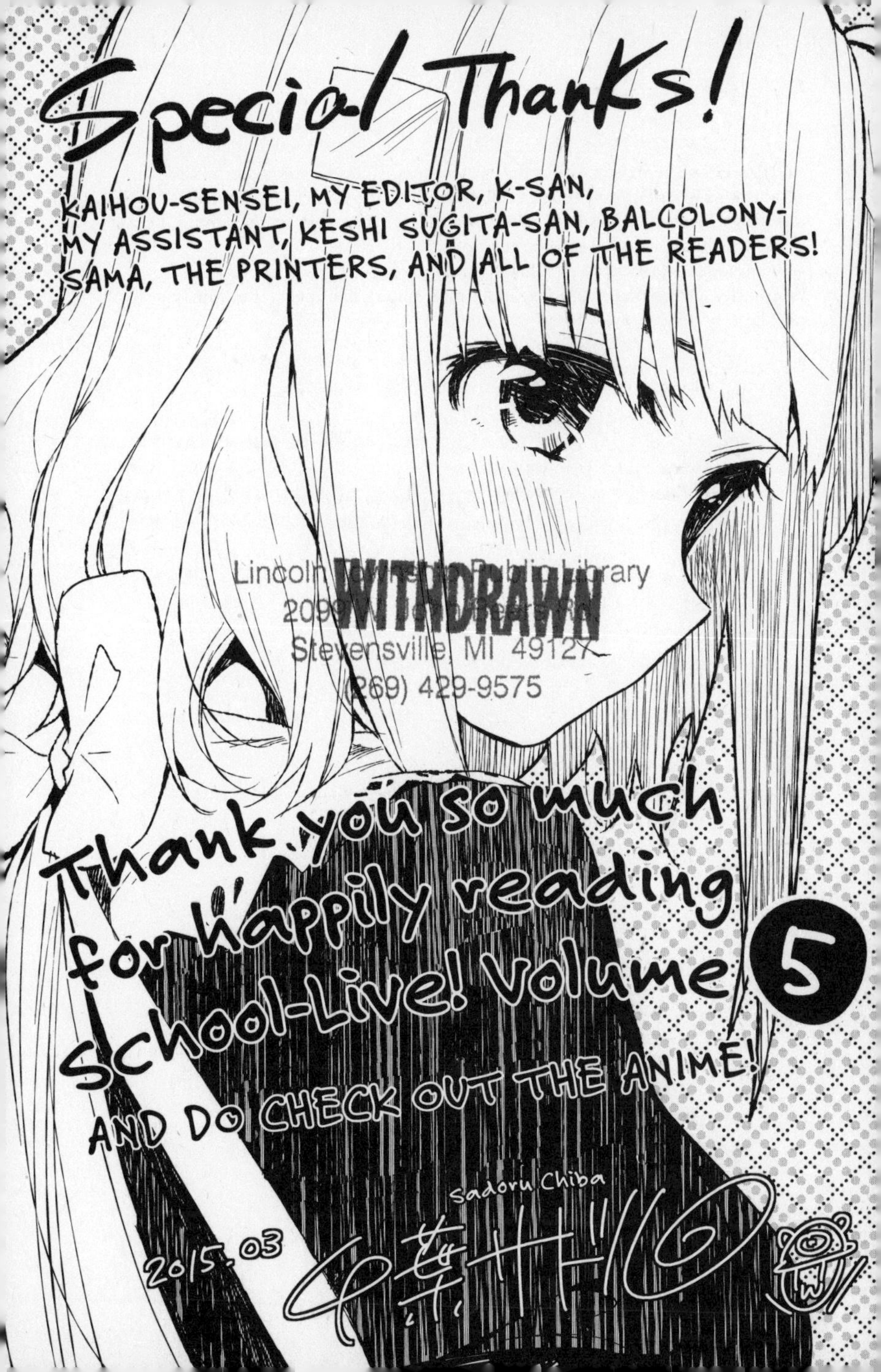
Special Thanks!
KAIHOU-SENSEI, MY EDITOR, K-SAN,
MY ASSISTANT, KESHI SUGITA-SAN, BALCOLONY-
SAMA, THE PRINTERS, AND ALL OF THE READERS!
Thank you so much
for happily reading
School-Live! volume 5
AND DO CHECK OUT THE ANIME!
Sadoru Chiba
2015.03

Translation Notes

Common Honorifics:

no honorific: Indicates familiarity or closeness; if used without permission or reason, addressing someone in this manner would constitute an insult.

-san: The Japanese equivalent of Mr./Mrs./Miss. If a situation calls for politeness, this is the fail-safe honorific.

-kun: Used most often when referring to boys, this indicates affection or familiarity. Occasionally used by older men among their peers, but it may also be used by anyone referring to a person of lower standing.

-chan: An affectionate honorific indicating familiarity used mostly in reference to girls; also used in reference to cute persons or animals of either gender.

-senpai: A suffix used to address upperclassmen or more experienced coworkers.

-sensei: A respectful term for teachers, artists, or high-level professionals.

-nee: Honorific derived from onee-san/-sama ("big sister"). When used alone after a name, *-nee* can mean closeness.

SCHOOL-LIVE!

NORIMITSU KAIHOU
(Nitroplus)

Translation: Leighann Harvey

Lettering: Alexis Eckerman

GAKKOU GURASHI! Vol. 5
©Nitroplus / Norimitsu Kaihou, Sadoru Chiba, Houbunsha. All rights reserved. First published in Japan in 2015 by HOUBUNSHA CO., LTD., Tokyo. English translation rights in United States, Canada, and United Kingdom arranged with HOUBUNSHA CO., LTD through Tuttle-Mori Agency, Inc., Tokyo.

English translation © 2016 by Yen Press, LLC

Yen Press
1290 Avenue of the Americas
New York, NY 10104

Visit us at yenpress.com
facebook.com/yenpress
twitter.com/yenpress
yenpress.tumblr.com
instagram.com/yenpress

First Yen Press Edition: November 2016

Yen Press is an imprint of Yen Press, LLC.
The Yen Press name and logo are trademarks of Yen Press, LLC.

Library of Congress Control Number: 2015952613

ISBNs: 978-0-316-31001-7 (paperback)
       978-0-316-31002-4 (ebook)

10 9 8 7 6 5 4 3

WOR

Printed in the United States of America